MERCHANTS OF DEATH

Merchants of Death

A Kate Dawson Mystery

John L. Flynn

OPEN ROAD
INTEGRATED MEDIA
NEW YORK

ISBN: 978-1-5040-8423-9

This edition published in 2023 by Open Road Integrated Media, Inc.
180 Maiden Lane
New York, NY 10038
www.openroadmedia.com

To Jackie Johnston and our late father, John, with love and admiration

MERCHANTS OF DEATH

PROLOGUE

At twelve-twenty-six in the afternoon, Officer Jamie Hartwell pulled his patrol car around the back of the Westfield Shopping Centre and parked in the alleyway near the Container Store. Hartwell, an eight-year veteran of the Army, had always wanted to be a police officer. He joined the San Francisco Police Department shortly after his discharge five years earlier. At thirty-three-years-of-age and single, he enjoyed helping people, and saw himself as one of the new breed of "peace" officers who lived and worked in his own community, assisting others on a day-today basis with problems, no matter how routine.

As he sat in the black-and-white unit, counting down the minutes to his lunch, he watched as several patrons of the store loaded storage and organization products into their cars on the loading dock and then drove away. Everything looked fairly routine to him. He reached for the microphone to his car radio, just about to call in a Code-7 (meal break) for the local Denny's restaurant, when he spotted a late model sedan sitting idle at the far edge of the loading dock. It was parked illegally across two lanes. In closer observation, he saw the windows to the car were rolled down and the driver's side door was slightly ajar.

Someone must have been in a real hurry to get into the

after-holiday clearance sale at the Container Store, he thought to himself. *They completely missed the sign warning patrons not to leave their cars unattended on the loading dock.* Deciding to investigate, Hartwell spoke into the radio's microphone, "Dispatch. This is 1-Lincoln-15. I'm 901 at Westfield Shopping Centre, requesting a 10-29 on a late model white Buick LaSabre, California Plate 4-9-0 Victor-Henry-George."

"10-4, 1-Lincoln-15," the radio dispatcher replied. A moment later, the voice on the radio added, "Vehicle is registered to Mahmud Ibn Suri, 57 South Ellsworth Street, San Mateo. No wants, no warrants at this time."

"10-4, Dispatch," Hartwell signed out, replaced the radio's microphone, and climbed out of the patrol car. Adjusting the police hat on his head, he walked slowly in the direction of the loading dock. Again, he surveyed the area from his vantage point. All the other cars had at least one customer from the Container Store associated with it, while only the one seemed like it had been abandoned.

Jamie Hartwell approached one of the clerks who was busy helping a customer load her station wagon with several utility boards and a closet organizer. The cop waited respectfully out of range. Only after she had pulled away, he walked up to the clerk. "My name is Officer Hartwell," he stated, pointing at his badge. "I'd like to have a word with the owner of the white Buick LaSabre."

"So would I," the clerk replied, spitting on the pavement.

"I assumed he was still in your store."

"A reasonable assumption, officer, considering how he's parked his vehicle," the clerk wisecracked. "My biggest sales day of the year, and this fuckin' rag-head pulls through two lanes of my loading dock and parks his car smack-dab in the middle. Then he and three of his buddies, dressed like sand rats, got out of the car, and headed north to Market Street. Never even went near my store. What the fuck do they think this is, a fuckin' public parking lot? This is a business! The loading dock is for my customers, not some fuckin' A-rabs!"

"Do you remember when this happened, sir?"

"Sure," he responded, with a smirk, "about an hour ago. I've been waiting for that camel-jacker to come back, so that I could lay him out."

Hartwell looked at his watch and nodded, then said, "Sir, I'd advise you and your staff to keep as far away from that vehicle as possible. Take no provocative action. I'll handle things from here."

"You gonna arrest him?" the clerk persisted.

The police officer did not respond immediately. He was too busy looking at the car from his new vantage point on the loading dock. When he finally did speak, Hartwell repeated his warning, "Sir, for your safety and the safety of your customers, I'd advise you to stay back. Out of range. The San Francisco Police Department will handle this, but I do need you to follow my orders."

"Sure, whatever you want," he replied, with a backward wave of his hand.

Hartwell turned to the microphone attached to the lapel of his uniform. "Dispatch, this is 1-Lincoln-15. I have a follow-up to my 10-29. Vehicle now appears abandoned on the loading dock behind the Container Store. It is parked across two lanes and may represent a hazard to traffic entering the lot from 4th or Market."

"10-4, 1-Lincoln-15," the dispatcher replied. "Be advised, the duty sergeant has been informed of your 11-54 (suspicious vehicle) and is en route. Let me know if a tow truck is required."

"That's a big 10-4," he said, almost routinely. "Checking the vehicle now. Will keep informed."

"10-4, 1-Lincoln-15," the dispatcher added. "Proceed with caution."

With his right hand cautiously gripping the handle of the 9 mm Glock17 he carried in a leather holster on his hip, Hartwell made his way towards the vehicle. At first, memories of his tour of duty in Iraq conjured up images of late-model Sedans booby-trapped with IEDs (improvised explosive devices) and gave him good reason to pause and maintain a wide berth from the abandoned vehicle. During the Gulf War, many of his fellow soldiers had been injured or lost their lives to homemade bombs wired to perfectly innocent-looking vehicles by the enemy. But after one complete pass, he didn't get that vibe. Other than showing extreme signs of neglect at the hands of its owners, the Buick looked clean.

Making a complete circle, he walked around the vehicle again and then moved in, looking in the open windows for some sign of its owner, Mahmud Ibn Suri. Under the dashboard in front, he found a police-band radio, tuned to the dispatch frequency most of the City police used. He tried the glove compartment, which was not locked, and pulled out a dozen different identification cards and badges, including two fake police IDs with presumably Mahmud's photo stamped on them. He also found a loaded Smith & Wesson revolver stashed under the passenger's seat, its serial number burned off with acid. And then, lying on the floor in the back seat under several blankets, he discovered a portable acetylene torch kit with oxygen and acetylene tanks. Taken together, Hartwell didn't exactly know to what the evidence pointed, but it was enough to suggest Mahmud and his three buddies were up to no good.

Officer Hartwell was just getting to his feet near the late model Buick when three men wearing ankle-length, white robes came sprinting across Market Street towards the loading dock, followed by a fourth man who had been delayed by traffic. Hartwell recognized Mahmud immediately from the identification cards he had pulled from the glove compartment, but his reaction was sluggish. He reached, as if in slow motion, for his service pistol, but he was not fast enough to outdraw the fourth man, Mahmud Ibn Suri. By the time he had pulled out his Glock and aimed it, his assailant had managed to click off two rounds. BLAM! BLAM! The bullets rang out as shoppers and pedestrians scrambled for cover. Still images, later released by police from surveillance video, showed Mahmud as the gunman straddling the crosswalk, taking aim and firing at the patrol officer at close range. In one photo, the suspect had moved up and was right next to the car with his sites lowered. In another, the gunman had fired two shots into Hartwell's body, while standing over him at point-blank range. The gunfight was over in a manner of seconds, leaving the veteran officer lying on the ground in a pool of blood, clinging to life.

"*Allah Akbar*!!!" ("God is great" in Arabic) Mahmud Ibn Suri shouted several times, as he leapt into the driver's seat of the Buick and started the engine. Quickly, his three men followed him, taking the open passenger seats. As the doors slammed shut, Mahmud fired several additional shots over the heads of the pedestrians still scrambling for cover and he and his men shouted, "Allah Akbar!" several times at the top of their lungs. With every one of the bystanders scared shitless, Mahmud shifted into D and floored the gas pedal. The late model sedan jumped forward from the loading dock onto the highway and blasted down Market Street, like a thoroughbred race horse that had been turned loose for the first time.

"Shots fired! Officer down . . ." Hartwell sputtered into his radio, as he clawed his way to the edge of the loading dock.

Despite being seriously injured and literally bleeding to death, he grasped his 9 mil with his left hand, took aim, and fired at the back of their vehicle, blowing out the rear window with his first shot. BLAM! He took aim and squeezed the trigger a second time. BLAM! His second shot hit one of the two terrorists riding in the back seat in the back of the head. The two other shots he managed to squeeze off ricocheted harmlessly off the pavement and lodged into one of the wooden pylons at the end of the loading dock.

With his last breath, Hartwell pushed the call button on his radio, and gasped, "Suspect vehicle is a . . . white Buick LaSabre. Last reported turning left onto Market Street . . . heading southwest . . . hell-bent in a heap of hurry. The occupants are four Middle Eastern men . . . armed and extremely dangerous . . ." Officer Hartwell blacked out before he could say anything more, never to regain consciousness, and was later pronounced dead at the scene. There were no other fatalities.

Several blocks away, the late model Buick clipped a student, while running a red light on Market Street; sent the young man sprawling. Dazed and in a lot of pain, he finally climbed to his feet and dusted himself off; the vehicle too far gone for a clear identification. His eyes darted to and fro, searching for someone who may have captured the incident on a cell phone and would make him a superstar on YouTube with his death-defying feat.

Rodney Grant's parents had warned their son a million times about riding his skateboard in traffic to school, but he rarely paid them any mind. At eighteen, Rodney considered himself invincible. With favorite champions such as Captain America and Tony Hawk, he continued to live his life on the edge; a young man with a death wish. He had no way of knowing that fate had already chosen him *and* several others to join Hartwell on a journey to Heaven. Instead, he just shrugged off his collision with the car and routinely started picking up his books from the pavement.

"I saw what happened back there," an overweight college coed named Judy Krebbs remarked, handing him one of the books she had struggled to pick up from the ground. "You know, you're lucky to be alive."

"Err . . . ah . . . thanks," Rodney replied without turning his head to acknowledge her presence, snatched the book out of her hands, and added it to his pile. Throwing down his skateboard, he hopped on and raced into the BART station, balancing his books like a circus clown from Ringling Brothers. Rodney Grant didn't get very far. In fact, few of his fellow travelers were actually moving. They were all bunched up at the Powell Street Station, waiting for their subway train to arrive. Some tapped their feet to counter the effects of boredom, while others checked their watches every few seconds to keep track of the passage of time. Then there were those who complained to perfect strangers about the important events on their schedules they were going to miss. Every one of them had somewhere to be or someone to meet. It never occurred to any one of them they might be living on borrowed time.

Rodney Grant kept his head down low so the "troll" who had helped him with his books wouldn't try to engage him again in conversation. He had nothing against overweight women. Heck, some of his best friends at City College were porkers. He just didn't like the sloppy ones who had let themselves go by binging on Happy Meals and slurping down 20-oz. Cokes. He actually found them physically disgusting and was determined to maintain his distance from her even if it meant walking up to the next station.

Finally, thirty minutes behind schedule, the 12:44 train on the Richmond line of the Bay Area Rapid Transit rolled into the

Powell Street Station on its way towards Millbrae, Daly City, and other points south. When the Red line was first completed in 1973, BART was considered one of the most advanced subway systems in the world. Its five lines connected San Francisco with Oakland and most of the other major cities and suburbs in the Bay Area. The Powell Street Station was just one of forty-three stations spread over four counties. Centrally located, the station was near the City's most popular attractions, including the cable cars, Union Square, Yerba Buena Gardens, the Moscone Convention Center, and the Westfield Shopping Centre. Now, forty-five years later, BART was beginning to show its age. Even though it carried more than fifty-thousand passengers every day, the subway system needed a face-lift, not the least of which was to its aging and nearly obsolete security infrastructure.

Balancing his books on the metal handrail, Rodney rolled onto the middle train car, slipped into a seat by the door, and quickly buried his nose in *Beyond Good and Evil* by Friedrich Nietzsche as the overweight college coed followed him onto the same car. He had been aware the "troll" had been stalking him for several blocks, but he purposely feigned disinterest as she trudged down to the end of the car and turned back around towards him. When she finally did stop moving, out of breath from her fastpaced trek through the BART station, Judy plopped down in a seat directly across the aisle from him. They exchanged a momentary glance, but the look of revulsion in his face said it all. He wanted nothing to do with her at all and did everything he could to discourage her from speaking to him.

Undaunted, she leaned forward, smiled and said, "Hello."

Grant merely turned away towards the window.

Judy Krebbs took out an inhaler and squirted a measured dose into her lungs to counteract the effects of her chronic asthma. As she started to breathe normally, the coed wiped the sweat away from her face with folded napkins that had been packaged with her Happy Meal from McDonald's. No sooner had she settled back into her seat, a third student from City College forced his way by her and dumped his book bag onto the seat in the middle, as if creating an unspoken barrier between the two of them. She watched as he then proceeded to unspool the ear buds to his iPad and disappear into the heavy metal music he had recorded earlier that day. She sighed deeply and wiped the tears back from her face. From her perspective, it appeared that no one was interested in talking with her, much less becoming her friend.

Several rows back, Saul Frishman, a pawnbroker in his late fifties with black, receding hair, glanced up from his newspaper long enough to witness their exchange and shook his head in confusion. He was convinced that he would never understand the younger generation. Back in his day, men and women were so much kinder to each other, even those who were relative strangers. They would have never been so cruel or rude to a perfect stranger, let alone someone they might know from school. Gathering the morning edition of San Francisco's Chronicle into his liver-spotted hands, he opened to a story on page four about a teenaged mother who had stabbed her boyfriend for abusing their ten-month-old. He guffawed aloud and leaned over to share the story with the woman sitting quietly next to him; chin resting on her chest, glasses balanced on the end of her nose. She stirred long enough to read the headline, then tapped his wrist and said, "That's nice, dear," before falling back asleep. Frishman did a doubletake at his wife and smiled. After thirty-eight years of marriage, he was still in love with the woman who sat next to him.

Out on the platform, two men wearing business suits exchanged a final hug and kiss goodbye before Ricardo Milan broke free from his older partner and headed toward the middle train car. He was impeccably dressed in a Brooks Brothers suit with thousand-dollar Tom Ford shoes and a $350 t-shirt from Yves Saint Laurent. He carried a model's portfolio of head shots and tear sheets from the modeling work he had done in New York and Los Angeles. With a quick brush of his left hand, he smoothed back his blond hair into a flowing coif. It was a move that had become one of his patented trademarks on the runways in Europe. But now, with so many male models copying him, it had become more of a nervous habit than a hot trend for looking sharp and ready. He passed several fellow travelers, including an elderly woman with fresh produce who was struggling to pull her grocery cart aboard the train, but never actually saw a single one of them. Ricardo lived in a world that was quite different from the rest of them and preferred it that way. Crossing the threshold, he didn't bother looking for a seat but took hold of the first strap hanging from the ceiling. The chiseled features on his face turned blank and empty as he stood there, a seemingly marble statue of some forgotten Olympian god.

A few feet away from where he stood, Gladys Stevens continued to struggle with her cart as the last of the travelers scrambled aboard. Several people brushed by the old woman on the platform, pretending not to see her, while others cut their eyes at her with the same sense of anger and annoyance they had shown other senior citizens in their community. Yes, they had seen her kind before—on street corners, inside fast-food restaurants, riding on public transportation—and wished that they were any place else but there. Stevens reminded them of their own mortality; a topic better left unexplored.

When Wanda Smith, an African-American charge nurse from San Francisco General Hospital, first approached the train car, she also turned a blind eye to the old woman's plight;

simply elbowed her way in and fought a Hispanic man over a seat on the left side of the car by the window. She won. But after settling back into her seat with the "Help Wanted" classifieds of Oakland's *Tribune*, she happened to look up and, for the first time, saw Gladys Stevens. "Shit!" she shouted aloud, the word echoing through the car as she jumped up and headed to the door. Wanda stepped out onto the platform and, with her left hand, took the handle of the grocery cart and literally carried it over the threshold. Thankful and relieved, the old woman toddled behind her, the epitome of a two-year-old child following her mother.

"Dat's right! Dat's right!" Smith said, as she returned to the seat now occupied by the Hispanic man. For an instant, she stood over him, flexing her muscles with a look that told him to find another seat. He quickly got the message and moved out of her way. Then she turned her anger towards the others in the car, adding, "Y'all dun saw dat po' woman strugglin' wid her cart, but no one dun lift a finger to help 'er. Just leave it fuh de niggah tuh do! Y'all should dun be proud of yo'selves. Real, upstandin' pillas of da community! I hate dis fuckin' city!"

All at once, the car went as silent as the tomb. The usual chatter and chit-chat between fellow travelers on a train had ceased and twenty-seven out of the twenty-eight subway patrons were still, listening and waiting for Smith to make her next move. She stood her ground, daring anyone to say or do anything to her. Finally, the tension reached its climax when a young mother, who feared that some racial incident was about to explode into a shooting or some other fatal nightmare, scooped up her three-year-old child into her arms and jumped off the train. A couple of other passengers followed her, but the rest stayed in place. Wanda Smith laughed aloud as she watched them disembark, then settled back down in her seat and buried her head back in the classifieds. A collective sigh resonated, and within a matter of heartbeats, people were talking to each other again.

After what was supposed to have been a brief, two-minute stop at the Powell Street Station to drop off and pick up new passengers, the train's familiar "ding-dong" sounded and the doors to each of the subway cars slid closed. The southbound BART No. 4 pulled out of the Powell Street Station slowly but gradually began to pick up speed as it headed south and west to its next stop—Civic Center/UN Plaza Station—six minutes away. Several blurred flashes from the lights above and a sustained blackout accompanied the subway train as it barreled down the tunnel at sixty miles an hour. When the train finally emerged from the last blackout, approximately one minute before it was scheduled to arrive at the next station, there wasn't a single soul stirring in the middle car. All twenty-four passengers were dead.

With only one or two exceptions, the seated corpses—their shoulders side to side like wooden martinets—faced towards the front of the subway car, the pupils in their dull eyes focused on the last thing they had seen.

Rodney Grant, seated near the door, gazed into the Nietzsche book, forever locked on page fifty-six, while Judy Krebbs had not taken her eyes off Grant, her corpse content to stare at him for all eternity.

The older Jewish couple sat next to each other, just as they had sat together all their married life; the old woman's chin still resting on her chest as though she was napping with her eyes open; Saul's directed where his newspaper had been, but it had fallen to the floor; its individual pages spread out all around his feet. News of stabbings, political appointments, or sports' scores no longer relevant to him; a man who had lived his life cashing in on the misfortune of others.

Perhaps, if Ricardo Milan had survived, he would have read the fashion review from Paris, but his corpse still hung from the strap in the ceiling of the subway car, his "perfectly-sculpted" body now stretched out beyond recognition.

Gladys Stevens and Wanda Smith sat a few seats away from each other, the old woman still clinging to her grocery cart; Smith buried under the newspaper, her search for a new job no longer necessary.

The corpses of the other travelers were also stationary, as if frozen in mid-action by some mighty winter storm, their eyes fixed forward, sitting row after row after row. One woman's body was turned, her arm draped over the backseat, cut-off in mid-conversation with the fellow female traveler behind her; another bent over at the waist, arms outstretched, forever scrounging for something in her travel bag beneath the seat. Everyone else was in his or her own seat, the quintessence of well-mannered second graders on the first day of school. Here and there, an arm was hanging loose in the aisle, or sitting idly on the armrest; some hands folded together on laps—all seated as any normal subway passenger, waiting for the next stop and points beyond. The spark of life there one moment, then, just as fleetingly, as the subway car plunged into darkness, snuffed out—poof. A profound stillness settled over the car.

For several moments, the BART train continued barreling down the track towards its destination. The sound of a solitary ringtone from one of the traveler's cell phones broke through the stillness of the car. It rang once, a second time, and finally, a third time before it stopped. An audible beep from the mobile device signaled a message awaited. Other than that, there had been no apparent sign of panic or struggle among the passengers. No sign of trauma or agony. No sign anything was wrong.

As the train slowly rolled into the Civic Center/United

Nations Plaza Station, scheduled to depart in less than two minutes for Millbrae, Daly City, and further on, passengers in the first three cars and in the last two scrambled out onto the platform and made their way swiftly towards the elevators, escalators, and stairs at the central hub of the BART station. Most were either connecting to another line or seeking local transportation to City Hall, the War Memorial Opera House, the Asian Art Museum, the San Francisco Public Library, Louis M. Davies Symphony Hall, or some other destination; choosing taxicabs, boarding buses, or making the decision to walk to their next stop.

No one got off the middle train car, even though its door was wide open.

While the car sat open on the subway platform, Wendy Angelino, a frequent commuter who visited her mother in Oakland twice a week, stepped aboard, carrying an umbrella. She looked around for a seat, but the dull eyes of twenty-four corpses stared back at her in silence. At first, Wendy thought she had stumbled inadvertently onto the set of a horror film that was shooting at the BART station. She loved zombie movies and especially enjoyed the artistry behind the scenes. But as the reality of her situation caught up to her overly-active imagination, Wendy screamed out in terror, turned back around, and fearing that she was now trapped, threw her umbrella at the corpse she imagined was guarding the door. She then jumped off the train and hit the platform, running, screaming at the top of her lungs.

"They're all dead!" Wendy shouted, trying to wave off other commuters. "The subway car is full of dead people."

CHAPTER ONE

A crowd had gathered outside the BART station, located at the Civic Center and United Nations Plaza, comprised of people drawn to the strange, bizarre, and tragic event of a subway car arriving with a full complement of deceased passengers. The crowd scene reminded most of Union Square at Christmas, San Francisco's large and popular shopping plaza, with lights flashing from row upon row of mobile news trucks that surrounded the central hub. All that was missing was a skating rink and the eighty-six-foot-tall tree.

Reporters from CNN, Fox News, MSNBC, CBS, and miasma of other cable television networks stood just outside the gates to the five subway lines on the cement curb talking into their news cameras. Some were interviewing family members of the deceased. Others were treating the event as a potential terrorist attack, like the ones in Europe, speculating about a link between ISIS and the tragic deaths of those aboard the subway car. The media feeding frenzy had just begun.

Kate Dawson drove her BMW 525.i southwest on Market Street, but just beyond Seventh, she was forced to slow her vehicle to a crawl as she began maneuvering through the piranha news trucks parked outside the crime scene. She turned her car right onto the flat, red brick expanse that comprised United Nations Plaza and headed towards the SHN Orpheum Theatre where the mobile command post had been set up. A uniformed patrolman who recognized Kate pulled aside a makeshift barrier, waving her through the labyrinth of police cruisers parked in front and on the opposite side of the street from the theatre. She pulled into the first available spot and paused for a moment to stare out the windshield at the usual crime scene festival.

Dozens of uniformed police officers and plainclothed detectives moved in and out of the station in a random but orderly fashion. Several of the crime scene boys had retrieved their equipment from an unmarked police van, while, at the same time, a police spokesman was talking with some of the local reporters.

Doctor Edgar Brogan, the chief medical examiner, had formed his techs from the ME's office into a small detail and was about to march them down a few flights of stairs to the actual crime scene. Several of his people were brand new, recent graduates of City College who had never actually been to a crime scene and had only trained on newly-deceased cadavers donated to the school. Kate looked at each of their bright, young faces and recalled the day she saw her first dead body. She was a young detective then, recently partnered with Frank Miller. When she arrived at the crime scene, Kate was still hungover from celebrating her promotion from the night before. The sight and smell of a human body, mutilated by a serial killer, caused her to puke her guts out. She wondered how Edgar's people would fare on their first assignment. They all seemed so . . . so inexperienced, or was it that she was getting older, more seasoned.

Dawson got out of her car and headed towards the crime scene. Familiar with a few of those in attendance, she nodded politely as they passed. In addition to the SFPD cops, she encountered several military types: TSA, suits from the FBI, CDC, Homeland Security, and, of course, the Department of Justice. Soldiers from one of the State's National Guard units, carrying M16s, formed a secure ring around the BART station. Kate Dawson wasn't the least bit surprised by the huge turnout of law enforcement officials and military personnel, considering the multi-jurisdictional aspects of the crime. She was just astounded something like this hadn't happened before. A couple dozen men and women found dead aboard a subway train was exactly the kind of scenario city officials had worried about for years, ever since the 9/11 attacks. And the fact that four Middle Eastern men, who were already suspected of killing a police officer in a separate, possibly unrelated incident, were now being sought as prime suspects, created the kind of powder keg that made her job more difficult. Not that the news outlets cared. The reporters were already busy sensationalizing the story by creating their own set of facts and conclusions. Fake news at its best.

With a deep sigh of irritation, Dawson walked past the media and followed the ME's team down to the subway platform. She emerged from the shadows of the stairwell into the commuter area where the five subway lines converged, then headed towards the Richmond line of the BART and found its platform had been turned into what appeared to be a gigantic hamster cage. Large bright lights flooded the area, which transformed the dull darkness into an odd reality, somewhere between day and night. A HAZMAT team from the Centers for Disease Control had rolled out a huge, plastic tarp and erected a barrier around the subway platform, securing the tarp to the concrete walls with several layers of a white reflective tape. In the middle of the platform, a makeshift opening had been cut into the

tarp, and a clear plastic tunnel, connected to the contami-
nated subway car, stretched out about thirty feet to a kind of
decontamination chamber, situated near the commuter core.
The plastic tunnel and the decontamination chamber looked
like they had both been made from Saran Wrap. On both the
inside and the outside of the plastic structure, several members
of the HAZMAT team, dressed in yellow "space suits," were
working feverishly to secure the seams with a heavy-duty tape.
Kate wondered why the CDC had gone to so much trouble to
contain the subway car, but then remembered from one of her
"disaster preparedness" briefings that it was standard protocol
to secure and contain any resource that may have been exposed
to a dangerous pathogen. Even Wendy Angelino, the commuter
who had first discovered the car full of dead bodies, sat off to the
side, encapsulated in her own bubble.

Doctor Brogan's team of crime scene investigators was waiting
for him on the subway platform, watching the HAZMAT crew
put the finishing touches to their containment barrier, when the
Chief Medical Examiner finally caught up to them. He wasn't a
young man any more, but Brogan knew that getting an update
from the director of the CDC was critical to the success of his
forensics team. He was still huffing and puffing when he finally
stepped out onto the subway platform. Kate Dawson scrambled
to keep pace, right behind him.

"Oh, Dawson. Good to see you," he grunted, turning to
his side.

"What's up, Doc?" she asked.

"We've got a really bad one, Inspector."

"So I've heard."

"That's not the worst of it," Brogan said, trying to catch
his breath. He paused at the top of the platform, and started
searching through his pockets, like an absentminded professor.

"My regular team is broken down in traffic, miles from here, and it's unlikely they'll arrive for several hours. I've got to get in there before all the trace evidence gets trampled under the heel of every Tom, Dick, and Uncle Sam, but I've got no one I can trust to work with me." All his pockets had been turned out. "I picked the wrong day to stop smoking."

Dawson looked at the fresh faces of the men and women who stood on the platform, the subway car a mythical beast contained in plastic looming behind them.

"Who are they?" she whispered to the Medical Examiner.

"Trainees. Not one hour of field experience among the bunch. I'd be better off with a group of trained chimpanzees from the local zoo, but the colleges just keep churning them out."

"You can't be serious?"

"Dead serious."

Kate Dawson looked at them again. "Well, let me know if there's anything I can do to help out."

"Count on it, Inspector."

"It's the subway car, isn't it?" one of the newbies, Andrew Wicke, guessed.

Brogan nodded. "The passengers on board are all dead."

Whispered words and nervous excitement rolled through the group, but that excitement was tempered by words from one of their own. He was a recent graduate from City College who subscribed to every conspiracy theory he heard on Talk Radio. How he managed to pass the licensing exam and earn a spot on the forensics team was a mystery to all his peers. "All dead?" he spoke up, cutting through the chatter. "You don't expect us to go in there, do you?"

"Yes, I do," Brogan replied, frowning at Wicke. He then turned his attention to the other team members but gave them a moment to settle down. When they were finally quiet, he said, "I assure you that it will be perfectly safe. I've worked with HAZMAT suits for many years and never experienced a problem. Besides, the CDC has already vented whatever gas was in the car and saved us several canisters for our study back at the lab. They've also tested for a variety of toxins and everything man-made they could think of. Our job is to go into the subway car, examine the bodies, and pick up the search for what killed them where the CDC left off."

"Bullshit!" Wicke exclaimed, getting in the ME's face. "Why don't you tell them why they're really here, Brogan? You owe them at least that."

The Chief Medical Examiner fixed Wicke with a death stare. "Another word out of you, Andrew, and you're out of here."

Wicke continued to hammer away, "Boys and girls, this ain't no typical crime scene. This is a line-up for a slaughterhouse. That subway car is nothing more than a way for the Federal Government to test out a new bioweapon the CDC has developed to pacify crowds in urban environments. You go in there, I guarantee, you ain't coming back out again."

"You must be out of your mind, Wicke," Kate Dawson interjected.

"I heard it on talk radio, Inspector, driving in," Wicke replied.

Dawson shot back, "And I heard one of those commentators say that pigs could fly, but that didn't make it true."

"Now tell me, is that any more outrageous than saying twenty-four healthy people got on at one subway stop and arrived dead at another?"

Brogan turned back to him, and ordered, "You're dismissed, Wicke. I don't want to see you back here again. Martinez, Carson, help Mr. Wicke find his way out, and then get back here double quick."

Martinez and Carson escorted Andrew Wicke, one on either

arm, from the crime scene with Wicke bitching and struggling the whole way.

"Anyone else care to join Mr. Wicke?" Brogan asked, as he glared at everyone on the platform. No one moved nor spoke. They seemed terrified of what he might do next. After a moment, he said, "Let's begin with the understanding that there is no such thing as the 'typical crime scene.' It does not exist. Even though the crime may be identical to many others—homicide, robbery, burglary, or sexual assault—each crime scene itself is different."

"Different in what way?" one of the new members of the team asked, his voice quivering with fear.

Kate Dawson spoke up, "Doctor Monroe, the 'Angel of Death' serial killer, was known for staging his crime scenes like a movie set. He enjoyed arranging his victim's bodies, their personal belongings, the furniture, other props, and even the murder weapon from the scene of one of his favorite movies."

Brogan added, "Inspector Dawson is the detective who first broke the case, and ultimately *ended* Monroe's killing spree."

The group of naïve forensics technicians broke into a spontaneous round of applause. Kate smiled faintly, hardly feeling the superstar. Those events, especially John Monroe, seemed so long ago, perhaps even a lifetime ago. She was no longer that rookie detective who had fallen under the spell of the clever and handsome serial killer. For a split second, Kate wondered if she'd ever feel that way again.

"Each crime scene has an individuality that sets it apart from all others," the Chief Medical Examiner continued. "Hazards abound at crime scenes. Every nuance must be a serious consideration. Forensics work is a dirty, dangerous job. I won't lie to you about that. If you ignore your training—if you try to wing it on your own—people are going to get hurt. They may even die.

You must follow the established protocols if you want to process a crime scene cleanly and still be able to walk away with the secrets you've uncovered."

"And the subway car?" one of the other technicians asked.

"There's nothing supernatural about it," Brogan replied. "No great, hidden governmental conspiracy. It's still just a crime scene."

"Really?"

"Yes, but I think you'll find that it has a story of its own to tell."

The tech swallowed down a deep gulp. "When?"

"Right now," he answered, with a twinkle in his eye. Doctor Brogan reached into his briefcase and pulled out a typed, single-spaced document. There were two columns with a total of fourteen names. Having made multiple copies, he began to pass them out to his team. "We're going to form up into groups of twos—"

"Why?" another one interrupted.

"Batman had Robin, the Lone Ranger had Tonto, Captain America had Bucky, and Starsky had Hutch," Brogan explained. "CDC protocol demands that we pair up in situations like this. It's called 'the buddy system.' Check the list for your name and find out who you're working with today."

"Who's Starsky and Hutch?" Carson asked.

"I think those were the guys who drove the 'General Lee' around," Martinez replied, "but it was definitely before my time."

"Marvel or DC?"

"I'm really not sure, but it would be my guess, with the Confederate Flag on the car, they were not from Gotham City."

"Good guess," Carson agreed.

"Doctor Brogan, who are you partnered with?" Martinez asked, not finding the Chief Medical Examiner's name on the list.

Brogan smiled. Good-naturedly, he had listened to the exchange between Carson and Martinez and had wanted to correct their misrepresentation of "Starsky and Hutch," but he just couldn't find the words inside him. They both seemed pretty clueless. He repressed the urge to laugh and turned to Kate. "Inspector Dawson and I are going to suit up in HAZMATs and make the first incursion into the subway car. I'll want the next pair prepped and ready to go when we return."

For a moment, Dawson did not understand. She continued to stand around, with her hands on her hips, and then, when the realization hit her, she scrambled to the ME's side. "Can't we talk about this first?"

Brogan shook his head and started stripping down to his t-shirt and boxers. "Didn't I just hear you volunteer to help out?"

"Yes, but—"

"You are qualified in all of the HAZMAT safety protocols. I signed the certificate that hangs over your desk."

"But that training was over a year ago."

"In my book, that makes you an expert," he quipped. "Besides, Kate, you're the only one out here that I trust with my life."

"You owe me *big time* for this one," Dawson replied, eyes flashing, as she stripped down to a black sports bra and matching panties.

Moments later, Dawson bent down and climbed through the entrance/exit to the decontamination chamber and was subsequently guided to a small folding chair by a technician from the CDC. Because the chamber was so small, she had to walk hunched over and was relieved to be able to sit down on the folding chair and stretch out her back. Brogan followed her into the chamber and zippered the plastic hatch shut. He then sat down on a folding chair opposite Kate and pointed at the small pile of yellow clothing next to her. The bubble helmet, which resembled a fish bowl turned upside down, sat just behind the pile.

"Kate, we are going to be using a Level A HAZMAT suit, just like the one you used in training," Brogan reported, matter-of-factly. He was all business, and whatever degree of apprehension or danger he may have felt was hidden beneath a veneer of professionalism. "The Level A suit is air-tight and offers the highest level of protection against vapors, gases, mists, and particles. The suit is constructed of several layers of Nomex, with a top layer of Tyvek. It is fully encapsulated, and its Self-Contained Breathing Apparatus is enclosed safely within the suit. Because it is air-tight, you will need to work a release valve so that the suit does not over inflate from the air exhaled by the SCBA."

Dawson had placed the HAZMAT suit on her lap. "You know, I'm still not crazy about the color," she said, sarcastically. Joking was her way of reducing the level of stress, and right at that moment, Kate was feeling very stressed.

"Yellow and orange are the standard CDC colors," he reminded her, not 'getting' it.

"I was thinking something more in black, so my ass doesn't look so big," she replied, holding the suit up against her body.

Brogan shook off a smile. "Your suit also has a two-way, voice-activated radio and a two-channel earpiece speaker for communicating with me and monitoring the operations channel."

"I don't suppose I could get some jazz piped in?" she quipped.

"Working in a HAZMAT suit is very strenuous, as the suits tend to be less flexible than conventional work coveralls," he stated, again all business. "With the exception of laboratory versions, HAZMAT suits can be hot and poorly ventilated—if at all. Therefore, Level A suits are limited by their air supply to around twenty-five to thirty minutes of very strenuous work.

We've got to get in there, conduct our investigation, and get out before our air runs out. And then, we've got another thirty minutes of decontamination to deal with."

"I don't suppose I can get you to reconsider your choice," Kate asked, looking for a way out of her predicament. "Any one of your new trainees would likely make a better selection than me."

Doctor Brogan ignored her last wisecrack. "Now, just like in training, I want you to do what I do to get into your HAZMAT suit. Follow my steps carefully, and if you have a question, please do not hesitate to ask."

Kate Dawson swallowed down a deep gulp.

The Chief Medical Examiner cast the HAZMAT suit out in front of him, and pulled on one leg at a time, sealing the elastic around each ankle with white reflective tape that had the consistency of duct tape. Kate watched him closely, then pulled on her own suit, one leg at a time. She had some trouble wrapping her ankles with the tape, but he helped her out before he continued. Next, he pulled on a pair of leather work boots, with steel toes and shanks that were covered with a yellow, Tyvek bootie, also taped to the suit and the boots. Kate mimicked, pulling on her boots and sealing the ankle seam with tape. Then Brogan pushed his arms through the arm holes and zippered his suit from bottom to top. He wound the tape around the joints several times to prevent any kind of exposure. Dawson did the same. Finally, he pulled on a couple of pairs of rubber gloves and sealed them to his wrist with the tape.

Nearly complete, Brogan reached over and finished wrapping Kate's gloves to the suit, asking her, "Are you okay?"

"I feel like a Thanksgiving turkey that's just been stuffed with Stove-Top stuffing mix and basted with butter," she replied, trying to make light of her discomfort. "I guess I'm ready for the oven."

Uneasily, Brogan stood up and put on his bubble helmet, snapped shut the sealer, and inflated his suit slightly with oxygen. He waited for Dawson to follow his lead, but when she failed to stand up, he grabbed her by the hand and pulled her into a hunched-over position. With the help of the CDC technician, he then put on her helmet and sealed her suit closed.

"Are you okay?" the ME repeated his question, his voice sounding vaguely robotic as he spoke to her through the elaborate two-way radio receiver embedded in the suit.

"You sound like Darth Vader in that helmet," she commented.

Brogan finally laughed. "Chalk it up to the marvels of modern-day science."

"I'm telling you," Kate added, holding her hands to the bubble helmet, "you're really creepin' me out with that voice."

"C'mon, let's go," Brogan encouraged.

Dawson advanced slowly, at first, shuffling her feet down the plastic tunnel until she was secure enough with her balance to walk. She stayed a few feet behind the Chief Medical Officer. With each step, she glanced around her surroundings and was reminded by the elaborate care taken by the CDC to seal off the subway car; that she was walking on highly toxic ground. Kate felt her pulse racing. Clearly, her worst fears seemed to be coming true. What exactly they were dealing with, she didn't know. The hazardous materials could have been chemical, biological, or nuclear. While she marveled at the precision of the operation, she could not help but feel anxious. Every inch brought her closer to the subway car and sudden death. The fact that she was wearing one of the yellow HAZMAT suits did not appear to alleviate any of her anxiety of being separated from oblivion by a thin layer of plastic.

When they had finally reached the subway car, Kate and Doctor Brogan did a full reconnoiter of the exterior, circling the vehicle at a safe distance. The forty-year-old relic had turned a dingy gray, a thin layer of soot running the length of the car. The once-bright, silvery rivets, which held its seams together, had turned brown with rust and shed ruddy tears along its lines. The windows had also yellowed and were now so nearly opaque, the interior light shined dimly through them. They made a complete circle, and then walked around the vehicle again.

Kate noticed some scratches in the aluminum frame and concluded they were new as they had not yet surrendered to the ravages of time. She followed them to the roof and, with some difficult maneuvering, found footprints in the soot, maybe three or four sets of work boots. They seemed to be concentrated around the escape hatch in the ceiling. She deduced that several men must have climbed down from a maintenance hatch and entered the subway car when it was in one of the tunnels. *But that would have required the subway car to be stopped or stalled in one place.*

They completed their second circle and stood in the middle of the platform, the hot lights beating down on them, as they surveyed the subway car. Both were breathing heavy, their chests heaving, gasping for breath. They waited and looked and listened.

"We've got to go in there," Brogan said, breaking the silence.

Dawson nodded her head in the bubble helmet. "I don't think I've got the nerve. Suppose I just wait out here for you?"

"Now what kind of message would that send to our brand-new recruits after I just lectured them about the buddy system," he reasoned with her.

"I'm a cop, Doc, not a crime scene investigator."

He stared her down. "You're one of the finest detectives in homicide and I need your expertise to help solve this case."

For a moment, Dawson thought about it. "Okay, okay! But

if I die in there, I want you to tell Roberts what a fine detective you thought I was. He still thinks of me as some kind of a 'screw-up.'"

"I'll send him a commendation letter for your file."

"Good," she said, with a grin. "That'll really piss him off."

Doctor Brogan entered first; Kate slightly behind him. From where they stood, at the entrance, they could look up and down the center aisle and see every seat, but what Dawson noticed first was the silence. Except for the gentle sound of the respirator unit in her suit, it was deathly silent. Nearly every seat was occupied with a dead body that regarded her with total indifference; its dull, lifeless eyes forever looking away from her at the front of the car. But there was still no sound. No rattling of newspapers. No whispered conversations. No nervous coughs or cleared throats. No ringing of cell phones. No sound at all.

They searched each other's eyes for clarification through their bubble helmets, without uttering a word. Aware of how much work there was to do, reality set in that the crime scene was far worse than either had imagined. Some unknown calamity had struck and killed everyone on board. Was it an act of God? Some force of nature? Or something man-made? Neither of them could say for certain. They had practically no clues, no real starting point.

For a long moment, all they could do was look from corpse to corpse, feeling hot and sweaty as the bright lights beat down on them through the heavy plastic.

Dawson suddenly blurted, "What happened here, doc? Why are all of these people dead?"

"I don't know," Brogan replied, with a shrug of his shoulders. "Infectious diseases are among the leading causes of death worldwide. Perhaps, that's as good a place as any to start."

"Are we talking about some kind of outbreak?"

"I'm not sure, Kate," he said, flatly. "At first, I thought it might have been some sort of fast-working pathogen, such as a new strain of bacteria or a virus. But that would have meant the infectious agent was most likely airborne, and airborne pathogens are notoriously sloppy. The mortality rate is high. Remember the Spanish flu that killed fifty million people in 1918? But because the pathogen was a biological one, the effect on afflicted groups was nowhere near one hundred percent. Someone always survives and provides the antigens to combat the infectious agent."

"But there were no survivors," she reminded him.

Brogan nodded. "Exactly. That's the reason why I don't think we can blame their deaths on a single pathogen."

Kate Dawson was beginning to regain her composure after the initial shock of seeing all the dead bodies. She was also beginning to think clearly in her role as the lead detective came into sharp focus. "What if all the oxygen in the subway car was suddenly, and deliberately, pumped out into space? They wouldn't be able to breathe. They'd choke to death, right?"

The Medical Examiner paused to consider her hypothesis. Absentmindedly, he reached up to scratch his head, but his hand was stopped by the bubble helmet that topped his HAZMAT suit. "Yes," he responded to her question, continuing to think about it. "It's possible we're seeing asphyxiation on a mass scale. Swift, painless, almost direct asphyxiation. But unfortunately, the evidence does not bear out your hypothesis. If a person can't breathe, the first thing they do is loosen their clothing, starting with the neck. Look at that man there," pointing at the pawn-broker, "he's wearing a bowtie, and he hasn't touched it. And that woman with the button-down collar," the pawnbroker's wife of thirty-eight years, "it looks like she's cold."

"You're right," Kate confessed, with a helpless shrug. "I guess I'm not very good at this game of yours."

Reassuringly, Brogan touched her on the shoulder. "Dawson, every crime scene has its own little secret. If we can unlock that secret, then maybe we can figure out what happened here."

She agreed with a nod. Her deceased partner, Frank Miller, used to say something very similar to her, and the ME's words were encouraging. She felt she needed just that to keep going.

The first body she came to was Judy Krebbs, the plump college student who had followed Rodney Grant on board the train. Her obese body had spilled over her seat, and partially filled the seats on either side of her. Kate reached around the young woman's waist to pat her down and came up with the inhaler Judy had tucked into the waistband of her sweats.

"Coronary?" Dawson asked, tossing the inhaler up in the air like a coin and catching it as it came back down.

Brogan had just finished removing the book from Rodney Grant's hand and glanced over his shoulder, eyebrows scrunched. "I doubt it. While it's true that millions of users carry inhalers for chronic obstructive pulmonary disease or COPD, just as many users rely on inhalers for asthma and other problems."

"Are you sure it wasn't a coronary?" she repeated, scrutinizing the body. "She's a big girl, with a high body mass index and an inhaler. She looks like a heart attack just waiting to happen."

"No, coronaries are painful," he said, shaking his head. "People who experience a heart attack grimace. They grasp at their chest or arms. Act like they are having trouble breathing. I see no evidence of that here. Besides if we rank this one as a coronary, what about the other twenty-three people who are not fat and carry no inhalers? How do we explain their deaths as coronaries?"

"But what if it was fast?" Kate persisted. "What if they didn't have time—?"

"Fast?" Brogan asked, scanning the interior of the subway car. "Take a look around. These people were cut down in mid-stride."

Looking around the cabin, the only thing that all of them had in common was that they all died instantly, at the same time. "They don't seem to be in a lot of pain," Kate observed, basing her statement on empirical evidence of what she actually saw. "In fact, they all look quite peaceful. Almost serene."

"I concur," he replied, the beam to his flashlight illuminating the pawnbroker's wrinkled features. "I think we can probably rule out sarin gas and other deadly nerve agents like it."

"What makes you think so, Doc?" she asked, with raised eyebrows. "I seem to recall sarin gas as being quite lethal in that Tokyo subway attack in 1995. If memory serves me correctly, twelve people died that day, and more than five thousand others were treated in local hospitals and clinics, some still in a comatose state. While many of the survivors did ultimately recover, some of the victims suffered permanent damage to their eyes, lungs, and digestive systems."

"Take another look at the passengers."

They stared back at her, indifferently.

"Exposure to nerve gas, like sarin, brings on seizures, cardiac arrest, and death within minutes," Brogan said. "An *extremely* painful death, in fact."

Kate tilted her head contemplating Judy Krebbs. Somewhere, in the back of her mind, she had forgotten something or ignored something. Some fact or detail that would have provided her with the answer Brogan was looking for. She didn't know what it was and wracked her brain to come up with it, then gave up. "I'll be damned if I know what you want."

"Look at them, Dawson. Look closely," he repeated, pointing

to Ricardo Milan, Gladys Stevens, Wanda Smith, and Rodney Grant. "There's not a single nosebleed among them. No foaming at the mouth. No vomit. No bulging eyes. Look at them. Do you see any sign of trauma? Any evidence of discomfort?"

"No. They appear to be calm, cool, collected."

"Poisons like anthrax, sarin, ricin or tetrodotoxin attack the central nervous system, the brain, and the lungs." The ME counted them off on the fingers of his gloved hand. "You'd not only see trauma written all over their faces, but some would be foaming at the mouth, while others were vomiting. This would be a very messy crime scene with vomit and excrement all over the floor."

She tried wipe that thought out of her head. "Then what are we dealing with here?"

"If I'm right, we're dealing with a new, weaponized neuro-toxin that is several orders of magnitude deadlier than sarin gas," Brogan answered, with a satisfied look in the ruddy complexion of his face.

"Deadlier than sarin gas?" she repeated, clutching her throat. "What could be deadlier than sarin gas?"

"Botulinum Toxin (BTX) is the most poisonous substance known to man," he said, matter-of-factly. "Produced by the bacterium *clostridium botulinum*, less than 1μg/kg body weight is sufficient to kill in large numbers. Microbial toxins promote infection and disease by directly damaging host tissues and by disabling the immune system. While some bacterial toxins, such as BTX, are among the most potent natural toxins known in the civilized world, they also have practical uses in treating dystonia and spastic disorders, as well as inducing muscular atrophy. But no one, as far as I know, has been able to produce a weaponized version."

"Until now," she said, completing his sentence.

"That's right. Until now."

Kate puzzled over the term 'muscular atrophy.' "Doctor Brogan, you've stated that BTX has its medicinal uses as well, like providing relief to sufferers of dystonia and spastic disorders. If a weaponized form of BTX was used, could that explain why our victims were found 'frozen' in place?"

The Chief Medical Examiner did not answer right away but stared off into space, thinking, tapping his finger. "We've been looking at commonplace answers when the real solution has been staring us right in the face. We've always imagined that our enemy would rely on a conventional weapon—nerve gas or a dirty bomb—to strike at us in one of our large cities. But what if they produced a microbial toxin in a bio-war facility that was so deadly, so dangerous, they'd have no way of testing it out first without endangering the lives of their own people. The only way they'd know if their new weapon was effective was by testing it on a small, isolated group of people, such as passengers on a subway car."

"The Manhattan Project," Kate nearly whispered.

"That's not a bad analogy," he replied. "You know, when Oppenheimer first proposed testing the atomic bomb, he didn't know what would happen. Many of his fellow scientists, including Edward Teller, were concerned they were going to create an unending chain reaction that would destroy the earth. Despite all their fears, Oppenheimer, Fermi, and the rest of them still went ahead with their test, successfully detonating the first A-bomb at the Trinity site."

Kate understood the implications.

"This was their Trinity test site," Brogan continued. "Secluded from a major population center, but still close enough to kill a large enough sample, the terrorists needed a plain, simple way to test their bio-weapon. They had no way of knowing just how successful their new neurotoxin would be."

"From what I'm seeing, their test was pretty successful." She waved open-handed at all of the dead bodies.

"Yes, and if I'm right, we are looking at a weaponized Botulinum Toxin. We should be searching for a well-equipped lab that can produce the neurotoxin safely in mass quantities. Botulinum Toxin is very complex and dangerous to make, but it can be produced by a trained chemist with chemicals and other elements that are readily available in the San Francisco market-place," the ME added, as he resumed examining each of the passenger's bodies, one at a time. "The only real problem that I can see for the terrorists is how to transport the neurotoxin without being exposed themselves. To reduce the risk, they'd likely transport it in a liquid solution, tightly covered. But it does appear they've solved that problem because we have not had any other reports of unusual deaths lately."

"We'll want to keep the local clinics and hospitals informed."

Doctor Brogan had dropped to one knee and was struggling to pull the pants off one of the dead male passengers who had been sitting upright. The man's body fell rigidly from his seat onto the floor of the subway car. Brogan loosened the man's belt and unzipped the fly, then pulled down the pants and underwear of the male victim. "Have a look at his buttocks, Inspector."

Kate did, but then turned her head away quickly.

"You'll never make it as a medical examiner," he quipped, leaning to one side and looking at her over his shoulder.

She turned back slowly; her face white as a linen shroud. "What was your first clue?"

"Kate, I need you to focus."

"I'm doing my best, Doc." She swallowed back the bile coming up.

"Typically, blood in a dead person goes to its lowest points,"

Brogan lectured her like she was a first-year medical student. "Postmortem lividity should appear as a bluish-purple or reddish-purple color. Do you see any purplish marks on his butt or thighs?"

"No," Kate replied, holding her right hand to the bubble helmet. She felt quite woozy.

"Exceptions to these colors often provide important forensic clues to the cause of death." He pressed his gloved hand against the white flesh. "For example, when we're dealing with carbon monoxide poisoning, lividity appears to be cherry red in color. Death due to intense cold, such as hypothermia, produces a bright pink color, and the same is true when a recently deceased body is locked away in a refrigerator prior to performing an autopsy. When a compound called methemoglobin forms in the blood, as occurs in exposure to lethal concentrations of potassium chlorate, nitrates, and aniline, lividity tends to be dark chocolate, brown color."

"Looks like dark chocolate," she added, her focus all but spent.

"Yes! You know, that's exactly what I thought."

Kate was close to vomiting in her helmet, but quickly moved her hand to blot out the image of the ME leaning over the dead body in order to steady herself. *Oh shit! I'm gonna hurl!* Dawson took a few steps backward but realized that they were no longer alone. Someone or something was moving by the sliding doors. *Did we miss one of the bodies? Maybe they aren't all dead after all? Or maybe just one of them had come back to life?* Her heart skipped a beat.

Shaking like a leaf with fear, Dawson started to turn slowly, giving that primal fight-or-flight response plenty time to work itself out. But as Kate's peripheral vision in the bubble helmet began to fill with the shapes of two large men in green

HAZMATs with weapons, she felt a rising terror in her gut. She reached for the service pistol that she routinely carried on her hip, but it was no longer there! Her chest heaving, her eyes wide, she demanded to know, "Who the hell are you!?"

"I'm sorry to disturb your work, ma'am," one of the Army men said politely, his voice clipped and somewhat mechanical. "But I'm going to need you and the other man to come with us."

"What's going on?"

"This is now a restricted area," the other Army man added, "and only military personnel above a certain grade will be permitted to remain."

Kate looked beyond the two men to the platform. An olive green military truck was parked there on an angle, and an Army private marched back and forth with a rifle on his shoulder in front of the rear door. Another uniformed private stood near the hatch to the decontamination chamber. To see through the bright light streaming through the plastic, she squinted her eyes and could distinctly see a M4A1 rifle in his hands. These guys may not have appeared to be the brightest crayons in the box, but they were playing for keeps.

"I demand to know what's going on!" she repeated herself.

"Ma'am," the first Army man said, his face blank and expressionless in the large bubble helmet, "for reasons of national security, this area is being quarantined and all those in that area are under martial law."

Kate hesitated for a moment, then said, "This is my crime scene."

"Not anymore," the second Army man replied, coldly.

"Less than an hour ago, your governor issued a state of emergency for the San Francisco Bay area. He instructed the BART to be closed temporarily and ordered the National Guard to cordon off several blocks around the site," the first Army man reported, bringing her up to date.

At that moment, Brogan climbed uneasily to his feet and stood between Dawson and the two soldiers. "What's going on here, Inspector?"

"Nothing but a couple of claim jumpers," Dawson answered, never taking her eyes of the soldiers.

The ME turned to face them. "My name is Doctor Edgar Brogan, Chief Medical Examiner of the San Francisco Police Department. This is my crime scene. Inspector Dawson is helping me with my investigation."

"You're out of the cast now, Hamlet," the second Army man joked. "Your understudy has taken over."

"I'm afraid he's right, Doctor Brogan," the first Army man added, dismissing the Medical Examiner. "This is now a military operation and you are both subject to summary execution."

"I want to see your authorization," Kate demanded, her hand out. She was not about to surrender her crime scene to a couple of Army pricks. Her determination was written all over her face.

"Authorization? You want to see my authorization," the second Army man asked, as he removed his Glock19 from its holster and cleared the empty chamber with a KAMerchants of Death CHINK! He pointed the weapon at Brogan. "You wanted to see my authorization? How about the United States fuckin' government?"

For a moment, Dawson looked surprised, and then she nodded, aware. "Oh, that's really mature," she stated, with irony. "Drawing on an unarmed man. Why don't you and I even up those stakes and then you try that one with me?"

"Anytime, you pinko bitch."

"Ma'am," the first Army man said, far more politely and diplomatically, "we would rather not arrest the two of you, but we are prepared to do whatever is necessary to secure the integrity of this site."

The second Army man grinned, a big toothless grin. "Whatever is necessary."

"Sergeant, this is still my crime scene," Kate tried to keep her voice low and steady, but she couldn't help it. She was upset by their damned arrogance and frightened for the ME. "Twenty-four civilians died here of unknown causes and I'm going to find out what happened to them. No matter what it takes."

"No matter *what* it takes," Brogan echoed her sentiment.

"Well, then, I'm afraid to say that one of us is going to be gravely disappointed," the soldier replied, with a smile.

Kate cleared her throat. "What are your orders, Sergeant?"

"We've been ordered to pick up all remaining civilian personnel," he responded, "and transport them to an assembly area on the other side of the cordon. Now, we can do that the easy way or . . ."

"We'll not give you any trouble," Kate promised the soldier, and she was more than true to her word. They were escorted down the plastic tunnel in their HAZMAT suits and scrubbed clean.

Outside of the plastic tunnel, at the exit to the decontamination chamber, Kate Dawson climbed out first and stepped firmly down on the subway platform. She was wearing a pair of Army fatigues, a couple of sizes too big. Brogan followed her out, also dressed in a drab, olive-green uniform. He scanned the platform for his students and was actually surprised that they were no longer waiting for him.

They were met by a small detachment of soldiers, carrying M4A1 rifles, who marched them up several flights of stairs and loaded them into the back of a small Army helicopter that was waiting for them.

Once airborne, Kate Dawson leaned over to the ME. "I

want you to call that friend of yours at the CDC," she said, in a whisper. "Tell him what we found and let him know that you think it's a weaponized form of Botulinum Toxin."

"Wouldn't you rather tell him yourself?"

"No, he's your friend," Kate replied. "Besides, I've got other things to do."

CHAPTER TWO

An hour later, as she walked into the Hall of Justice, Kate Dawson passed by the Chief of Police's Lincoln Town Car parked at the curb and realized that her late day had just gotten more complicated. She climbed several flights of steps and turned left toward the bureaus. She was half expecting Roberts to glare at her from his glass-enclosed office when Dawson entered the Homicide Bureau, but that familiar, almost agitated look on the Lieutenant's face was nowhere to be found. Kate headed directly to their small cantina and poured herself a steaming cup of coffee, added a couple of sugars and a shot of milk from the refrigerator, then opened several of the cabinets, scouring for donuts or something else sweet but came up empty-handed. Disappointed, Kate headed back out with her cup of coffee in hand.

Ramirez appeared to be the only one left in the Bureau. He was sitting at his desk, typing a report into his computer, when she approached him. An open bag of greasy donuts, with the name "Dynamo Donuts" stenciled on the side of the bag, was sitting on the corner of his desk.

"They're in the Conference Room," he said, with a slight Hispanic accent.

"Thanks, Jorge," Dawson said, attempting to snitch one of his donuts. "I don't suppose I could trouble you for one of those donuts. I missed dinner again this evening, and something tells me that this is going to be a long night."

"*Si*," Jorge Ramirez replied, nodding his head, then reached across his desk for the bag and held it wide open for her.

Licking her parched lips, Kate looked inside the bag, then pulled one out with a wax-paper wrapping. She took a big bite. "Sticky buns," she said with a sigh as she swallowed it down, nearly whole. Dawson took a sip of her coffee, then another bite of the surgery confection. "My favorite." Her words came out warbled since her mouth was full. "You must have known I was coming back here after my visit to the crime scene."

"Yep. The Lieutenant wanted me to send you right into the Conference room when you arrived."

Kate Dawson finished eating the first sticky bun, licked her fingers, had another sip of her coffee, then started devouring a second one. In between bites, she managed to find out from Ramirez who was in the Conference room with Roberts—the Chief of Police and some young analyst from Division.

"He's running a real tight ship today," he added.

Kate patted him on the shoulder. "Thanks for the heads-up, Jorge."

"Oh," Ramirez remembered, and handed her a manila folder. "They found the getaway car abandoned in the Mission District. Impound has it now, but they'll be dropping it off first thing in the morning for the ME."

Dawson nodded.

She stood silent for a long moment, looking through the folder, contemplating what it all meant. Slurping down the last of her coffee and crumpling the cup into the Dynamo Donuts bag, she disposed of it all in the first empty trash can and squared her shoulders in anticipation.

Walking into the Conference room and quietly closing the door behind her, she briefly locked eyes with Lieutenant Roberts, then sat down in the chair opposite the Chief of Police, folding her arms across her chest.

Not pleased, Chief Gates resumed his discussion, "The truth is . . ." With a degree of hesitation, he paused for a moment to swallow down hard an ample measure of humiliation, wiping his mouth with the back of his hand. "Hell, we're just not ready! We've suspected that ISIS would strike a major target on the West Coast for a while now. The government has thrown all its intelligent services into the mix, and we have been collaborating with MI6, Mossad, the Deuxieme Bureau, Interpol, and others to determine their next move. The good money is on a strike right here."

"In San Francisco?" Lieutenant Roberts asked, eyes as wide as saucers. Gates affirmed, "Intel is suggesting a sporting event or outdoor concert."

"The Super Bowl," Kate said, not entirely surprised, peering from face to face. When she reached the young woman seated next to the Chief of Police, Kate stopped and stared. In her late twenties, extremely beautiful, and dressed in formal blues; the creases in her uniform were perfectly pressed to razor sharpness. "They're targeting the Super Bowl."

With a sense of somber confidence, the young woman said, "That's what I'm here to find out."

"Inspector Dawson wrote the initial report about the possibility of a terrorist strike on Super Bowl Sunday," Roberts stated, as he passed her report around the conference room table. He appeared to be proud of his detective's work, but only as far as the Chief was concerned. "She agrees with you."

"Thank you," the young woman replied, with a roll of her eyes.

Setting protocol, Nelson Gates stood up at the end of the table. The Chief of Police was a stocky man in his early fifties with salt-and-pepper hair that was combed back over a bald spot. While he often wore the formal dress blues, today he was dressed like a stockbroker in a black pin-striped suit, with a white shirt and red tie. He smiled at the young woman next to him, and said, "Alex Starke took over the City's Counter-Terrorism Task Force six months ago. She may look young to you, but she's produced some outstanding results in the short time she's been on the Force. I've discovered that, when I want to get certain things done, I turn them over to Alex, and they get done. That's how I plan to proceed here."

The Chief sat back down, but his words hung heavily over the conference room table, making it abundantly clear to the others that Starke was in charge as far as he was concerned.

Alex Starke leaned forward in her chair and opened her own manila folder on the table in front of her. "The initial descriptions of that poison gas attack on the BART subway car and the execution-like shooting of Officer Hartwell by Jihadists from a local sleeper cell appear to the public to be two random events, and we're going to let them continue to think that. But most of our experts agree that the two events are most likely part of one larger, coordinated attack, orchestrated by terrorist mastermind, Abu Baker al Baghdadi."

"Christ, almighty!" Roberts exclaimed, nearly in shock. "He's killed more people than the black plague."

"As the former number two man at Al Qaeda, he's believed to have plotted the 9/11 Benghazi attacks and is suspected in coordinating the Paris and Brussels attacks with other former Al Qaeda operatives," Starke continued.

"Al Baghdadi is alleged to be the current leader of the Islamic State of Iraq and Syria, or ISIS."

The Chief of Police added, "If he did plan that poison gas attack, then it's safe to say that others will likely follow."

"It wasn't poison gas, Chief," Kate corrected him.

"Then what the hell was it?" Gates responded gruffly, looking at the seasoned inspector with doubt.

"It was a weaponized form of—" Dawson started to respond but was cut off in mid-sentence by her younger rival.

"—Botulinum Toxin," Starke concluded. "The neurotoxin is considered to be one of the deadliest substances known to man, and from what the CDC reports, deadlier than what we could have imagined. Our experts believe that it was probably manufactured right here in the States, maybe even San Francisco, by a trained chemist with materials smuggled in through the Mexican border."

Kate Dawson glared at her. Not only had the Chief's girlfriend stolen her words, but she had also made Kate look insignificant—worse, redundant. She was beginning to wonder where this woman got her intel from. After all, Kate had just come from the crime scene. *Had Starke been monitoring communications with the Chief Medical Examiner the whole time we were there?* Now, she felt like she was being ridiculous, paranoid. *Just because you're paranoid, she thought to herself, doesn't mean they aren't still out to get you.*

Starke went on to say, "My priority, from the very beginning, has been to develop some kind of defense strategy."

"Are there no known antidotes?" Roberts asked, his face blanched white in fear.

"We've been working on plans to neutralize the neurotoxin, including one radical plan to immunize large portions of the population, but many of those plans are still on the drawing room table," the young woman confessed.

"So, then," the Lieutenant interjected, "nothing we have now can stop them?"

Gates exhaled loudly. "We expected much more lead time."

"We've just got to hope that we can stop their operatives at the border," Starke said, tilting up her chin in determination.

"How long have we been complaining about the border and doing absolutely nothing about it?" Roberts asked.

Kate Dawson had heard enough. "Those chemicals and other raw materials don't have to come through Mexico, Chief," Kate said, repeating Brogan's words. "They're all readily available right here in the local market."

Now, with situations reversed, Starke glared at her.

"In fact, if I were conducting this investigation," Kate added, with a slight smile. "I'd start by looking right here for a well-equipped lab that could produce the neurotoxin safely in mass quantities."

"We've already initiated a preliminary study of local area businesses that might have links to Al Qaeda or ISIS," Starke responded.

Gates barely reacted as he measured both women for a beat. "That's brilliant," he replied dully. "Roberts, I don't know how we could possibly fail with two such energetic talents working for us."

"If this is the work of ISIS, then God help us," Roberts conceded.

"Let's not complicate this any more than it needs to be by bringing God or 'Allah' into the picture," the Chief of Police warned him. "We've already got one group of religious fanatics that want to kill us. By invoking God's name, we run the risk of igniting a holy war."

"They call it 'jihad' for a reason," he reminded his boss.

Gates grunted. "I am familiar with the term, but it is up to us, as police officers, to keep the peace. We'll bring in those four men who are suspected in the death of Officer Hartwell and they'll receive a fair trial. But I will not tolerate a witch hunt for their known associates in the Muslim community," he said, in no uncertain terms. "The San Francisco Bay Area has one of the largest Muslim populations in the United States. Nearly two hundred and fifty thousand Muslims live in the six counties around the City. Many work in Silicon Valley; others teach, own businesses, drive cabs. They worship in their mosques, care for their families, send their children to school, pay taxes, and have nothing in common with the radical Islamists in the Middle East that seek to destroy us."

"Understood, Chief," Roberts acknowledged.

"I refuse to let San Francisco become another Palestinian war zone. The majority of Muslims in this City must know that we stand solidly with them against those few terrorists who undermine the peace. To prevent another San Bernardino or Orlando, we must encourage our Muslim neighbors to partner with police. That very message will form the basis of my press conference tomorrow afternoon."

"We stand behind you, Chief," Roberts added, but it wasn't entirely the truth.

"I'm counting on it, Roberts," Gates replied, his words creating another natural pause which hung over the room.

"I'd like to see the subway car as soon as possible, Lieutenant," Starke said finally, the tone in her voice more of a command than a request. She stood facing the head of the Homicide Bureau, tapping her foot, waiting for a response.

Roberts was deliberately slow in answering her. "We'll talk about that later."

Kate Dawson shook her head, and said, "Lieutenant, the Army has taken over the crime scene and invoked martial law. I doubt if any of us will be getting in there anytime soon."

"Then I want to examine the getaway car," Alex pressed. "I understand Hartwell got off a couple of shots. Maybe he got lucky?"

Gates and Roberts exchanged glances and shrugged.

"Impound's got it now," Kate reported, surrendering the manila folder to Starke, "but it should be in the ME's possession by morning."

Alex snatched the folder out of her hands and slammed it open on the table.

"Dawson, you're dismissed. Go home and get some rest. We'll take it from here," Roberts ordered, cold as ice. "On your way out, find Starke an empty desk in the Bureau. Preferably one with a working computer. Then have Ramirez assign her a login and password. She thinks she can find that lab. Let's give her the tools she needs and see what kind of intel she develops."

"Yes, sir," Kate replied.

She rose to escort the young woman to the door.

"Sir?" Starke asked, exchanging a look with the Chief of Police.

"I have a lot to cover with Roberts," he said, with a sigh. "Why don't you let them find you a desk and start looking for that lab?"

"Yes, sir," she replied, somewhat deflated.

Kate Dawson held open the conference room door for Starke, then followed her out.

After the door had closed, the Chief of Police proudly said, "Keep your eye on her, Jim. You've just had your first glimpse of the future of law enforcement. They're educated, knowledgeable, self-assured, opinionated, and, yes, a little ruthless. She's one, very impressive young woman."

Roberts grinned. "I don't think I've ever seen that twinkle in your eye before, Nelson. Sure, she's very impressive, knowledgeable, even cocky, but we've seen other women like her. What gives?"

"Not like this one."

"If I didn't know you better," the Lieutenant said, with a wink, "I'd say you got a real hard-on for this one."

"Ah, what I wouldn't give to be twenty again," Gates confessed, a wrinkle of a smile crusting his fifty-year-old features. He paused, thinking about it for a few moments. "But I'm more than twice her age—an old man—and she has her whole career ahead of her."

"I'm glad you recognize that, Chief."

"Ah, I've struggled with that fact every day of my life since I first laid eyes on Alex Starke at the Academy. Still, there are plenty of older men who end up withyounger women every day."

"That's just not you, my friend. You're a family man."

"You don't understand. I'd be willing to give that all away for one torrid night with her between the sheets."

"C'mon, let's go back to my office," Roberts said, opening the conference room door for the Chief of Police. "I've got a bottle of Pappy Van Winkle's twenty-year-old bourbon in my desk. One sip and, I guarantee you, you won't mind going back home tonight to Alice and the kids."

"Alice who?" he jested, exiting the room.

"Your wife of *twenty-six* years," Roberts reminded him, as they made the short walk to the Lieutenant's office.

Gates spied Alex Starke across the room and hesitated. She was seated at a computer in the empty room, with Dawson and Ramirez hovering over her. "Did I mention that she finished at the top of her class at the Academy?"

"Alice?"

"No, Alex," the Chief of Police corrected him. "Do you know that every bureau head has been clamoring for her? You're the only one who hasn't said anything. She'd make you one hell-of-a lead detective."

The Lieutenant raised an eyebrow. "I already have one *hell-of-a* lead detective. But don't bother telling her that. Dawson already thinks she's the best and reminds me every chance she gets."

"You never did like her, did you?"

"It wasn't a question of 'like,' sir," Roberts defended himself. "I've just never respected her investigative skills. Frank Miller, God rest his soul, partnered with her, and used to speak highly of her detective work. But to me, she's always been somewhat of a loose cannon, a maverick who felt the rules didn't apply to her."

"She does have an impressive arrest record."

"What good is 'an impressive arrest record' if she's left huge gaping holes in her cases for appeal?"

"And exactly how many of those cases were overturned on appeal?"

"I'm not really sure, Chief," Roberts replied, reluctantly. "A lot."

"Only two of her cases in the last year have been overturned on appeal."

"Two? I was convinced that it was a lot more than that."

"You know, she's taken and passed her lieutenant's exam," Gates reported, shifting his gaze to Dawson, watching her at a distance as she interacted with Starke, nodding to himself. "Most of my people think she's ready to run a bureau, with the right mentoring."

"There's an opening available?"

"Robbery. It's hers, if she wants it," the Chief of Police replied, simply. "Hasn't she told you?"

Roberts snorted out his nose and shook his head, seemingly resigned to the inevitable. "She'll made a fine lieutenant, Chief, despite my personal misgivings. The Robbery Bureau would be lucky to have her."

"You may want to tell her that. We're still waiting for her decision. She's been stonewalling everyone, including me." Entering his office, Roberts went right to the metal file drawer behind his desk and reached into the middle drawer for the bottle of Pappy's. He unscrewed the cap and sniffed inside, savoring the smoky flavor of the maple-syrup-colored spirit. To him, it smelled like heaven. He poured a shot of bourbon into a paper cup, and handed it to the Chief of Police, then filled his coffee mug with a hefty pour.

"Here's to swimmin' with bowlegged women," he said, raising his coffee mug to the Chief as a toast.

Gates swallowed down his drink in one gulp. "Ahhhhhhhhhhh," he said, with great satisfaction, and licked his lips. It tasted mighty good to him. "I was fifteen when I first heard that toast," he said, feeling good. "I never knew what it meant until I got to college and had my first date with an upper classman. She was bowlegged as hell, and it turned out to be one of the best nights of my life."

"Women were simpler then," Roberts reminisced. "All you had to do was decide whether you wanted a blonde or a brunette, pick out the height, the weight, and the size of their tits, and let nature take its course. There was no bullshit about condoms, diseases, or morals. You just had to find a place to do it, and she was all yours. Ready, willing, and able."

"I think I'm in love with Alex Starke," Gates confessed.

Roberts shot him one of his patented steely looks. "You and I had better have another drink," he said, with a sense of resignation. He poured two more shots, and both slugged them down together. "I'm beginning to understand why you want to make Starke my lead detective, so you can keep her close by without raising any objections from your staff, and you know she'll be safe and sound with me in a high-profile position."

"At the same time, Lieutenant," he added, "your protégé gets a well-deserved promotion and takes over the Robbery Bureau."

Roberts scratched the stubble of beard growing on his face, then reached up to adjust the small, horned-rim glasses on the end of his nose as if to bring the faraway image of the female police inspector into focus. Dawson was still working with Starke on the far side of the Bureau. "I doubt she'll ever take that promotion, Chief. She seems to have found her niche right here in Homicide."

"Well, then, you need to kick her right in the ass. For her own good."

"Sir?" the Lieutenant queried.

"Dammit, Roberts, you know that promotions around here are rare. Usually, someone has to die before one opens," Gates said, reasoning with his bureau head. "And with all the new, young hotshots, like Starke, fighting for a place of their own, Dawson could quickly find herself standing still next to one of them. She's only fucking with her career."

"I'll talk to her, sir," Roberts promised.

"You do more than talk to her, Lieutenant," the Chief of Police ordered him. "You light a fire under her ass; a fire so hot that she'll be jumping out of the flame into the frying pan before it's all through."

James Roberts slowly blinked his agreement, while out in the vast collection of computers and desks that made up the Homicide Bureau, Alex Starke glanced up at Dawson and lifted her hands palms-up.

"I don't know exactly what I'm looking for," she confessed, looking back at the computer screen, "but I'll know it when I see it. It will either be a spike in the power grid of utilities for Pacific Gas and Electric customers at a new location in the City or it will be an increase in residential trash pick-ups for a neighborhood in decline. I'm also running down reports that neighbors have filed about local area burglaries. You'd expect a decline in a community where guards with AK47s are routinely patrolling a home lab during the late-night hours."

"I suppose you might also run across complaints that residents had made to their local HOAs about the influx of strangers walking around their streets with Russian-made semi-automatic rifles," Kate added, looking down at her. She had meant it as a joke, but the humor had completely evaded her younger counterpart.

Alex Starke did a double-take over her shoulder. "I hadn't really thought about that one," she said, totally oblivious, "but it makes perfect sense."

Kate Dawson patted the rookie on the back. "Well, it sounds like you've got a lot of work ahead of you, Starke, so I'll just leave you to it. I'm going to go home and catch a few hours of sleep before I have to report back here tomorrow morning."

"I've reviewed your duty roster for tomorrow," the young woman reported, turning in her chair to face Dawson. "Inspector Clark and Detective Jawara are both available. Since they just wrapped up a three-month investigation into those deaths at the City's Power Plant, they've not been given a new assignment. I want them both to work for me, knocking on doors and doing surveillance."

Kate barely had a chance to react. Very tired and unprepared to listen to Starke dictating personnel decisions, she swallowed down the woman's words, like something stuck in her craw, and replied, "That's a matter you'll have to take up with the Lieutenant. He makes those decisions."

"But you're the lead detective, aren't you?" Starke asked, full of guile. "I just assumed that the two of you consulted on all personnel matters. I can see now that I was simply mistaken. Sorry."

"Frank Miller was our lead detective," Kate explained, sober and aware. "He consulted with the Lieutenant on all decisions that were made and did a damn good job for twenty-two years. He was killed in the line of duty while we were working under-cover at the Black Rose, trying to bring in the 'Angel of Death' serial killer. Over the years since then, I've helped Roberts with some of his decisions."

"The 'Angel of Death' murders. Yes, I read about them at the Academy," she said, almost purring with delight. "You left your partner alone, didn't you? You abandoned him so that you could pursue the department's number one suspect through the club. But then, you were in love with him, weren't you? Not Miller. I mean Jay Monroe, the serial killer."

"*John Monroe* was a monster."

"But you were in love with him? Weren't you?"

"Is there anything else that you'd like to know?"

Alex Starke smirked. "What was it like making love to a serial killer?"

Dawson had heard enough, but she refused to surrender her veneer of collegiality to the young upstart in dress blues. "I'm tired, Starke, and I'm going home now. I'm sure you can find your way out of here, or perhaps you can just wait for the Chief of Police to drive you home."

"Nelson will make sure I get home safely."

"Oh, I'm sure he will."

"Tell me one last thing, Inspector," Starke said, deliberate and cunning in her approach to the senior detective. "From every-thing I hear, the Homicide Bureau is the bureau! None other like it. I've heard that careers are made in Homicide, more so than any of the other bureaus."

"Why do you ask?" Kate asked, raising an eyebrow.

Starke restrained glee but barely. "The Chief promised me

any job I want after this investigation is wrapped up. And from where I sit right now, the opening in Homicide looks pretty damn good to me."

"We don't have an opening in Homicide."

"You will," Starke replied, turning back to the computer at her desk. Then, a moment later, she muttered under her breath, "Roberts needs a good lead detective that he can trust and I'm going to make myself indispensable to him."

Dawson heard her words yet refused to acknowledge a response. Instead, she walked away from her rival and headed out the door.

Kate Dawson was nearing the turn-off for Bayside Village Apartments and home, when she realized that she had spent the last thirty minutes in traffic obsessing over Alex Starke. *Never have I met a more irritating, egotistical, and arrogant bitch in all my life.* But her dislike for Starke went far deeper, almost to a primal level, which was all about survival. Her instincts told her that Starke was bad news. The fact that Kate had devoted her entire career in law enforcement trying to find the essence of humanity in everyone was completely lost on Starke by her obnoxious and conceited persona. Dawson wondered if beneath those watery, baby-blue eyes and physically-perfect physique laid a murderous robot programmed to make her life a living hell. Credit her neighbor Lenny for introducing her to the *Terminator* films.

She was still obsessing about Starke when she pulled into a parking spot in front of her building and shut the ignition. Kate climbed the steps to the third floor and walked down the length of the corridor. As she approached Lenny Provolone's apartment, she paused for a moment outside his door. She hadn't seen him in nearly a week and wondered how he was doing. When Dawson knocked on the door, the door swung open on its own. Instinctively, she reached for her service pistol, and got down into a crouch. Lenny's body was on the floor.

"Lenny!" Kate screamed.

With her gun still in hand, she knelt down on the floor beside her neighbor's crumpled body and stretched her left hand to feel the carotid artery in his neck. Provolone was still alive, but just barely. She looked down at his stomach where his hands were wrapped tightly around the hilt of a large butcher knife, which appeared to be deeply embedded, but Dawson knew better than to try to remove it since it was actually helping to stem the blood flow. Pulling it out would increase blood loss and cause further injury to internal organs. "What the hell happened to you, my friend?" she said aloud, but he was unconscious, unable to respond.

She looked out into the darkness of the apartment, sighting her Beretta back and forth at imaginary targets. The room had been tossed, like someone was looking for something Lenny had. When she was satisfied that Lenny's assailant was no longer in the apartment, Kate holstered her weapon. She reached for her cell phone and dialed 911 immediately.

"911, what is the nature of your emergency?" the operator responded.

"This is Kate Dawson," she said into the receiver. "My neighbor has been stabbed with a kitchen knife. He is a white male, approximately five-feet, six-inches tall, forty-years-old. Bayside Village Apartments, #13."

"We've got a vehicle en route to your location."

Kate Dawson then reached across Lenny's floor to where clothing lay scattered and pulled a jacket to her, tucking it under Lenny's head so his airway was open and unobstructed, then stretched him out by pulling his legs straight. Finding a bath towel, not caring if clean or dirty, she pressed it firmly down around the wound to keep it from bleeding.

Within twenty minutes, the ambulance was outside Lenny's apartment and two EMTs were caring for him. His injuries were serious, but not as life-threatening as Kate had first imagined. Her mind raced at who could have done such a thing to him. The first name that came to mind was Rebecca, an old and possibly deadly foe.

CHAPTER THREE

In the morning, Kate Dawson awoke in a chair outside the Intensive Care Unit at UCSF Medical Center, her body nearly folded into thirds like a pretzel in the standard wooden chair. She had spent the night, sleeping on her purse as a makeshift pillow and a thin, cotton sheet as a blanket pulled over her head in the hallway. Kate would not have spent the night outside the ICU for just anyone, but she had been so worried about her friend and neighbor that she refused to leave the hospital while he was there, clinging to life from a stab wound from an unknown assailant. Now, as the late-night shift changed to morning, she climbed to her feet, stretched, and stole a peak in his room. Lenny Provolone was still unconscious, resting, the veins in his left arm feeding hungrily on his IV drip.

Dawson backed out of the room and searched for the duty nurse. She found her coming out of another patient's room. "What can you tell me about Mr. Provolone's condition?"

"Are you a member of his immediate family?" the nurse asked.

"No," Kate replied, reaching for her SFPD badge.

"Well, I'm afraid that this patient's records are confidential."

Kate Dawson held her badge up. "Nurse, I am the detective

who found Mr. Provolone and called it in. He is my neighbor and my friend. When I found the door to his apartment ajar, I entered, and discovered his body on the floor. He had the stab wound and was basically unresponsive."

"Your friend was very lucky that you just happened by," the nurse said, acquiring Lenny's chart. "Even though the stab wound missed all the vital organs, the emergency care physician found it necessary to stabilize the wound and reduce bleeding before treating the injury. Traumatic stab wounds can be very serious. We're just lucky we caught and treated this one fast."

"What's his long-term prognosis?"

The nurse, thumbing through the different pages, replied, "Generally good. We'll continue to administer intravenous fluids as well as a full round of antibiotics. He should be up and around in a couple of days and be ready for discharge by the end of the week."

"Thank you."

"You know, we won't discharge him unless we know that he'll be able to maintain long-term aftercare," the nurse added. "He'll have to keep the wound dry and clean and re-bandage it daily. And he must maintain a high degree of personal hygiene, including lots of hand-washing and bathing. We must keep the wound free from infection."

"That will be a first," Kate said, sarcastically.

"And then, there's the pain management."

Kate Dawson readjusted her stance. "I think I got the picture. I'm his friend, not his caretaker. If Lenny needs extended home healthcare, he can work that out with his case worker. That's not my decision."

"Long term treatment for stab wounds generally includes follow-up care with the patient's primary care physician," the nurse concluded.

"Thank you," Kate said, her smile beginning to wear thin. "I think we'll just leave the rest up to Mr. Provolone."

The nurse returned Lenny's chart. "Whatever you say, Inspector."

Dawson turned away from the nurse, heading towards the exit. As she walked through the Emergency Room and out the rear door, she dialed her cell phone. "Dispatch, this is 20-William-15. I am requesting two officers to be posted outside Room 316 in the Intensive Care Unit at UCSF Medical Center."

"Acknowledged, 20-William-15," the dispatcher replied.

"Make that around the clock," Kate added.

"Patient's name is Len Provolone. I'm concerned that his assailant, who is still at large, may try to finish the job. Keep me informed. Out."

An hour later, after a quick shower and change of clothes, Kate Dawson was back at the Hall of Justice. When she walked into the darkened, deserted detective room of the Homicide Bureau, she half-expected to find a blurry-eyed Alex Starke hunched over her computer station, still working on proving her theory about the terrorists. But Starke was nowhere to be found. Clarke and Jawara were apparently late again. Lieutenant Roberts must have been at City Hall with the Chief of Police. The only detective still holding down the fort was Jorge Ramirez. Of course, his face was flat on the desk, out cold, but under him were detailed drawings and architectural blueprints for several older buildings in the Tenderloin and the Mission Districts. They were spread out across his desk; the one next to it coated with notations and addresses in red "flair" pens. Kate reached around Ramirez, typed several letters on his keyboard, and pressed the "enter" key. The computer's flashing icon started processing information, whirring through the files in the SFPD data banks, and processed the top six entries for "chemical labs." She reached over and pressed the "escape" key, but the computer was determined to complete its initial command and processed the top six entries for "increased energy consumption" for Pacific Gas & Electric. Each time Kate pressed the "escape" key, the computer processed more information, until it was finally complete.

Still standing over her colleague, Kate cleared the screen to his computer and opened a separate window with an interactive map of San Francisco. She typed in the first entry and cross-referenced it with the top picks for several other entries. Almost immediately, the map came alive, highlighting a location—a warehouse building in the Mission District. She repeated this over and over, identifying at least seven different targets. Kate had been skeptical about Starke's theory, but the answers were right there in front of her. She couldn't exactly run down a fellow detective's work that was so inspired.

"You're a damn genius," she said, exasperated, praising the work of her rival, all the while hating her for it.

Jorge Ramirez began to stir to life. "What did you say, Kate?" he asked, lifting his head from the table.

"I just called you 'a damn genius,'" Dawson lied.

"Thanks," Ramirez said, half asleep, then closed his eyes again.

"I would have never thought—" she continued, evaluating the records on the computer display.

"Thanks," Ramirez repeated, lifting his head slightly, "but I really can't take credit. It was all Starke's work."

"What are you saying?"

"I mean, I helped her run the numbers. We all did. Roberts, the Chief . . . but in the end, the detective work was all hers."

Dawson pursed her lips in understanding.

Ramirez rubbed his eyes, forcing himself awake. "Then, a couple of hours ago, when the rest of us were all spent and ready to call it a night, she started shouting, 'I got it! I got it!'" he explained. "I asked her, 'Got what?' And Starke replied, 'Well, I've managed to access the city's power grid computer and this electrical substation here,' pointing at an area on the map, 'shows massive power drains during off-peak hours. We're talking power enough to run a dozen, fully-equipped meth labs. For a district that's made up of warehouses, which are supposed to be closed at night and open during the day for regular business hours, this is really damned peculiar.'"

Dawson looked closely at the grid on the computer. "So, you're saying she's narrowed its location to this neighborhood."

"No, I'm saying she narrowed it to this block," Ramirez corrected her, tapping a single box on the grid.

Dawson focused on the one city block, and then said, "So, what are the Chief's orders?"

"Kate, you'd better take that up with him. I'm officially off-duty," he replied, as his head slumped right back down on the table, landing on top of the detailed drawings and architectural blueprints. Ramirez closed his eyes as he fell back to sleep.

"Jorge! Jorge!" she demanded, nudging him to wake up, but he simply didn't respond to her gentle coaxing. For an instant, Dawson looked down at her partner, and considered another approach. She could always lean over and scream loudly in his ear, but she thought better of it. Ramirez must have spent much of the night, working with Starke and the others, and that could not have been easy. Finally, she just decided to let him sleep.

Kate Dawson looked back at the computer monitor and made a mental note of that one city block. She recognized a section of the Mission District that belonged to the homes of working-class families, recalling that most of the industrial warehouses were just south of 16th on Folsom Street. If members of a terrorist cell were using one of the warehouses for their chemical weapons lab, then they were probably held up in one of the homes nearby. She counted the homes on the satellite map—forty-one. Somewhere in one of those homes was the terrorist cell that she was looking for.

As Dawson climbed into her car parked on the curb outside the Hall of Justice, she couldn't help but notice plumes of black smoke billowing upward into the southern sky. She wasn't the only one. Other people had stopped to look as well. The black smoke was threatening to blot out the morning sun as it rose in the east and started its long climb overhead.

She cranked her car and slowly pulled away from the curb, turning right onto Bryant Street, then reached into the glove compartment and pulled out a microphone to her police-band radio. "Dispatch," she spoke into the receiver, "this is 20-William-15. Request a 10-24 with the Chief."

"Acknowledged, 20-William-15," the dispatcher replied. She went silent for a moment, presumably to establish a routine car-to-car transmit with the Chief of Police, then came back on the line. "Unable to make contact at this time. Chief appears to be 'out of pocket.' Will continue to monitor the situation and get back to you when a connection can be made."

"10-4," Kate replied, acknowledging the dispatcher's message had been received and understood. As she braked for a traffic signal at the next corner, she glanced up over her shoulder, and again looked at the dark sky overhead. "Dispatch, what's with all the black smoke?"

"There's a 10-80 in the Mission District," the dispatcher said, revealing both a fire and an explosion. "A third alarm was called in at five thirty-six this morning and all traffic is being routed around the scene now as we speak. If you plan on traveling anywhere near that neighborhood, proceed with caution."

"That's a big 10-4," Kate said, signing out, then returned the microphone to her glove compartment and turned on her car radio.

"Bay Area commuters, if you're now just joining us, we've got important news about your commute to work today," the female voice on the radio announced, all business. Sixteenth Street is now closed between Mission Street and Florida Street, and all east-west commuters are being asked to take Market Street or the 101. Folsom Street is also closed between 16th Street and 24th Street. City Officials have also asked us to remind drivers about emergency vehicles. If you see an emergency vehicle approaching your location, you are required by law to move your vehicle over to the right side of the roadway in order to make room for the emergency vehicle to pass. Failure to yield the right of way to an emergency vehicle could result in heavy fines and even the loss of driving privileges. In the next few hours, while they continue to clean up the warehouse fire in the Mission District, there are going to be dozens of Fire and Rescue vehicles moving through the area . . ."

Dawson drove her car about halfway down the block, then rolled to a stop behind a line of traffic that has trying to make the left onto Harrison Street. She glanced down at her watch and shook her head. "This is ridiculous."

Impatiently, Dawson clicked to the next channel.

"Repeating our top story," a male broadcaster reported, "an explosive fire at an industrial warehouse overnight has prompted the evacuation of about two hundred residents in the Mission District and, at one point, knocked out power for thousands of customers in the central city area . . ."

For an instant, Kate drummed her finely-manicured finger-nails on the top of the steering wheel, then changed stations again. She inched her car along the street and was now seventh in line to make the turn.

"The remains of the building look like a war zone, after a massive chemical fire destroyed a warehouse in the Mission District," another male on the new station repeated the lead story of the day. "According to an eyewitness report from the district chief with the San Francisco Fire Department, the massive ware-house fire began with sparks from a house fire on 16th Street. He says a three-bay garage behind the home was burning when fire trucks first arrived on the scene. By then, of course, the fire had already crossed the fence line to the adjoining industrial ware-house, A-1 Custom Paints on Folsom Street. Minutes later, thick black smoke was spreading to the south, heading towards the residential area, and the Galleria mall beyond . . ."

Dawson listened to the reports, so spellbound with the news coverage that she not only missed her chance to move up in line, but also found herself several cars back, as two late model sedans pulled around in front of her, then jockeyed to claim her place in line. When she finally did look up from the radio, she was surprised to see that she was no closer to making the left turn onto Harrison than before. Dazed and more than a little confused, she struggled to stay in the moment, her mind being pulled in two different directions, but it was the loud, annoying horn from the car behind her that finally snapped her out of her reverie.

"That's enough!" she shouted, at the top of her lungs, turning around and giving the driver behind her a dirty look.

Once she settled back in the driver's seat, she decided it was time to turn on the siren. She leaned forward, reached under the dashboard of her car, and then began cutting through traffic, siren wailing. Brought back instantly to the crisis at hand, she continued to listen to the grim news on the radio, afraid one of her friends on the Force may have been numbered among the casualties.

"Several people are reported dead in the huge fire. Only one home, believed to be the one with the detached garage, had significant damage. Fire crews spent several hours and utilized thousands of gallons of water protecting residential structures in the nearby community from the burning warehouse," the disembodied voice on the radio continued to make his report. "Residents living closest to the warehouse say they were awakened during the night by a series of distinctive pops, which sounded like firecrackers, and then they started seeing flames. Others claim the pops sounded more like small arms fire as if two rival gangs were shooting it out. A first alarm was called just after 4:20 am, followed subsequently by a second at 4:51, and a third at 5:36. Most of the residents were told to evacuate their homes around 5:00 am. Local police are working jointly with fire officials to clear the area . . ."

"Damn it to hell!" Kate exclaimed, punching the next button on her radio. "I want to know more about the casualty count!" Irritated, the police inspector breezed through several other radio stations, listening for a few seconds, then clicking through to the next channel. No one seemed to be talking about fatalities from the fire and her concern about her friends escalated with each new broadcast.

"A spokesperson for Pacific Gas and Electric says its work crews have restored power to the residential community near the warehouse fire. But they have also reassured us that crews will continue working throughout the morning . . ."

Click.

"Powerful fireballs that could be seen as far away as Oakland shot up from the burning warehouse last night . . ."

Click.

"Families with small children and pet owners are being warned to keep their loved ones indoors, away from pools of standing water and ditches in the area. Dangerous chemicals from the warehouse fire may have seeped into the ground or been part of the runoff water . . ."

Click.

"At this hour, reports are still flooding into the newsroom about that deadly fire in the Mission District, but there is at least one piece of good news to report," a female commentator announced to her listeners. "According to Michael Shannon, spokesperson for the San Francisco Police Department, police officials under the leadership of Nelson Gates, Chief of Police, were able to mobilize dozens of their off-duty police officers and office personnel to assist residents in the evacuation of the predominantly Muslim community adjacent to the fire. With the power and lights out, and fire officials battling the third-alarm blaze, I understand the police went literally door to door at considerable risk to themselves and carried children and elderly residents to safety. Even S.W.A.T. teams participated in the evacuation. Here's a big shout out to our heroic men and women in blue: Way to go guys!"

Dawson, proud of her fellow officers, reached down and turned off the radio. If members of the news media had planned to say anything about casualties, they would have said it already. She had to be content with that false narrative until she knew something more concrete.

Kate pressed her foot down on the accelerator and raced through traffic with her siren sounding and her lights flashing.

Within twenty minutes, after fighting through heavy morning traffic and numerous road closures, Dawson finally turned the corner onto Folsom Street, and followed the cloud of smoke and debris to the city block where the warehouse had once stood. She pulled her BMW next to an Army Humvee and several soldiers who were guarding it and turned off the siren. The sight of the camouflaged vehicle and uniformed troops carrying M16s in front of the charred, skeletal remains of the warehouse sickened her. It brought to mind a recurring nightmare Kate had of limping through a bloody mosaic of chaos and mass destruction from a nuclear blast in the city of San Francisco, which often ended with her getting violently ill from the radiation poisoning and dying on the trash heap called home.

She closed her eyes and shuddered.

When Kate opened them back up, they were all there, all the friends she had feared were lost in the conflagration. She breathed a deep sigh of relief. First, she saw Doctor Brogan and several forensic investigators from the ME's Office sifting through the twisted steel, burnt wood, and cooling ashes for bodies and any other evidence of a crime. Then she saw William Clark, scribbling in his notebook, while Mikhail Jawara and Matt Balardi stood around drinking coffee from Styrofoam cups and joking. The Chief of Police was there, too, off to the side, conferring with other police officials, including her boss, Lieutenant Roberts, and several men in green army fatigues, while a couple policemen maintained flanking positions on either side of him. They seemed to act as a buffer for the Chief from any reporter bold enough to cross the police barricade. And finally, she spotted Starke, Alex Starke.

Starke was dressed all in black, wearing black tactical pants and vest, a black long-sleeve fatigue shirt, and black laced leather boots. She wore her Glock G41 .45 caliber pistol on a black web belt with a baton and radio around her waist. With the exception of the black S.W.A.T. baseball cap, which she wore backwards on her head, she could have been mistaken as a member of the S.W.A.T. team, even though Kate was the only one who knew better. She appeared to be off in her own little world, poking through the rubble but not really looking.

At the edge of the perimeter, where the skeletal remains of the warehouse were still smoldering, Dawson stepped out of her car, paused, then flashed her police badge at the army sentries. They didn't react at all but continued marching back and forth. Pulling the yellow caution tape over her head, crossing through, she recognized one of the uniformed officers who stopped long enough to wave her on but then went right back to work wrapping the caution tape along the street side of the building as a kind of barricade. She walked past the coroner's investigators kneeling in the mud, collecting trace evidence.

"How's it going, boys?" she asked, stopping long enough to say a word.

"Not bad," one replied, gazing up at her. "I'd be happier doing my job if we weren't under the watchful eyes of those gorillas with guns."

"Yeah," the other one answered. "The U.S. Army doesn't have any jurisdiction here. They can fuckin' go home."

"Hmmm, I wouldn't want to be the one to tell them that."

The two investigators laughed at her joke, then went right back to work.

Dawson swallowed a smoky/sooty taste, intently watching Alex Starke, her black S.W.A.T. uniform silhouetted against the charred, smoldering remains of the warehouse. She was still kicking items over in the rubble but not really looking for any evidence on her own.

Dawson pulled a small container of Vicks Vapor Rub from her jacket and rubbed a smear under her nose. *It's gonna be bad.* Her friend, Rosa, who had worked with the ME office before she died, taught her the trick to keep from hurling from the stench.

She made her way across the debris field until she reached the opposite side, ignoring calls from Jawara and Clark.

"What the hell happened?" Kate demanded, taking Starke's arm, as she walked up behind her. The junior detective tried to shake her off, but Dawson pulled her up short. "When I left you last night, you were still looking for the location of a warehouse where they could build their WMD. You didn't say anything about forming a strike team and going after them, like street vigilantes."

"Situations change," Starke replied coldly. "Last night, I made the call when I found the warehouse."

"Ramirez showed me your findings," Kate said, releasing her arm.

"Excellent piece of detective work, Starke. Worthy of Dick Tracy or the Dark Knight. I'm sure the Chief of Police is very pleased with you."

"Thank you, Dawson," Alex replied, unclear of her two pop culture references.

"But finding the location of the warehouse was always going to be followed by other steps," Dawson explained, patiently. "Next, it was our responsibility to find 'probable cause' before we sent in a strike team. That team would have been armed with a search warrant, and an arrest affidavit would have been filed with a local magistrate or judge. Those documents protect the evidence we seize. Right now, as things go, any evidence we find is inadmissible in court. You should have learned all about that in your first year at the Academy."

"To hell with the courts! I made an executive decision, and I don't care how many rules I've broken to protect my country!" she declared, the perfect fascist. "Radical Islamic Terrorism is the enemy of anyone who embraces peace and freedom. I exercised my prerogative as head of the City's Counter-Terrorism Task Force and mobilized a team to take out the terrorist cell.

That's what real leaders do. They learn, adapt, and apply themselves in constantly changing conditions."

"The early bird gets the worm, eh?" Kate interjected.

"Well, I sure as hell wasn't going to wait around until after you crawled out of bed this morning and finally rolled into the bureau to launch our strike team," Starke said, with her eyes flashing. "Clearly, if I had waited for you, we would have lost the initiative in our war against the Jihadists."

"You seem to think this is some kind of competition."

"*Everything* in life is a competition," Alex replied, confident in her statement. "We start by competing in the sandbox for the most toys, then later we compete for the highest grades. We're always competing for love, whether it's the cutest guy in class or the one who has the most money. We compete for the best job and to have more than our neighbors. Everything is about winning. Life's a competition in which there is no prize for second place."

Dawson got right to the point and right in her face. "Well, stop competing with me, Starke!"

Her youthful rival shot Kate a sideways glance, mere inches from each other's faces. "Natural selection is so ingrained into our DNA that I could no more stop competing with you than I could give up living or breathing. To survive, you must be the best. That is why the most competitive women are often the most successful."

"I've read *Cinderella* and *Snow White*. You're still competing for your daddy's love, aren't you?"

"Oh, that's really original, Dr. Freud," Starke spit back, hands on hips.

"Well, that fairy tale world of yours doesn't interest me, detective," Dawson replied, taking her stance. "I compete with *no one*, except myself. I run my own race. I have no desire to play your game of being better than anyone else. I just aim to improve myself, to be better than I was before."

"I'm sure losers tell themselves that all of the time. But the fact of the matter is, individuals best adapted to their environment are more likely to survive and reproduce, while those that cannot adapt, do not survive."

"You've got it all worked out, don't you?"

"I leave *very little* to chance."

"What about love, family, and seeking a deeper meaning to life?" Kate prodded. "Cooperative efforts between people and nations are what make the world go 'round, and competition is nothing more than a sideshow."

"Bravo," Starke said, mocking her rival with fake applause. "I've got your *participation* trophy right here, Dawson. But when everybody gets a trophy, no one really wins."

"You want to know what you can do with that trophy?"

"Now, now, that's not very polite."

All at once, Dawson felt her Banshee struggle to come out, hands coiled, ready to strike, but she hesitated just long enough for common sense to replace anger. "Tell me, Starke," she said, instantly reclaiming her cool. "Did you have to nuke the whole block just to flush out one terrorist cell? Or was that something you enjoyed? Personally? Maybe get lucky and burn a few residents' homes down in the process? After all, they're Muslim, right? So, who really cares?"

"You are way out of line here, Inspector," Starke said, nose to nose with Kate, forcing her backwards.

"Why don't I just put it into terms that only you would understand?" Dawson replied, shoving Starke back with the palms of her hands.

Alex struggled to stand firm. "My strike team and I had nothing to do with the warehouse fire. That structure was already burning when we arrived. So was the three-bay garage on the other side of the fence."

"You don't really expect me to believe that, do you?"

"I don't care what you believe," Starke responded, enraged. "It's the truth, and that's exactly what I'm going to put into my report. No matter what else you may say about me, I'm not a liar."

"So, you're saying those men over there," Kate replied, pointing at the half dozen or so charred bodies lying face-down in the mud and ash, "died of old age or boredom? They look like they got shot up pretty bad in a firefight and then finished off execution-style, each a bullet to the head."

Starke grunted. "That was my assessment, too."

Kate Dawson took a couple of steps away from her rival, inspecting the crime scene again with cool, dispassionate eyes. There were eight, no actually, nine men who appeared to have shot it out in the warehouse; presumably more who may have gotten away. She started where each man had fallen and traced their steps back to the egress points where they may have gained access to the building. It was her assessment that one group had clearly gotten the drop on the other in what appeared to be a surprise incursion, but those men were successfully repelled by superior firepower of the others, resulting in a total of nine men dead.

Kate dropped to one knee and picked up a small assortment of shell casings. As she examined each round that had been spent during the firefight, she matched the shell casing to a weapon in her mind. They had primarily used Kalashnikov AK 47 assault rifles, with an assortment of small arms, like the 1911 Colt .45 semi-automatic, the 9 mm Beretta, and the 9 mm Glock 43. None of the shell casings matched those weapons carried by Starke's strike team. Kate was beginning to think that Alex Starke had been straight with her.

Starke approached Dawson and pointed down at one of the bodies that had suffered third-degree burns over eighty percent of its mass, but there was still plenty of charred flesh stretched across bone to make the face recognizable. The stench was unbearable. "That's Mahmud ibn Suri," she said, as a matter of fact. "He's been wanted for several of the nightclub bombings throughout Europe and in Eastern Turkey. He was also our number one suspect in the murder of Officer Hartwell and those passengers on board the subway car. A Sunni Muslim, he was devoted to the teachings of the Prophet Mohammad, and, we believe, the leader of this terrorist cell."

Dawson didn't say a word but pulled out and put on latex gloves, bent over, patted down the body, and came up with a 9 mm Glock 43, a silencer, a handful of cash, a couple of stolen credit cards, and some fake ID's, including two bogus passports. "Looks like Mahmud ibn Suri was getting ready to run."

"This is Hassan Abu Abdullah," Starke added, taking a few steps through the rubble of the warehouse, then stopped to turn over the corpse. She pulled a rag from her pocket and wiped the mud from his face. "They called him 'the handsome one' partly because the name 'Hassan' means 'beautiful' in Arabic."

"Nice face," Dawson said, after examining him more closely. She also patted his body down for weapons and contraband.

Starke wadded the rag and shoved it back in her pocket. "He was a Shiite from Iran, where he took his orders directly from the Ayatollahs, whom they regard as a sign of 'Allah' on earth. He was also the leader of a rival terrorist cell, working clandestinely in the City of San Francisco. Both men were Muslim, both sworn enemies of the United States, and yet both men were ideologically at war with the other."

"Muslims have been killing each other for hundreds of years,"

Kate said coldly, rather dismissively. "Shia or Sunni, I could care less which group decided to take the other group out. My only real concern is the Botulinum Toxin and putting the terrorist cell that is producing it out of business."

"We should be concerned for the day when these different factions of Islam stop fighting each other and unite against a common enemy," Starke warned.

"So, what happened here?" Dawson pushed for some answers. "I'd guess that Hassan's strike team used the element of surprise to get the jump on the rival cell in the middle of the night and caught Mahmud's team sleeping. Then Hassan made a play for the Botulinum Toxin first and Mahmud shot him?"

"Of course, if Mahmud got to the toxin first, then Hassan was killed trying to get it from him," Alex offered a feasible alternative. "In either event, there was a shooting match in the warehouse between both groups and Mahmud was the only one to come out of it alive—wounded, but alive."

"But he got caught in the fire?" Dawson suggested.

"I believe he started the fire to obliterate any evidence of the toxin," Starke added, walking her rival through the only scenario that fit the evidence at hand. "His plan was to burn down the whole block, destroy any sign of a lab or terrorist cell, and hide out until he could get away with the toxin, but he got caught in his own fire and was burned nearly beyond recognition. Oh, yeah, he got caught all right."

"But that doesn't explain what happened to the toxin," Kate said, voicing her objections and surveying the devastation, "or who shot each of the bodies point blank in the head."

"There must have been someone else here," Starke replied.

"A cleaner."

"A person who 'cleans up' after a crime to physically erase their trace? We were taught to call them 'fixers' at the Academy."

Kate squatted down and examined the gunshot wound to the head of several victims lying in the mud. "Well, he was here, that's for sure. I think you and your team may have interrupted his 'clean up' because he left incriminating evidence at the crime scene."

"Evidence? What evidence?"

"Take another look," Kate said, pointing at one of the foreheads. "He picked up all of his shell casings, but left bullets behind in each man's skull. A really efficient cleaner would have removed those bullets to the head with a pocket knife in order to keep them from showing up on a ballistics report."

"Unless he wanted them found," Starke suggested.

"Well, hopefully, ballistics will be able to tell us something," Kate said, glancing up, catching the eye of Doctor Brogan as he and one of his student investigators from the Medical Examiner's Office trudged towards them through the muck. "I'd be willing to give up a week's salary, at this point, just to find out who our mystery guest was working for."

Brogan stopped just short of the bodies. "If you dear ladies are through making your mud pies, I've managed to wrangle a willing volunteer here who's going to help me bag 'em and tag 'em for transport."

Dawson smiled, faintly. "Let me know when you've completed your ballistics report, Doc. I've got a real interest in knowing who shot these men execution-style after they were already down."

"You got it, Kate," he replied.

Dawson heard a couple of familiar voices coming her way. Clark and his long-time partner, Jawara, were approaching. They seemed to be arguing, but Clark clearly had the upper hand.

"The vast majority of the 1.6 billion Muslims in the world are Sunni, or roughly eighty-seven percent of the total Muslim population, with less than ten percent of the remaining Muslims who prefer to be identified as Shia," Clark said to Jawara, sounding more like a professor at Berkeley than a homicide detective. "The conflict between Shia and Sunni Muslims goes all the way back to the seventh century and the death of the Prophet Muhammad and has nothing to do with current political boundaries."

Jawara shook his head. "Nope, I don't believe it."

"Clashes between the Shia and Sunni sects have been aggravated by politics but by and large are the result of a fundamental disagreement in religion that dates back thirteen hundred years."

"I'm telling you, I don't believe it."

"Don't believe it then, but it's true," Clark said, confounded by his partner's basic lack of understanding. "The argument originated in 632 A.D., shortly after the death of Islam's founder, the Prophet Muhammad. Tribal Arabs who followed him disagreed over who would succeed him. The majority believed that Muhammad's rightful successor was his father-in-law and close friend, Abu Bakr, but a small group believed the Prophet's successor should be Ali ibn Abi Talib, his cousin and so-in-law and father of his grandchildren."

Kate jumped into the discussion. "The Sunni majority got their way and Abu Bakr was named as successor of the prophet."

"Thanks for sticking up for me," Mikhail grunted.

Kate and Jawara exchanged glances. "I thought you would have learned by now not to question Clark's eidetic memory."

"I keep probing the limits of that finely tuned mind of his," Mikhail confessed, with a tooth-filled grin, "but so far I haven't found a subject that he doesn't know something about."

Clark stuck his hands in his pockets and shyly said, "There's *plenty* I don't know."

"Partner, compared to the rest of the world, you're a fuckin' genius. One of these days, we're goin' to Vegas and I'm gonna prove it to you. Ain't no one gonna best you in the Trivia Bowl."

"Promises, promises."

"You guys have been talking about Las Vegas for as long as I can remember," Kate said. "Why don't the two of you go already and stop just talking about it. Enter the Trivia Bowl and make us all rich."

"In time, sister, in time," Mikhail promised. "Right now, I'm grooming him like a fine race horse for the big event."

"A race horse?" Clark was shocked.

"That's just a figure of speech, Partner," Mikhail defended himself.

"Inspector Clark has an eidetic memory?" Starke asked Kate, with Clark standing right there in front of her. She could have just as easily asked him but chose instead to question Dawson. Starke didn't bother to lower her voice or cloak the question in other terms. To her, William Clarke was little more than a bug under her microscope. "But he's always taking notes."

"William remembers *every* detail of his life," Dawson defended her friend. "In fact, he can cite you chapter and verse for every day going all the way back to the moment when he was born. But sometimes he has problems remembering details of other people's lives and events that are cross-wired with his own. He takes notes to keep the information straight in his head."

Clark turned to the young detective. "Things can get a little scrambled in my head without notes."

Alex Starke's jaw dropped. "Oh, oh, okay," she stammered, utterly surprised that the specimen under her microscope spoke.

"We've talked with the neighbors," Matt Balardi reported, as he and a uniformed officer walked up and joined his fellow detectives in a huddle. "Some of the folks said they were awakened around 3:15 a.m. by a series of distinctive pops. Pops that sounded a lot like—"

"Firecrackers," the uniformed officer said.

"Yeah, probably some kids with firecrackers," Balardi continued. "But a couple of others thought the pops sounded more like—"

"Small arms fire," the uniformed officer added.

"Yeah, small arms fire," Balardi repeated, "as if two rival groups of gangbangers had decided to shoot it out."

Starke folded her arms across her chest and pivoted towards Kate. "They weren't local kids with firecrackers or gangbangers with small arms. They were professionals with silencers," she informed the others. "We believe this was a hit, one terrorist cell taking out another cell."

"I guess you were right, Clark," Jawara confessed.

"What did I tell you? Muslims have been killing each other for years," Clark replied, waving his notebook in hand. "Shia or Sunni, it doesn't really matter. God help us if they should ever decide to work together."

"This information is confidential," Starke reminded the others. "You are not to speak with anyone about this case."

"Well, that's it then," Roberts growled, tense and irritable as he approached his team of detectives, but he made every effort to hide those feelings behind a gruff exterior. "The United States Army is now calling the shots. They've just pulled the plug on our investigation."

"No!" Starke said, as her mouth dropped in surprise.

"Don't take my word for it, Starke. Go ask the Chief himself."

"I will," she replied, marching past Roberts and the other detectives.

"Can they do that, Lieutenant?" Jawara asked.

"They took over my crime scene yesterday," Kate said, sourly.

"They represent the federal government," he replied. "They can do anything they damn well please."

"Jurisdictional mandate," Clark said, but no one was listening.

Roberts decided it was time to get the show on the road. "Let's get all of our people packed up. We're moving out. I'll expect full reports from each of you when we meet again this—" All at once, the Lieutenant stopped barking orders, in the middle of his team, unmoving, staring off into space with a blank look on his face. Most of them had long ago accepted the fact that their boss was a plodder. They'd seen him sitting in his office for hours on end, thinking, planning his next move before he would take the next step in an investigation. Rather than being labeled a "slowpoke" by his colleagues or those who knew him best, his loud mouth and bluster made him appear to be thorough and hardworking. The fact that he also lacked imagination when it counted, most didn't escape anyone at the Hall of Justice. He was part of an older breed of administrator that was gradually being phased out and replaced by younger bureau chiefs with a keen eye for detective work and community policing.

William Clark who had served him the longest period also knew him best. When Roberts hadn't come out of his stupor in a few moments, Clark opened his notebook, and said, "Sir, what was that about a meeting?"

The Lieutenant did not respond but stared hard at Clark, as if struggling to find his next word. Finally, he said, "Afternoon."

"Very good, sir," Clark replied, trying to sound routine. "We'll meet in the bureau conference room at 12:30 p.m."

"Thanks . . . William," Roberts added, gradually returning from a faraway land. He struggled to move, to break free of the big block of ice that had seemingly encased him. He felt pressure all over his body and could not easily move any muscles or speak more than a word or phrase. He was fully aware though, and with his boss only a few yards away conferring with Starke, he fought hard to appear normal. With great difficulty, he turned his head just a few degrees towards the medical examiner, and asked, "Edgar . . . what . . . did . . . you . . . find?"

"We've scoured the ruins of the warehouse for other bodies, Jim, but these are the only casualties we've found," Brogan reported, pointing at the nine body bags laying near and around his feet. "The bodies were all concentrated right around here. It must have been one hell of a fire-fight. Here's what I can tell you . . ."

"Save . . . it . . . for . . . later . . . today," Roberts ordered, struggling for every word. Brogan leaned in closer, lowering his voice, and crossed his arms across his chest. "It happened again, didn't it?"

"Yeah . . . yeah," the Lieutenant replied, rolling his eyes in his head. It seemed like that was all he could do to make this point.

"You know that it's only going to get worse," Brogan said, with genuine concern in his voice. "One day, you won't recover from it at all and you'll end up on a slab down in the morgue."

"I'm . . . starting to . . . feel better . . . already," he stammered.

The Medical Examiner shook his head. "You need about five or six weeks of uninterrupted rest and a good statin drug to reduce the risk of heart attack, stroke, and even death from heart disease."

"Would you settle for a long afternoon of flyfishing?"

"No, your heart simply isn't strong enough," Brogan objected. "You need palliative care, with lots of bed rest."

Roberts was moving again, stiffly. "In case you hadn't noticed, doctor, we've got a real crisis on our hands."

"Let's face it, Jim, you've always got a crisis on your hands, but you also have an excellent team of detectives. Clark,

Dawson, Jawara, any one of them could handle the heavy lifting, while you're out for a few weeks," Brogan said bluntly. "But if you don't stop now and take your health more seriously, the next time we're all gathered together will be at your funeral at Woodlawn Memorial."

Lieutenant Roberts hung his head; knew he was right but felt indispensable.

"Sir, if you'll not be needing me right away, I'd like to head back to the Hall of Justice." Having moved closer to the two men, Kate Dawson politely interrupted her boss and the medical examiner. She barely made eye contact with Roberts.

"I need a word with you, Inspector," Lieutenant Roberts said, almost bitterly, like a man who had been given six months to live.

"Yes, sir," Kate replied, swallowing the lump in her throat.

"Jurisdictional mandate, my ass," Jawara scolded his partner, as the two of them headed back to their car. "Where do you come up with this shit?"

"Hell, I was prepared to cite *Weston v. Georgia* as an example of how the Federal Government, with the active support of the President, can take over a crime scene under the auspices of national security."

"Shit!" Jawara was pissed. "No one cares, Clark."

"Hey, guys," Balardi called, running over to their side.

"What's up, Matt?" Clark asked, turning.

Winded, Balardi choked down a couple of deep breaths. "I guess I picked the wrong week to give up smoking cigarettes."

"You should take better care of yourself," Jawara quipped.

"Speaking of care," Balardi said, breathing easier, "What did you think of the old man? He didn't look so good."

Clark checked his notes. "Third time in as many weeks."

"I'm hoping that Brogan can talk some sense into him," Jawara said.

"Someone had better say something to him before he keels over dead right in front of us," Balardi added, with little to no tack.

Roberts waited until the rest of his detectives had exited the burnt-out remains of the warehouse and the Chief of Police was out of hearing range before he said anything more to Kate. His speaking ability had improved considerably, but mobility was the next major concern. He still felt like his body was trapped inside a block of ice with pressure baring down on him from all sides. Roberts tried moving his hands and found his fingers, an arduous process that seemed to tap the last of his strength. His bones creaked as he tried to move his legs.

"It didn't escape my notice, nor that of Chief Gates, that you and Alex Starke had a physical altercation," he said, after a momentary pause. "I'll not have my detectives fighting with each other at a crime scene. If you want to put on gloves and go ten rounds in the gym with her, I can arrange that, but that kind of aggressive behavior in public is simply unacceptable. You don't have to like each other to work together. You're both professionals, and I expect the two of you to behave like professionals when out in the public eye."

"Yes, sir," she replied, respectfully, in compliance.

"Alex Starke is more than just another graduate of the Police Academy. In a class of about seventy cadets, in which fifty-two police and sheriff's recruits averaged ninety-two percent or higher on the academic portion of their academy training, Starke received the top academic honors with an overall score of 99.87%," Roberts reported. "She also proved to be just as imposing on physical prowess, beating out every other cadet, male or female, on all seven sections of the exam. All this talent at age twenty-six."

Dawson thought a moment. "Let's not forget the obvious, sir. She's also a very beautiful woman who the Chief of Police has decided to take a personal interest in."

The Lieutenant grimaced, gritting his teeth as he spoke, "I'll have no more talk like that!"

"Yes, sir."

A moment of awkward silence passed between them, during which Roberts struggled to compose himself. "Alright, what's your general impression of Starke?"

"She's . . . impressive." Kate was shocked she'd be asked the question. She had spent so much time building a case against Starke in her own mind that the thought of evaluating her fairly had never occurred to her. "She clearly knows her stuff, Lieutenant. Earlier today, she not only identified the leaders of the two rival cells by name, but also had supplemental knowledge about each man that may prove invaluable to this investigation."

"I detect a degree of hesitancy in your response," Roberts noted, attempting to play devil's advocate.

"Sir, do I have your permission to speak freely?" she asked removing the gloves and shoving them in her pocket.

"Self-expression was never one of your problems, Inspector," he joked, a hollow joke that totally missed its intended mark. "You can speak freely, Dawson. Just keep it relevant to our discussion. In other words, I don't want to hear any more speculation about Starke's relationship with the Chief of Police."

"A moment ago, I used the word 'impressive' to describe her, and I still stand by that one-word description. At times, she has the power to excite attention, arouse intense admiration, and leave us feeling breathless by her awe-inspiring display of skills. If she were a superhero, we'd call her 'Miss Marvel.' That desire to leave us feeling breathless in her wake is also what I see as her weakness." Kate cocked her head and peered directly into her superior's eyes. "Alex Starke is a world-class prima donna, sir, who must not only dominate the center spotlight with her massive ego but also be the star of the show. She is vain, arrogant, a bit reckless, and difficult to work with."

The Lieutenant was amused. "You know, Dawson, that's what some of the detectives used to say about you."

"Impossible!" Kate exclaimed. "The two of us are nothing alike. You must have me confused with someone else."

"Maybe . . . The person I was thinking about had just sailed through the Police Academy with high marks on both the academic and physical portions of her training. All her instructors were convinced she'd make detective on the first round of exams, and I was looking to recruit a fresh face for the Bureau. The fact that she was somewhat of a loner didn't bother me," Roberts explained, painting a rare portrait of his one and only female detective. "But when I started to hear scuttlebutt about her not being a team player or considering herself to be too good to do certain tasks, that's when I started to question my decision to bring her into Homicide."

Kate Dawson shifted her stance uncomfortably, struggling with a hand on her forehead to shield her eyes from connecting with his. Roberts towered over her, a big hulk of a man.

"I was actually prepared to cut her loose when Frank Miller pulled me aside, and said, 'I think she needs supervision,'" Roberts' recall of events was nearly one hundred percent accurate. "Now Frank and I may have disagreed about a lot of things over the years, but I always respected his work mentoring young detectives. From what I saw, he took a cocky, self-centered graduate of the Police Academy and transformed her into one of the finest detectives that I have ever had the pleasure of working with."

"Thanks, Lieutenant." Kate struggled for words, remembering the last time she had seen her partner alive. "I learned a lot from Frank Miller, and I still miss him to this day."

"Would it surprise you if I said that I miss him, too?"

Tears glistened in the corners of her eyes and she reached up to brush them away. She was not ashamed of having feelings for her late partner. In many ways, she still felt responsible for his death, but didn't feel comfortable sharing that with Roberts. He had bullied and provoked her, lied to her, made fun of her, and put her life in danger far too many times for the two of them to share a "kumbaya" moment together. She regarded him with disdain and, like others in the Homicide Bureau, counted down the days to his retirement. The irony was not lost on her that she still looked to him for praise of a job well down.

Roberts smiled slowly. "Now, you know if Frank Miller had lived, he would be wondering why you're still working for me in Homicide. That thought had occurred to me several times, and when the Chief of Police asked me last night what you were still doing here, I didn't have a satisfactory answer for him."

Dawson crinkled her forehead. "You and the Chief of Police were talking about me last night?"

"No, not exactly. He just wanted to know if you had given any thought to your future career choices."

She gazed at him intently. "Sir?"

"You've taken and passed the Lieutenant's exam. So, we were both wondering if you'd thought about a promotion? Maybe even submitting the proper paperwork to take over one of the bureaus?"

"I haven't given it much thought," she lied, looking out,

beyond the crime scene. Even with the rub, the smell was getting to her. It still confounded her that smells did not bother the guys much. She watched as Doctor Brogan and his team of investigators packed up the last CSI van, and departed the scene.

"Robbery needs a new bureau head," Roberts reported, putting it out there. "The Chief of Police and I think it would be a good fit for you."

That's it! "You can tell Gates that I'm not interested in Robbery."

"I think you're making a mistake, Dawson." He pointed towards Alex Starke, who was still talking with the Chief. "I want you to take another look at Starke. She represents the future of law enforcement. Those cadets coming out of the Police Academy today are full of drive and ambition—impatient, ruthless, and willing to take risks to get ahead. By standing still, you could very easily find yourself falling behind them. And I can tell you, they don't give out trophies or plum assignments for second place. But if you were in a leadership role, as a bureau head, you could help shape their careers. Really make a difference."

"I thought that I was already making a difference."

Roberts cut through the crap and his tone of voice changed. "I want you to reconsider your decision."

Kate Dawson was still staring into the street.

"Did you hear me? I said—"

"I heard what you said, Lieutenant, but no amount of intimidation from you or the Chief of Police is going to change my mind."

"I'm not trying to intimidate you, dammit. I'm asking you to look at your career objectively, so that you make the best decision. Understand?"

Dawson tore her eyes away and finally looked at her boss. "Understand? Yeah, I understand. With all due respect, *sir*, I know exactly how this works, and I'll be the one who makes the final decision."

"Don't take too long, Dawson. The clock's already ticking."

"I know."

CHAPTER FOUR

Shortly before lunch, Kate Dawson returned to the Hall of Justice and found Dr. Barry Glass, the staff psychiatrist, out on the promenade, leaning back in a metal chair from the Department of Public Works, eyes closed, listening to "La Traviata" on his iPod, drinking in the warm rays of the sun. The sixty-three-year-old, balding, ex-hippie was wearing one of his expensive, trademarked Hawaiian shirts from Tommy Bahama and handmade, leather Birkenstocks. He sported a white beard that he kept neatly trimmed and wore, what was left of his hair, in a long white ponytail. While his appearance and dress were eccentric, to say the least, for an official member of the police department, Dr. Glass was the very model of professionalism. After completing his residency at Berkeley, he became a consultant at San Francisco General and an honorary board member on the State Board of Psychiatric Health in Napa.

Dawson placed a Cobb salad and a bottle of water down on the metal table, also from the Department of Public Words, and slid into the chair next to him, trying not to disturb his reverie.

Glass felt her sit down, leaned forward in his chair, and removed the ear buds from his head. "Violetta's aria from 'La Traviata,' particularly as sung by Maria Callas, is one of Verdi's most sublime pieces of music," Glass said, turning off his iPod. "It always makes me think of what Heaven must be like, with all of those Angelic voices singing."

"I'm sorry for breaking in on your lunch hour, like this," Kate apologized, "but I really need your help."

Glass spied her Cobb salad and reached across the table for it. "Did you pick up any salad dressing? Maybe a plastic folk and knife?"

Kate sighed in resignation and rummaged through her purse. She had hoped to eat the Cobb salad for lunch herself but knew she couldn't refuse him. She came up with a set of plastic utensils, wrapped in cellophane, and a couple of napkins and passed them over to Glass, asking, "Care for a bottle of water?"

"Evian?" he responded, nibbling on a slice of crisp bacon.

"No, it's just generic tap water," she replied, without thinking. "I clean out my plastic water bottles every night and refill them. Just doing my part to save the environment."

Dr. Barry Glass bobbed his head. "Ever since the City banned the sale of plastic water bottles, I've been drinking Evian. Evian's bottles are made of glass and still disposable. Recycling your plastic water bottle may seem like the 'green' thing to do, but the truth of the matter is reusable water bottles harbor more germs than your home toilet. Recent laboratory tests of just ten refillable water bottles at Berkeley identified a buildup of more than three hundred thousand colony-forming units of bacteria. We're talking dangerous germs like E.coli and salmonella. Do yourself a favor, Kate, get rid of all of your plastic water bottles, and start drinking Evian."

"I had no idea, Doc," she revealed. "But I'll be honest with you. I don't really like the taste of Evian water."

"I'm not surprised," Glass added, as he chowed down hungrily on the salad. "Its low sodium content and balanced mineral composition are foreign to the palate of most Americans. They've been drinking water from a sewer so long that they don't know what good water really tastes like. Bottled at the source in the French Alps, Evian remains completely untouched by man throughout the entire process. So, when you drink Evian water, you are drinking the naturally pure and refreshing taste of real water."

"You sound like a commercial."

"I just know what I like," he replied, taking another bite.

Dawson leaned across the table, eyeing her lunch. The psych was practically inhaling the chopped salad greens, tomato, and fresh slices of grilled chicken breast. Each time he pushed the avocado, chives, or hard-boiled eggs to the side, she made smacking noises with her lips in anticipation, but then he'd go back and gobble them up. She closed her eyes, imagining the savory red wine vinaigrette splashed over the Roquefort cheese.

"So, Dawson, what was it that you wanted to talk to me about?" Glass asked, through a mouthful of food.

Kate was silent for a long moment, then jumped in, "I took the Lieutenant's exam recently and passed."

"Oh, yes, I saw your name on the list. Not only did you pass, you received the highest passing grade. Congratulations!"

"I put everything I had into passing that exam." She tucked a stray strand of her gorgeous blonde hair behind her ear. "I've pushed myself hard these last six months and sacrificed a lot to get this far. Am I wrong in taking a moment to catch my breath and decompress a little?"

"No, not at all. Your hard work has obviously paid off. It's perfectly natural to want to pause and reassess your life," he replied, truly happy for her.

"I just can't seem to turn it off, Doc. Everyone keeps making demands of me, but no one wants to hear what I want."

"Has your relationship with Lieutenant Roberts changed at all since you passed the exam? Have things become more collegial?"

"Well, that's one of the problems," Kate responded, choosing her words carefully. "At times, he still rides me hard, like a cadet fresh out of the Police Academy, not the seasoned professional that I've become. But lately, he and the Chief of Police have decided they know what's best for my career and have been trying to coerce me into taking a new job that I don't really want."

"What's the position they want you to take?" asked Glass, as he finished the last of Dawson's sustenance.

"Robbery. They need a new bureau head for Robbery."

"A bureau head? Interesting," he remarked, raising an eyebrow. "The SFPD needs good leaders. Particularly now. I don't see the downside, Kate. It looks like a great opportunity for you."

Kate protested, "But I'm not ready to leave Homicide. I like what I do, and I enjoy working with the people in the bureau."

Glass gave her his knowing smile. "Change is inevitable, Dawson. You can no more stop the hands on the clock from moving than you can prevent the earth from spinning on its axis through the universe. I know it's not easy to walk away from something to which you've devoted your career, but that's the way of all things. There'll be new people and other opportunities for growth in your next assignment, and eventually that will become your norm. And, as hard as it is to accept, the Homicide bureau will go on just fine without you."

"I'm not ready for that yet, Doc."

"I'm sure someone's already told you how rare promotions are in the SFPD," Glass explained. "A person has to retire or die before a deserving position becomes available."

"Yes, more than once."

"And of course, you know that it's not unusual for a person to experience some anxiety, maybe even a little fear, when confronting a new job. But I guarantee you, those feelings will gradually subside."

"This isn't a panic attack."

He wiped his mouth and wadded the napkin in the snap-lid container. "Well, I sense something else here. Something you're not telling me. Something that's holding you back."

"That's really none of your business," she shot back, angry.

"Well, just remember, you came to me," he said, abruptly pushing away from the table, "and in doing so, you *made* it part of my business." Glass seemed to be surprised by her sudden outburst. To him, their brief meeting was of two old friends who had been out for a leisurely stroll in a meadow that had turned into a mine field and *he* had stepped on the land mine.

"I'm sorry. I really am," Kate pleaded, as she began to settle down. Then, after a few moments, she shrugged, figuring Dr. Glass might as well know everything. "I met my husband right out of the Academy. He was an artist living in Haight-Asbury, and he reminded me a lot of my father. We fell in love, got married, and I had Stephanie, all in less than a year. The marriage didn't last long."

"How long?" he asked, sitting back down.

"Not long at all," she replied, with a few sniffles. "He had a real problem with drugs, and no matter how many promises he made or how many treatment programs he took to fight his addiction, he always ended up right back in the same place. It's difficult being married to an addict, with all of the mood swings and personality changes; it's even worse being divorced from one and sharing custody."

She looked at the staff psychiatrist for a fleeting moment, engaged his eyes, then quickly looked away.

Dawson continued, "You already know the part of the story about when he took my daughter hostage to get back at me."

"Your daughter, Stephanie, was shot dead with your service pistol during a domestic dispute with your ex-husband and you spent two years on administrative leave," Glass recalled, from one of their sessions. He made a point of catching her eye and holding it. "Is that what this is about? You're worried that you'll make another mistake, and someone else will die."

"No, not really. It has more to do with a promise that I made to Stephanie on the day she was laid to rest."

"You never really forgave yourself for her death, did you?"

"No, I haven't," Kate confessed, biting down hard on her lower lip. "I promised her that, at the first opportunity, I would start another family. I'm going to turn forty in a few months, so my biological clock is ticking. I've thought about this a lot, sometimes waking up at night in cold sweats. I don't dare take on the responsibility of running a bureau if my mind is focused on getting pregnant."

Dr. Barry Glass, at last, understood. "Don't worry, Kate your secret is safe with me."

"I figured if I stayed in Homicide, I could always take a leave of absence just prior to the third trimester and come back after the baby was born. I mean that's what FMLA is for, right?"

"Who's the lucky guy?" Glass asked, still smiling.

"Well, actually, I haven't met him yet," Kate replied, "but when I do, he's going to be a truly amazing man."

The police psychologist's smile turned upside down. "I'm sure he will."

Dawson stood up at the table, and said, "Thanks, Dr. Glass. I really do appreciate your taking the time out of your busy schedule to talk with me. I feel so much better about things now."

"Feel free to call me any time," he replied, also standing up.

She acknowledged him with a nod and headed back upstairs to her office. Barry Glass remained behind, concerned, shaking his head.

At twelve-thirty in the afternoon, Kate Dawson walked into the conference room at police headquarters, and put her stuff down. Because she had missed lunch, she grabbed a cup of coffee and a couple of donuts from the cantina at the back of the room and sat down at the far end of the table. Most of the detectives from the Homicide bureau were assembled around the table, including Clark, Jawara, Ramirez, Balardi, and several others she didn't know well. Lieutenant Roberts sat at the head of the table, conferring with Alex Starke. She wasn't a part of the bureau, so the cops in the room eyed her warily, as they would any stranger from the outside.

Roberts had the honor of introductions and didn't waste time getting the meeting started. "She's already worked with a few of you, but I thought that I'd take a moment to introduce the rest of you to Alex Starke. Starke is a special assistant to Chief Gates, and she also runs the City's Counter-Terrorism Task Force. Don't let her age fool you. She finished top of her class at the Academy, and in the short time she's been with the Force, she's produced some excellent results."

"Ms. Starke," asked Balardi, always troublesome but especially with new people, "would you mind if I ask you a question?"

"That's what I'm here for, detective," she replied. "And for the record, it is Officer Starke."

"Do you have any practical experience in dealing with Islamic terrorism?"

Every cop in the room thought the same thing: Starke

seemed awfully young and inexperienced to be placed in such an important role, but then this was not the first time the Chief of Police had used his office to promote a young woman he fancied. Dawson looked from face to face, hoping no one would actually say it. Leave it to Matt Balardi to bring it up.

"After high school, I spent two years as a paratrooper in the Israeli Defense Forces, fighting Hamas," Starke reported, as a matter of fact. "My parents hold dual U.S./Israeli citizenship, as do I. Israel requires its citizens serve in the military when they turn eighteen. Those living outside Israel, whether they hold Israeli citizenship or not, can apply for the IDF if they meet requirements, including no criminal record, a high school diploma, and the ability to speak Hebrew."

"You speak Hebrew?" Kate asked her young rival.

"Yes. I also speak Farsi, Arabic, French, and of course English."

"Ah," said Balardi, timidly. "Good enough."

Roberts took control and spoke directly to Starke. "Chief Gates and I have already briefed you on the basics of the case, and since you were working with Dawson out at the crime scene earlier this morning, I think we'd all be interested in hearing what you have to say, maybe what observations you'd like to make."

"It's really quite simple. Elementary, in fact," Starke said, sounding every bit like Sherlock Holmes. "We believe the murder of Officer Jamie Hartwell and the deaths of those twenty-four commuters on the BART subway car are related. Hartwell was responding to a routine traffic violation at the Westfield Shopping Centre when he was confronted by Mahmud Ibn Suri and his three associates. Eyewitness reports claim that Suri and the others came running across the parking lot, traveling northeast to southwest, when Suri opened fire and shot the officer. They then drove off in Suri's late model Buick LaSabre, shouting '*Allah Akbar.*' The BART station at Powell Street is located about two blocks northeast of the Westfield Shopping Center and is the station located directly before the BART station at the Civic Center and United Nations Plaza. We believe Suri and his accomplices planted a neurotoxin on the southwest-bound subway car, and then somehow triggered it to explode, killing all those people on board before it reached the next station."

"*Claro,*" Jorge Ramirez acknowledged in Spanish. "Has Mahmud Ibn Suri been picked up by authorities yet?"

Kate Dawson shook her head. "An APB was issued for his arrest following the terror attack on the BART subway car, but he was never arrested or charged. However, we are reasonably certain that Suri is dead. His body was among those recovered from the warehouse fire."

"He's dead then?" Balardi was watching Starke, as if he didn't quite trust her. "How did that happen?"

"We believe that Mahmud Ibn Suri was the leader of one of the two local terrorist cells operating in the San Francisco Bay Area," Starke stated, opening one of the classified reports in front of her on the conference table. "Intelligence reports also suggest that his cell was operating the lab that produced the neurotoxin used in the subway attack.

Once Inspector Dawson had confirmed the specific neuro-toxin they used, the focus of our investigation shifted to finding that lab. What we didn't know was that a rival terrorist cell was also looking for Suri and his men. Sometime this morning, members of both groups shot it out for control of the neuro-toxin, and they all ended up perishing in the warehouse fire."

Only William Clark seemed to get this. The faces of the other detectives looked back blankly at Starke. Most of them had been out to the warehouse fire, but it still had not registered.

Mikhail Jawara raised his hand in a school boy manner and risked the ridicule of the others for looking stupid. "Does this have anything to do with the ongoing feud between the Shia and Sunni factions of Islam?"

"The two factions have been at war with each other for hundreds of years due to a fundamental dispute over Muhammad's rightful successor. Mahmud Ibn Suri was a Sunni Muslim, devoted to the teachings of the Prophet Mohammad, while Hassan Abu Abdullah, the leader of the rival cell, was a Shiite from Iran, where he took his orders directly from the Ayatollahs. I guess it doesn't matter now which side was right because they're all dead."

"Clark tried to explain this to me, but it really didn't make a whole lot of sense," Jawara confessed. "Their war is with the West. Why don't they just join forces, and fight their common enemy together?"

"It's far more complicated than you realize," she said, fixing him with a look.

"Maybe we should just sit back and let the two factions kill each other off?" Matt Balardi said aloud, what everyone else was thinking.

"Yeah, sure. Pistols at dawn," one of the other detectives weighed in.

Balardi smiled broadly. "That's what they used to do to settle disputes. If it worked for Hamilton and Burr, who are we to disagree?"

"You boys can't be serious?" Starke asked them.

"I am."

"Damned straight, I'm serious," Balardi replied. "Every time there's a conflict over there, the U.S. military gets called in to settle it, and we lose American lives. The next time, we should give each Arab combatant a tank, and let them slug it out. Better yet, give 'm each a nuke, and let them hammer it out. I'll guarantee you they won't be comin' back for more."

"Right on, brother."

William Clark thumbed through his notes. "Do we know what neurotoxin was used to kill those commuters?"

"Was it sarin gas?" Jawara asked, interrupting his partner.

"It was far worse than sarin," Starke replied. "What could be deadlier than sarin gas?" Jawara fired back.

"Botulinum Toxin. BTX is the most poisonous substance known to man. Less than $1\mu g/kg$ body weight is sufficient to kill in large numbers."

"How much did we recover from the warehouse fire?" Clark asked.

"Not a drop," Starke answered.

Balardi breathed a sigh of relief, and said, "So, is it safe to say the threat has been contained?"

"No, I don't think you understand," she objected. "Whatever amount the lab had produced during its operation is gone. Missing. We didn't find a drop because we think someone else may have gotten to it first."

The conference room fell suddenly silent as each detective considered the implications: The world's most deadly toxin missing from a terrorist cell in San Francisco.

"Do we have any leads?" Lieutenant Roberts asked, cutting through the bullshit. He had been so respectfully silent during Starke's presentation that most of the other detectives had forgotten he was among them at the table. He leaned forward in his chair and stared first at Starke and then Dawson. "Well?"

"We believe there was a third man," Starke offered.

Dawson jumped in, "We don't know who he is or which side he works for, but it appears that he may have been brought in from the outside as a 'cleaner.' Those men who were wounded during the raid on the warehouse but not killed were executed by him with a single shot to the head."

"There's really not much there," Alex concluded.

Roberts directed them to the next thread of evidence. "Do we know how they triggered the neurotoxin?"

"No, sir. Again, there's not much to go on."

"I've reviewed the casework that was written on the 1995 Tokyo subway attack. There does appear to be a great many similarities between the two attacks," William Clark reported, glancing up from his notes.

"What have you got, Clark?" Roberts asked, curtly.

"On Monday morning, March 20, 1995, five members of the Aum Shinrikyo, a doomsday cult bent on hastening the end of the world, launched a chemical attack on the Tokyo subway system during the peak of rush hour," he explained, his notebook in hand. "Each member carried two .9-liter packets of liquid sarin wrapped inside a newspaper and an umbrella with sharpened tips. At predetermined stations, the sarin packets were dropped and punctured several times. Each perpetrator then got off the train and exited the station to meet his accomplice with a car. The sarin affected passengers, subway workers, and all those who came into contact with them. Twelve people died, another fifty were severely injured, and five thousand others suffered temporary vision lost. The attack was considered to be the worst act of domestic terrorism perpetrated on the Japanese people since the end of World War II."

"Well, now, at least we know where Mahmud Ibn Suri got his idea for the subway attack," Starke said.

Roberts threw his hands up in the air. "Were any of Suri's associates carrying umbrellas with sharpened tips? Did they deploy sandwich-sized bags filled with a liquid form of the neurotoxin?"

"No, sir." Clark turned red, a sheepish look on his face.

"Then it's irrelevant!" Roberts shouted.

"Dawson and I have developed a theory that—" Starke started to say but was cut off in mid-sentence.

"Who gives a shit?" the Lieutenant growled, growing more and more impatient. "Goddammit, I've had enough of listening to your theories. Let's just stick strictly to what we know. Understand?"

"Yes, sir," Starke replied, the good little soldier.

"Understood," Dawson responded, with surprise.

The room went silent and everyone's attention was on Roberts. In the past, he had often spoken with such authority and force that they had come to accept it as his way of shaking things up or kicking ass to make a point. But the coarseness and profanity in his language made him sound like a man possessed by some unknown demon, as if he had exchanged places with a mirror-universe version of himself. He was definitely not the man that they knew.

"Now, exactly what do we know? Point one," he said, raising his thumb to enumerate the first point, "an unknown quantity of the world's deadliest neurotoxin is missing from the warehouse fire."

Dawson nodded, following his points.

"Point two," Roberts added his index finger, "Mahmud Ibn Suri, the chief suspect in the subway attack and the murder of Officer Hartwell, is dead. Apparently, he and his rival, Hassan Abu Abdullah, suffered injuries in a pre-dawn raid on the warehouse and both perished in the fire."

All the detectives acknowledged his second point.

"And finally, point three," the Lieutenant said, adding his middle finger to the other two. "A third man was present at the crime scene but left no evidence behind as to his identity or purpose."

They were all in agreement with him, whoever he was.

Roberts knitted his brow in concentration. "In the absence of hard evidence, we need to follow the money trail," he said finally, on fire. "Where did the money come from to fund the lab? Pay for the chemicals? They must have been expensive. Deadly. What company delivered those items to the lab? You wouldn't have contracted with UPS or FedEx to make that delivery. Also, there must have been a lease on the warehouse. Who signed the lease and paid the rent each month? What about utilities? You'd expect that someone in the Muslim community must have known about the warehouse. Who knew and didn't say anything to authorities? What about the rival terrorist cell? How much did they know?"

"Hold on!" Jawara shouted. "Slow it down!"

William Clark had opened his notebook and was feverishly writing everything down that the Lieutenant said. "Could you repeat that last one?"

"I'm still not clear which group was which," Balardi commented, looking for some degree of clarification. "I still don't understand . . ."

One moment, James Roberts was sitting forward in his chair, shouting out questions randomly off the top of his head. The next, silence as the look on his face changed. The stern, steely-eyed appearance was replaced with a grimace as pain and an unusual squeezing sensation seized his chest. Without thought or volition, he clutched at his heart with both hands, and muttered, "Oh, no." Everyone around the table heard his utterance, but few had time to react to him before his face turned beet red. Sweating and shortness of breath followed. In less than a minute, the Lieutenant had tumbled from his chair, and was lying sprawled out on the floor of the conference room, out cold.

"What the hell!?" Jawara yelled.

"What's wrong with the boss?" Balardi added.

Kate knew exactly what was wrong and sprang to her feet and started barking orders, "Clark, grab the portable defibrillator! It's mounted on the wall, near the elevators."

"Right!" he replied, scrambling out of the room.

"Starke, call Brogan immediately, and get his ass up here. Extension 1138 . . . and then call an ambulance, 911."

"I'm on it," Alex responded, heading to the conference room phone.

"Jawara, Balardi, give me a hand with the boss. I want to straighten him out on the floor."

Balardi shouted, "Do you think we should move him?"

"He's had a heart attack, Matt," Kate said sternly. "The quicker we can get CPR started, the better his odds are. We really don't have time to discuss this."

"I hope you know what you're doing," he said, shaking his head.

Kate Dawson was already down on one knee, cradling Roberts' head. "C'mon, boys, I want him flat on the floor, with his legs straight and his arms at his sides."

As they straightened out his crumpled body, Dawson stripped off her Versace jacket, and tucked it under Roberts' neck, so that his head was tilted back at a slight angle. She then opened his airway and leaned over him to check for breath, but with the flurry of activity around her, she was finding it hard. Roberts, a big, hulking man who weighed over three hundred pounds, slumped in the middle where his belly fat had rolled over the top of his leather belt. The body was all dead weight as they attempted to flatten him out on the floor. Ramirez and the other detectives in the Homicide bureau scrambled to clear away chairs and personal belongings in the way. Eventually, several others pitched in and helped maneuver Roberts safely. He was completely unresponsive.

"He's not breathing," Balardi reported.

"Dammit, Kate, he's not breathing!" Jawara exclaimed.

"Can't find a pulse," one of the others said.

Acting quickly, Dawson straddled her boss' upper torso, pumping his chest with her fingers laced together as one, elbows locked, pressing down with all her weight just below the sternum. She counted one compression per second for fifteen counts, allowing each compression to return on its own. Under her breath, she repeated the lyrics to the Bee Gees' song "Stayin' Alive," as a way to keep track of the number of compressions she did on his chest.

Then Kate moved to Roberts' side, tilted his head back, and pinched his nose. She sealed her lips over his mouth, and gave him two rescue breaths, blowing hard enough for his chest to rise. She then climbed back on top of his body and resumed pumping his chest. That was only one round. Kate knew she wouldn't be able to keep up that pace for long.

The Lieutenant had not responded at all to her actions.

At that moment, Clark ran back into the room with the AED. "I've never used one of these," he confessed, offering it, "but I have taken extensive notes on how the AED is supposed to give the heart an electric shock when someone's heart has stopped."

"I've been trained to use a defibrillator," Alex Starke said, as she pushed Clark aside and laid the AED out on one side of the floor. She unzipped the cover to the bag and flipped open the lid to the device. Immediately, as she turned the power on, a recorded voice reminded her to "Call for help, now."

Kate stopped pumping his chest, breathlessly asking, "Are you ready?"

"Nearly," Starke replied, taking the electric pads out of a sealed pack. "Get his shirt off. We've got to attach the pads directly to his chest."

Kate grabbed the two sides of Roberts' Oxford dress shirt, and rather than unbutton each button one at a time, she pulled hard and ripped the shirt in half, sending buttons flying, then tore through his white undershirt. "Okay!"

"Wipe away any sweat from the chest," Starke ordered, reading from the instructions.

"With what?"

"I don't know. Use the corners of his t-shirt."

"Done."

Starke removed the backing paper from the first pad. "Place this pad on his upper right side, just below the collarbone. The adhesive will force the pad to stick to his chest. Just make sure you attach it in the right place."

"Got it," Kate replied, after sticking the pad in place.

"Place the second pad on the left side, just below the armpit," Alex instructed Kate, handing her the second pad. "Make sure you position the pad lengthways, with the long side in line with the length of Roberts' body."

"Done," she again replied. "Okay, everyone, stand clear!" Starke shouted, and then watched as everyone took a step back away from the body.

The AED sounded a brief alarm, then shot a bolt of electricity through its pads. The body jolted into the air from the shock and came back down hard on the floor. Kate leaned back in and resumed chest compressions and rescue breathing, as the AED charged itself for a second try.

"Stand clear everyone," Starke repeated, waving people back.

Again, the AED sounded its alarm and a second bolt of electricity shot into the chest of Lieutenant Roberts. The body jolted but remained unresponsive.

"C'mon," Kate shouted, as she went back to pumping his chest.

"What's happening here?" Doctor Brogan demanded, as he and one of his technicians raced into the conference room. Most of the detectives were standing around the floor watching the two women work.

"Roberts had a heart attack during our meeting," Starke said, rather cold and unemotional with her details. "Dawson's been giving him CPR and we've just used the defibrillator twice now to jumpstart his heart. No response."

"Cardiac arrest," Brogan said to his technician, bending down over the body and pressing two fingers against the side of his neck.

"He doesn't appear to be breathing," the technician noted.

"Hey, I've got a pulse," Brogan exclaimed. "Get me one hundred cc's of adrenaline."

At once, the two men sprang into action. While his assistant filled a syringe from a bottle of adrenaline, Brogan swapped places with Kate and began administering CPR. The technician instantly followed his lead. Once he had finished injecting the Lieutenant with the stimulant, he pulled a small, lightweight respirator from his equipment pack, placing its black rubber mask over Roberts' mouth, and renewed attempts to restart his breathing by pumping a squeeze bag, in and out.

Nothing.

Kate bent over him, at the level of his head, and gently stroked his short, gray hair. As much as she despised him for what he had done to her over the years, she could not seem to muster any anger or hate for the man who lay there before her. *Pitiful man, what kind of life have you known?* She reasoned that James Roberts must have joined the police force back in the seventies, at a time when police officers were called "pigs" and spat upon by college students and hippies. In his face, Kate saw the person that he used to be before he succumbed to the temptations of power and corruption. She saw a man who must have started out with a tremendous amount of integrity and humility and served the force with an unswerving devotion to principle and duty. Then the world changed, policing changed, but he was unable or unwilling to change himself. He must have clung to his principles for as long as he could, and when overwhelming adversity made that impossible, he must have started down a long road of compromises that led him right there. Roberts wasn't an evil man; just a man who had simply chosen the path of least resistance. The fact that he also lacked imagination had led him to become the lowest of all lifeforms, a bottom feeder.

"Come on, breathe!" the technician cried out, plying him with fresh air.

Nothing.

"He's not responding. We're going lose him. Come on, dammit!" Brogan swore at him, pounding on Roberts' large chest cavity.

"You're hurting him!" Kate shouted at Brogan, compelled to do something, other than just stand there.

Clark held her back. "No, they know what they're doing. Just let them work."

Brogan continued to pound on his chest.

"Breathe, dammit! Breathe!"

"Come on, breathe!" his assistant repeated.

Kate Dawson stared down into her boss' face. His big, round boyish features had gone pale, almost ashen. Panicked, she looked from Doctor Brogan to his technician and cried, "Help him!"

Frantically, the Chief Medical Examiner and his assistant struggled to keep him alive as his features grew more and more pallid.

"Fight, dammit!" Brogan shouted, pumping hard and fast on his chest with the palms of his hands.

"Fight!" his assistant completed.

Kate reached out to her boss, gently squeezing his hand. "You can't just die on me like this," she whispered in his ear. She thought about her words for a moment, then added, "You've got to help us solve this case."

Roberts's eyelids fluttered.

"Jim!" she cried, squeezing his hand tightly.

Brogan continued CPR. In a matter of moments, or perhaps mere heartbeats, his face twitched, and his hands clenched and unclenched in spasm. The color was returning to the ice-cold features of his face.

"Come on, you can do it!" Brogan urged.

Kate added, "Lieutenant, you can do it. Don't quit on me now."

Finally, with a feeble cough, Roberts pushed the mask away from his mouth and started to breathe on his own. He choked at first, struggling for each breath. But then, gradually, the big, hulking man began to breathe in and exhale the fresh air in his lungs, with some difficulty, weak as a newborn baby.

"All right!" the technician exclaimed.

"Thank God," Brogan prayed, perspiration dripping from his face. "I thought we'd lost him."

Kate and the others couldn't believe their eyes, but the proof was right before them. It seemed impossible that he was still alive, but Dawson was beginning to believe that anything was possible.

With a tremendous weight lifted from his shoulders, Doctor Brogan stood straight, his head tilted up, eyes closed in thanks; his face crimson, his shirt soaking wet.

The technician ran his hand through his hair, relieved, smiling from ear to ear. Nearly everyone was crying tears of joy.

"Thank you," Brogan said to Kate, with a slight nod of his head.

"Don't give it another thought," she replied modestly.

"C'mon," he ordered, still out of breath. "We've got to get your boss to a hospital!"

"Right," his technician agreed, attempting to comfort and console Roberts until the Rescue Squad arrived.

Kate was concerned. "Will he be okay, Doc? You wouldn't believe it, but just a few minutes ago, he sounded like a man possessed."

For a moment, Brogan looked down at Roberts, then pulled Kate off to the side. "Your boss didn't have a heart attack, although that may have contributed to the problem. He experienced sudden cardiac arrest, a very serious trauma to the heart that a significant number of people never fully cover."

"I always thought they were the same thing." Dawson was confused.

"People often use these terms interchangeably, but they *are not* the same thing," the Medical Examiner explained to her. "A heart attack occurs when the blood flow to the heart is interrupted or blocked, while cardiac arrest is when the heart malfunctions and suddenly stops beating unexpectedly."

"Sounds the same."

"No, no. A heart attack is a 'circulation' problem and sudden cardiac arrest is an 'electrical' problem."

"But will he be okay?" she asked, wiping tears from her cheeks.

"I think so," Brogan replied, patting her on the shoulder. "Cardiac arrest is reversible in most victims if it's treated within a few minutes. You know, over three hundred thousand people in the United States die every year because there's usually no one around who knows what to do, but your quick thinking may have doubled or even tripled Roberts' chances of survival. That was good work, Dawson. Damned good work. I'm really proud of you."

Kate smiled through her tears. "It was a team effort, Doc."

"Who are you kidding?" Brogan could see right through her. "Without your leadership, Dawson, this man would be dead right now."

"I think you're overstating things a bit."

"Not at all." He put his arm around her shoulders. "I just hope when my time comes, there's someone responsible like you around."

"Thanks."

A few minutes later, the Rescue Squad was wheeling Roberts on a gurney toward the bank of elevators, IV and oxygen in place. Kate walked alongside, holding his hand in hers. Clark and Ramirez were a few steps behind. They all hoped, after a few weeks in the hospital, followed by a couple of months of rest and rehabilitation, the Lieutenant would be able to return to his duties in the bureau.

"You're going to be okay. There's nothing to worry about," Kate reassured him. "Brogan will accompany you to the hospital."

"Dawson," he said weakly, "you are not a very good liar."

"No, I suppose I'm not," she confessed.

"I've spent a lifetime learning how to lie," Roberts revealed, "but I guess my heart was never really in it."

"We picked good jobs, didn't we?"

Roberts smiled and, in turn, so did Kate.

When they reached the elevators, Kate Dawson pushed the down button and almost immediately one of the elevator cars going down appeared. She helped them as best she could, then quickly said her goodbyes before the elevator continued on its journey.

"Take good care of him, Doc," Kate said, shaking Brogan's hand.

"You know I will."

"I'll stop by the hospital tonight."

"He should be stable by then," Brogan assured her.

As the elevator door closed, Kate Dawson turned to Clark, who was standing right at her side, and said, "Well, I guess I should get used to calling you boss, William. Do you want me to get them all rounded up and back in the conference room? We've certainly got a lot of work to do."

"Thanks, Kate, but let's be clear about one thing."

"Sure," she replied with a shrug.

"I'll serve as the Old Man's Interim Bureau Chief until he's healthy enough to return to the job, but I won't accept a permanent assignment. Truth be told, I really don't want the job. Too many headaches, far too much paperwork. I'd rather continue to serve in this bureau than lead it," Clark confessed.

"Okay, but why tell me?"

William Clark smiled broadly. "You know damned well, Dawson. You're the one who should be running this bureau."

"Well, I doubt if Balardi or Corcoran or Farris would agree with you."

"You're probably right, but then again, this isn't a popularity contest," Clarke replied, the smile still crusted on his face. "It's a job that takes a certain amount of hard work, discipline, compassion, tenacity, and finesse to do it right. No one else but you possess those traits."

"I've thought about it—" she started to walk away.

"Hey, Kate, do me a favor."

Dawson stopped, and half turned toward her fellow detective. "Anything for you, William."

"Think about it some more."

Kate Dawson smiled. "Okay, I will."

Twenty-five minutes later, the detectives who comprised the Homicide Bureau and Alex Starke were gathered around the conference room table, chatting with each other, sipping coffee or looking through notes. Scuttlebutt around the table was that Kate Dawson was going to take over as Interim Bureau Chief, with Clark's blessing, but when she entered the room, followed by Clark, most realized who their new taskmaster was. Clark closed the door behind him and sat conspicuously in Roberts' chair at the end of the table, with Dawson sitting down right next to him. Balardi, Corcoran, and Farris turned their gaze to Kate, but she fixed them in place with a glare.

"Well, we've certainly had an event-filled afternoon," Clark said, modulating his voice and tone to set the right mood for the meeting. "I'm sure you'll be happy to learn that Lieutenant Roberts was admitted to UCSF Medical Center just a short time ago and is undergoing a slew of tests. They tell me that his prognosis is good, and that he should make a complete recovery." When William Clark had finished speaking, he clapped his hands, and ignited a round of applause from everyone sitting around the table, including Kate. He waited until everyone had settled down again, and then said, "During the Old Man's absence, I'll be taking over as Bureau Head."

"Is that true?" Starke asked, looking up and down the table.

Balardi's features squeezed out of shape with surprise. "You?"

Ramirez smiled, saying, "*Bueno*," while Corcoran, Farris, and one other homicide detective snickered aloud.

William Clark and his partner exchanged glances.

"I don't really want to do it," Clark added, as if talking directly to Mikhail Jawara. "But in lieu of an equally-qualified candidate, I serve at the pleasure of the Chief of Police."

Jawara nodded. "It's cool, partner."

Kate Dawson breathed a sigh of relief, but at the same time, felt an emptiness in the pit of her stomach. *Maybe, Clark was right?* She looked at Balardi, then Corcoran, Farris, and the other detectives at the table. There was no one else better quali- fied to run the bureau than her. She decided that she'd talk to the Chief of Police about the position at the earliest possible time.

Just then, the door to the conference room swung open and Doctor Brogan, fresh from his trip to the hospital with Roberts, stepped through the threshold. "I came as quickly as I could."

Kate Dawson shot a worried glance at the ME. "How's Lieutenant Roberts doing?"

"Stable," he said calmly, directly. "Resting."

"Thank, God," she said, closing her eyes.

"Thank God as much as you want," Brogan replied, patting her on the back. "I'm just grateful that someone with your experience was there. Otherwise he'd be lying on a slab in the morgue. Dead."

"Doc," Kate whispered, "*please—*"

Clark listened politely to their exchange, then decided it was time to get the meeting started. He turned his gaze to the Medical Examiner, and said, "Doctor Brogan, thanks for agreeing to meet with us today under such short notice. Now, I know your investigation is still ongoing, but I was hoping you could bring us up to speed with your findings."

"Certainly. Once the warehouse fire was contained earlier this morning, my forensics team and I scoured the ruins for bodies. We found nine of them, including one we believe is the chief suspect in Officer Hartwell's murder, Mahmud ibn Suri. All nine bodies were concentrated in the southwest corner of the warehouse; the remains spread over several large rooms. We also found evidence of a firefight, including the actual weapons they used and hundreds of rounds of shell casings from several Kalashnikov AK 47 assault rifles, and shell casings from several smaller arms, like a 1911 Colt .45 semi-automatic pistol, a 9 mm

Beretta, and a 9 mm Glock 43. My team is presently hard at work matching ballistics with the weapons that we seized and hope to have a more comprehensive picture by tomorrow."

"That's very good, doctor," Clark complimented him.

"Starke and I searched that area, too, and would like to hear your take on what happened there," Dawson added.

"The evidence suggests that a rival cell, possibly led by Hassan Abu Abdullah, stormed the warehouse shortly after 3 a.m. We found his body among those of his men, shot-up almost beyond recognition," Brogan said without a tick of emotion in his voice. "Neighbors remember hearing 'popping' sounds, what they called 'firecrackers,' which could have been small arms fire channeled through silencers, about that time. Hassan's strike team took out the one or two guards who were still awake and got the drop on Mahmud's team that was still sleeping. Both groups shot it out for control of the Botulinum Toxin, and Mahmud was the only one who got out alive; wounded but alive."

"I think he may have gotten caught in the fire," Dawson suggested, "but Starke thinks Mahmud actually started the fire to obliterate any evidence of the toxin or the lab or his terrorist cell."

Alex Starke jumped in, "But then, he got caught in his own fire and was burned nearly beyond recognition."

"I congratulate both of you on some outstanding detective work. Your description of events is an excellent reading of the evidence," the Medical Examiner said, agreeing with their conclusion. "But there's only one problem with your theories. They don't explain what happened to the toxin they produced."

Starke said dourly, "We know they used a small amount to kill those people on board the subway car, but there's really no telling how much the chemist produced in that makeshift lab of theirs."

Kate stated dejectedly, "We may never know if it was a few ounces or several tons."

"Exactly," Brogan and Clark agreed.

Jawara got in on the act, leaning back in his chair, and smiled affably at the overweight ME. "Doctor, is there any evidence that suggests the toxin was stored in the warehouse? Could it have been produced there, then stored safely at another location other than the warehouse? My gut tells me that it's locked away in a safety deposit box at the bank or stored in a public locker at the airport."

Brogan was unruffled by the question. "Anything's possible, Mikhail. My team and I have been working under the assumption the terrorists produced the BTX in a specially-equipped lab at the warehouse and then subsequently stored their product on the premises. We've found evidence of the lab in equipment at the warehouse. We just haven't found the toxin itself."

"The rival terrorist cell seemed to think the toxin was there," Clark reasoned, as he read back over his notes. "Otherwise, Hassan Abu Abdullah and his team would have had no reason to attack the warehouse."

Starke crossed her arms. "Maybe Hassan was just looking for a good excuse to take out his rival, Mahmud ibn Suri?"

"This is like a damned moebius loop," Jawara said. "Just when you think you're getting somewhere, the loop turns back on itself."

"Well, you're not going to like this any better," Kate replied.

"Oh, no. You wouldn't do that to me," Jawara voiced his objection.

"Sorry, Mikhail," she said guilelessly. Dawson held Jawara's eyes for a second, then looked down at the table. "On our way out of the crime scene, I insisted on having another look at each of the bodies. We found that, in addition to the wounds sustained during the firefight, each victim had a single gunshot wound to the head, point-blank range. That suggests a third-party shooter."

Starke interjected, "We refer to this third man as 'the fixer' or 'cleaner.' We believe he was hired to ensure nobody talked."

"Hired by whom?" Clark asked, staring down at a blank page in his notes.

"We just don't know," Starke confessed.

"Fixers work for Mafia bosses," Jawara said, with a smug look. "They don't generally take 'help wanted' ads on Facebook or Home Advisor or hire themselves out to terrorist cells."

"We're hoping that Doctor Brogan and his team can tell us more," Kate said.

The ME exhaled loudly, then said, "You'll have the autopsy and ballistics reports tomorrow, but in terms of your third-party shooter, I don't think we're likely to know much more about him. Mikhail's right. Fixers by their very nature are very secretive people. They offer their clients the highest degree of discretion and privacy. If he doesn't want to be found, he won't be found."

His words hung in the air.

Kate Dawson leaned over and whispered something to Clark. He thought about it for a moment, then shrugged.

Kate stood up from the table, walked over to the white board, and wrote several words with the dry-erase marker, then said, "The way I see it, we've got four distinct investigations. First, we've got to find the remainder of the Botulinum Toxin. We know the lab was up and running for several weeks, but what we don't know is how much of the weaponized BTX was produced. More importantly, where is it now? And who has control over it?"

"Kate, if it's all the same to you," Ramirez said, "I'll work on that part of it."

Rather than acknowledge his request on her own, Dawson turned to her boss, and waited for him to act. Clark nodded his approval.

Relieved, Dawson said, "Thanks, Jorge."

"You're going to need some additional help with that, Jorge," William Clark added. He looked around the conference room, and his eyes landed on Matt Balardi.

"Matt, why don't you give him a hand with that?"

"Swell," Balardi said, with a frown.

"Next, we know that BTX is a very complex and dangerous neurotoxin to make, and that only a skilled or well-trained chemist with the right chemicals and other elements would attempt to produce large quantities in a makeshift lab. Starke seems to think there are only two or three chemists in the Muslim community who have the skillset to pull this off. I agree with her." Dawson turned to her new boss, with eyebrows raised like question marks.

William Clark tapped his pen. "What do you say, partner? You'll have to scour that whole neighborhood to find the chemist."

"Sure. Why not?"

"Don't sound so glum, Mikhail. I'll still be around to help you out."

"Great! With our own Bill Nye, the science guy, how can we miss?" Jawara quipped.

Kate smiled brightly, visibly pleased. "Next, we've always worked under the assumption that the chemicals and other elements to make the BTX neurotoxin were readily available to the San Francisco marketplace. What we don't know is the exact list of chemicals needed. Where were they purchased, or if any of the more dangerous elements had to be smuggled in from outside the country? We should have two or three guys look into this—"

"Corcoran, Farris, and . . . It's Walker, isn't it?" Clark reached over the table and shook hands with him. "I'd like the three of you to take a crack at this."

The three of them acquiesced, reluctantly, but not one of them seemed overly excited about the assignment.

"Was that about it, Kate?"

Dawson hesitated a moment. "Nearly, boss," she said finally, staring at the white board. "The only thing we haven't covered is the third-party shooter."

"Why don't you and Starke work on the identity of the fixer?" Clark was all business. You could hear the determination in his voice as he barked out the last orders. "I want to know who he is and what he was doing there."

Starke replied curtly. "You got it, boss."

Dawson nodded. "We're on it."

Without expression, Clark stared at the detectives gathered around the conference room table. "So, now that you've gotten your individual assignments, I don't think there's much point in discussing any more. As Lieutenant Roberts used to say, 'Get out there, beat the grass, and see what turns up.'"

CHAPTER FIVE

At three fifty-four in the afternoon, Kate Dawson pushed her way through the crowd that had gathered on the steps outside the main entrance to the Hall of Justice and stood next to William Clark and the other bureau heads and detectives behind the empty podium where the Chief of Police would make his remarks to the press. Together, with the handful of well-dressed dignitaries from local and state governments, including the Mayor, the head of the City Council, City Council members, and the State Representative, she joined a semi-circle that flanked the center stage on both sides of the steps. As Kate stood peering through the crowd, Clark said a couple of things, but the noise level was so loud she didn't hear him. She merely nodded at him or smiled while the remainder of people stood stiffly by, reminding her of mannikins in the huge store windows of the Benny Gold Department Store.

Nearby, members of the press straddled the white, marble steps behind their portable television cameras and micro-phones, each vying for the most optimum location. Police officers had very little trouble containing the crowd of about seventy people who stood directly in front of the podium; some huddled together in small groups talking with each other.

Meanwhile, protestors carrying signs—"Hate is NOT an American Virtue," "Immigrants make America great," "I'm Muslim. I'm not a terrorist, but a proud American," and "Muslim Refugees Are Welcome Here"—walked round and round on the sidewalk in front of the entrance. Muslim women wearing their traditional hijab walked proudly, holding their children's hands, their voices raised in solidarity. Dozens of bearded men either walked with their families or held their signs up high enough so others could see them.

At exactly four o'clock, Nelson Gates, dressed in his formal police uniform, walked out of the main entrance to the Hall of Justice and stepped up to the podium. He took a brief moment to acknowledge those gathered around him, catching Kate's eye, then pulled a couple sheets of paper from his jacket pocket. He leaned forward into the microphone, and said, "Early this morning, members of the San Francisco Police Department, working in close collaboration with Fire and Rescue, were dispatched to the Folsom neighborhood of the Mission District and assisted residents in the safe and orderly evacuation of this predominantly Muslim community adjacent to the warehouse fire. Most of the officers, detectives, 911 phone operators, and other city workers who participated in this unique mobilization were off duty personnel who volunteered to help out in the crisis. With the power and lights out and fire officials battling the third-alarm blaze, these volunteers went literally door to door at considerable risk to their own lives and carried children and elderly residents to safety. Even S.W.A.T. teams participated in the evacuation, ferrying those with disabilities to local shelters. I am enormously proud of the heroic men and women in Blue who took part in this effort. Our law enforcement officials deserve our gratitude and respect. Without their willingness to place public safety above personal security, local government simply could not have met its most critical responsibility of protecting American lives. This morning, they saved hundreds of lives, and demonstrated to the world that we San Franciscans are not separated by our religious or ethnic beliefs, or isolated from each other by our individual communities, but are indeed one people, the residents of this great city of San Francisco, united in our solidarity against those who seek to divide us."

Gates paused briefly to drink in the adulation and applause of the crowd—some clapping hands, others cheered, and a few remained silent—and then launched into the next section of his speech. "Some have sought to use the acts of terror perpetrated earlier in the week to sow the seeds of division among us by suggesting that one group alone is responsible. This is unacceptable and inconsistent with what America is all about. Muslims and Arab Americans helped to build this great city of ours and have strengthened it, day in and day out, for more than two hundred years with their enormous commitment. They have served as police officers and firemen, teachers and business owners, civic leaders, doctors and nurses, dockworkers, hotel clerks and housekeepers, cooks and waitresses, taxi drivers and cable car operators, soldiers and sailors in every conceivable role, strengthening their local communities and safeguarding our city great. The cooperation of our Muslim neighbors has been essential in identifying and preventing terroristic threats. We must never lose sight of this. And, as we work to create a brighter and more prosperous future, we must not forget to recognize those who have fallen."

There were more claps and cheers as the audience responded to the speech from the Chief of Police.

"Now, I know there is no question or doubt that threats to our national security, as well as to the security of this great city, are real," Gates continued. "Together, we have mourned the loss of our fellow Americans in New York City, Boston, Washington, D.C., Schwenksville, San Bernardino, and Orlando, Fort Hood, Texas, and in cities around the world. We now also mourn the life of Officer Hartwell, who was gunned down in the line of duty, as well as the lives of those twenty-four commuters who boarded the BART train and perished before they reached their final destination. Both of these attacks were shameful acts of cowardice and fear, inspired by a corrupt ideology, one that seeks to twist and pervert the peaceful teachings and traditions of Islam into radical Islamic terrorism. But as you and I both know, the vulgar actions of a handful of misguided individuals do not reflect the values of an entire faith or people. And while violence, especially violence that results in the loss of innocent lives, often triggers more violence, we must work together to temper widespread anger and bigotry, and to eliminate acts of vengeance and retaliation."

Again, the Chief of Police paused, hoping to give his audience a chance to react positively to his words, but the smattering of applause, largely from his own people, suggested that he had taken his speech too far. He looked out at the community leaders, and then the protestors, and was met with blank stares and silence. For the first time, when he looked again, Gates actually read the words on their protest signs; not all but enough to begin to understand their concerns. Some of the words resonated with him in a way they had not before. He folded the two sheets of paper in half and placed them into his jacket pocket.

As all watched what his next move would be, Gates ran his tongue over parched lips and began again, "Ours is a nation of immigrants. In fact, I'm the grandson of Irish immigrants who fled Ireland at the turn of the last century when the potato crop failed, and famine and disease killed over a million men, women, and children of my countrymen. We had no choice but to come to the United States, and when we arrived in cities like New York and Boston, we were reviled and hated like no other people on the planet. Not only did the predominantly Protestant Americans mistrust us for our Catholic religious beliefs, but we were unskilled workers who had spent our lives toiling in fields. Oh, there were some who were blacksmiths and stonemasons, but the majority of us had no formal training at anything. If you walked around the streets of those Eastern cities, you'd see dozens of handwritten signs, not unlike your posters, that would read 'No Irish Need Apply.' And if a police officer was killed or some other terrible event happened, the Irish were always blamed for it, whether they were responsible or not. The Irish were the scapegoats for everything wrong with society. Eventually, that sentiment changed as community leaders reached out to include the Irish, and the Irish took jobs as policemen and firefighters, miners and coal workers, in sanitation, as steamfitters; basically the jobs no one else wanted.

"The American people have proven, time and again, that our progress as a nation is rooted in welcoming those who are new and that our country's greatest successes happen only when there is a genuine willingness to reach across lines of division and exclusion." Gates swallowed hard. "Sometimes that doesn't happen fast enough. But then, we are only human, with our own fears and foibles. If we are going to realize our nation's promise, and if we want to heal persistent wounds and overcome new threats of our democracy, then we must learn to work together."

Some of those who were gathered in front of the Hall of Justice responded positively to Gates' off-the-cuff remarks; others remained silent, while the protestors were anxious to get their rally ramped up.

"One of you is carrying a sign today that really speaks to the heart of what I am trying to say. That sign reads, 'I'm Muslim.

I'm not a terrorist, but a proud American.'" The surprised protestor waved the sign up and down. "Regardless of color or creed, we are all Americans. And to the extent that relationships between Muslim and non-Muslim Americans are defined by differences, those who sow hatred rather than peace will, no doubt, prevail. But we cannot—must not—allow that to happen. I do realize that this is easier said than done. This requires great courage and an open heart. But I am confident that together we can confront and overcome threats to our fellow citizens, to all innocents. We are bigger than the problem we face. So, I call on all community members, not just Muslim-Americans, to help us prevent all forms of terrorism and political violence. United, we can bring about a lasting peace for the citizens of San Francisco and be an example for the rest of the world."

The steps that led to the entrance of the Hall of Justice exploded with raucous applause and cheers as Nelson Gates brought his speech to a close. He paused to wipe the perspiration from his forehead, then smiled down on the Muslim-American community leaders from his vantage point on the top step. They appeared to be "satisfied" by what he had to say; not overjoyed but not disappointed either. He felt that he had struck the right balance between familiar rhetoric and personal anecdote that allowed him to relate to Muslim-Americans. After all, his Irish grandparents had faced a similar kind of prejudice when they first came to the United States. The Muslim-Americans who carried the protest signs out on the sidewalk were less than "satisfied" as they resumed their vocal protests. Even though Gates was the consummate politician, he knew that it was going to take a lot more than a few speeches to stem the tide of violence and bigotry. Members of his police department were going to have to produce results and bring in those who were responsible, without creating a witch hunt.

As he made his way from the podium, Gates exchanged the usual small talk and pleasantries that courtesy demanded in situations like this. He shook hands with the State Representative first, the head of the County Council, City Council members, and finally the Mayor, with whom he exchanged a few whispered remarks. Gates then continued on down the line of dignitaries and officials, shaking hands, smiling, and repeating, "Hello, nice of you to come" in a well-rehearsed, cordial manner. Had there been a baby in the audience, he would no doubt have kissed it. The Chief of Police was campaigning, not for political office but good will.

With her right hand outstretched, Kate Dawson approached him. She seemed anxious to congratulate him, but he just brushed by her, taking the hand of the person standing right next to her. For an instant, she was miffed, but then Michael Shannon, spokesperson for the San Francisco Police Department, came up behind her, and whispered in her ear.

"Are you serious? The Chief has agreed to meet with me?" Kate repeated his words back to Shannon, loud enough for Clark to hear them.

William Clark nodded, and gave her a big "thumbs-up."

"Yes, Inspector," he replied, taking her by the arm. "This way."

"Where are we going?" she asked, leaving Clark behind.

"You'll see," Shannon replied, hustling her along.

As the Chief of Police continued moving through the crowd, glad-handing well-wishers and sidestepping questions from reporters, they followed closely behind him, never any more than a few steps. Near the bottom of the stairs, Gates broke free from the throng. At first, he nodded over his shoulder at Shannon, then slipped down a service entrance.

"Ladies and gentlemen of the Press," Shannon interceded, mere moments after pushing Dawson towards the same service door. "Chief Gates will not be entertaining any questions at this time from the Press. But I will be happy to respond to any questions or comments you may have."

Dawson felt obliged to take the same escape route and followed Gates down the old service entrance to the basement. Back in the thirties and forties, she had heard police officials would back their "paddy wagons" up to the door and then march their most hardened criminals into soundproof cells reserved strictly for solitary confinement. She imagined the place was later converted into a bomb shelter in the fifties by city planners to relieve Cold War anxieties, and then totally abandoned afterwards. Tight, small places made her uneasy, and as Kate walked along the dark service coordinator, she kept glancing over her shoulder for the fastest way out. At the end, she found herself face to face with the Chief of Police. He seemed to be purposely hiding in a cloak of shadows.

"Congratulations, sir," Kate offered, again extending her right hand. "That was a most inspiring speech."

"What the hell are you doing here?" Gates demanded, clearly concealing something under his formal jacket.

Kate put her hand down, and replied sourly, "Your administrative aide said you had agreed to speak with me, sir."

"Well, then, I guess the joke's on me, isn't it, Inspector?" he said, stumbling out of the shadows, the fly to his pants down, a river of urine at his feet. "I just pissed myself, and I don't give a fuck who knows about it."

"Sir, you're intoxicated," she said, her face flushed red with embarrassment.

"You didn't actually think I was going to go out there and face all those assholes, sober, now did you?"

"I don't know what to think."

"I've been drinking the hard stuff for hours, Dawson. You

might want to give it a try sometime. The thing of it is, drunk or sober, we Irish never really lose our composure. I can keep it up better than any man you know."

"Oh, I see."

"Yeah, well, you just let me take care of my business with the 'man,'" he replied to her, sounding drunk, maybe even a little hung over, as he struggled to close the zipper to his trousers. With that one task finally accomplished, Gates gave up all his efforts to conceal the flask from Dawson and took another deep drink, using the sleeve on his police uniform to wipe away the excess from his lips. "Pappy Van Winkle's twenty-year-old bourbon. Your boss and I were just toasting each other's health last night with bourbon and now he's lying in a hospital bed with wires out the yin-yang. Isn't it strange how the hands of time move us inexorably, hour after hour, toward our doom, and yet we have no control over them?"

"Lieutenant Roberts is supposed to make a full recovery," she reported. "I spoke to his doctor right before your speech."

"He should have been born an Irishman. He would have been able to handle his booze better," the Chief lamented.

"Sir, maybe we should go to your office—"

Gates leaned toward her and whispered, the boozy smell of alcohol, "I was beginning to wonder how long it would take you. Hell, why don't we just fuck right here? No one ever comes down here."

"I wasn't suggesting we go to your office for sex," Kate said, with disgust. "You're a married man with a wife and family at home—"

"Exactly!" he exclaimed, unbuttoning his jacket. "And you're a single woman. Hey, that's good thinking. We'll go to your place."

"I'm not going any place with you!"

"I could make it worth your while," he replied, draining the bourbon in his flask.

Kate shook her head back and forth. "Oh, no! Tell me you didn't just say that."

"I know you want to be a bureau chief, Dawson, so I could endorse a request that makes you head of Homicide in Roberts' absence."

"I'm not for sale, Gates," she said firmly, "at any price."

"A woman of integrity," the Chief of Police replied, mocking her, making fun of her commitment to honor and truth.

Then, like a venomous snake striking its victim from a safe distance, he reached out and grabbed Kate's arm, pulled her into an embrace, and kissed her, deeply. For all of his act about being drunk or intoxicated, Gates seemed to be pretty fast on his feet and alert for a man who had been drinking all day. He was also easily twice her weight, so when he pinned her against the wall, she wasn't getting free any time soon. He pushed his tongue in her mouth and slobbered all over her. Dawson struggled to break free fighting back with every ounce of strength that she could muster. She clawed at him with her fingernails, jabbed him with the one elbow she managed to free, and eventually slipped out of his grasp long enough to land a well-placed knee to his groin.

All at once, he went limp in her arms, staggered backwards against the brick-n-mortar wall, still reeling, holding his groin with both hands. He slid down the wall, and when he hit the floor, Gates tucked himself protectively into a fetal position, rocking back and forth in an extreme amount of pain.

Kate's first thought was to draw her service pistol, but even before a second thought came to mind, her police training kicked in, like a genetically, hard-wired instinct for survival. She grabbed Gates by his left wrist and pulled his arm up behind his back, not far enough to break it but just high enough to remind him that she could. With her other hand, she grasped a scruff of his salt-n-pepper hair and pulled his head back against the wall. She could have easily smashed it like a pumpkin on the brick-n-mortar, but Dawson just held his head there, as she squatted down right beside him, her mouth inches away from his right ear. She wasn't about to give him another opportunity to overpower her, and kept him close to her.

Kate screamed, "Don't you fuckin' move!"

"Dawson, please—" he pleaded with her, turning white as a sheet.

"Don't do it! Don't you dare move a muscle!" she raged, tapping his skull lightly on the wall, playing with him the way he had played with her. "You wanted a little excitement. How's this? That old adrenalin pumping? Good boy. You still want to fuck me? Well, let me see what you've got left there, chief!"

"I'm telling you, it was just a joke," Gates cried, tears in his eyes.

"Then why am I not laughing?"

Nelson Gates seemed to pale even more. "I'll give you whatever you want. Everybody's got a price. Just name it."

With her eyes squeezed together, Dawson looked down at Gates, channeling that Clint Eastwood spaghetti western look. Such a badass. It would not have taken much for her to break his arm or crack his skull against the wall. Hell, she could have set off an atomic bomb down there and no one would have been the wiser. But then she realized that the "candy-ass" chief of police wasn't worth her effort.

"C'mon, Dawson" he begged her. "What are you going to do? Kill me?! Break my arm? Crack my skull. It was just a joke. Nothing was meant by it."

"Yeah. Suppose I get my strap-on, just for fun, and fuck the shit out of you!" she demanded, angry as hell. "Would you still think it was a joke?"

"All right, I get it. You're pissed off," he stammered, struggling in her grasp to break free. "You feel humiliated. Used. I get all that. What do you want? What can I do to make it all go away?"

Dawson slammed his head against the wall. "I warned you not to move a muscle."

"Okay, okay!" Gates screamed, in agony. "I'm taking charge of Homicide," Kate stated. "You'll submit the proper paperwork through HR, along with your own personal endorsement. If a member of the City Council objects—and I doubt seriously they will—do whatever it takes to secure that position for me. For the record, I did just pass the lieutenant's exam, at the top of my class, and I am next in line for promotion. William Clark won't put up a struggle. No one will ever question your decision."

"You must be mad," he gasped.

"It might seem like that," she confessed, "but then, how would you describe the behavior of the chief of police who goes off on his nut one day and sexually assaults one of his female officers?"

"I see your point," Gates replied, deflated.

"Good."

"And Roberts? What about him?"

She thought about that for a moment, then said, "You're going to find him a nice, cushy desk job where he doesn't have to think too much. You've got several openings on your staff. Assign him to one of those."

"That's pretty cold, Dawson."

"Believe me," she replied, remembering all the years with Roberts as her boss, "it's better than he deserves."

"And what about my protégé, Alex Starke? What happens to her?"

Dawson hesitated. "She'll remain in Homicide. She's got the makings of a good cop and would benefit greatly from

mentoring with a senior detective. Besides, I know how important she is to you."

"What makes you think that I'm going to go along with any
of this?" Gates asked, his confidence level growing as he sobered
up. "Suppose I just have you arrested and jailed indefinitely for
striking a senior officer?"

"You got as much to lose as I do. Maybe even more."

"If they believe you."

"Let me ask you something," Kate enquired, after another
moment's pause., "did you ever meet the former chief of police?"

"No, I never met him."

"His name was Ruiz Aguilar," she reported, releasing the
scruff of hair she had held, but not the arm behind his back.
"We were rumored to be having this torrid affair, even though
I never cared much for the prick myself. His wife reported him
missing one night. They found his Mercedes parked in the
garage at the Mark Hopkins, but they never found his body.
When Roberts and his boys discovered from hotel records I had
called his home that night from my room at the Mark Hopkins,
they searched the room and found Aguilar's severed head in my
bed. In the end, the circumstantial evidence wouldn't have held
up in court, and I was never charged with his murder."

Gates shook his head. "I don't believe you."

"Next time you're having a drink with Roberts, ask him,"
Kate dared the chief of police to find out for himself. "I warn
you though, once you find out the truth, you're never going to
be able to sleep soundly again."

"Bullshit, I don't believe any of this!" he started to get up.

Dawson shoved him back down on the floor and grabbed a
tuft of his hair. She then pulled his head against the wall.

"The next time," Kate said, unaware that she was shouting at
the top of her lungs, "I'm going to crack your skull wide open!"

"Holy fuck!" Gates shouted, slouching away in her grasp.

Kate Dawson leaned closer as he cowered in fear and took his cheek in her right hand. "If you ever mention a word of this to anyone," she said coldly, adding a hard slap to his cheek, "I'm going to find you and I'm going to kill you, and then leave your severed head for your wife to find. You got that? Nod your head if you understand me. Nod, you fuckin' asshole!"

Gates nodded, grudgingly.

"Now, there's just one more thing, Chief."

"Who the hell do you think you are?" he scowled, dropping any outward façade of civility. "Dictating terms to me!"

"If I ever hear that you've done this to another woman— tricked her into coming down here and coerced her into having sex with you—I'm going to cut your dick off and feed it to my goldfish."

Gates looked back at her, astonished, speechless.

"Later," Kate said, as she released him and stormed away.

Kate was still shaking, her heart pounding deep within her chest, as she emerged from the old service entrance to the basement and stepped out into the bright afternoon sun. She paused and felt the warmth of its radiance on her face and skin. Sunlight was said to be the best disinfectant, and at that moment, she needed a thorough cleansing to wash away the dirt and filth of Gates from her body. *Bastard! What gave him the idea he could to do that to me?* she asked herself. She had never once flirted with Gates or given him any indication she was interested. *Maybe*, she figured, *he thinks he's was one of those men in a position of authority who assumes he can do anything he wants to a woman without consequence! Ha! He definitely got more than he bargained for!*

Angry, and more than a little confused, she walked down to the end of the block, and stopped. *What's going to happen now? Will there be a formal inquest? Maybe an arrest warrant for assault and battery, sworn out by the Chief, waiting for me at the Hall of Justice?* Kate knew she had done nothing wrong, but those things always had a way of twisting themselves around. *After all, it's my word against his, and who'll believe me? Perhaps, if I just keep walking, maybe just drive away, I can leave it all behind?* Kate didn't have a clue about what she should do.

She was back in the Homicide Bureau within the hour, hunched over a computer terminal at her desk in the darkened, deserted room. She had written both a letter of resignation and a formal complaint, but she didn't seem in that much of a hurry to press the button to send either one. Her fingers rested on the keyboard as she stared blankly at the computer screen. The cursor winked at her, waiting for a response, but she did not see it. Her mind was awash in a kaleidoscope of images as she kept going over and over again the details of Gates' assault and her retaliation. Kate wondered if there was anything else that she could have done differently. She never took her eyes from the screen as the minutes ticked by on the clock.

"Shit." Kate Dawson breathed quietly, suddenly aware of her surroundings and the cursor that was flashing on her monitor.

She stood up, stretched, then walked over to the lady's room. Slipping in, Kate turned on the light and locked the door behind her, then filled the basin with cold water, splashing her face several times. As she hunched over the sink, water dripping, she looked at the image in the mirror, barely recognizing her own reflection. Her features were pale and drawn; the flesh around her eyes loose and sallow. Worse, she looked and felt like one of those hateful women who cut their hair short and ran around castrating men.

"What have I become?" she asked herself.

Less than an hour earlier, Dawson had not only threatened to kill the Chief of Police but also promised to leave the chief's severed head for his wife to find in their marital bed. To make matters worse, she had also demanded that he appoint her to a position she was more than well-qualified to earn on her own, without the heavy hand. She must have sounded like a petulant child who had just gone off the deep end with all the pretty, little choices at Willy Wonka's Chocolate Factory. *What the hell was I thinking?* Admittedly, Kate was surprised by the chief's boorish behavior, but she didn't blame herself for his actions. She would have done it all again in exactly the same way. He was the one who had provoked her. About the only real thing she regretted was not kneeing him in the groin a second time, once for herself and once for all those vulnerable women he had probably brutalized over the years. No, she didn't hate men. She wasn't a radical feminist. A misandrist. She just hated those men who used their positions of authority to abuse women.

Dawson splashed herself with more cold water and came up smoothing the strands of blonde hair on each side of her face with her hands. She looked deeply into the mirror for answers, some easy solution to her dilemma that wouldn't cost her a job, the pension she had worked so hard to build, or her own personal integrity. But every idea that Kate thought of as a solution proved to be equally distasteful to her. She could either humble herself by asking him to overlook her bad behavior and beg to keep her job, or she could blame it all on hormones, PMS. She wasn't really happy about either choice and wondered just how long she could maintain the Dirty "Harriet" persona before losing it altogether.

Then, as she thought about it some more, she realized the bastard deserved it. *Why in the world am I beating myself up over actions that were more than thoroughly justified by his assault? Why did he force me to defend myself?* she asked herself, but the answer was right there. She was an armed and dangerous woman who had threatened Nelson Gates' all-masculine world order.

Kate would have continued to stand there, looking in the mirror, for the next few hours had her trance not been broken by a knock at the door. She figured it was probably another woman working late, but then again, it might have been the Chief of Police looking to get even with her. "Just a minute!" she cried out. Grabbing a handful of paper towels from the dispenser, she quickly wiped her face, cast the used paper towels in the trash, then checked her face and hair once more. Dawson reached for the handle and cautiously opened the door, bracing for the worst, her eyes wide and intense.

"Sorry to disturb you, detective," the cleaning woman said, a mop in one hand and scrub brush in the other.

"That's okay. You've got a job to do," she said, exhaling a deep breath, relieved that it wasn't Gates.

"Sugar, if you need to get back in here, I should be done in a jiffy."

"No, it's okay. Take your time," Kate replied, glancing at her watch. "It's getting late, and I should be heading home."

"Have a blessed day," the cleaning woman added, with a smile.

Dawson walked back to her desk and looked down at the monitor. Her resignation letter and the formal complaint against Nelson Gates sat side by side on her computer screen. She reached down to her keyboard and struck the delete key twice, purging both documents from her desktop, then gathered up her purse and briefcase, and headed to the exit.

By the time Kate Dawson reached the UCSF Medical Center, the late autumn sun had set for the day and the long, dark shadows of fall were quickly upon her. She followed an ambulance, its sirens screaming, down the long driveway around the back and braked as the it pulled in front of the emergency room entrance of the large city hospital. Doctors and attendants with gurneys came pouring out of its double glass doors. It was easy to see why the UCSF Medical Center had been ranked seventh among the nation's premier medical institutions for the fifteenth straight year in a recent *U.S. News & World Report* survey. They always seemed to scramble when lives were at stake. She pulled her car around the back and parked in one of the spots normally reserved for police officers.

With her badge worn conspicuously on her hip, Kate walked in through the emergency room door, strolled through the enormous lobby and waiting room, and rode one of the elevators up to the eighth floor. She then took a left out of the elevator and headed to the hospital's east wing where all the private rooms were since Lenny had been moved from ICU to 814. She couldn't help but notice all the pain and suffering from other patients on the floor. One by one, she heard them moaning and crying out. Turning the corner, Kate immediately came on guard. His two police guards were missing. *They would have never left him unattended!*

Dawson hazarded a glance through the glass on the door and saw that her friend was asleep, for the moment, in the semi-darkened room. His waist was all bandaged up, and he was attached, like a hybrid car, to the hospital's equipment. Just then, a hospital orderly carrying a syringe came out of the bathroom and moved to the side of Lenny's bed. Kate ducked down to keep from being seen. *Since when did orderlies at UCSF Medical Center administer shots to patients?* she thought to herself, reaching for her Beretta. *Never!* Kate knew she had to stop him before he had the chance to inject Lenny.

Thinking quickly, Dawson crouched down, her shoulder against the door, counted down five seconds, then blasted through the door. She hit the man in the lower abdomen with her shoulder, causing him to fumble the hypodermic needle targeted at Lenny's IV, which dropped harmlessly to the bed. She rolled into a tuck, and came to her feet, facing off against him.

"Hold it right there, asshole!" she yelled, holding the gun out in from of her in the combat stance. The muzzle was trained squarely on the assailant's chest.

The assailant said nothing, just looked straight through her, seemingly in a trance of his own. He was young and powerful, his muscles chiseled into shape, like those of an Army Ranger. It was obvious to her that he had been in life-or-death situations before, maybe in Iraq or Afghanistan. He knew how to fight; had been taught to defend himself. Kate didn't have a chance in hell of beating him. If he fought back, she'd have to shoot him as she was no match for him physically. She took her eye off him for a split second and spotted the bodies of the two police guards on the floor of the bathroom. Both looked dead.

With flawless precision, the assailant executed a perfect drop swipe at Dawson's feet. As the police inspector fell, she dropped her gun. The assailant quickly wrapped his legs around her neck and squeezed, forcing the air out of her. Stunned, she struggled to get free, her arms flailing in every direction. But the harder she struggled, the more his vice grip tightened, relentlessly increasing the pressure against Kate's throat. She felt her body going limp, and she couldn't even gasp anymore as her eyes started to slide up into her head and darkness was closing in all around her. She had strength enough for one last play, if she could keep herself from passing out.

She clasped her fingers together and hammered down with

all her remaining strength on his groin, stunning him for a second, but that was all she needed to drumroll her body out of harm's way. Then, as she scrambled to her feet, she reached for her Beretta and held it out between them. The assailant's eyes flickered open.

"Okay, now I want some answers!" Kate demanded, gasping for breath.

"Doctor . . ." Lenny croaked, eyes barely open. From his perspective, someone appeared to be standing at the end of his bed.

"Go back to sleep, Lenny," she reassured her friend.

With cat-like reflexes, the assailant snatched the hypodermic needle off the bed, and plunged it into his jugular, pumping a deadly poison into his own body. He smiled at Kate, for a heartbeat, as if to say, "Fuck you, bitch," then his body broke out into spasms as the poison quickly worked its way through his system. Finally, he went down hard, his eyes folding back into his head.

"Son-of-a-bitch," she cursed under her breath, lowering her gun, just as three nurses charged the room.

Within the hour, Lenny Provolone had been moved to another private room down the hall, while his former room was transformed into an official crime scene. Even though there wasn't actually much to see in either room, police officers were posted outside both doors to keep curious onlookers from stopping in the hall. The forensics team worked the crime scene for clues and trace evidence. In the center of the floor, Brogan knelt over the body, while Ritchie, the official police photographer, snapped off pictures over his shoulder. One of the CSI boys had bagged and tagged the hypodermic needle and the other was dusting for prints on the apparatus that held the IV bag overhead. A third member of forensics was examining the two officer's bodies in the bathroom, while his partner concluded a routine sweep for prints and trace evidence. Jawara, Ramirez, and Balardi stood around in a half circle, listening to Dawson give her official statement. She sat in the chair near the window with Clark crouched down in front of her taking notes.

"It all happened so fast! I was momentarily distracted when Lenny woke up," Dawson explained, "and that was all the time the assailant needed to grab the syringe and inject himself. He was dead in a matter of seconds. There was really nothing that I could do about it."

"Kate, there's no reason to beat yourself up," Clark said. "We've all lost suspects in the past to suicide."

"Thanks, boss."

"Do you want to keep going or do you need to take a break?"

Kate said resolutely, "Let's keep going."

"What is your relationship with Mr. Provolone?" Clark asked, a routine question for his notebook. "He is my next-door neighbor," she replied, then added, "and my friend."

"Why did you come here this evening?"

"I dropped by the hospital on my way home from work to check on his progress. You see, I was the person who found him, called 911, and stayed with him all night. If it hadn't been for me, he would be a dead man now."

"Are you acquainted with the deceased?"

Dawson glanced over at the body. "No. Never seen him before in my life."

"Do you know of any reason why the deceased would have wanted to bring harm to Mr. Provolone?"

"None whatsoever," she replied, with a shrug. "I can only assume that he wanted to complete the job from the night before."

Clark paused, thumbing back through his notes. "Have we

already established a connection between last night's attempt on Mr. Provolone's life and this evening's effort to kill him in his sleep?"

Dawson shook her head. "No, William. It was just idle speculation."

"Officer, are you almost done with your investigation?" one of the doctors interrupted. "I've got patients up and down the hallway who need to be settled down for the evening. They won't get settled down until there is absolute quiet on the floor."

Clark nodded. "One or two more questions? We're just about done."

Dawson looked between Clark and the doctor. "We can always finish this up tomorrow, William."

"Whatever you say, Kate," he replied, closing his notebook and standing up.

"Thanks," she replied, running her hand through her hair.

"Ladies and gentlemen, I'm going to have to ask you to leave," the doctor shouted over the din of activity in the room.

William Clark hesitated only a split second before acknowledging his request. "The doctor's right. We've got to clear out of this room, so that patients on this floor can get the rest they need. This investigation is over for tonight. If you didn't get everything you need, you can come back tomorrow. The room will be sealed, and they'll be two guards posted at the door. For now, get your equipment packed up, and let's get these bodies on ice."

Brogan's men, one at a time, brought in a gurney for each of the three men, while the others packed up and sealed their equipment Mikhail Jawara exchanged a glance with his partner, then ran his thumb and forefinger through his goatee. "So, what do you say, Clark? Let's go get a drink at McGinty's. My treat."

"Thanks, Mikhail, but I'll pass."

"What about you, Jorge?"

"I promised my wife I'd bring her some real gelato."

"What is she, pregnant again?"

"No, just fat," Ramirez replied, sourly, as he left.

Jawara shrugged. "Guess that means no, huh? Well, I guess I'll stop by the liquor store and buy a bottle for home. If anyone has second thoughts about sharing a glass with me, you all know where I live." He shuffled off, his shoulders slumped with fatigue, trailing in the wake his partner.

With the room finally cleared of cops, Dawson was the last one out the door before two police officers sealed the room. She conferred with Lenny's doctor and nurse for a moment, then left alone. As she walked down the hallway to the elevators, Kate was struck by how quiet things were at the hospital in the early morning hours, not unlike the Hall of Justice. The corridors were empty of doctors and nurses; their places taken by a handful of janitors and cleaners who only worked that late shift, day in and day out. The only sounds the low hum of wet vacuums and other machines used to sanitize the floors.

Dawson went home for a couple of hours. Not even bothering to shed her clothes, she laid across the top of her unmade twin-sized bed and pulled one of her pillows to her head, yet slumber was held at bay for hours.

Her cell-phone alarm went off about the time she actually fell asleep—5:00 a.m. After a cold shower to revive herself, she returned to Lenny's hospital room with a couple of coffees and a bag full of Dynamo Donuts for the two cops on duty. She then entered the room and stood at the end of his bed, appraising him from head to foot.

With his head resting comfortably on the pillow, Lenny lay flat on his back attached two long, flexible plastic tubes wrapped over his ears, carrying oxygen to the nasal cannula in his nose.

Lenny was breathing, albeit faintly, but at least he was breathing. Behind him, a monitor kept routine track of his respiration, blood pressure, heart beat, and other factors related to his own body's efforts to normalize and recover. Overhead, one IV bag fed him valuable nutrients in liquid form, the other supplied the right concoction of antibiotics and pain meds. He looked comfortable, or at least as comfortable as he could be under the circumstances. With a serious stab wound to the stomach, she didn't think he was going to be cosplaying Obi-Wan Kenobi at one of his science fiction conventions any time soon.

Kate Dawson stripped off her jacket and shoulder holster and placed them gently on a table near the window. She then stretched out on the chair by the window, placing her .9 mil safely on her lap, and slept another hour.

At 7:00 a.m, Lenny's nurse entered the room, startling Kate momentarily, who sat bolt upright in the chair weapon in hand. The nurse barely flinched in the confrontation, having seen the inspector enter the room an hour before, and threw open the curtains to reveal another bright but fog-shrouded day in the Bay area.

Realizing who it was, that there was no real threat, Kate settled back down and smiled warmly at the nurse. "What time is it?" She glanced down at her stopped watch.

"It's just a few minutes past seven," the nurse replied, kindly. "If you're looking for a cup of coffee or breakfast, our cafeteria is located on the ground floor just opposite registration. Your officers can eat there, too. Mr. Provolone is safe with me and the other nurses at the duty station."

"Thanks, but I'll just stay right here."

The nurse pulled Lenny's chart up on the computer, made a few notations, then said, "Suit yourself. I'll be back in about an hour or so to check on him again." She swept out of the room in much the same way she entered. Not thinking much of the nurse's bedside manner, in protest, she reached up over her head and pulled the curtains closed. Pointedly, she also looked at Lenny Provolone who never stirred. She relaxed back in the chair, again closing her eyes. She didn't have to wait long before she was asleep. Twenty minutes later, she heard a knock at the door and woke to find her two replacements. Barely awake, Kate exchanged glances with the two uniformed cops.

"Morgan and Ochs?" she queried, reading their name badges.

"That's right," Ochs responded.

"Yes, ma'am," Morgan replied.

"You know, Lieutenant, neither us had much of a breakfast this morning. Do you mind if one of us picks something up at the cafeteria?" Ochs inquired. "It should only take a couple of minutes."

Dawson nodded her head. "That's fine. In fact, when you're down there, get me a black coffee with a couple of sugars."

"Right," Ochs replied.

Kate climbed out of the chair and stretched her arms and legs, then opened the curtains back up and was nearly blinded by the light. The morning sun had been working hard to burn off the leftover fog. Over her shoulder, she heard her friend stirring to life.

"I wanted to say thank you, Kate," Lenny said, upon waking. He spoke quietly; his voice deep and broken-concrete horse.

"It's the least I could do, Lenny," she replied, leaning across the bed. "How many times have you helped me out in a pinch?"

"But you saved my life," he added, astonished. Kate smiled wryly. "Twice. But then who's counting?"

"I owe you a life debt," Lenny said, with built-in melodrama. "No, I actually owe you two life debts."

She held up her hand to stop him. "We're not going to discuss it further. Forget about it."

"But how will I ever repay you?" he whined.

Dawson pulled her Beretta from its holster, put the gun to her friend's face, and said, "Now, if you don't shut up about this, I'm going to claim both of those 'life debts.' And it won't be pretty!"

At that very moment, there was a tap on the door; Officer Ochs with her black coffee. "I've got your coffee, Lieutenant," he reported.

Dawson holstered her weapon. "Bring it on, Ochs."

Handing the coffee to his senior officer, he pulled Kate aside and whispered, "Is everything okay, Lieutenant?"

"Fine, Ochs," she replied quietly, her voice soft and gentle.

"If you need me, Lieutenant," Ochs said, "I'll be right outside."

"Thanks," Dawson responded, as she mixed the two packets of sweetener into her cup of black coffee. She took an initial sip for taste, then swallowed down a big gulp.

Lenny Provolone scratched his beard. "I don't suppose I could ask you to shave me?"

"Nope, sorry," Kate replied, standing over him. "I draw the line at saving a man's life. Are you finally going to shave the beard off? I think you'd look ten years younger without that awful beard."

"No, I'm just looking for a trim," he replied sourly.

"If it's just a trim, Lenny, you should ask your nurse. I'm sure she'll be more than happy to help out."

"I doubt it. Most women just want to shave it off."

She shrugged. "I'm afraid I can't help you, friend."

"What does a guy have to do to get a box of Cap'n Crunch or Lucky Charms cereal for breakfast?" he asked rhetorically.

"I'm afraid to tell you that you're on a liquid diet until the wounds to your abdomen heal."

"I don't like yogurt," Lenny complained.

"In a few days, you'll wish you could have some yogurt. But right now, you'll get all of your nutrients from an IV drop."

"What kind of hospital is this?"

Kate Dawson gave her friend an annoyed sneer for a fleeting moment, then looked away. "I need to ask you something, Lenny."

"I want someone to tell me why I can't get a box of Cap'n Crunch or Lucky Charms for my breakfast."

"This is important," she added, engaging his eyes.

"So is this," he persisted, like a child in kindergarten trying to wear down his teacher, unable or unwilling to let it go.

Dawson shook her head slowly. "Okay, I'll tell you what, Lenny. You answer all my questions truthfully and I'll make sure that when you can have solid foods again, you have your choice of breakfast cereals."

Lenny's eyes narrowed in suspicion. "No Cheerios. It's got to be Cap'n Crunch or Lucky Charms."

"Okay, buddy, I promise," she said, crossing her heart.

Begrudgingly, Provolone asked, "What do you want to know, Kate?"

"A couple of nights ago, I found you nearly dead on the floor of your apartment, your hands wrapped tightly around the hilt of a large butcher knife. The knife was wedged deep in your stomach and there was blood everywhere. For all intents and purposes, it appeared that you had committed suicide. But then I also noticed that your apartment had been tossed, like someone had been searching for something, and the front door was open. What is the first thing that you remember from that night?"

Lenny stared ahead. "I don't remember much from that night."

She shot a worried glance at him. "Did you mean to kill yourself?"

"No, of course not," he replied hastily.

"Then what was that butcher knife doing in your hands?"

"I don't know. I don't remember!" he shouted at her.

"Well, which is it? You don't know, or you don't remember?" Kate leaned over the bed, her eyes focused on him like a powerful laser beam. She was angry and hurt at the same time. She couldn't understand why he was refusing to cooperate with her after all the years they had been friends.

"Stop asking me all these fuckin' questions!"

"What is your problem?" Dawson was very close to losing it herself. She fought to control her emotions, but where her friend Lenny was concerned, she completely lost all objectivity. "I'm trying to help you. Don't you understand that? Why won't you let me help you?"

"I don't want your help! *I don't need any help!* Do you understand me?" he exclaimed through a burst of pain, between gritted teeth.

"Yes, you do," Kate insisted, immediately at his side, pumping the button that released morphine into his IV. "Something's going on with you. I need to know what that is."

"Why is it so important to you?" he growled, leaning back in bed. The morphine had chased the pain away.

"Someone tried to kill you, Lenny, not once but twice!"

Provolone paused, closing his eyes in thought. Finally, as if lost in some distant memory, he said, "She refused to call me Lenny. She insisted my name was 'Peter,' as in 'Peter Pan.' To her, the name 'Lenny' was always 'Lennie Small,' that clumsy, gentle giant from *Of Mice and Men* who unintentionally breaks the neck of Curley's wife when she comes onto him. But she was always 'Wendy.' She wanted our romance to be a happy one, full of flights of fancy, not one of tragedy and death."

"Did Rebecca give you any reason for stabbing you, Lenny?" Kate asked.

Lenny dropped completely out of his reverie and smacked the table hard, challenging his interrogator with a death stare for a full half minute, thirty seconds of dislike and disbelief. He managed to keep the anger out of his voice, but not the incredulity. "Rebecca? I never mentioned Rebecca. She doesn't have anything to do with this. In fact, I haven't seen her for over a month."

"I'm sorry, Lenny," she apologized. "I just assumed that it was Rebecca who had stabbed you because of her volatile personality."

"No," he replied coldly.

"So then, this other woman's name was 'Wendy'?"

"Her name was Gwendolyn," Lenny corrected. "Gwendolyn Bush, but most people just called her Wendy. Actually, I'm beginning to doubt now that was her real name. I caught a glimpse of her driver's license once; her last name was Devereaux, not Bush. Maybe Bush was a married name? I don't know. I guess that I'll never really know."

"Where did you meet her?"

"Liberatore's Restaurant in Westminster," he fired back, without a moment's hesitation, but then paused, thought about it for a moment, then added, "Actually, we met online at Match. com. I had created a full profile, using the website's proprietary algorithm, and included a half dozen pictures or so. 'Scientist Seeks Next Great Discovery' was my headline, and after about three weeks' time, without getting any hits, I thought about pulling the profile."

"Then you heard from her?"

"Yes, I heard from her."

Kate Dawson stopped pacing and turned around.

"Remind me to get her profile photo from you."

Lenny shrugged. "She didn't have one."

"I'm familiar with those dating websites, particularly Match.com," Kate said, having had a recent, real-time experience with online dating. "The site administrator requires everyone to post a photo with their profile."

"That was the funny thing about Wendy," he confessed, thinking more about her and how they met. "When I asked her about her profile photo, she claimed that she had received thousands of responses from her initial ad and had chosen to pull her profile photo in order to limit the number of responses. Wendy told me that she was a very beautiful woman; that men were always following her, crossing the street to meet her. Said she had grown tired of that kind of man and was only looking for a sincere man looking for a wife."

Kate Dawson closed her eyes and shook her head. "I suppose there's one born every minute."

"Call me a sucker then because I bought everything she was selling," Lenny said, his voice rising in anger, "hook, line, and sinker."

"Lenny, *please*," whispered Kate.

"Let me finish. I've seen what I look like in the mirror. Most women take one good look at me and run away, screaming into the night. I'll never be confused with a handsome, leading man. That being, I've had to spend my life developing my intellect just so I had an even playing field with most of those shallow assholes—"

"Lenny!" implored Kate.

"It's true. All of it," he whimpered, a tear in one eye. "So, I figured who would understand a truly beautiful woman, like that, better than a man, like me. We were, after all, two sides of the very same coin—Beauty and the beast. Here was someone who was looking for a sincere relationship with a man where appearance was less important than character, and here was I, someone looking for a woman who just seemed so genuine in her approach to a relationship with a man."

Kate patiently listened, let him talk. She, too, had tears in her eyes. Finally, she asked, "Were you right about her?"

"Maybe . . . in the beginning . . ." he said calmly, directly. "We agreed to meet at a small, Italian restaurant, and when Wendy came walking through that door, she was undeniably the most beautiful woman I had ever seen. I fell in love with her right then and there. We sat for hours, just talking. In fact, I couldn't remember the last time I had just talked with a woman. Maybe it was that first night after you and I met. Anyway, she asked me all the right questions, and told me everything I wanted to hear. By the second date, I would have given her anything she wanted . . . including my soul. But the fact of the matter is all she wanted N.E.M.E.S.I.S., and she would have done anything to get her hands on that technology."

"Oh, I'm so sorry, Lenny."

Provolone folded his arms across his chest. "She didn't ask for it right away," he added, feeling defensive. "First, she told me that she had read an informative article about me and my satel-lite system in *Scientific American*. That article was already a year old; much of the information already out of date. But she knew enough about the National Emergency Management Electronic Surveillance Intelligence Systems or N.E.M.E.S.I.S. to not only write a follow-up article but also conduct a symposium about the next generation of surveillance satellites at Northrop Grumman. I just didn't see it at the time, but the red flags were all there."

Kate sighed, mind calculating.

"Then one night at my apartment, after we had made love in front of the fireplace, I caught her going through the trash in my study, reading discarded schematics like a first-class engi-neer. She claimed that she was having trouble sleeping and was looking for something heavy to read that would put her to sleep. I gave her one of the textbooks I had authored, but I could tell she wanted something more. She wanted my personal notes about N.E.M.E.S.I.S."

Dawson was astonished at his naivety. "What do you know about her, Lenny? Could she have been a spy, working for a foreign government?"

"That's just the thing. I don't know anything about her."

"Nothing?"

"Well, not really," he admitted, his head whirling. "Wendy told me once that she was born in Baltimore to working-class parents who had both worked at Bethlehem Steel before the plant closed. She had an older sister and was married before to a cabinet maker in Gettysburg, Pennsylvania. His name was Bush. She didn't talk that much about her past. We never really talked about the past. Mostly, we stayed focused on the present, and there was always a lot going on."

"Did you ever meet any of her friends or coworkers?" Kate inquired.

"No," Lenny replied, a stray tear running down his cheek.

"What about family members? Her sister? Her ex?"

"No, but she talked once about scheduling a flight to visit her sister in Baltimore. Apparently, her sister had remarried."

"How long were the two of you together?"

"Three weeks, more or less."

"So, for three weeks now, you've been dating a ghost; a ghost with no family, no friends, no real history."

"With the exception of the other night, the last three weeks have been the best three weeks of my life," Lenny said, miserably. He gazed at Kate with wide, red-rimmed eyes that he kept wiping away with the palms of his hands. Finally, he had no choice but to look away from her as the flood gates opened. At that point, he spoke haltingly about her. "Wendy once said to me that if she were dying and only had three weeks to live, she'd want to spend her last moments with me. She said she found me to be strangely comforting."

Kate Dawson didn't reply right away. Instead, she handed her friend a few tissues. "Well, let's talk about what happened the other night."

Provolone was silent for a long time, then whispered, "I don't think I can."

Kate sat on the edge of the hospital bed and put her arm around his shoulder. She whispered in his ear, "This woman doesn't love you, Lenny. She is not capable of loving anyone. She seduces people by telling them what they want to hear. She manipulates them by using their weaknesses against them. She'll do anything or say anything to get what she wants from you, including murder."

"I'm not dead yet," he said.

"She took a butcher knife from your kitchen and stabbed you with it. When she realized that she had failed to kill you, she hired an assassin to poison you at the hospital while you slept," she continued, trying to talk some sense into him. "Doctor Brogan was able to lift a couple of prints from the butcher knife that were not yours and we've got a stiff down in the morgue, pumped full of his own poison. What more do you need to know about this woman?"

Lenny wiped his face. "But this woman loved me, Kate. I know she loved me. It was real." Kate kissed his forehead lightly. "I know that it seemed real to you, as real as anything you've ever known, but it was all part of a game, a con."

He shook his head, slowly, reluctantly.

"What happened the other night, Lenny?"

"She asked to borrow the key to my apartment," he told her

finally, surrendering the last details. "She said she was going to surprise me by making me dinner. She tidied up my dining room, much like you've done on occasion, and set out a beautiful arrangement of dinner wear, including candles. I never realized that I had such a nice set. I could smell Chicken Marsala baking in the oven, and for desert, Angel Food Cake. We never got a chance to eat any of it."

"What happened?"

Lenny exhaled heavily, realizing what a fool he had been; hated to admit to the truth. "Man," he said with an empty laugh, "there really is a sucker born every minute."

"Don't think about it, Lenny. Just tell me what happened."

"Well, when I went to put my book bag down, I noticed that my computer was still on. I never leave my computer on as part of my security agreement with Northrup Grumman," he said, feeling used. "Individual pages of documents were out of order on my desk and several schematics had been clearly traced by pencil. I confronted Wendy with what I found, but of course she denied everything. She told me that I was just being paranoid and asked me why I thought she had done anything. I then noticed that several of my drawers had been opened and searched. When I returned to the kitchen, she stabbed me with the butcher knife and left me for dead."

Kate Dawson slid off the edge of the bed and began pacing the hospital room floor. "What was she looking for? Why did she tear your place apart? This is really critical, Lenny."

Provolone shrugged his shoulders. "It's a shame we won't be able to ask her about it." She looked into his eyes. "You know the answer. Just think."

Lenny thought about it for a moment, and replied, "I must be losing my mind. She was looking for my WEP-key."

"WEP-key? What's a WEP-key?"

"It's not literally a key, but a 236-bit encryption protocol designed to ensure that only authorized parties can access secure data on my computer or the mainframe at Northrup Grumman," he explained, sounding like a college professor. "You see, access to N.E.M.E.S.I.S. is protected by the WEP-key."

"Did it look like she had found it?" Kate asked, concerned.

Lenny's eyebrows were scrunched in thought. "I don't know. I had secured it under one of the drawers in case I ever needed it myself. Normally, I just use a login and password, like everyone else, but it's best to keep a WEP-key also."

"You need to call your boss today and tell him what happened."

"I can't do that," Provolone said, visibly shaken at the mention of his supervisor. "If anyone at work learns about what I've done, I'll not only be terminated from the project, I'll also lose my security clearance. I'll get fired by Northrup Grumman, and the Military will prosecute me for espionage."

Dawson rocked her head back and forth. "I know somebody who might be able to help. Let me see what I can do."

At that moment, Lenny's nurse swept back into the room. Her eyes were bright with mirth as she seemed to float just above the floor with the perfect mixture of joy and happiness. She paused to look at her patient. "Well, how are you feeling today?"

Provolone was unapologetic. "I want to go home." The nurse studied his face for a long moment, then said sweetly, "It's nothing worth crying about, dearie."

Kate looked at her watch, the hour and minute hands still frozen in place. "Lenny, I've got to go. In fact, I'm already late. We'll talk about this later. Promise me that you'll try to get some rest."

"I promise."

Kate Dawson kissed him softly on the cheek. "Good." She fumbled for the keys to her car, found them, and headed for the door. "Now, please do everything your doctors and nurses tell you. And rest. You're going to be feeling a lot better soon. I promise you."

"Kate, thanks for saving my life," he said, sniffling.

"Let's not go down that road again," she insisted. "I'll be back to check on you. In the meantime, there will be two officers guarding your room 24/7."

"Kate—"

"Get some rest," she told him again.

CHAPTER SIX

After the death of Jonathan Prinze, the benefactor who had helped Kate break the G-20 case wide open, she vowed that she would never step foot in Chinatown again. He had died so tragically at the hands of the Morag Tong that the image of his lifeless body floating in their hot tub had haunted her dreams for nearly a year. As she inched her car towards the Gateway Arch, or Dragon Gate, on Grant Avenue at Bush Street, the heavy traffic going into Chinatown was the least of her worries. She was concerned that one of the Morag Tong would recognize her, especially if they were watching from one of the green-tiled, pagoda-shaped roofs. She drove past the pair of Chinese guardian lions, or "Foo Dogs" as they were called, and made a wide U-turn in front of the Chinese Imperial Palace restaurant. Dawson didn't dare drive her car any further. Beyond the Dragon Gate lay a completely separate world; an enclave that still retained its own customs, languages, places of worship, social clubs, and identity. She referred to Chinatown as "the land that time forgot."

Kate Dawson wheeled the BMW to a halt in front of a nondescript building on the opposite side of the street. She pulled on Grant street, facing south, secured the parking brake, and she and Alex Starke stepped out of the car. Dawson did a full reconnoiter of her car, walking nearly all the way around it, and joined Starke on the sidewalk, looking back at Bush Street.

"Why are we parking here?" Starke asked, her complaint loud enough to be heard by everyone going into Chinatown. A few had turned in their seats and flashed expressions of surprise. "There are at least a dozen other parking spots, and even a parking garage beyond the gate. Besides it's not like the meter maid is going to ticket your car."

"Even so, I think we'll be safer here," Kate replied, as she watched the parade of tourist vehicles pass through the Dragon Gate. She had survived her last visit to Chinatown; Prinze had not. That was more than enough reason for her to be afraid and cautious at the same time. But then she recalled how three members of that ancient guild had tried to run her off the road into San Francisco Bay, while another two had tried to assassinate her. No one knew the treachery of the Morag Tong better than she, or the consequences for anyone who survived. To have survived the blade of one assassin was pure luck or fate; to have survived the blade of multiple assassins was "joss." Joss was an ancient, Chinese household deity who brought good karma or good fortune to those who deserved it. A combination of circumstances, events etc., operating by chance to bring good to a person, was how the modern Chinese viewed "joss." But it was never wise or acceptable to tempt fate more than once because Joss was a divinity who would just as easily turn that good fortune to bad. Dawson was keenly aware that she was living on borrowed time when it came to the Morag Tong; knew they were likely still after her and dared not tempt joss one more time.

"You don't believe all that mumbo jumbo about Chinatown, do you?" Starke asked Kate, studying her face for a long moment before she looked away. "I mean, I've seen a lot of strange stuff in my life, but I've never seen anything that made me believe there were 'mystical forces' working behind the scenes. To me, there was always a more rational explanation why certain things happened."

Dawson's features hardened. "I don't know, Starke," she lied. "I lost a good friend in Chinatown last year. He was killed by the Morag Tong, an ancient guild of assassins who were renowned for their skills with a blade and their unique ability to disappear completely in plain sight. Jonathan Prinze was literally killed right in front of me and I never saw it."

"I'm sorry, Kate," Starke replied. "And I don't mean any disrespect, but c'mon, 'disappear completely in plain sight'?"

"That's what I said."

"Do you know how crazy that sounds?" the younger detective asked, with a grin. "You do realize that it was probably nothing more than a lot of simple parlor tricks and misdirection. Superstition is what makes us think it was something more. But I assure you that none of it was real."

"His death was real enough," Kate demanded.

"I don't doubt it was real, but that whole story borders on the fantastic. The Chinese want us to believe the boogeyman exists, so they spin these tales about the Morag Tong. It's all just for the tourists," she said, walking down the street, avoiding eye contact with Kate.

"The boogeyman *does* exist," Kate stated emphatically.

Starke was taken aback. "I would have never taken you, of all people, Dawson, for someone who believed in any of this hogwash."

"I hope you never have to find out the truth for yourself."

The two detectives had crossed Bush at the middle of the street. In a matter of minutes, they had walked through the Dragon Gate and were headed into the heart of Chinatown.

The modern world gradually vanished into a world of legend and superstition as Dawson and Starke crossed Sacramento and Grant Streets. The "Willie Woo- Woo Wong" playground on the right—a playground bustling with Asian children and their parents in modern dress—was the only landmark that seemed out of place. The two homicide detectives kept a steady pace without saying a word. Eventually, they passed Clay Street, where a series of sacred pagodas shared the street with a dozen Chinese restaurants and bakeries. Reaching the end of the street, they paused outside what was arguably one of the largest Chinese markets in North America. Lon Hua's Grocery Store anchored the market on the left side.

Starke's smeller was on overdrive with all the outside vendors. "I'm hungry," she said, licking her lips. As she looked up and down the rows of vegetables, her eyes were as wide as saucers. "Maybe we could stop at one of the restaurants and order some Chop Suey. Better yet, why don't we get a fresh platter of veggies from here?"

"We're not here to eat," Kate admonished her.

"Wait, wait, don't tell me," Starke said, with a wide grin. "You're superstitious about the food, too?"

"No, I happen to like Chinese food," she defended herself from her younger rival, "but we're here on business."

Carefully, she scoured the market for the sign Colonel Shears must have left for her; a series of numbers with several Chinese characters, hung above one of the market stalls. It didn't take long to decipher it. She knew the Chinese characters, written backwards, were an abbreviation of the street, while the numbers added up to an actual street address.

"Suppose I order some Sichuan-Style Shrimp to go?"

"C'mon, we've got to hurry," Kate said firmly, taking Starke by the arm, pulling her away from the market, and directing her down Stockton Street. "I don't want to risk exposing Shears and his operation any more than I have to. Besides we can always feed your stomach later."

"Promises, promises," Starke replied, breaking free from her partner's grasp. "Who is this Shears anyway?"

"A very well-connected spook."

"Are you saying this guy's a. . . ?"

"A what?"

"Spy?" she whispered loudly. "Well, I wouldn't get too buddy-buddy with him, Starke," Kate warned.

"When I was in Israel, I worked with an elite team of Mossad agents."

"Good for you," Dawson replied; much too blasé, brushing off Starke's statement like it was another childhood boast to be believed. "Just forget anything you think you know about intelligence gathering. Shears and his team don't operate by the rules. Last year, when I needed information from a Chinese foreign national, Shears and his men abducted him right off the street and 'waterboarded' him for several hours at a safehouse to obtain that information."

"But that's illegal," Starke reminded her. "The use of enhanced interrogation techniques, such as waterboarding, was banned by the Obama Administration in 2009, and deemed a violation of human rights in 2015."

"You, of all people, are going to start quoting chapter and verse to me?"

"I figured someone ought to."

"I'm telling you, Starke, Shears and his team don't operate by the rules. They're not interested in medals or citations. They're only concerned with results."

Starke vehemently disapproved. "I can't believe you went along with them, Dawson. That just doesn't sound like you."

"The man had information that I desperately needed." Dawson's strides caused Starke to double-time every once and a while to be able to hear her. "That information broke the case wide open and saved countless lives. If I had it to do over again today, I wouldn't change a thing."

"But you broke your oath of office!" she exclaimed, breathlessly.

Kate proudly stated, "I also took another oath when I signed up to be a cop. I took an oath 'to protect and serve' the people of this city. As far as I'm concerned, that's exactly what I did."

Starke rushed to keep up. "I don't understand."

"Someday, hopefully, you will," Kate said, purposefully.

"Are you sure this 'Shears' is on the level?"

"Absolutely. I trust him with my life."

Starke recognized the twinkle in Dawson's eyes. "You're in love with him, aren't you, Kate?"

She didn't reply or react in any way, just kept walking.

In the next block, they came upon an old-fashioned Chinese laundry. Dawson produced a couple of fake claim checks that Shears had given her and made it look like she had returned to pick up some overdue laundry. As they opened and stepped through the front door, both women were surprised to see the laundry process was still being done entirely by hand. From the initial washing (in water which contained a detergent or other chemicals) to agitation, rinsing, and drying, and ultimately, pressing (with an iron) and folding, several Chinese workers moved the laundry down a long table which resembled a makeshift conveyor belt. The work appeared to be backbreaking, especially the initial washing and agitation, but the workers remained silent, almost stoic, as they completed each step, total professionals. At the final step, a sole worker wrapped each item of clean laundry in brown paper, and tied it shut with a ribbon. The parcels were then stacked in the corner for pick-up. If they hadn't seen it themselves, they would not have believed it.

Kate Dawson stepped up to the counter and surrendered her two claim checks to the laundry attendant, a short, round Chinese man whose smile seemed to be plastered on his face. He bowed his head politely several times, then excused himself. He was replaced by a hulking, Caucasian man who looked totally out of place in the Chinese laundry. He could have been one of Shears' men, even though she didn't recognize him. Eyes locked, the tension crackled between the two of them, like heat lightning on a summer's eve, but she wasn't about to back down.

"Tell me, big boy," Kate inquired, softly, "you still putting Chinamen in jail for spitting in the laundry?"

"*What did you say*?" the giant growled, a little hard of hearing, his speech impeded by words larger than three letters.

Kate spoke louder, "You still putting Chinamen in jail for spitting in the laundry?"

The giant grunted once—something totally unintelligible—and lumbered away, eventually disappearing into the back room.

Starke approached Dawson from behind, "What did you say to him?" she asked, her voice barely a whisper.

Kate whispered back, "I asked him if they were still putting Chinamen in jail for spitting in the laundry?"

"What is that, some type of Chinese fortune cookie?"

"No, it's a line from Roman Polanski's movie *Chinatown*," she confessed. "Shears is a movie buff. In fact, I don't think 'Shears' is his real name. I looked it up once on IMDb.com. There's a 'Colonel Shears,' played by William Holden, in *Bridge on the River Kwai*."

"You mean, 'Shears' is a character from a movie?"

"Apparently so," Kate revealed.

"Great!" Starke exclaimed. "No Colonel Shears? So then, for all we know, he's just some nut job rattling your cage."

"I'm Colonel Shears," he said, emerging from the back room.

There was a long moment of silence and unease. Alex Starke stared at the tall, broad-shouldered man without expression. She had little doubt in her mind that the affable, clean-cut, and handsome persona mask he wore cloaked a much darker figure. She wanted to reach up and snatch away that expressive leather face to reveal the brunt umber, re-sculpted features of a man who had long ago surrendered to cigarettes and booze and moral ambiguity. Whatever earnest qualities he once espoused with his wholesome, all-American appearance yielded only cynicism now, with a great potential for gloom and corruption.

Starke asked slowly, "You're Colonel Shears?"

"Let me guess?" Shears said, as he leaned in, eyes boring into hers. "You were expecting Marlon Brando from *Apocalypse Now*? Common mistake. We're both colonels, but his last name is Kurtz."

"Alex, this is my friend, Colonel Shears," Kate said, as she brought the two of them together. "He's agreed to help us with our case. Shears, this is Alex Starke."

"*Tzahal* (צה״ל), right? Israel Defense Forces," he said, taking a drag on the cigarette that was cupped in his hand. "You spent two years as a paratrooper in the IDF fighting Hamas. You showed some real *cajones*, Starke."

She nodded curtly, surprised at his knowledge of her background. "That's correct." They were in a stare down, as if they were trying to see into each other's skull. Shears was clearly better at it than Starke and enjoyed it so much more.

"Now show some sense," he said, his voice an octave lower, "and let us pros handle things from here."

Nary a blink, her eyes never left his face. "Just don't fuck it up."

Colonel Shears escorted the two detectives to the back room of the Laundry and cleared off a small table. He then pulled out a couple of chairs for them to sit and opened a manila folder on the table. Their personal casino dealer, managing a successful Blackjack table, he dealt out a series of photos and dossiers, and didn't waste any time getting to the point.

"Eight months ago, an elite five-member unit of the 75th Ranger Regiment, also known as Task Force Red, stationed at Bagram Airfield in Afghanistan, was given the task of delivering a cache of diamonds to an Afghani warlord in the Parwan province. The cache of diamonds was payment for the location of the Taliban leader who had been targeting NATO bases in the area with suicide bombers," Shears explained, taking another hit on his cigarette. "Unfortunately, the payment never reached the Afghani warlord. Task Force Red was reportedly ambushed somewhere near Charikar in the Parwan province and every member of the team was killed. We are told their bodies were stripped of uniforms, weapons, and anything valuable by the local Afghani people and left to rot in the high mountain dessert. But the cache of diamonds completely vanished without a trace."

"How much are the diamonds worth?" Kate asked.

"Thirty million dollars," Shears speculated, taking a drag. "But in the Golden Triangle, where Afghani warlords buy raw opium from the Brotherhood of the Snow Leopard in exchange for diamonds, that thirty million dollars is worth a half billion on the streets of New York City."

Alex Starke shot him a sideways glance. "Are you shitting me?"

He shook his head "no." "You could easily turn a huge profit in a matter of days, and still have your initial investment of thirty million in diamonds, even if you paid retail at any diamond exchange in Manhattan."

"I don't believe it," Kate said, surprised.

"Trust me. It can be done."

Dawson shook off his objection. "And what makes you such an expert at smuggling opium all of a sudden?"

"I know people who have done it."

"Like who, for instance."

"A guy I knew once," said Shears, taking a long, heavy pull on his cigarette.

"Yeah," Kate replied, with a healthy dose of skepticism, "I'd like to meet up with him sometime and swap stories."

"Sometime," said Shears, the crinkles showing in the corners of his eyes. "But then again, he does carry a top security clearance. Well above your pay grade."

"I just knew you were going to say that." For a few minutes, Starke watched the two of them. Dawson and Shears seemed to actually be enjoying the banter, the pursuit, capture, and retreat that came out of their words and phrases. If she didn't know any better, she would have mistaken their banter for some form of dating game or courting ritual between the inspector and the rogue intelligence agent. She got the feeling, and there was little doubt in her mind, that Dawson was having the time of her life. Starke caught the twinkle in her eye again, then quickly looked away.

"I still don't believe it," Kate repeated. "There are too many variables."

Starke leapt into the fray, interrupting their banter. "The biggest problem I see is that you have to find a way to move your product—a half billion dollars' worth of raw opium—from one of the most dangerous places in the world to one of the most controlled and regulated. I don't doubt you could get it out of

Afghanistan with the right connections and pay-offs, but there's just no way you're going to get into the United States without running into a lot of road blocks."

Colonel Shears smiled thinly at her. "It's not as big a problem if they think you're already dead."

Starke thought about his words for a moment, then it hit her. "The five members of Task Force Red are still alive."

"Exactly."

"I don't understand," Kate confessed, sitting up straight. "How is that possible?"

"Instead of delivering the cache of diamonds to the Afghani warlord, as ordered, they stole it for themselves," Shears told them the rest of the story. "Then, in order to disappear in the middle of a war zone, they staged their own deaths with an elaborate hoax. They reported being ambushed in a desolate region of the high mountain dessert and purposely gave the wrong map coordinates so there was no possibility of a rescue. Then they strategically scattered thousands of rounds of spent ammunition and explosives and bloodied uniforms to give the impression there had been one hell-of-a firefight. Task Force Red then struck their own deal with the Brotherhood of the Snow Leopard, using the cache of diamonds they were to have given the warlord as their down payment. They packed hundreds of pounds of raw opium in the aluminum caskets that were meant to ship their bodies back to the United States and tagged each casket with a warning that the bodies had been exposed to sarin gas during the ambush. The warning would have been enough to keep even the most curious Army official from opening the caskets and potentially exposing others to the dangerous gas. Then once the caskets were on the ground at Dover Air Force Base in Delaware, all they had to do was bribe the civilian funeral staff here or pay off the mortuary technicians, also civilian."

"Brilliant," Kate said, most impressed. "Military families make requests about sealed caskets all of the time."

"It's ingenious," Starke echoed Dawson's sentiment.

Shears added, "The operation went off with such perfect, military precision that the five members of Task Force Red agreed to work together on other high-risk targets. In the last eight months, they've stolen millions of dollars in military-grade weapons, munitions, armaments, and equipment. And with each success, they've gotten bolder and are hitting even bigger targets. Instead of high jacking truck convoys or robbing trains, they are now targeting aircraft in flight."

Dawson slapped the table in disbelief. "You've got to be kidding me?"

"No, I wish I were," he replied sourly. "That plane crash in Cologne, Germany last month was one of Task Force Red's latest targets. A hundred and twenty-five people were killed so they could snatch a hunk of weapons-grade plutonium that the Russians had agreed to surrender to the U.N.'s decommissioning efforts."

"What was plutonium doing on a commercial aircraft?" Starke demanded.

"You're going to have to take that up with the FAA. But I can tell you in advance, you're not going to like the answer."

"Why haven't they been caught?" Kate asked, similarly incensed. "Surely, the Army must have fingerprints, photographs, dossiers on each of these men? They can't live off the grid forever."

"That's all here," Shears said, pushing the photographs and dossiers towards the ladies. Dawson and Starke each picked one up and started thumbing through it. "But just remember that you're dealing with five Army Rangers—the best of the best— who have been trained to survive behind enemy lines. Their intelligence and counterintelligence training are the finest in the world. If they don't want to be captured or detained, there isn't a force on the planet who can stop them."

Kate Dawson held up her hand to stop him. "Why are you showing me this?"

Shears tried to hide his face, but she could see right through him. He smiled wryly. "Just remember, I'm only the messenger."

"Tell me," she insisted.

"Based on the Ballistics Report submitted by Doctor Brogan, the third-party shooter at the warehouse used a Glock 19 to execute those injured men," Shears said, at last. "For the past year, U.S. Army Rangers have carried the Glock 19 as their primary sidearm. When issued to Army personnel, each weapon is test fired with a Winchester .9 x .19 mm semi-automatic Full Metal Jacket round, and that bullet with its unique rifling marks is photographed and filed with the Ranger's personnel records. Since bullets fired from the same gun carry the same rifling marks, medical examiners are able to compare recovered bullets from autopsies with the original bullet."

"Dammit, Shears, I know all about rifling marks. I did graduate from the Police Academy."

"According to Army records, the Glock 19 that was issued to Captain Gideon McMaster was the weapon that was used to kill those men. McMaster was the fifth member to join Task Force Red."

Kate shivered. It was hard to tell if it was from the frigid temperature in the back room of the shop or the information she had just learned from Shears. As she rubbed her hands up and down her arms to keep warm, she glanced through the photos and dossiers of the elite team. Their exploits chilled her even more, as Dawson made a concerted effort to commit their names and faces to memory: Samuel Armbruster, Major,

Ranger Division; Victor Franco, Captain, Ranger Division; Herbert T. Jefferson, Lieutenant, Special Forces; James "Tex" Denton, Major, Ranger Division; and finally, Gideon McMaster, Captain, Special Forces.

"So, you're absolutely certain that my shooter is part of this elite Task Force Red?" she posed a rhetorical question. "What could they possibly hope to gain by killing those wounded men?"

"That should be obvious," Shears replied, shrugging his shoulders. "The Botulinum Toxin. In the right hands, sold by an arms dealer on the black market, it's worth more than plutonium or a whole cache of weapons."

"Who did the Army find to go after them?" Starke asked.

Colonel Shears smirked. "Oh, you know the Army. They've probably talked some poor, dumb son-of-a-bitch into doing it."

"Alex, could you give me a moment with Colonel Shears?" Dawson asked, looking up from the table and the photos.

"Sure. I'll be up front when you're ready."

Everyone stood as she left.

Shears gave no sign of having heard Kate's request. Instead, he focused on lighting another cigarette with the shiny, silver Zippo lighter, sporting a four-leaf clover. He then sat down in the chair, opposite Dawson, staring at her, searching her face for a sign, some symbol of what was to come. "This had better not be some kind of lecture or pep-talk about me doing my job. I won't stand for it."

Kate waved him down. "I wouldn't dare tell you how to do your job."

"Okay, so, what's on your mind?" Shears asked, blowing a long line of smoke.

"I need a favor."

"Sure. It's the least I can do, Kate, considering how much of a mess I've left you with—all of this crap," he replied, reshuffling the photos and dossiers.

"I've got a friend named Lenny Provolone," she said slowly.

"Provolone," Shears repeated the name, like it meant something to him.

"He's gotten himself in way over his head with a woman."

"A woman!?" He frowned.

"No, no, it's not what you think," Kate replied, putting on the brakes. For a moment, she hesitated, then tried to start again. "This wasn't just any woman; this was a woman who seems to be well-connected to the mob or some foreign government. Bottom line, she conned him into surrendering his access to a satellite system he made for FEMA, and then she has tried to kill him twice; the last attempt by a former Army Ranger. I've written it all down for you."

Shears was silent for a long time, then started rummaging through some papers on the corner of his small table. "What do you want me to do about it?"

Dawson shrugged her shoulders. "I want you to find out who she is and pay her off or frighten her off for me. She's running some kind of scam, and my friend is simply not man enough to handle a woman like that."

Shears bobbed his head. "Well, it looks like your friend may be in far deeper than you thought," he added, handing her a telex.

"Oh, no. What has the damn fool gotten himself into, this time?" she said sourly, reading through the printed message.

"Provolone is wanted on several counts, including espionage, by the U.S. Army."

"But this can't be right," Kate protested, clutching the telex in her hand. "I know this man. I've known Lenny for years. He's no spy."

Shears nodded as if agreeing with her. "Okay, let's assume, for the moment, you're right. What possible reason would a branch of the United States military have for issuing an arrest warrant for your friend? It just doesn't add up, unless the Army is trying to pick him up and put him into protective custody. Kate, think about it. This may not be as bad as it looks."

Dawson was thinking about it. "That woman still scares me. She's evil. She's brilliant. She knows that she's failed twice. I'd feel a lot better if I knew she was out of the picture altogether."

"Okay, I'll assign one of my best men to it." She snatched the cigarette from his lips and took a long drag; something she rarely ever did. "I was hoping you'd handle it for me. Personally."

"I'm afraid I can't," he said, as he reclaimed his cigarette from her. "I've got another assignment."

"Let me guess. You're the 'poor, dumb son-of-a-bitch' the Army found to go after them," she said, picking on him.

Shears pushed himself away from the table, angrily. "The Army's not just looking to stop Task Force Red, but they also want to find out the identity of the arms dealer who has been paying them off."

"You didn't have to volunteer for this assignment. There are plenty of other men, younger men, who could have done this."

"It's what I do, Kate."

Dawson was waiting at the make-shift door to the back room when he finally put out his cigarette. He fumbled in his pants pockets for another smoke, but he came up empty; not even a crumpled pack.

Suddenly, Kate turned towards him, put her arms around his waist, pulling him close. There were tears in her eyes. "I don't know how to say this, so I'll just say it. You damn well better take care of yourself, Shears. Look at that. I don't even know your first name."

His eyes darted over her features, dumbfounded. "It's John."

"I don't want to lose you, John. I can't lose you."

Shears put his arms around her shoulders and pulled her close, saying in his deep, craggy voice, "Now, don't get any strange ideas, sweetheart. I'm not the marrying kind, but I'll love you till the day I die."

"What more could a woman ask for?" she replied, kissing him deeply.

He returned her kiss, and then said, "Promise me, you'll be careful. Those men are trained killers; killing a woman is nothing to them."

"I promise." She kissed him quickly, one last time, softly on the lips. "Good. Now you promise me, you'll come back in one piece."

"I promise," he replied, brushing the hair from her face. Shears held back the sheet that separated the two rooms and led the way to the front of the laundry.

Kate Dawson managed to stay out of trouble in Chinatown. By the time it took for Starke and her to walk back to the car, a long line of traffic, mostly tourists leaving Chinatown, had backed up for a mile or more behind the exit for the Dragon Gate. Kate simply pulled away from the curb and headed down Bush Street. She stayed ahead of the afternoon rush-hour traffic and dropped Starke at police headquarters with a lunch bag full of Chinese vegetables and white rice. Dawson herself didn't stop at the Hall of Justice but drove straight to the UCSF Medical Center. She was very worried about her friend, especially after reading Shears' telex. She parked her car in the lot near the Emergency Room entrance and got out.

An ambulance pulled into the bay, lights flashing, and several paramedics swept through the door, pushing a gurney with a victim strapped to it. Dawson scampered in behind them. The lobby was one big mess with patients screaming out for help. Gun-shot wounds, accident victims, and attempted suicides crowded the halls with chaos.

A self-important, young intern, carrying a clipboard, stopped Dawson at the door, stating authoritatively, "You can't come in this way, ma'am. Visitors are around the front."

"No, it's okay, doctor," Kate replied, reaching into her jacket for her police badge. She pulled it out of her pocket and showed him, then slipped it through a beltloop on her hip so that the badge would be visible to all. "I'm here to follow-up with a knife-wound victim."

"Name?"

"Lieutenant Kate Dawson."

"No, I need the victim's name," the intern said.

"Leonard J. Provolone," she reported.

The intern walked over to a computer terminal at the desk, typed a few words, and shook his head "no." "He's no longer here. He's been transferred."

"Transferred?" Kate repeated, a frustrated look on her face. "No, there must be some mistake. Lenny wouldn't have gone to another hospital. He was in a private room on the eighth floor. Room 814."

"The only mistake is the one you're making."

"But I'm telling you that I was with him just this morning."

The intern came around and blocked her.

"Get out of my way!" she demanded, but when the startled intern failed to move aside, she shoved past him, strode directly to the bank of elevators, and pushed the "up" button, daring him to just try and stop her. Right when she boarded the elevator, she heard a "ping" on her cellphone indicating a new text message. She didn't recognize the number, so she quickly put it away. The message would have to wait. Some things take priority in her mind. Kate pushed the number 8. Hospital security was waiting for her when the elevator door opened.

"Ma'am, you're going to have to stop right there," the first security guard said, right hand resting on his holstered weapon.

"We need to see your identification," the second guard added.

Dawson looked from face to face, and then at the faces of the frightened nurses who were retreating behind the central nurses' station. "My name is Lieutenant Kate Dawson, San Francisco Police Department," she said, flashing her badge quickly at the two men. "I have a stab wound victim under protective custody in room 814. His name is Leonard J. Provolone."

"Lieutenant, let's just take things real easy," the second guard said. "Starting with that badge of yours."

Kate handed her badge over to the second guard who, in turn, handed it to the first. They both examined it, and when both of them were satisfied, they returned the badge to her. She clipped it back on her hip.

"Sorry, Lieutenant. It's just routine," the first security guard apologized.

"Nothing personal. Just routine," the second guard added.

Kate breathed a sigh of relief. "Thanks, guys. Now, if you don't mind, I'm going to look in on him while I'm here."

"I'm afraid your man is no longer here," the first security guard said, with a shrug. "He was moved out this afternoon under very heavy guard. All the paperwork was there. Signed and notarized. So, we just assumed you knew. We figured he was being moved to a more secure facility."

"Moved? Moved where?" she demanded.

Both hospital security guards were clueless, but the second man volunteered a possible answer. "You should ask down at the main desk," he said. "Sometimes they keep information like that down there."

Dawson's cellphone "pinged" a reminder that she had a text message waiting for her to read. She clicked on the message: "If you want to see your friend alive again, come alone to 74 Cargo Way. Just you. No backup."

At half past eight in the evening, Kate Dawson stood at the corner of 74 Cargo Way, looking down at her cellphone. She had no bars or cellphone signal. She was literally at a dead end, as far away from the nearest cell tower—and civilization—as she could go in the City of San Francisco. She wondered what all this had to do with Lenny and the mystery woman he had met.

A long, black limousine was parked midway along the block on the opposite side of the street, its motor still running, the passenger side door open. A big, hulking mountain of a man stood outside the door, smoking a cigarette, the orange glow from each puff illuminating a scarred, tragic face. He looked like one of those victims of an IED from Iraq or Afghanistan that had exploded in his face, his body remade and reconstructed into that of a killer.

"What are your orders?" he asked, leaning into the door.

"Kill her," the man in the back seat ordered.

He took one last, long drag on his cigarette, and cast it away. He then took a six-shot, Smith & Wesson .45 caliber revolver out of his shoulder holster and confirmed that each and every chamber was loaded. Snapping the cartridge into his pistol, he stood up straight, a mountain of a man, ready to kill.

Kate Dawson blanched white and recoiled at his sight. She knew what it meant, but it took a few seconds for that "fight or flight" imperative to register in her gray matter. Finally, she bolted down Cargo Way, heading east, and at her first opportunity, jumped the chain link fence that separated the street from the large, industrial warehouse district. She ran toward the front of the warehouse and raced around the corner of the building towards the door. Two bullets fired from her assailant's gun whizzed by her head, narrowly missing her.

Dawson pounded on the doors to several warehouses, then ran into the first one that was open, gasping for breath. Out of shape, she had spent far too much time at McGinty's, drinking beer and swallowing down bourbon chasers, and not enough time at the gym. She slammed the door behind her, locked it, and quickly scanned the warehouse for a place to hide. Other than a handful of boxes and crates, the warehouse was empty. So much for the idea of hiding out and waiting for the cavalry to arrive. She checked the bars again on her phone; still out of range.

Dawson ran to the back of the warehouse and found the door that opened onto the train platform. She was out of luck as it was bolted shut. She glanced out one of the small windows in back—a ladder leading up to the roof. Right then, she decided that she'd use the ladder only as a last resort. She was too frightened to climb up to the roof; to try escape that way.

Outside, she heard the sound of breaking glass, and for an instant thought her assailant was coming through a window. Then she recalled the fire axe on the wall. He must have smashed the glass with his fist. Then Kate heard the first blow of the axe, as he began furiously pounding at the door.

She ran back towards the front of the warehouse; decided to make her last stand there. After all, she had nine shots in her service pistol and one in the chamber. If that wasn't enough to stop her assailant, then she'd probably have to consider another line of work. Kate began piling up some boxes and crates along the side as a kind of barricade, like the Alamo. *Then again, maybe the Alamo isn't the best choice of names for it.* She remembered seeing the movie version with Billy Bob Thornton;

everyone died. She thought long and hard about it. *Fort Apache. John Wayne didn't die at Fort Apache. It was just cowboys and a long cattle drive.* She was probably on much safer ground going with the name Fort Apache.

Her assailant was making progress. The lock on the door was beginning to give way with each furious blow. Dawson looked behind her. The window with the ladder leading to the roof was beginning to look more and more appealing, even though she hated heights. It was dark out, and just maybe she'd make it to the roof before that overwhelming feeling of vertigo kicked in and spelled certain doom for her. Kate looked down at her barricade, at the boxes and crates, at the fort she had built herself. It was clear that she was scared and had no idea which way to turn.

Outside, her assailant—that big, hulking mountain of a man—was still swinging the axe furiously, landing blows on the door lock with every swing. He was like a crazy man, single-minded and possessed. At last, the lock gave way. Her assailant threw down the axe and kicked the door open. Taking out his gun, he advanced cautiously on her through the shadows.

He stepped into the cavernous warehouse and dropped down to one knee behind a large FedEx box, craning his neck to look around.

Nothing.

He then stood up and began making his way to the barricade very cautiously. Quickly, he looked behind it, gun out in front of him.

Nothing.

Disgusted, he spun about, gun trained on any object in focus, surveilling the rest of the warehouse, even pushing over other cardboard boxes and crates.

Satisfied that Dawson was not in the warehouse, he walked to the back wall and spotted the ladder leading to the roof, smiled, and began to climb the narrow rungs.

Reaching the top, he poked his head up and surveyed the flat roof through his gunsights.

Empty.

Breaching the roof, he stood tall, scouring and listening. A hundred warehouses seemed to stretch for miles along the railroad lines, from San Francisco Bay to points south and west. Realizing there was no way for Kate to have gone back down while he was standing there, he figured she had already fallen to her death or was clinging to the side of the building, waiting to make her move. Carefully, he walked along the edge of the roof, cringing at the crunching sound with each step.

Desperately, Kate Dawson hung there in the air, her fingers numb from clutching the roof's water-logged gutter, her body banging against the side of the building as the cold winds swept in from the Bay. Her feet kept scrambling to get a footing before she plunged to her death.

Footsteps.

At that moment, Kate regained her footing and clambered back on the roof. Hearing her, he pivoted and aimed, but she had the advantage. Holding the gun out in front of her in a combat stance, she had the muzzle of her 9 mil trained squarely on the man's large torso.

"Hold it! Don't move, or I'll shoot!" she exclaimed.

Amused, he started laughing maniacally, his eyes glinting blood red, and started to raise his gun slowly, pointing it at Kate center mass. Without hesitation, Dawson fired once, the report of the gun echoed through the warehouses. The bullet slammed into his chest. Staggering in shock, his hand automatically went to the pain and came back dripping in blood. Round two sent the man over the side, plunging to his death. The weight of the body produced a loud thud that could be heard for blocks away.

From the rooftop, Kate watched as the limousine pulled away.

An hour later, Dawson found herself right smack in the middle of another crime scene spectacle as the press and members of the San Francisco Police Department descended on the warehouse parking lot. At first, the press treated the story as a random shooting incident, the kind that never makes the lead on the nightly news and often gets buried at the end of the newscast. Then the story got a little bigger, when they learned a cop was involved. And finally, a full-fledged, leading story when they discovered the cop was a woman. It struck Kate, as she repeated the facts for the third time to officials, that they'd have been a great deal happier if she had turned up as the victim in a gang-land shooting. Stories with the right amount of pathos, under-world violence, and the death of a promising, yet inexperienced young cop always made the best news.

The San Francisco Police Department chose a completely different approach. Within minutes of the shooting, police cruisers were everywhere. Uniformed officers established a perimeter around the body and held back curious onlookers before the cops finally erected yellow caution tape. Doctor Brogan rolled into the crime scene in an unmarked sedan, followed by the CSI van and his team of forensic investigators, the crime scene boys, and Richey. Detectives from one of the bureaus—in this case, homicide—usually strolled in last, looking for coffee and donuts. The detective who lost the coin toss was often the one who ended up talking to the press.

Matt Balardi lost the coin toss. Jawara, Ramirez, and a couple of uniformed cops were standing around, listening to Kate Dawson give her official statement. None of them looked happy to be out this late again on a weeknight. This was the second time in as many days that Kate was personally involved in a homicide. Clark hunched down next to her, writing the account in his notebook.

"I didn't get a good look at the limousine driver, but I could tell he was wearing a plain black suit with a driving cap," she said, recalling details to mind.

"What about the mastermind? What did he look like?" Clark asked.

"He sat in the back seat, behind the driver. I didn't see him, but I'll never forget that voice. It was cold, calculating. When he ordered his man, 'Kill her,' the little hairs on the back of my neck stood up. Literally, I could not move, as moments in my life flashed before my eyes."

"Can you tell me anything more about the voice?" Clark pressed her.

Kate thought about it. "His voice sounded English, no Bostonian. Brownstone, Upper East Side. Prep school."

"In another words, 'rich.'"

"Yes," she agreed with his assessment. Then, as she continued to think about it, she added, "It was a Lincoln Town Car, not a Cadillac. The limousine was definitely a Ford. Top of the line, with all the options."

Suddenly, the ringtone on Jawara's cellphone went off; the theme from Isaac Hayes' "Shaft" played continuously until he picked it up. "Yeah, baby. You know Daddy's still workin.'"

Dawson nearly jumped out of her skin. "Is that about Lenny?" she demanded, pointing at Mikhail. She bit her lower lip, waiting for an answer.

Jawara held his hand over the receiver, and whispered, "No."

"I need to know that he's all right," she proclaimed, on the edge of panic. "Those people at the hospital weren't very helpful."

Ramirez tried to reassure her. "Don't worry, Kate. We've mobilized all our resources. We'll find him."

"Thanks, Jorge."

"We can stop, Kate, and do this another time," Clark said.

"No, William. Let's just keep going." Although she was spent, Kate had to take care of business.

"What happened next?" Clark continued to question her.

"My assailant wasn't in much of a hurry," Kate replied, trying to regain her focus. "He finished smoking his cigarette, then checked his weapon. From where I was standing, it looked like a six-shot, .45 Smith & Wesson. I was actually surprised by his choice of weapon. If I worked as a professional assassin, I would have chosen to use a semi-auto Glock or Beretta. But then, as I thought about it, older men do prefer high-caliber revolvers. 'Wheel guns' support the highest calibers available; they also don't jam during operation, like semis, and if you need more than six bullets, you'd better find a different profession."

Clark agreed with a huff. "Sounds like he was very deliberate in his approach, and not the least bit concerned with the outcome."

"Yeah, I'd have to say that was true," Kate said, with a shiver. "He sure did scare the shit out of me."

"So, you ran?"

"Yes, I ran," she replied indignantly. "I had purposely parked my car a few blocks away just in case it was an ambush. But when he came after me, I realized that I wasn't going to be able to out run him. So, I jumped over the fence and took advantage of the first open warehouse."

William Clark paused, glancing back through his notes. He was very methodical and most determined to provide a precise, orderly flow of events for anyone to follow. He took his time with the official report, justifying statements that Kate had made earlier with those she was eventually going to sign her name to under penalty of perjury. Early in his career, Clark had applied to work for Internal Affairs, on three separate occasions, and was turned down by IA three times. He would have made a topnotch investigator for Internal Affairs

"The guy looked like a fuckin' giant," Jawara commented.

"Goliath," Ramirez added. "*No es que la verdad*. [No shit.]"

"Yeah," Dawson said sourly, "he was pretty big."

Clark found what he was looking for, and said, "According to your account, you built a barricade in the warehouse, out of boxes and crates. You then waited for him behind the barricade with your service pistol, drawn and ready to fire. But then, in an earlier statement, you say you abandoned the barricade in favor of catching him out in the open on the roof? What really happened there?"

"I did build the barricade out of boxes and crates that I found in the warehouse; even named it Fort Apache," she said, going back over the details in her head. "But as I sat there, listening to him whack away at the door with an axe, I sure didn't feel safe. He was such a big man, and I was worried that he could have just as easily cut the barricade in half with one or two blows of it."

"Axe?" Clark asked, returning to his notes.

Kate nodded her head. "He had a fire axe, and at that moment, he was busy using the axe to break down the front door of the warehouse."

"Okay," he muttered, writing down the word 'axe.'

"He had an axe," Jawara whispered to Ramirez.

"*Qué coño*. [What the hell.] An axe," Ramirez replied, his voice lowered.

"So, I ran to the back of the warehouse," she continued her narrative, "and I looked out one of the windows. There was a narrow ladder that led up to the roof. In that split second, I realized that I'd have a better chance confronting him on the roof, and I abandoned my makeshift fort."

"So, you climbed to the roof?" Clark noted.

"Yes," she acknowledged, with a nod.

William Clark didn't look at Kate. He was busy writing her account of the homicide in his notes. Finally, he asked, "What happened next?"

"I hid out on the roof, and when he finally came after me, I waited for just the right moment to jump out and catch him by surprise. I didn't have to wait for long."

"When you finally confronted him, did you identify yourself as a member of the San Francisco Police Department?"

"More or less," Kate replied, playing fairly loose with the truth. "I demanded that he surrender his weapon to me, but he refused. Instead, he raised his gun to shoot me but I shot him first."

"One shot?" Clark inquired. "Two shots," Kate replied, red-faced. "Fired at close range. The second shot sent his body over the side of the roof."

None of the men there had to be told what a shot from a .9 mil would do to an average man's body, much less two shots. They were all experts, checked out on the police range once a month.

"Give me your gun, Kate," William said, almost apologetically.

"Dammit-it-to-hell, Clark," she said, handing over her weapon. "Why can't you just take my word for it?"

"You know, this needs to be done by the book." Clark examined her weapon closely. Satisfied that she had fired the handgun twice, he handed it over to Jawara. Jawara started his examination by ejecting the clip, and counting her bullets, one at a time. In turn, he passed the weapon over to Ramirez, who confirmed Clark's finding. They all agreed that Kate's weapon had been discharged twice.

"Let the record show that Lieutenant Dawson's standard-issue firearm has been examined by three detectives from Homicide, and their conclusion is that the weapon was fired twice," Clark stated, for the record.

She looked from face to face, and said, "Well, if you're satisfied that my weapon was only fired twice, can I have it back?"

Clark did. "Sorry, Kate," he said. "It's just procedure. Now Doctor Brogan may also want to examine your firearm. Run it against his ballistics report."

"I know," she said, with a bob of her head. Kate slapped the magazine back in and charged the slide by pulling it all the way back and releasing it, then slipped it into her shoulder holster. "Was there anything else you needed?"

"No," Clark replied, "unless there's something else you'd like to add to the official record."

"Not a damn thing," she said, with disgust.

Dawson wasn't necessarily angry with Clark. He was merely doing his job. She was angry with the whole system that required cops to prove their innocence first in a routine shooting. Unlike the court system and the court of public opinion, police officers were always presumed guilty when a civilian was shot in the course of an investigation. Cops had to prove that there was no malice behind their actions, and that they were completely justified. The rush to justice on the part of the press, the mayor, and city officials made it doubly difficult for them to do their jobs without filing lengthy action reports. There was no greater humiliation for a cop to know they hadn't done anything wrong but still were unable to prove their innocence beyond a reasonable doubt in the court of public opinion.

Matt Balardi strolled up, smoking a cigarette. "The Press are asking about you, Kate."

"Well, they can go fuck themselves," she said, still angry.

"It's not about you, Dawson," he said smugly, taking a heavy pull on his cigarette, releasing it slowly, deliberately dragging out the time. "It's about that friend of yours."

"Lenny?" Kate asked, the features in her face twisted out of shape.

"He's been arrested by the Army for treason and espionage," Balardi reported, the purveyor of bad news and gossip. Although his face didn't reveal it, he took great pleasure in delivering the bad news to Kate.

"Where?"

"The U.S. Army Garrison at the Presidio of Monterey."

The U.S. Army Garrison was located in Monterey County in the city of Monterey, California, on the Pacific coast, approximately 120 miles south of San Francisco; eight miles from the Ord Military Community, where the majority of students and permanent post military personnel lived in military housing on a portion of the former Fort Ord. The Monterey Peninsula was favored by naturists and had a rich history that stretched back over two hundred years to when the Spanish first settled there. Few spots anywhere could match its year-round moderate climate and its beautiful, rugged coastline.

Kate Dawson would have enjoyed the two-and-a-half-hour drive along US 1 to Monterey if her mind hadn't been so focused on Lenny and his predicament. She hoped that Shears was right, and that he had just been brought in for his own protection. But she had the feeling, deep within her heart, that it was much worse than that. She also knew there wasn't anything she could do to help him, except perhaps find him a good civilian attorney who could represent him in a military court. She didn't trust the JAG (Judge Advocate General) corps to assign him anyone but a trainee. A trainee in her mind was the kiss of death. Kate figured the only thing Lenny had going for him was the fact that he was a civilian employee of a government contractor. While treason and espionage were among two of the most serious charges—both punishable by death or long terms of imprisonment with a stiff fine—the military court tended to go much easier on civilian employees than soldiers. However, according to the UCMJ (Uniform Code of Military Justice), civilian employees were subject to immediate dismissal, loss of medical and pension benefits, and revocation of their security clearances. Article 106a of the UCMJ spelled out the punitive actions of the court in more detail than Kate could swallow in one reading. Suffice it to say, if he had indeed committed treason and espionage, Lenny was up the proverbial creek without a paddle.

Dawson pulled up to the Private Bolio Gate of the U.S. Army Garrison at the Presidio of Monterey (POM) and showed her police badge to the Sergeant on duty. He directed her to the Visitor Control Center, adjacent to the Bolio Gate, for identity verification and vehicle passes. Kate parked outside the building in a visitor's parking spot and went inside the building to sign in. Thirty minutes later, she was sitting in a small room, waiting to talk to Lenny.

An Army Private escorted Kate to a cubicle in the infirmary and pulled back the privacy screen where Lenny Provolone was dozing. His right hand was cuffed to the roll bar and his feet were chained to the bottom of the bed; an intravenous-drip from an IV bag overhead fed his left hand, and two long, plastic tubes, connected to a machine behind his bed, supplied oxygen through his nose. He was wearing a pair of his old, gray, moth-eaten underwear, a single, white sheet pulled to his waist. Dried blood from an injury was caked on his t-shirt about chest level. With his unwashed face and beard, he looked like a home-less man who had been picked up for vagrancy in the Mission

District. Lenny was also missing a couple of teeth where he had been struck in the mouth. Dawson had never seen her friend looking this bad. All her worst fears had come true.

"Why the hell is he in his underwear?" Kate whispered, as Lenny began to stir. She could see that he was shivering.

"Suicide watch, ma'am," the Private reported, as he pulled out a chair for her to sit down.

She looked at the soldier with contempt. "You get him some proper clothes right now!"

"You'll have to file a request with his advocate on your way out," the Army Private droned as he made his way to the exit.

"Count on it, Private!" Kate exclaimed, then settled into the chair in front of her friend's hospital bed. She waited for him to be fully awake before she asked, "How are you holding up, Lenny?"

"They're accusing me of something that I didn't do," he replied, groggy, not entirely himself. "I never betrayed my country. I'm not a spy. Please believe me, Kate. I'm innocent."

"I believe you, but then, I'm not the person you have to convince. In a military court, there is a five-member panel of Army officers who make up the jury. You'll have to convince them if you want to gain your freedom."

"Then you've got to get me out of here, Kate!" Lenny demanded.

"I have no jurisdiction here. I can't just flash my badge."

"You have no idea what it's like here," he said, his voice lowered to a whisper. "Two nights ago, the guards let three inmates into the infirmary and helped them beat the crap out of me. They tore my stitches wide open and broke a couple of my front teeth. They all laughed and called me a traitor."

Dawson buried her face in her hands, and trembled. "Oh shit, Lenny!"

"What the fuck does it matter?" he sighed. "The doctors are all sadists here. They withhold our meds, and then place bets on how much pain each of us can endure without them. But then, the nurses are no better. They make us sit in filthy bed-pans until they're good and ready to clean us up. The record is sixteen hours, and you're looking at the current record-holder."

Kate stared at him a moment, disbelieving. "You've got to report these incidents to your attorney, and anything else they do to you. They're trying to intimidate you, but you've got to fight them. You can't let them win. You've got to show them just how strong you are."

"That's really easy for you to say! You're out there! I'm stuck in here! In this jungle where everyone is a predator," he said, sniffling back tears.

"Lenny, don't let them see you crying."

"Kate, if you can't get me out of here, then I need you to do me a favor," he said, in a whisper.

"I guess it all depends on the favor," she replied, exasperated.

"I want you to kill me." Dawson did a double-take. "Are you out of your mind?"

"I'm quite sane," Lenny responded, looking like someone who was very troubled, "but I won't be if I have to spend another day, another hour, another minute, let alone thirty long years, in this place. I'd rather be dead."

"You don't know what you're saying."

"I know perfectly well what I'm asking," he protested, fighting with the handcuffs that held him prisoner to the bed. "You could smuggle a razor blade in to me, so that I could slit my wrists. Or shoe laces, so that I could hang myself. Or rat poison, disguised as tooth paste. What do you say? You'd be doing me a tremendous favor."

"*Stop it!*" Kate shouted, putting her hands up to her ears. "I don't want to hear another word!"

Lenny shook his head. "You don't understand, Kate. I don't have anything to live for," he replied, pleading with her. "They took away my job. They've stripped me of my security clearance, and they've given N.E.M.E.S.I.S. to a bunch of hacks who don't have a clue about how my system works. I've lost my pension and whatever money I still have in the bank is going to get gobbled up in a lengthy court battle. When this is all over with, regardless of how much prison time I have to serve, the only job I'll be qualified to do is as a greeter at Walmart. For that matter, *who's* going to hire someone like me with a prison record?"

Dawson wanted to seize Provolone by his thin shoulders, pull him roughly out of his bed, and slap the shit out of him, but she was forbidden from touching or otherwise engaging with him physically. "You chicken shit, son-of-a-bitch! Did you always think that life was going to be easy? Fair?"

"I'm better off dead, Kate. Can't you see that?"

"That's the bullshit I said I didn't want to hear from you, Lenny."

"But it's *true.*"

"That's your problem, Lenny," she barked, steel-tipped with hostility. "You've always taken the easy way out of life and cheated yourself from what you possibly could have learned from it. The saddest thing in this world is wasted talent. Rather than have a woman your own age who may have loved you and challenged you to develop as a man, you've chased after little girls half your age because they were always easier to get. A year ago, I caught you bidding on a sex slave. You were going to buy a woman, rather than develop a real relationship with one!"

Lenny Provolone paled. "You know, women don't like me.

They never have. They take one good look at me and run away, screaming into the night, like I'm some kind of monster."

"Is that any wonder with the way you treat them?"

"I'm warning you, Kate. I don't want to have this conversation now."

"Well, we are going to have this conversation!" she insisted, her eyes bloodshot and aflame. "I've watched you take the easy way out of just about every aspect of your life, and it has sickened me. Rather than develop a personality of your own, you've highjacked the personalities of your favorite movie characters and played dress-up. First it was Humphrey Bogart and then Obi Wan Kenobi. I've often wondered if you've ever had a genuine moment as Lenny Provolone."

His lips were quivering. "He's nothing but a loser. When people see me on the street, they look right through me. It's like I'm not even there. But when I'm dressed as Bogie or Obi Wan, at least I'm somebody."

"That's really sad, Lenny, but don't think, for one moment, that life is any easier for the rest of us. Every one of us has had to fight and claw and scratch out some kind of meaningful existence for ourselves. No one is giving us free money or 'get out of jail free' cards.

"You've been charged with treason and espionage," she told him, in no uncertain terms. "I'm not going to let you take the easy way out this time. You are going to stand trial like a man and take whatever punishment is due you. They may throw the book at you; they may decide to bury you in the deepest dungeon, but you're not going to take the easy way out."

Quaking, he began crying like a baby. "I don't know, Kate. I really don't know what to do."

Kate Dawson slammed her hand down on the bed to get his attention. "You can act like a man!"

For an instant, her disgust for him registered, then Provolone slumped, deflated, as if all the life in his body had leaked out of him. His eyes, which had been glazed over with tears, were now black, completely devoid of life. The warm fluid that once flowed through his veins had long since dried to a powder. He was one of the "hollow men," headpiece stuffed with straw, an effigy of himself, waiting to be set ablaze.

She continued to stare at him for another couple of minutes, unable to think at all, then stood up and went out the door. Never looked back.

Outside the Visitor Control Center, Dawson reclaimed her car and drove part of the way back home along the coast. Just outside of San Jose, she picked up Interstate 280 and followed it home to San Fran. Kate refused to think of Lenny, not even once, the whole way.

CHAPTER SEVEN

During the early morning hours, Kate Dawson received a text message from one of Shears' men, the one who had been assigned to look into Lenny Provolone's psycho girlfriend-turned-assailant. Kate read the message and immediately deleted it from her inbox. She had had enough of her friend and neighbor to last her until the end of the year. She laid her head back down on the pillow. But the more she thought about it, the more she wanted to know about the woman. She woke up long enough to recover the text, which included a time and location, then went back to sleep. For the rest of the night, Kate tossed and turned in her small, twin-sized bed.

Dawson got to Pier 54 before Morgan did. She waited in her car, watching for him in between five-minute power naps. She was still tired from the night before. Not long after, Major Morgan, Shears' second-in-command, pulled his vintage 1958 red Cadillac up alongside Kate's BMW and blew the horn. He then leaned over and opened the passenger-side door.

"Get in!" Morgan shouted to Kate.

Dawson slid in next to the ex-military major and could immediately tell just by the look on his face that Morgan had something, something pretty big. Major Morgan was "old school" military, but his traditionally stoic face radiated excitement.

"I've got a lot of intel that's going to interest you, Dawson," he said, pulling away from the Pier and turning into the traffic for the Bay Bridge and the East Bay.

"Great," Kate said sourly. *And just when I felt I was finally rid of Lenny*; only Morgan didn't know that. "So, whatcha got?"

"Don't rush me, sweetheart," he replied. "We have a date with a horse."

"A horse?"

Golden Gate Fields was the best horse racing track in Northern California. Straddling the cities of Albany and Berkeley, along the shoreline of San Francisco Bay, it compared favorably with its sister racecourse at Ascot, where the Royal Ascot Grand National horserace had been run every year since 1711. Golden Gate Fields attracted its own top game trainers and breeders; a whole host of wealthy, politically-connected folks and celebrity faces, fashion designers, dot.com millionaires, wine and food experts, and those rare connoisseurs of the "good life."

By the time they got there, in the late afternoon, the grounds around the grand racetrack were a wash of gentlemen in luxury suits, women in figure-hugging silk dresses and lavish accessories, and elites from nearly every walk of life. Ex-patriots from South Africa and Europe rubbed elbows with a bustling throng of the loud and proud citizens of the Bay, each one betting money on their favorite race horses on this special day, like money was being printed and handed out on the parking lot. Everyone came to Golden Gate Fields with the hope of winning a small fortune. The prime position to watch the race was on the fresh green turf, located near the horse pens, and, of course, the expensive box seats where the rich and famous held court at every race. Those placing single bets or playing only single tickets were pushed together in the bleacher section.

Upon arrival, Dawson and Morgan were assaulted by the high-pitched voice of an over-enthusiastic female, "Come on, *Dover*! Move your fuckin' ass," one woman shouted aloud from the bleacher section.

"My money's on *Jinx*!' C'mon, *Jinx*! Go! Go! Go!" a second woman exclaimed.

The two women were feverishly watching the race in their beautiful floral dresses, calling out the names of their horses, when Major Morgan escorted Kate Dawson into the bleachers section. They were each dressed rather plainly for their visit to Golden Gate Fields, carrying military-grade binoculars. They pushed past the two women, heading for the far end of the bleachers. Morgan put the binoculars up to his eyes; turned to the right, facing the crowd. Kate did what he did. Had anyone been watching them, instead of watching the race, they would have looked ridiculous, facing the wrong way. But with the size and overwhelming motion of the crowd, no one noticed. Well, almost no one noticed.

"Your boyfriend's looking the wrong way," said a blonde floozy who was smacking her gum. "The horses are over there."

"He's got a system," Kate reassured her.

"System? What *kind* of system?" Blondie was instantly alert, thinking there could be an inside scoop. "Do you see those flags flying above the box seats?" Kate said, pointing to the pennants that topped the overhang. At one point, the pennants were flapping in the wind, and in the next, they were still. "He likes to bet on horses that would benefit from an extra push from the wind." You had to admit, Kate was quick on her feet.

"Smart! Very smart!" she exclaimed, squinting her eyes, then bolted to the top of the stairs to get a better look. She put on her sunglasses and craned her neck. "Thanks!"

"What did you tell her?" Morgan asked, as Blondie waved at them excitedly. Kate's lips curled in satisfaction. "I told her about your system."

"System?" His eyebrows shot up.

"The one where we watch the flags flying above the box seats," she replied, pointing up.

Kate glanced over at Morgan, expecting to see him squirming, all ready with some clever comeback, but he stood stock still, the binoculars fastened to his face set completely in stone.

"I just hope your blonde friend doesn't come back looking for a tip on a horse because I don't know the first thing about horses or horseracing," he confessed, focused on the box seats.

Dawson perked up. "Really? I would have taken you for an expert handicapper any day of the week."

"Surveillance is my game."

Kate continued to look through her binoculars and spotted a short man in a finely-tailored, black tuxedo. "With the cane, is that Devereaux?" she asked, scanning back and forth for another suspect.

"Yes," Morgan said, adjusting his vision to find him, "that's Robert Devereaux."

Robert Devereaux was a short man, well under six feet tall, mid-forties, strikingly wavy brown hair and a handsome but pudgy face, with piercing blue eyes against a pale, almost albino complexion. He was engaged in conversation with a handful of high-society types who stood with him in his large, private box at the racetrack. He seemed to be enjoying himself, with several bottles of wine open; content to pouring for his new friends.

"Born in Bordeaux, France, he and his twin sister, Renée, were orphaned at age two when their parents died in an automobile accident," Morgan reported, revealing what he'd learned yet never taking his eyes off him. "They were taken in for several years by a senile old aunt who lived in Paris but found themselves in the French foster care system where the courts continually sought to separate them. Madly infatuated with each other—not simply as brother and sister—claiming to have developed a strong psychic bond while growing up apart; they always knew when the other was in some kind of trouble. They became 'bad seed' orphans who murdered or terrorized their way out of foster care. They fled to Dresden, Germany, at age ten and fell under the influence of the Roma, where the two of them learned how to lie, cheat, steal, and intimidate others, mostly tourists, throughout the region. Robert eventually rose to command one of the largest crime syndicates in Europe, with his sister right at his side."

"The old rags-to-riches story," Kate interjected, with some degree of cynicism. "We've had our dealings with the Roma or 'gypsies' for years in Southern California. Those who are involved in criminal activity live mostly in the shadows, running petty scams up and down the coast, mostly on tourists who don't have much recourse to stop them. I do think it's kind of rare for the Roma to trust anyone who's not a 'gypsy' or 'traveler,' like themselves."

Morgan nodded in agreement. "I doubt they shall do so again, though," he said. "Robert and René Devereaux made a lot of money for the Roma when they were two runaways just looking to get by. But when Robert took over, he became very ruthless and also paranoid. He killed off most of the senior-level bosses, fearing they were out to get him, and put his own men in place but soon began to fear his own men. So, after he made his first score for the Roma, smuggling more than a billion dollars in cocaine into Eastern Europe, he and his sister escaped to America with thirty million of their dollars in gold. Here, they built their own empire. They used half of the stolen money to take over the drug trade they'd built in Europe and used the other half to blackmail several small countries in Africa into selling them munitions. They parlayed those first munitions sales into a world-wide munitions and drug empire that brings in fifty million a month. With that kind of income and fast living, you'd think they'd be fairly content."

"Live fast, die young, and leave a good-looking corpse behind," Kate remarked. "I know the philosophy all too well."

"They are both geniuses to the point of being insane. Robert is a manic-depressive who uses drugs to modulate his behavior, and Renée is a sex addict who sleeps with her brother and many, many other men. The siblings live an opulent lifestyle, spending money like there is no tomorrow," the major concluded. "I'm surprised that none of the U.S. government's law enforcement agencies have been able to close them down."

Morgan shook his head. "Both the FBI and the Justice Department have ongoing investigations, but there's simply not enough evidence. You have to remember that they are both very, very smart. In the last two years, for instance, we know they've laundered millions of dollars through a failing winery located on the southeast tip of San Francisco, but we haven't been able to prove it. They operate legitimate vineyards, bottle and ship their own wine, serve it at events like this, and pay their federal and local taxes. But like most shell corporations, there's no way the Devereaux winery makes the kind of money they claim it does."

Dawson continued to monitor their box with binoculars.

"Who's that with him under the hat? Is that Renée?" Kate shouted above the noise as the horses behind her entered the next-to-the-last lap; the excitement of the crowd reaching its crescendo. Morgan turned his attention to the reserved section as a strikingly beautiful, petite brunette strolled into the box seat and moved next to Robert Devereaux. "That's Renée. She's never far from him," he replied, pointing at her. "French passport and speaks at least five languages, no accent."

Dressed in a bright, floral-patterned dress from Hubert de Givenchy, with a stylish, cream-collared hat and black sunglasses, Renée Devereaux looked like a runway model who had just escaped fashion week in Paris. Her skin had a deeper, richer complexion than her brother, clearly highlighting her glamorous, movie star features. Her eyes were blue, much like Robert's; lips full and red; cheekbones plumed-up with blusher to stand out. She was clearly the most beautiful woman in the section, if not for all of Golden Gate Fields.

"I can see why your friend was attracted to her. She's a real looker."

"You mean, she's a real mankiller," Kate whispered, eyebrow raised slightly.

"Whatever. Anyway, it's nice to finally see her in person," Morgan said. "The photos I got from Interpol and the Deuxieme Bureau really didn't do her the kind of justice she deserves. She's a beautiful woman."

"What's the chance of my getting a face to face with her?"

"None," Morgan said flatly. "She's too well guarded. They both are. Besides, we don't want to tip our hand." Kate guffawed. "You don't think they know they're under investigation."

"Oh, I'm sure they know they're being watched, but I see no reason to poke a hornet's nest if we don't have to."

"You got something else in mind?"

"Absolutely," said Morgan, with a smile.

"*Magnificent Fury* has come from nowhere as they race for the line!" shouted the announcer over the loud speaker, stirring up the crowd in the final, few moments of the race. Kate and Morgan lowered their binoculars and turned to the finish line as the crowd of people around them climbed to their feet, excited, happy, cheering on the horses on the final furlong.

The woman next to Morgan gripped his arm as she waved her ticket in the air. "C'mon, *Dirt Devil!*" she cried.

All eyes were on the thundering hooves of the horses as they galloped by the bleacher seats in a fury towards the finish line.

"And as they cross the line, it's *Magnificent Fury* way clear of *Stud Finder* and *Saratoga*! First Number One, Second Number Two and Third Number Five!" called the announcer excitedly at the finish.

The wail of applause and the cry of dismay were familiar sounds to those patrons who regularly attended horseracing tracks around the world; no different in tone or texture between Golden Gate Fields or Ascot. A million hopes and dreams had been made and lost in those last few seconds of the race. The woman cheering for Dirt Devil wasted no time in tearing up her ticket, dropping the shards to the floor and giving the final group of horses a bitter look, much to Major Morgan's hidden amusement. Blondie, who had been smacking her gum earlier, walked by them, shaking her head sadly. She had been crying. Her teary eyes met Kate's eyes as she shrugged her shoulders, making her way towards the exit.

"Oh, ma'am?" Kate asked, as she momentarily reached into her pocket, then bent over and pantomimed picking up a ticket from the bleacher steps. "I think you may have dropped this on the steps."

Blondie opened the ticket, and her mouth dropped. "*Magnificent Fury!*" she said with astonishment. "It looks like you're a winner," Dawson said. "Congratulations!"

"I won!" the woman shouted, holding up her ticket. "I won!"

"Softie," Morgan whispered to Kate.

"Do you have any idea how much time and paperwork that winning ticket would have cost me?" she replied, smiling.

As Kate and Morgan exited the bleacher section, they were joined by an older man in his mid-sixties, dressed for the occasion in a formal suit with a rounded face and a cheery smile, tipping his hat to them for their return.

"It's unbelievable," the man sighed. "In all my thirty-five years coming to Golden Gate Fields, I've never seen a horse run such a fast, last furlong. Magnificent Fury could be the next Triple Crown winner." Kate Dawson turned to face him as she extended her hand. "Mr. Norman Gertsen," Morgan introduced Kate who took note of the man's powerful handshake. "He does an occasional job for us. In real life, though, Norm owns a chain of convenience stores in Northern California and Nevada."

"One hundred thirty-three stores, to be exact," Gertsen said cheerfully.

"Wait a minute," Kate replied, as she thought about the name. "I know you. You're 'Storm'n Norm'n.' I stop in your convenience stores all the time to buy coffee and donuts."

"'Storm right in and get everything you need from Norman,'" Gertsen recited the corporate jingle from his stores. Dawson bobbed her head in recognition. "You're famous."

"Thank you," he replied humbly.

"We've asked Norm if we could use his convenience store empire as a cover to infiltrate a couple of operatives into one of Devereaux's corporate events, and he has agreed to help us out," Morgan explained, as they all walked slowly, through the throng of packed people, towards the parking lot. "Robert and Renée Devereaux hold a semi-annual, three-day wine tasting event at their estate on Hunter's Point for some of their richest friends and invite local business owners to sample their wine and beer with the hope of attracting new business partners. Of course, it's all for show because they could care less about selling wine, but the show keeps the bean counters at the FBI and Justice happy."

"They invite me every year, but I've always been busy with other things," Norm added his two cents to the conversation.

Morgan rubbed his hands together, in anticipation. "This year, however, Norm is going to announce his retirement and tell his stockholders that his niece is going to be taking over the business."

"Her description tactfully adjusted to favor me," Kate replied, amused. "Exactly," Morgan replied, glad to have her aboard. "When?"

"Next weekend."

The grand Albion Castle at Hunter's Point, thirteen miles southeast of San Francisco, was where Robert Devereaux and his sister Renée had chosen to host the wine tasting and auction of their latest offering of featured and reserved wines and was the perfect place for the rich and the famous to gather and celebrate their good fortune. Built in 1870 by John Hamlin Burnell, a young English immigrant with plans to create a large brewery to supply the eight hundred saloons that had sprung up all around the city. Beer was a popular beverage among the working class of San Francisco, with several local breweries already competing for business, but Burnell's new property had a secret advantage: an underground aquifer that provided pure cold water, perfect for brewing. He built himself not only the workspaces for the Albion Porter & Ale Brewery, but also a castle home, modeled after the Norman fortifications Burnell loved back home, with a distinctive six-story tower built from stones taken from the ballast of several cargo ships. Under the castle, Burnell dug out two stone cisterns, each capturing eight to ten thousand gallons of spring water each day. The two hundred-foot pools were accessed by a cave entrance and a network of tunnels, which connected back to the house, and still, to this day, provide fresh, clean drinking water. Albion Castle was surrounded by hundreds of acres of land that were later converted into vineyards.

The property changed hands several times over the years, and also changed purposes. During Prohibition, the brewery was forced to close down, but it was soon reborn as the Albion Water Company, providing bottled drinking water from its underground cisterns. In 1935, they started harvesting grapes, producing wine in several delightful vintages. In 1938, the castle was bought by Sculptor Adrian Voisin who remodeled the living space, adding much of the beautiful woodworking and medieval-inspired interior that makes Albion Castle look like a grand French Château today. He lived and worked there for some twenty years and spent thousands of dollars on the many exquisite treasures and furnishings brought from Europe and are still on display and in use even to this day. In 1961, the castle nearly fell victim to a highway construction scheme that planned to bulldoze the building and pave over the vineyards, but the property was saved by "green party" activists who argued the fresh water source under the building could be the only noncontaminated source of fresh water in the event of a nuclear attack.

In 1998, the property was sold again to another artist, this time sculptor Eric Higgs, also known as one of the founders of CitySearch. Higgs added a number of unique touches of his own to the property. Until 2005, the castle and vineyards were used as a residence, art studio, B&B, and occasional party location, then it was sold at auction for $2.1 million dollars to Robert and Renée Devereaux who decided to sell their own vintage of wine. Their semi-annual, invitation-only, wine tasting weekends were the talk of the town in San Francisco, Monterey, Oakland, and the rest of Northern California, and attracted mostly the rich and famous.

At the furthest edge of her world, Kate Dawson traded her BMW for a Lincoln Town Car and driver, her fondness for Starbucks coffee and sticky buns for champagne and caviar, her counterfeit-label clothes and jewelry for real couture from Givenchy and Marc Jacobs, and her identity as a Homicide inspector for Angeline Gertsen, the new CEO of all the 'Storm'n Norm'n' convenience stores. In fact, when she stepped out of Sebastian's newly opened shop in Soma, the makeover made Kate look and feel like Audrey Hepburn's "duchess" from *My Fair Lady*. A completely different woman, she was honestly surprised when a man crossed the street to not only get a better look at her but also to ask for her number. Kate Dawson also felt better about herself, and for the first time in a long while, she felt like a woman and not just a female detective. She imagined that there was actually a real man out there with a heart of gold who wanted to share his life with her, unlike the dozens of rejects she had met over the years. Was it too much for her to hope that there was a charming prince waiting for her; modern Cinderella at the grand ball?

Kate Dawson sat dozing in the back of the Lincoln Town Car as Alex Starke, dressed like a chauffeur in a dark grey uniform, directed the gleaming black limousine up onto I-280 at Mission Bay, taking the long way around Potrero Hill to avoid the heavier traffic and flooding that was commonplace. A giant, sixteen-wheeler zoomed by them at breakneck speeds and threw up a great wall of debris and water, which nearly engulfed the limo. For a moment, Starke thought they may have missed their exit as the entire windshield was covered in dirty water. She slowed, not able to see a thing and turned the windshield wipers on fast. Gradually, the water slung away the road filth and visibility cleared.

The rain was still coming down hard when traffic started backing up through the interchange for the UCSF Medical Center at Mission Bay; crawling at twenty-five mile-an-hour crawl through Dogpatch. Starke could see the train yards that stretched all the way back to AT&T Park and watched as individual trains, with only a few boxcars, moved at their own pace through the storm. She picked up speed through the Central Waterfront area, then made the turn into Hunter's Point just past Cesar Chavez Street. The only sound she heard was the rain tapering off lightly on the roof as she drove up the mile-long drive surrounded by artistically trimmed bushes, marble statues, and the odd horse grazing out in the open. Then the storm clouds gave way to blue skies; another perfect morning dawning, dotted by small wispy clouds; an Eastern sunrise shining brightly over the vineyards that stretched for miles.

Like out of a dream, the grand Albion Castle loomed over Hunter's Point. If not for the long, black limousine and the paved road, Kate Dawson could have easily imagined a scene from Europe in the Middle-Ages with armored knights on horseback, riding to their fair ladies in the field. As they drew closer, the beautiful daydream faded from view.

"Dawson, we should be there in a couple of minutes," Starke reported, glancing in the rearview mirror. She could see Kate stretching her arms and legs in the back seat.

"Do you remember the plan?" Kate asked, adjusting her dress and fussing with her hair. Although she could be a model, she rarely had to dress up.

"Of course, I do," Starke answered, a bit perturbed. "We've been over it a hundred times. How could I forget?"

"I know, I know, but a lot can go wrong. We've got to be prepared to improvise."

Starke's eyes narrowed in the rearview mirror. "Sometime

after the formal reception and dinner tonight, I'll slip away from the others and make my way down to the grotto where the two large cisterns are. If I run into any of the staff, my story is that I was looking for the ladies' room and got turned around. Otherwise, I'm not to take any provocative action."

"Exactly," Kate confirmed. "Document as much as you can of the underground, including rooms and storage compartments, which could be used to store drugs and munitions. We know that there's a maze of tunnels down there—some dating back to the 1920s and Prohibition—but no one that we know of has been down there in nearly a hundred years. So, you're going to have to move fast if you want to cover a lot of ground before you're missed by anyone."

"Don't worry," she said, defensively. "I know what I'm doing."

There was no other way, so Kate had to hope she did. "I'll be looking for the office and any records or computer files that I can get my hands on. We need to find something, anything that ties the Devereaux's to drugs or arms smuggling. I also want to find out what she was doing with Lenny's satellite system."

"We may not get another shot at this," Starke reminded Dawson. "Yeah, and just remember we can't count on the Bureau for back-up," Dawson reminded Starke, with a thin smile. "There are no cell towers out this far. Our phones are going to be inoperative."

"I've got your back, boss," she said, reassuringly.

"And I've got yours, Alex."

Once they passed through the final gate and onto the approach concourse outside the castle, Kate could see two figures waiting patiently behind a small table by the front steps leading up to the wide-open door. The rest of the arrival area was a flurry of activity, as porters and other servants carried numerous pieces of luggage from cars parked at the front, while members of the household staff, including butlers and under-butlers, supplied new arrivals with refreshments, in the form of wine and beer. Starke circled the driveway around a small fountain and pulled up in front of the check-in party as the small graveled stones crunched under the weight of the limousine's tires. Starke killed the engine, then got out of the car and walked slowly but deliberately to the rear where she opened the door for her mistress. Just as soon as Kate Dawson stepped out of the limousine, she straightened up and looked around in delight. A small Chinese woman, dressed in what appeared to be traditional wear, walked up to Kate with a small card, bowing slightly to both her and Starke, whilst trying to decipher the name engraved on the formal card.

"Madame 'An-Gee-line Gert-son'?" she asked, politely.

"Angeline Gertsen, my dear," Kate corrected her, with a cheery smile.

The woman nodded politely and started back inside. She passed another small Chinese woman, dressed almost identically, standing outside the large main door with a well-dressed man at her side.

As Kate entered the foyer, a tall man sauntered down the stairs to greet them with no apparent urgency. He had wavy black hair, grey-green eyes, and an impeccably polished set of white teeth. But the moment Dawson noticed the small scar on his left cheek under the eye socket, she didn't see any else. It absolutely transfixed her. For the romantic in her, she liked to imagine he won it in a duel over a pretty woman, or maybe it happened in a racing accident, driving Formula 1 racecars through the streets of Monaco, or maybe he was a gypsy who had squared off against a rival gang in a knife fight? He held out his strong hand as he walked towards Kate, taking hers into his. Rather than shaking her hands American style, he appeared to kiss the air just above it, as if she was European royalty. He seemed very charming and unusually formal.

"My name is Damien LaMarca, head of security."

Kate Dawson smiled demurely. *That explains the scar.* "How do you do, Mr. LaMarca?"

"Damien, please," he replied, with a smile of his own.

"Damien, as you wish," she repeated his first name. "We have a room for you at the Château."

"Oh, splendid," smiled Kate, glancing around at the gorgeous surroundings.

"By the way, the preview is already in progress," he remarked, cordially. "We are offering several vintage wines that date back to the founding of the winery in 1870 by John Hamlin Burnell. The prices are actually quite reasonable and would make excellent investment properties for you."

"Oh, is that right?" she asked innocently, putting on the charm, playing the part.

"We also have a century-old Bordeaux and several reserve wines that I think will please your palate. They have all been well-received in Europe by some of the best families."

"What better praise can there be, truly?"

"Let me escort you there." Damien led with his arm, in the direction of a large, breathtaking building that was, by comparison to the Château, little more than a country annex.

Dawson looked over her shoulder, acknowledging Starke who simply waited by the car, busying herself with the remainder of the luggage. Kate followed Damien across the drive to the grand and decorous annex. Walking along the gravel track, they passed through the open archway into the main courtyard where a dozen or so stages had been temporarily erected, each designed and built to showcase a different assortment of wines and beverages. The annex itself was a grand design, covered by

Middle-Aged carvings, brickwork, and sculptures. Makeshift lights, giving off a warm, comforting glow, had been fitted and installed around the main court. The grounds were covered with dry hay and sweet fruit, which produced a rich, pleasant smell to Kate's senses. A number of other buyers, wine tasters, and pundits were walking around sampling the wine and chatting with experts about the quality of the vintage. No doubt they had been hired by the Devereaux's to close the deal.

Damien picked up a thick catalogue from a tray, placed on one of a number of wooden tables around the court.

"Catalogue of the sales," he announced, handing it to Kate.

"Thank you," she replied, feigning interest, perusing the beautifully produced catalogue. "Tell me, Damien, is that century-old Bordeaux you mentioned in here?"

"Yes, as a matter of fact, it is." Damien pointed to a page in the catalogue, indicating the very rare wine. "It's one of the outstanding items in the auction and will be among the last shown. We expect the bottle to fetch over $100,000. A similar vintage sold at auction in 1985 for $156,000. It was the most expensive bottle of wine ever sold at auction, and our Bordeaux is comparable."

"A hundred thousand dollars?" Kate gasped.

Damien extremely accommodating to the beautiful woman, asked, "Would you like me to see if there are any samples left from today's preview?"

"Oh, no. I think I can manage. Thank you," she said sweetly, turning the page in the catalogue. It was then she began following a couple of the other buyers, from stage to stage, pretending to note each different wine as she went past to the information in the catalogue.

"If you need further assistance, please call me," he said, mere inches behind her.

"Thank you, Damien. I appreciate your attentiveness," she said without a backwards glance.

Kate Dawson made a full circle around the wines that were on display, sampling one or two of them, enough as to establish her identity as a buyer. She said "hello" and exchanged brief words with a couple of the other buyers and listened intently to several of the wine connoisseurs as they spoke with authority about the brand. Kate confirmed her suspicion from earlier: the experts had been hired to render very positive testimony about the wine, beer, and other beverages, and the other buyers were retailers from the San Francisco Bay area.

By the time she returned to the front of Albion Castle, and the entrance to the Château, Damien LaMarca was busy helping other guests. He paused briefly to deliver a short and simple message to her, "Madame Gertsen, the Devereaux's have been regrettably detained. However, they did want me to express how anxious they are to meet you at the reception in the Château gardens later, at seven."

"I look forward it," Dawson said, making sure she caught his eye. She spotted Starke returning from a trip to deliver luggage to the room, and snarled at her chauffeur, "I do wish you'd hurry with that luggage. You always manage to keep me waiting."

"I'm sorry, Madame," Starke replied, playing along with masquerade.

"Your driver may stay in the servants' quarters," Damien proffered, watching them, perhaps a bit too closely.

Kate turned to Alex Starke, now holding the last of her three bags, "I'm sure that will be more than adequate. What do you say, Alex?"

"Thank you, Madame."

"Good. Whenever you're ready, Alex."

Inside the Château, the history and grand scale of the

aristocracy was evident in every turn and in every room. The light, egg-shell blue carpet covered the floor with a soft touch, complimenting the sandy brickwork and marble finishing of the walls and high ceilings. The hall was awash with antique furnishings, famous paintings and jewel-encrusted chandeliers and light fittings. A large mirror hung on the far wall making the hall appear even larger than it was. Two large staircases with plush burgundy carpeting led up, curving one to the left and one to the right, leading guests and dignitaries to other areas of the six-story castle building.

As Kate Dawson passed by one of the windows, she peered out and saw that a number of the house servants were busying themselves out in the gardens, preparing tables and erecting small marquees outside for the reception. Two porters were carrying a large decorative brass sculpture from the grounds through to the garden; a positively gaudy piece. She continued up the set of stairs to the right with Alex struggling up behind, still carrying the three pieces of luggage. Her face was all flustered and rosy red; sweat forming on her brow. Starke, a good sport, muscled through the role.

Kate listened as Starke directed them down a long corridor lined with expensive golden pillars and mirrors. Smaller hallways lead off in both directions, further into the heart of the Château. It really was a grand building. Eventually, they came to an ivory door and opened it with no effort, despite the door looking heavy. Dawson strolled inside, as if she did this kind of thing every day and was greeted by a luxurious view over the front of the Château thanks to a large, open French window leading out to a stone balcony. A cream sofa was situated in the room across from an oak table displaying a selection of reading material. The large, four-poster bed took center stage at the rear of the room dressed in real silk drapes. A couple of arm chairs rested in the corner along with a large wardrobe and drawer space. An open fireplace lay dormant in front of the sofa. Starke, close behind, set the bags at the door. The rest had been stacked near the dresser.

Before Dawson said another word aloud, she raised a finger to her lips, indicating the possibility that the room could be bugged. The two of them looked around the room quickly, quietly, starting with the most obvious places where a wireless, miniature microphone could be hidden or concealed. They checked under the ornaments and around the bed, even in the complimentary fruit bowl by the window. A common listening device could actually be hidden anywhere to monitor the room, and it was biggest concern Kate had. One wrong word could result in their covers being compromised and the mission being canceled. Dawson wished she had a tracking device for bugs and imagined, if she had asked Shears, he would have provided her with one, but hindsight was always twenty-twenty.

They continued to diligently search the room. Starke was the one who came up with something in the bedside lamp. She motioned to Kate who, in turn, inspected the lamp. There it was, a small mic planted directly in the middle of the lamp above the light bulb; as small as a thumbnail and easy to overlook as an integral part of the lamp. But to the trained eye, unmistakable.

"Well, don't just stand there, Alex," ordered Kate, "start unpacking!"

"Yes, Madame!" Starke jumped to it.

"You heard what Mr. LaMarca said. There is a reception at seven," Kate said, loud enough for everyone to hear. "I will need the Marc Jacobs gown and the black beaded shoes."

"Yes, Madame." Starke played along, handing Kate a designer cosmetics bag by Henri Bendel she had purchased at Neiman Marcus.

Dawson took the bag from her assistant and set the medium-sized case down on the bed next to her. It seemed unusually heavy. She removed a handful of luxury beauty products, from foundation to lipstick, and placed them strategically around the his-and-hers sink in the bathroom. She even removed an old eye shadow-caked canvas bag, which never seemed to come clean no matter how many times Kate washed it, from deep within. She then unsnapped a series of hidden snaps from the bag's frilly leather base. Especially-made for her by one of Shears' men, based on designs stolen from MI-6, her cosmetics case hid a false bottom where she often carried her Beretta and several rounds of ammunition for undercover assignments. She retrieved her service pistol and a fresh clip from the hidden compartment, and handed Starke's Glock-19 off to her partner. Now, they were both ready for action.

On the ground level, inside a small security office located on the other side of the castle, away from the state rooms, Damien stood in silence with a young man who was wearing headphones. The young man was wired up to the latest in observational and surveillance security equipment. A dozen or so small monitors were linked up in front of him overlooking all secure areas of the Château. Numerous digital discs and recorders were linked up to one large computer. Dutifully, Damien checked the monitors for any unusual activity, clicking through several images like an impatient television watcher with a remote control, while the young man who was listening to a recorder on his large headphones, started jotting down information on his pad. "Mr. LaMarca," the young man said, interrupting Damien's concentration. "Mr. Johnston in Room 914 has confirmed with his broker that he'll go to a hundred thousand for the century-old Bordeaux."

"Good," said Damien. "Anything from Gertsen?"

"Nothing about the sale, sir," the operator reported. "Mostly gibberish about women's cosmetics and shoes. Yuck!"

Damien LaMarca smiled thinly. "Keep on it."

The string ensemble in the Château Gardens played a light but pleasing melody of continental and classical music on harps, violins, and cellos. Wait staff moved gracefully around the exquisite grounds, serving mostly wine and beer and a few appetizers to those rich and famous patrons. At every turn, Kate Dawson could see Robert Devereaux in conversation with a rich oil sheikh or industrial giant, while Renée Devereaux, who was always close at hand, spoke with film celebrities or well-known entrepreneurs. The conversations were not very deep; seemed mostly for show.

Kate kept her distance, surveying the whole proceedings discreetly, lest she blow her cover. She went by the bar, and noticed the bartender was only serving drinks, from nonalcoholic cocktails to rich sparkling champagne and the finest Ports and wines, from the Devereaux brand. They were really pushing the company brand, lending a great deal of legitimacy to the wine tasting and auction.

She admired the golden silk drapes hanging across the gardens; a large, soft lattice, crisscrossing the paths. She strolled under it to a large walkway by the waterfront of the Château's lake, which had been erected to provide a romantic, breathtaking amble tended by eager butlers who waited only to provide their guests with the best.

Dawson rounded the corner and nearly ran into Robert Devereaux arguing with a stunning, African-American woman dressed in a light tan blouse, cream-colored jacket, and a skirt that rested just above her knees. The clothes were Versace, but Kate recognized them as counterfeit. The woman's hair fell to her shoulders, very thick and shiny, but Kate had seen enough extensions in her life to know the hair was also fake. Even the small handbag she carried under her arm, with the large Fendi logo, was an imitation. Kate faded back, pretending to listen to the string ensemble, but continued observing the woman from her peripheral vision. She was as much of a fake as Kate, and at the event for reasons of her own.

Kate tuned into the argument, picking up key words: "husband" several times, "soldier" once or twice, "combat mission," "died," "loyal member of the team," and "cash settlement," among many. From what Kate Dawson was able to piece together, the woman's husband had died during a mission and she was expecting compensation from Devereaux. *No, it has to be more than that.* Kate's thought processes went into overdrive, constructing a scenario much deeper than she had originally imagined. This woman's husband had stolen a cache of weapons for Devereaux during his final tour of duty in Iraq or Afghanistan and died before he could collect. She was there to shake him down or go to the police with what she knew.

"Son-of-a-bitch," Dawson breathed quietly, though she wasn't really surprised. "Mrs. Fake" was now very much a person of interest in Kate's investigation.

Dawson scrambled to catch up as nonchalantly as possible. Devereaux had her under the arm, leading her forcibly down the walkway. As his pace increased, his grip did also; she seemed to be dragged, not escorted. All discussion between the two of them had ceased and, for all intents and purposes, "Mrs. Fake" appeared to be headed to the Château under house arrest.

As the two of them passed near the bar, a very large, burly man with a mustache stumbled into their path. Dressed very casually in a checkered jacket, open Western shirt, and Levi jeans, displaying a gold, blingy pinky ring, he appeared to be drunk but was only drinking beer. Devereaux tried to steer "Mrs. Fake" clear from talking to him, but his large frame blocked them from moving forward. Kate Dawson seized the chance to slide onto one of the barstools.

"Mr. Devereaux," the man shouted, in a Southern drawl, "Squeeze Play all set?"

Robert Devereaux froze in his footsteps. For a few heartbeats, his face flushed but he didn't move. Then he sheepishly looked around at his other guests, and said, "We'll know more at the end of the month. Now, enjoy yourself. I think you'll find the young ladies make stimulating company."

Devereaux shot him a killer look to end the conversation, and escorted "Mrs. Fake" into a large conservatory area, shut off from the rest gardens.

Kate climbed off her barstool and was about to follow when the rude man turned back around to the bar, slammed his beer mug on the counter, and shouted, "*Beer*tender, get me another beer!"

"'Tex,' don't you think you've had enough?" Damien asked, as he emerged from behind a small congregation of guests.

"I'll be the judge of that!" he exclaimed. Kate never cared much for men who couldn't handle their liquor, and even less for loud, obnoxious drunks. She eyed him with disgust, but a split second later, she scrutinized his features. *I've seen his face before. Yes, but where?*

Damien stepped over to him and put his arm around the man's shoulder. "'Tex,' why don't you let me order you some coffee?"

"I want another beer!" he demanded, pounding the edge of the bar, very drunk, out of control. "Who the hell do I have to kill to get another beer?"

Acting quickly, Damien reached for a pressure point at

the base of the man's neck, known as the subclavian artery, and pressed down. The pinch—an ancient martial arts technique—blocked blood and nerve responses from reaching the brain, leading to unconsciousness. The security chief not only subdued the potentially violent man but put him out for the rest of the night.

That's it! James "Tex" Denton, Major, Ranger Division! Dawson remembered seeing his face among the photos that Shears had shared with her and Starke and what she read in his dossier. *He's one of the five members of Task Force Red.* Now everything was starting to come together. The two cases that she had been investigating separately were now one: Task Force Red stole the munitions, including several large caches of military-grade weapons, ammunition, equipment, and stores, that Robert and Renée Devereaux then, in turn, sold on the black market to rogue countries and terrorist organizations. In fact, Kate was even willing to go out on a limb and say the Devereaux's had purchased the raw heroine that put Task Force Red into business in the first place.

"Enjoying our little party, Madame Gertsen?" Damien asked, as he and his men cleaned up the mess.

Kate cleared her throat. "Immensely, Mr. LaMarca. Quite a party." She indicated the embarrassment with her head, then spun about and headed towards the conservatory. He turned to watch her with suspicion, then cautiously moved away.

Alex Starke waited for the cover of night to slip away from the other chauffeurs, valets, and servants. Dressed in a black jacket, a black turtleneck, and slacks, she quickly crossed the grounds, and waited near the Lincoln Town Car to proceed. She could hear the reception near the Château was still in full swing and made a conscious note to maintain her distance so that she wouldn't run into Kate or one of the other guests. It was quiet on the grounds, except for the creatures of the night in the vineyards—chirping insects, intermittently hooting owls, and the occasional whinnying of the horses in the stables—a relaxing ambience. She waited to see if security had dispatched any guards to patrol the grounds. After a few moments, Starke realized that she was pretty much on her own.

She crossed the makeshift parking lot to the horse stables and crept down the isle of stalls. Based upon intel provided by Shears, there were two entrances to the underground maze leading to the grotto and the two large cisterns: one in Albion Castle, the other at the back of the stables. Starke figured the one inside the main house was heavily guarded or otherwise secured. Her best bet was through the stables. The hay smelled fresh and the cobbled floor was clean, obviously swept and washed each night. A couple of horses were grazing from their pens into feeding bags, but they paid her no attention. Starke approached the back of the stables and stood by the last pen where there had to be some kind of switch or lever to open a secret door.

Starke slowly unbolted the door, hoping it would not creak, to the last stall from inside, swung the door open and stepped in. The wooden floor creaked under her feet, but there was still nothing apparent to Starke that caught her eye or aroused suspicion. Fresh hay in the corner and a feeding bag nailed to the wall suggested the pen had been recently used. It was then a large wooden box along the rear wall, scattered with more hay and grass, caught her eye.

No, can't be. A glimmer of steel.

Kneeling down to inspect what looked like sheet metal underneath the hay, Starke was so focused that she didn't register the tall figure in the shadows. Standing up slowly, still searching and oblivious, the figure charged her. Seeing him just in time, Starke side-stepped him. As he passed, she struck him in the back of the neck with a karate chop, and he went down hard. A black belt in martial arts, she learned to protect herself in close quarters while in the Israeli Army. She bent down to look at her attacker and discovered he was nothing more than an ostler. Following procedure, she patted him down for weapons, then she tied him up, gagged him, and left him in one of the stalls.

Starke ran her eyes and hands along the wall for the mechanism that operated the lift. At the back of the stall, almost to the floor, she found an indented black box with several levers. Pulling on one of them, she heard the sharp whine of motors as a section of the floor began to descend slowly. She released it and peered down the dark hole at a metal double door. Climbing down the elevator shaft and out onto the floor, she wedged her fingers and pulled hard, easing open one of the doors.

Pitch black. Patting her hands along the wall, she found the light switch but chose not to use it. Starke's vision began to adjust and she concentrated on all that was around her. The room smelled like a Medical Examiner's autopsy lab. Dozens of gleaming metal cabinets and large metal tables with various loose instruments and bottles came into view. *Ah, this is an operating theater built specifically for Devereaux's horses.* Horses from the stables above were transported down into the hospital to be operated on. *This certainly keeps nosy visitors from the racetrack at bay. And if a wounded soldier was brought in from the battlefield by one of their buddies to be patched up, the outside world would also never know.*

Starke headed straight to the opposite end of the room to another door. Listening behind and through the door, she waited several heartbeats, then turned the knob to find the tunnel.

Dark and narrow, off to the left, it seemed to climb towards the surface and the guest rooms at the Château; to the right, the tunnel was all downhill. She followed the tunnel down, deeper and deeper, into the earth.

By the time Kate Dawson reached the conservatory, night had settled in. She crept by two lovers who were leaning up against one of the trees, making out, and snuck around the side to the gardens. The only light was coming through the blinds of a small office. All of the other rooms were dark. Kate sidled up to the side of the building and cupped her hands against the window and her eyes. There sat Devereaux and "Mrs. Fake."

Dawson watched Robert Devereaux scribble his name on a check and tear it out of its book, said something to "Mrs. Fake," and handed it over. She replied something Kate couldn't make out and smoothly slid it inside her handbag. They both stood, shook hands, and readied to leave. Kate slipped around the corner and crouched down, watching them walk away.

As a handful of guests approached, strolling through the gardens, Kate got back to her feet and acknowledged them, pretending to be out taking a leisurely stroll herself. She'd stop occasionally, run her fingernails through her hair and fluff it back, and take deep breaths, drinking in the intoxicating smells of the garden. Once they were out of sight, she placed her hand on the brass handle and snuck inside the small office.

The room was a dark chestnut with few furnishings but had plenty of wealth and taste on display. A few small tables dotted the room, each with a small flower or decorative bust. The desk on the near wall was small yet covered in files, a modern computer system, and a number of small books. Two large paintings of the Devereaux siblings, in Renaissance period costumes, posing outside their estate gate, hung on opposite walls behind the desk. Amongst other things, a lamp made of gold and a figurine of a medieval knight on horseback were on display. Two of the bookshelves, which flanked either side of the office, were filled with expensive, leather-bound books. Two plush, leather chairs, upholstered in dark burgundy, had been placed facing them. The threat of someone coming back was minimal but not impossible, so Kate wasted little time.

Peering quickly over her shoulder, she beelined for the desk Devereaux had sat behind just minutes earlier and opened the drawers, searching for the checkbook. Her hands traced over the various papers and clippings before finding it, emblazoned with the Devereaux Wineries logo, in the bottom drawer. Opening the book to the last blank check, she found no notation of the amount nor the name of the person to whom the check was written. Combing the top of the desk for a pencil and a blank sheet of paper, she found both, wanting to create a rubbing of the check. With the pencil at a twenty-degree angle, she lightly rubbed the white piece of paper over the top of the check to make a manual scan of what had been written. The imprint from Devereaux's writing left a fresh, clear image of the check— $1,000,000 made out to Sierra Jefferson.

Jefferson? Another familiar name. Wheels turning, it came to her in a flash. Like Tex, she had heard the name Jefferson during Shears' briefing. *Herbert T. Jefferson, Lieutenant, Special Forces, the third member of Task Force Red. Was he dead now? Was "Mrs. Fake" the grieving widow come to collect?*

Kate Dawson placed the checkbook exactly the way she found it, folded the etching and stuffed it in her bra, then guardedly retraced her steps out of the office.

Near the bottom of the tunnel, Starke began hearing the distinctive sounds of automation. At first muted, but as she approached the end, they became louder, nosier, more threatening. *Smoke? Burning diesel fuel!* She covered her mouth with a dark handkerchief to keep from gagging. The ground beneath her shuddered and she braced herself. Advancing towards the bottom, the steady sound of thudding machinery far below kept repeating itself over and over again. Instinctively and silently, she opened the next door in her path. Moving through a small archway, the sounds and smell of machinery drew her into a large warehouse located hundreds of feet beneath the grounds. Sensing movement, Starke crouched down and flattered herself against the wall, her Glock-19 in hand.

Two men with rifles paced across the warehouse floor, carrying flashlights to illuminate their path. Dressed in brown coveralls, much like factory workers or longshoremen, they looked more like caretakers for the estate; one big and well-built and the other small and wirey. Not finding anything, they continued their patrol.

Once they'd passed, Starke returned her pistol to its ankle-holster and slipped deeper into the warehouse. Dozens upon dozens of wooden crates were stacked high on shelves, standing a good twenty feet high, nearly to the ceiling, each one emblazoned with Devereaux Winery on the sides and top. *Hard to believe each crate holds a dozen or more wine bottles in thick layers of padding. Maybe a couple of dozen crates, but not several hundred to a thousand crates.* She spotted a conveyor belt carrying a dozen wooden crates on it and followed it out to a dry dock carved out of the cavern stone. When voices were heard echoing down the corridor, she ducked under the conveyor belt; listening, waiting, watching.

About to step into the courtyard from the gardens, Dawson nearly bumped into the two lovers who had been making out. They were holding hands as they scurried along the path, desperately not wanting to be seen. Kate let them pass without acknowledgement, then continued her evening stroll nonchalantly around the gardens, taking in the beautiful night air.

"You were looking for something?" Damien asked firmly, with a slight smile, as he emerged from the shadows.

"A full moon," Kate sighed wistfully, "and a handsome prince."

LaMarca adjusted his black tie, and said, "Perhaps you'll permit me to escort you through our gardens?"

"That would be lovely—"

Suddenly, Robert Devereaux came out of nowhere, and stood between his security chief and Kate, with a cold killer's stare. Devereaux's eyes seemed to burn right through her, like a great x-ray machine, revealing every flaw and defect just below the surface. Dawson felt the intense heat as it radiated over her body. She shifted her weight, moving her arms and legs in an attempt to strike a more modest pose, but she definitely felt compromised as the look on his face stripped away every level of decency. For the first time, since her ordeal with serial killer John Monroe, Kate was truly frightened. She had no way of knowing whether Devereaux was going to kill her or expose her for the fraud she was. She could only claw and scrape to seize that last ounce of courage within herself, determined not to let him see her sweat or turn misty-eyed in front of him.

"Madame Gertsen, allow me to introduce myself," he said soft and smooth. "I am Robert Devereaux."

"Mr. Devereaux, it's a great pleasure," Kate smiled demurely and reached out to shake his hand, a routine formality she had carried out dozens of times in the last hour, but he seized her hand and refused to let it go.

Devereaux tucked her hand firmly under his arm, and then,

with a backwards glance, addressed Damien. "Would you see that Mrs. Jefferson gets the proper sendoff?" he insisted, dismissing his security chief from the conversation.

"Of course," Damien said, bowing slightly at Kate, "If you'll excuse me?"

"Another time, Mr. LaMarca."

"Damien!" he shouted after her.

Rudely, and with very little charm or grace, Robert Devereaux dragged Kate away from the courtyard in front of his private office. They left Damien standing there, staring after them, lost in his own thoughts, as his boss pulled her roughly along like a puppy on a leash for the first time.

For just an instant, Kate Dawson hazarded a look at Devereaux, her deep blue eyes sweeping over him, trying to slow him down, but he just ignored her; so cool and collected in his sophisticated white dinner jacket and tie. In fact, he carried such a personal sense of confidence and charm that it appeared he could get away with anything, especially murder, and no one would say a word. His grip just tightened on her hand as he escorted her forcefully along the path.

Kate could no longer hold back, "You're hurting my hand."

"Oh, say, it isn't true," he feigned ignorance of any wrong-doing. "You should really take a walk in my gardens."

"I did," Kate replied, not the least amused, wriggling to gain her hand back. "Ah, and did you find what you were looking for in the office?"

"The office?" She tried to put on her innocence to no avail.

All at once, his face turned grim and he twisted Kate's hand at the wrist, forcing her down to the ground on one knee. At the same time, he raised his other hand high up in the air, then released it, like a coiled snake, striking her across the face with his open palm—not once, but twice; back and front.

"Don't insult my intelligence again, Madame!" he shouted, right in her face, spittle hitting her eyelid. "I know you were in my office tonight."

Face on fire and eyes tearing uncontrollably, she whined, "I was looking for the powder room."

"Don't lie to me!" Devereaux shouted, raising his hand again.

"I'm not lying," Dawson insisted, bracing for the next blow. "I wandered into your office by mistake. I was looking for the powder room."

Alex Starke remained hidden under the conveyor belt as the wooden crates snaked their way around the room, traveling from near the entrance where she came into the warehouse to the dry dock. She clasped the palms of her hands over her ears to protect them from the intense noise reverberating off the stone walls as well as being in such close proximity to the belt's mechanisms. Starke glanced up once or twice to see if she could see what was going on but instantly flattened herself on the floor, unmoving.

"Carl. Dieter," Damien LaMarca addressed two of his security guards by their first names, "take Mrs. Jefferson out beyond the point in the launch and cast her coffin into the Bay. Make sure no one sees you. The crate is weighted and sealed and should sink almost immediately to the bottom."

"During our drive in the limousine from the airport, I seem to remember Mrs. Jefferson talking to us about one day being reunited with her husband," Carl said, speaking formally, reverently, like a funeral director; hands clasped in front, holding his weapon.

Dieter agreed, "Yes, she really did miss him." Damien played along, "Well then, see that her burial at sea is a special one without any slip-ups."

"Yes, sir," the two guards replied in unison.

The three of them lifted a wooden crate off the conveyor belt and placed it upon a small speedboat tied up to the dock. Damien watched as his two men sped away, then headed back to the surface.

Alex Starke backed up under the conveyor belt, staying hidden, until she was certain she was alone. Her eyes flew over every square inch in view; ears tuning in to whatever sound not matching the norm. *I have to get a look in one of those crates.* Braving the moment, she shot out in search of a prying tool.

With her adrenaline on overdrive, working swiftly with an acquired crowbar, Starke struggled to open the top of one of the crates sitting on the conveyor belt, but the wood splintered into several pieces and broke off several of the nails that held the top firmly in place. Her mind flew in fifty different directions holding the three splintered pieces in her hands. *How in all hell am I supposed to seal the crate now? Fuck!* Dropping them, Alex tossed aside the layers of padding and reached into the crate, expecting a bottle of wine. Instead, she yanked out a brand new, military-grade AR 17 assault rifle, grease still in the barrel; five more, just like it, in the crate. Exactly as they had surmised, Devereaux was smuggling military weapons and other munitions in crates marked 'wine.' Starke had thought it was surreal to find such a precision factory warehouse, full of noise and machinery, located under the beautiful and idyllic Albion Castle, but now it all made sense.

Placing the assault rifle precisely where it came from, she considered the three splintered pieces of wood. Once she had returned the packing material, she shoved the splintered pieces down and hammered with the crowbar on the bent nails until the top of the crate was sealed. Any idiot, not even looking for it, would notice the damaged box and instantaneously suspect intruders in the warehouse. Panicking, heart pounding, she spun side to side, seeking a place to hide the crate. *Perfect!* A small niche, just wide enough for the crate, was visible under the motor that powered the conveyer belt. *They'd have to look hard to find it, which would give me plenty of time to get away with Dawson.*

At seven pounds apiece, plus the crate itself, Starke struggled to pull over fifty pounds off the conveyor belt. Once up and over the side, she let gravity take hold and it crashed to the floor. When no one responded, she felt safe enough to drag it over and shove it into place, breathing a deep sigh of relief. She then rearranged the other crates so there was no gaping hole to suggest a crate had been removed.

Inching amongst the shadows, Starke made her way out of the warehouse and back into the tunnel, creeping and keeping low; mindful of the two guards assigned to the grounds. Taking the elevator to the next floor, she jogged past the horse stalls, stopping between the stables and the main Château to catch her breath. Only a few lights could be seen twinkling in the numerous windows, and still the insects chirped and whistled around her. The servant's quarters were to the right, exactly where she belonged, and the main building to the left.

"Don't lie to me!" Robert Devereaux growled at Kate.

"I'm not lying—" she cried out. Dawson could feel her Beretta strapped in its holster to her thigh, but she was fighting the urge to use it on him. She swore if he hit her one more time that would be the last thing he'd ever do. The pain was nothing, but that sense of humiliation was almost more than she could bare.

"Am I interrupting something?" Renée asked sarcastically as she strolled up to find a woman on her knees in front of her brother.

You could hear the crossing of swords as Robert and Renée Devereaux exchanged glances. Even though they were brother and sister—and lovers—no one understood her brother's proclivity for unrestrained sadism better than she did. While anyone else would have been surprised, or even repulsed, at seeing the great Robert Devereaux beat, torture, or force a woman to submit to his will, Renée took it all in stride. She drew the line at finding his female victims in bed with them. Incest was one thing, but she would not tolerate threesomes or any form of swinging. People of a certain social class, wealth, prominence, or upbringing were clearly above such reproaches.

Robert Devereaux jumped back from Dawson, startled, as if he had just been given an electric shock. "Not at all, dear. I was just showing Madame Gertsen the gardens."

"Oh, is that what you were doing? I wasn't quite sure," Renée said, cocking her head, scrutinizing the subservient Gertsen.

"Renée, it really isn't any concern of yours."

"Robert, you're neglecting your other guests," she reminded him, backing away from the two of them. "Say goodnight to your 'friend,' and come with me—now."

"Goodnight," he said simply, straightening his suit, and left, no backward glance.

Renée Devereaux took control. "Madame Gertsen, come by my office in the morning and I'll assist you personally with putting your order together for Devereaux wine. I assure you the discounts will be very favorable in exchange for your discretion. Shall we say nine o'clock sharp?"

With a quick pivot, she did not wait for a response, but took off to catch up with her brother, guiding him along the path to the Château.

Kate sighed visibly relieved . . . but for how long.

Just after midnight, Starke checked her watch. *Shit! I'm way late.* If anyone asked her where she'd been for the last three hours, she'd have a difficult time selling the story that she went for a walk around the grounds. She bent over at the waist to calm herself, catch her breath.

Hustling, she took the main pathway, avoiding the garden lamps and illuminated fountains. Not stopping to think, she thundered along the path and looped around behind the gardens. Instead of going through the main door, where she'd be noticed, she climbed to the second-floor balcony and let herself in the door. She found her bed among the other servants and climbed in; clothes and shoes still on. Satisfied no one heard her, Starke pulled the covers over her head and fell asleep.

Kate Dawson struggled back to her feet, brushing the embedded pebbles from her knees and hair from her tear-stained face, and followed the same path back to her room, shaking uncontrollably. With her arms crossed across her breasts to hold herself together, as well as from the chilly night air, she ran through her thoughts, *Clearly the Devereauxs are involved in munitions smuggling and, more importantly, working with Task Force Red. But why did Renée use Lenny so unmercifully? What does she want with N.E.M.E.S.I.S.? And how am I going to get him off the hook?*

Seeing no way to gain entry through the front door of the Château without being seen, Dawson struggled along the pebble drive in her high heels, up to the main driveway, and snuck around the side of the building, eyeing every window and door for a way in. Bingo! A small window, open enough to pry apart with her fingers, she hiked her dress and pulled herself onto the ledge, tittering on her tiptoes, holding onto the frame. Listening for movement or voices, the drapes were pulled aside and she climbed through; pausing only to readjust her dress and close the window before heading upstairs to her room. Glancing left and right, she silently turned the door knob to suite and readied for bed. With all that was on her mind, Kate dozed restlessly, mostly staring at the clock, waiting for a shoe to drop.

"I told you not to disturb us!" Devereaux shouted, cracking open the door to his suite in the tower of Albion Castle. His face was flushed red as he struggled to pull on his plush, velvet robe.

Damien LaMarca, on the other side of the door, apologized, "Sir, I'm sorry, but it's very important. We found a groomsman tied up in the stables and there have been intruders in the warehouse. One of the crates is missing."

"How the hell could someone steal one of the crates right out from under our noses?" Devereaux demanded, out of his mind.

"I don't know, sir," Damien replied.

Devereaux turned to his sister, listening in, now tying her robe. "Put Security on full alert," Robert barked out his orders, pausing only a moment to think. "The only two people who are new to our guest list are Gertsen and her personal assistant, Alex. I want a complete read-out of their whereabouts for the last twelve hours."

"We've been watching them, sir," Damien responded. "I always thought there was something a little odd about them."

"Good. Well, maybe now we'll find out."

Robert Devereaux left his suite with Renée right behind him as they started down the main staircase past the bedrooms.

"What makes you suspect them?" she asked.

"I saw her snooping around the office after my meeting with Mrs. Jefferson," he replied, still livid. "When I questioned her about it later, she lied to me; told me that she had been looking for the powder room."

The three of them bounded down the stairway towards the lobby area.

As Devereaux turned a corner, Renée stopped him by the arm, her eyes wide and gleaming. "She was the woman at the racetrack!" Renée blurted out. "You know how I never forget a face. Well, her features have been altered slightly, but I swear that was the same woman watching me through binoculars."

Devereaux blew out a frustrated breath, shaking his head in disbelief, "And we led them right into our operation."

Renée turned to Damien. "I want a complete workup on Gertsen by morning—fingerprints, DNA, the works. I have a meeting scheduled with her at nine, and I want to know exactly whom I'm dealing with by then."

"Yes, ma'am," her security chief replied, politely.

Once they reached the ground floor, the three of them walked into the small security office. There, a young man with headphones rested with his head on the desk, half-asleep with fatigue, while a dozen or so small monitors in front of him clicked on and off with images overlooking the secure areas of the grounds. Digital recordings were being made from those monitors and stored on a main hard drive and in a cloud server.

Mortified to find one of his men asleep at his post, Damien pounded on the desk to rouse him, but the young man reacted sluggishly, as if he was drugged; did not even jump nor was he upset at being caught. Surrendering the headphones to his boss, Damien listened to one as he clicked through several channels to reach the bug.

Robert Devereaux was furious about the security breaches and blunders. His unkempt hair hung across his forehead and his face was flushed. He'd killed for less incompetence. Renée, on the other hand, stood next to him, concerned but cool as a cucumber.

"Well, do you have her or not?" he demanded.

Damien clicked on the overhead speaker. "If you listen

closely, Mr. Devereaux, you can hear snoring. Sounds like she's been asleep for a while."

"Wake her, dammit! We'll settle this right now!" Robert ordered, the impatient child shining through.

"No," Renée countermanded his order. "I have a meeting scheduled with Gertsen in the morning. I'll find out what she's up to. In the meantime, I want that complete security check done on her. No mistakes." She waggled her finger, which meant not one.

"Yes, ma'am," Damien replied, standing erect.

Robert Devereaux made it perfectly clear, "But if that woman turns out to be someone other than who she claims to be, *I'm* going to kill her."

"Yes, dear," Renée sighed, patting his arm. "Now let's get to bed."

CHAPTER EIGHT

Kate Dawson was already awake, feasting on a small breakfast of scrambled eggs, crispy bacon, whole-wheat toast, fresh black coffee, and orange juice, when one of the household servants hand delivered a message to her; a reminder that she was scheduled to meet with Renée Devereaux in the office at precisely nine o'clock sharp to discuss business. With her morning meal out of the way, she showered and dressed in a beautiful, floral sundress from Marc Jacobs, flat shoes, and few pieces of tasteful jewelry. She felt a cold wave of perspiration flush over her body as suspicion ran wild through Kate's mind. Why would an extremely wealthy business woman, such as Renée Devereaux, schedule a private meeting with the owner of convenience stores to discuss a paltry order for less than ten or twelve thousand dollars? Even if it was part of the plan, and things did seem to be progressing accordingly, Kate couldn't shake the feeling that there was an alternative motive, and that thought troubled her. Then she recalled where the etching of the check was. She slipped it in the palm of her hand and made ready to hand it off to Starke.

Kate left her room at eight fifty-five and made her way down towards the study. When she walked across the front lobby, past two household servants who were cleaning and dusting the room for guests, she saw her Lincoln Town Car parked out on the front driveway. Starke had stripped off her chauffeur's jacket and had sleeves rolled up, polishing the hood. Getting Starke's message that it was time to "clean things up," she made a point of walking out to Starke to whisper "tally-ho," and palm the note to her. She didn't say anything else; nothing else was needed. Kate was quite proud of herself, knowing that she was on her way to break the case wide open; that it was time to call in the cavalry.

The mere idea of being in the same study made Kate's anxiety return. *Were there cameras in the study? Was I caught going through Devereaux's drawers? Could this be a clever ruse to trap me; to call me out for the burglary? Or perhaps Starke's break in at the warehouse had aroused suspicion?* She really didn't know what to expect as she neared.

Taking a small corridor by the far stairwell, Dawson reached forward and gave a gentle yet firm knock. Nine-oh-one. She was late, but not precipitously late, only a minute. Kate could hear the tapping of computer keys, then footsteps, seconds before the door opened. Renée Devereaux filled the door with her charming smile.

"Good morning," Kate smiled, shaking her hand. "Thanks for taking the time out of your busy schedule to meet with me."

"Actually, the pleasure is all mine," Renée said, returning the handshake. She led Kate into the study and indicated a single leather chair on the other side of the desk, to which Dawson sat and made herself comfy. Renée sat behind the desk, with a computer front and center. "We've tried numerous times in the past to persuade your uncle to carry our line of featured or reserved wines in his convenience stores, but he's never responded to any of our offers."

"I'm afraid that Uncle Norman is very 'old school,'" Dawson

replied, hinting that she knew more about the family and store operations than she actually did. "He always stocked his convenience stores with items that customers needed in a hurry, like milk, bread, and toilet paper. You know, convenience items they could run in and pick up quickly. I have a completely different approach and a slightly different marketing plan. I want to continue to offer my customers their convenience items, but also offer them more than what they need."

"Very wise," Renée said, hands folded on the desk.

"I want my customers to think about their spouse toiling away at home on dinner, see a bottle of your Merlot, and then decide to pick up that bottle of wine to make dinner a special occasion," she said, painting a vivid picture. "I want a couple who have been invited to dinner to stop off at the convenience store to not only pick up flowers but that rare bottle of Cabernet Sauvignon Reserve wine for their hosts."

"Yes, yes, I'm beginning to see your vision."

"Great! And then, I want my customers to think investment as well as value. If they see an expensive Bordeaux advertised at my store in San Jose, I want them to buy that bottle with confidence for a future investment."

"I have the Liv-ex Fine Wine 100 Index on the computer; it represents the price movement of 100 of the most sought-after fine wines for which there is a strong secondary market. You'll find several of our wines on that list," she boasted, logging into the computer with several keystrokes. "With access to the Wine Stock Exchange & Price Index and Vinfolio's Wine Prices as well as Cellar Watch, I have the most comprehensive and up-to-date online resource guide for auction and retail prices, with over four hundred thousand prices for the last eight years."

"Incredible," Kate remarked. "This compilation of data might be helpful to you in selecting your purchase this afternoon," she began hitting random keys on the computer, maintaining eye contact with the screen. "As I see it, you'll need a dozen of our featured and reserved wines, with several bottles for each store of those 'investment' wines. Give me a moment or two, and I'll print out my recommendation list for you."

Kate Dawson sat back in the leather chair, but after a couple of minutes, she got fidgety and began looking around the room. The study was not much different from how Kate had seen it on the previous night. The chair she was sitting in was new, but all of the other furniture and furnishings were exactly where she remembered it. As Renée Devereaux smiled to herself, hitting numerous key buttons, Kate took in the two large oil paintings of the Devereaux's behind the desk, taking up a good portion of the wall space. In the one painting, Robert was dressed in armor, like a knight astride a huge stallion on the grounds outside the castle. In the other, Renée was adorned like a fairy princess in a period gown from the Renaissance outside Albion Castle. They really did see themselves as wealthy patrons "to the manner born."

While building her list for Angeline Gertsen on the computer, Renée was alerted about a new email in her inbox. She responded to a couple of prompts. Within a few seconds, a complete dossier filled her computer screen, pushing all other data to the side. "KATHERINE 'KATE' DAWSON, LIEUTENANT, SAN FRANCISCO POLICE DEPARTMENT, HOMICIDE DEPARTMENT . . ." As Renée Devereaux read through the text on her screen, she let out a small, bewildered laugh, keeping her amusement under control. She clicked on a grainy, black and white image of Dawson, which opened up to a full color image of Kate wearing her dress uniform. She clicked through several other pages worth of information about her guest, including a set of fingerprints, personal data, and service record.

"I find a computer indispensable," she looked up at Kate, grinning. "I used to hire expensive brokers to provide me with daily reports about the market, but now I do it all myself with a couple of keystrokes. I can isolate and identify individual strengths and weaknesses in the market, determine new opportunities for growth, and separate out threats that need my personal attention."

"I know what you mean," Kate reciprocated. "I'm lost without my computer." Dawson noticed the look on Renée's face change throughout their conversation and felt danger rising.

"We have several investment wines that might interest you," she chuckled to herself about her discovery.

"Splendid," Kate shifted in her seat, uncomfortably.

Renée Devereaux's computer continued uploading data and she read through each field in the report. In the end, there was the assessment. ". . . THREAT ALERT: HIGH. INDIVIDUAL: DANGEROUS. PROCEED WITH EXTREME CAUTION . . ." The wording took Renée's breath away. On the monitor, the image of Dawson was covered with the bold warning: "Dangerous." Nodding to herself, she clasped her hands and turned back to Kate, a satisfied look crossing her face. "I think you'll be pleased to know that we have all of those wines in stock."

"Excellent news," Kate answered, with a forced half smile.

Devereaux printed out her list of wines with discount prices and handed it across the desk to Dawson. "I've priced all of them very competitively for you, with deeper discounts for the reserve wines. You'll find many of the collector's wines listed on page two with their price point breaks."

Glancing through the list, Dawson feigned interest. "I can see that I have a lot of decisions to make. Would you mind terribly if we meet again this afternoon to complete our business?"

"Not at all," Renée concluded, rising and simultaneously hitting the monitor's power button so the screen went blank. Regarding the wall clock, she announced, "It's time for my morning massage. Why don't we meet again at four sharp?"

"Good idea," Kate agreed, standing up. She had never sat so long in one place in her entire life and was quite relieved to be back on her feet. She had feared the worst throughout her meeting with Renée Devereaux, and now that it was over, she was breathing a bit easier. Being undercover as Angeline Gertsen was hard and Dawson was always on edge, concerned that the mask she was wearing would not sustain her. In fact, as she strode across the floor, Kate smiled confidently at her host, and Renée even smiled back as she reached for the door. But as it opened, all of her pretenses crashed. The masquerade was over.

With their guns drawn, Damien LaMarca and two of his security guards were waiting for her. They took Kate Dawson immediately into custody—patting her down and seizing her Beretta—and marched her downstairs one level to a group of Medieval cells, each one partially carved out of rock and finished off with metal bars. The floor was solid rock. Damien opened the middle cell door with a special key he carried and the two guards dragged her into the cell, kicking and screaming for her life.

"Holy shit, Damien!" Kate shouted, struggling with the two guards, her face red with anger. "I'm a cop. You know this isn't right! You're never going to get away with this! What the fuck—"

With a single, backhand blow, the first security guard sent her tumbling to the far corner. Pushing herself upright, blood trickled down the side of her mouth, landing on her dress. In two long steps, he hoisted her up by her throat, held her high in the air, then slammed Kate against the jagged rocks, hard.

"Are you out of your fuckin' mind?" Dawson screamed, gasping for air.

The second security guard came in next, kicking her in the stomach with the pointy edge of his boot. Having the wind knocked out of her twice in quick order, she struggled for air, doubled over in pain, hands clutched to her belly. He waited for her to relax, then kicked her again and again with his boot. Each blow brought her closer to losing her breakfast. He got right down in her face and said threateningly, "Don't you dare puke! If you puke, I'm going to shove your face in it, and make you eat it back up."

Finding focus on his face, his eyes were pure blind rage. Fear pulsed through her as she tried to pull it together. "You son-of-a-bitch!" she screamed at him.

The first security guard pulled her to her feet and body slammed Kate, her head smacking against the rocks, sounding hollow. She folded, calculating that much more of this and she would black out.

They continued to punch and kick her until she was just a piece of quivering meat lying on the floor of the cell.

"Okay, that's enough," Damien said to his men. "We'll let the pain from her wounds soften her up."

A day and a half later, Kate Dawson began to stir. She tried to open her eyes, but the left one seemed to be welded shut where she had been backhanded by one of Damien's goons. She touched the wound gently with her fingertips and discovered that it was not only swollen but crusted with blood all around the socket. Her lips were bloodied and swollen as well where she had been struck in the face several times. Kate tried to sit up using her right arm, which felt as weak as a blob of jelly, but she could not overcome the spinning sensation in her head. She groaned and held her head with her good hand. Her breathing was also weak and shallow. With the way they had been punching and kicking her, she suspected a couple of broken ribs, if not a punctured lung. Wanting to cry, no tears could be mustered. Slumping back down, she prayed God would have mercy on her and let her die peacefully. Life was much too painful to continue.

Feeling sorry for herself, she could have sworn she heard someone snoring, a man snoring. With her one good eye, she scanned the room. Shears lay sprawled on the floor in the cell nearest hers, dressed in rags that appeared to be women's clothes, and he had had the shit kicked out of him, too. Shears was the toughest man she knew, and if they had done this to him, they could get to anyone. That was truly frightening.

Dawson reached through the cell bars and nudged him.

No response on the first nudge, he began to stir and open his eyes on the second. When he recognized Kate, he tried to sit up, but he felt weaker than a newborn kitten.

"Are you all right?" Kate asked, slurring her words. *Maybe a couple of missing teeth or a broken palate?*

"I'll be fine just as soon as the guy in my head turns off his jackhammer."

"That's just what I was going to say," she said, struggling with pronunciation.

"Starke reported that you were okay," he said, sizing her up. Shears could see that Dawson had been severely beaten, probably by guards, and it pissed him off. "What the hell happened?"

Kate tried to smile, but it hurt too much. "Then she got through?"

"Got through? Are you kidding me? She's a real trooper, that girl," he replied, incredulous. "When she learned that security had disabled the Town Car, she stole one and dove off the cliff at Hunter's Pointe, then swam the nine miles across San Francisco Bay to the Coast Guard base at Alameda."

"I don't believe it," Kate said, trusting every single word.

Shears grimaced from the pain. "Hell, she wanted to come back with me, but the Chief of Police grounded her. So, me and my men made the trip across the Bay in scuba gear, riding on two two-man submersibles."

"Your men are here?" she asked, a relieved look on her face.

"Yeah, they're hiding out, waiting for word from me."

"Good."

Shears struggled to lean up. "Now, are you going to tell me what the hell happened to you?"

"I blew my cover," Kate said, flatly, shaking her head. "Devereaux came on to me with some sick, twisted game of his and I panicked. I should've played along with him; done anything he asked, but his game reminded me too much of the games that John Monroe used to play on me. They're both sadists, you know. They both get off from inflicting pain or degrading others. The difference is that Monroe is six feet under and Devereaux has yet to experience my wrath." Her throat was parched; her lips so dry she felt they would split if moved too much. It hurt to move, to breath, to live.

"Let's not make this personal," Shears reminded her.

Dawson glared at the army colonel, trying to swallow. "Maybe you can turn things on and off like that. I can't. Those men beat me, humiliated me, and left me for dead. They might just as well have raped me because they took away my last ounce of dignity. The only thing I still have going for me is rage. And the next time I see Robert Devereaux, I plan to make him crawl and scream for help before I put a bullet through his head."

"Okay, killer. Let's just make sure there is a next time," he said, climbing painfully to his feet. Shears examined the lock on his cell door. "Have you got a hat pin or a nail file or a probe of some kind?"

"What the fuck do you think?" she fired back, angry, resentful.

"Well, you don't have to bite my head off!" It was then he spied her ears. "Let me have your earrings."

Kate Dawson took each of the earrings off and handed them through the bars. Rage a'nd vengeance was keeping her alive, nothing else. All she could see was that evil bastard's head exploding from front to back.

Although her face was a bloody, swollen mass, Shears could see the rage in her one good eye and decided it was time to change the narrative. "Tell me about your mission," he suggested, working with one earring.

She thought about it for a moment, then answered, "In the beginning, the mission went according to plan. With our identities established, as the owner of a chain of convenience stores and her personal assistant, we were able to join the lifestyles of the rich and the famous as their equals and infiltrate their operation with little difficulty. The first discovery we made was that the Devereaux's were using sales of wine from their very legitimate wineries to launder money from their arms deals. We quickly established that two of the five team members of Task Force Red were working directly with the Devereaux's. In fact, I met the Ranger they called Tex at the reception on Friday night, and I saw Devereaux write a check for a million dollars to Sierra Jefferson, the widow of the Ranger who died in combat."

"Starke delivered your copy of the check. That was good thinking. Where did you learn how to do that?"

"Dick Tracy."

Shears laughed, all the while picking at the lock. "Starke was supposed to check out the caverns below Albion Castle for a huge cache of munitions," she continued. "We believed weapons were being stored in wooden crates labeled with the Devereaux Wineries logo. But I never got the chance to corroborate what she found."

Shears paused. "I hate to disappoint you, Kate, but I've checked Devereaux's warehouse. It's empty."

"That son-of-a-bitch!" she cried out in rage, her voice cracking.

"For the last two days, planes with the Devereaux Wineries logo etched on the side of the fuselage have been taking off every two hours from San Francisco International Airport," Shears reported, squinting his eyes to refocus, head pounding. "And two freighters, which stopped and loaded crates from Devereaux Wineries at the Port of San Francisco, cleared the Golden Gate Bridge last night around midnight and were last seen heading out into international waters."

"They're moving everything out."

"To where?"

"That's what we've got to find out, and fast," Kate replied, with renewed determination.

Shears went back to working on the lock. After a moment, he looked up and said, "You do realize that without one of those crates of munitions we don't have a case. It's mostly hearsay, your word against Devereaux."

"We could have the Coast Guard stop one of those freighters at sea," she recommended, "and search those crates."

"Without any evidence, we'd never get a warrant to search them," he countered Kate's recommendation. "And if either of those freighters are registered in a country that doesn't recognize our extradition rights, we'll never even get close to them. Unless of course, you had piracy in mind."

"Fuck, Shears, isn't there anything we can do?"

"No," he said, shaking his head. "There's a reason why the Devereaux's have been operating as long as they have. They're very lucky. They'll just move their whole operation to some place, like Venezuela, for a few years, and back the authoritarian regime of Nicholas Maduro, until it's time to move again. They are the 'Merchants of Death.' As long as there is a conflict or war some place in the world, they'll always have customers ready to pay them top dollar for arms and munitions."

"That's pretty cynical, Shears."

"Truthful, Kate," he replied. "The only real way to stop them is to be out in front of them, somehow; to catch them in the act."

Kate's mind reeled. *All that work we put into catching these assholes and they are going to get away with it?* Her head wobbled back and forth, angry and hurt at the same time. No, it was much more than that. Kate was close to losing it altogether! She fought to maintain control; a drunk fighting the urge to take another drink. Drunk! And then, all of a sudden, she remembered Major Tex Denton. "Shears, I just remembered something. It may be important."

"What?" He froze in anticipation.

"At the reception on Friday night, I ran into Major James Denton, one of the five members of Task Force Red," Kate sputtered, desperate to get the words out. "It was a chance meeting. He had been drinking. A lot! I'd have to say he was inebriated. I heard him mention the words 'squeeze play' to Devereaux, who was making the rounds of the party. It ruffled his feathers; made him stop dead in his tracks and his face turned red. I'd say it was the only time I saw him come close to being unglued. He said, 'We'll know more at the end of the month,' and quickly changed the subject, but the words were already out there."

"'Squeeze Play,' what does that mean?"

"I don't know," she confessed. "I was hoping it meant something to you."

Shears stopped working on the lock to ponder the term.

"The only 'squeeze play' I know is a term from Major League Baseball. It's a play in which the batter purposely bunts the ball, expecting to be thrown out at first base, so that his sacrifice gives the runner on third base the opportunity to score. It's a risky play that doesn't always work. But when executed with perfect precision and skill, it is a real wonder to behold."

"Baseball? That can't be it," Kate dismissed. "It's got to mean something else."

"I'm open to suggestions."

All at once, the door opened, and Damien LaMarca entered the room, followed by two of his security guards with MAC 10s.

"What do you want?" Shears demanded, cupping the earrings.

"How are you feeling? Hope I didn't slug you too hard?" Damien said sardonically, with a fake smile devoid of any kind of humor. "The boys did try to rouse you, but you were out cold. You know, if you're gonna act tough, you should learn how to take care of yourself. You really should."

"You son-of-a-bitch!" Shears braced himself, fists ready. "How about the two of us go a couple of rounds? I'll show you what tough is. You sure as hell won't be able to clip me from behind without your boys holding me down." Damien chuckled. "Another time, brother. Another place."

"Where's Devereaux?" Kate insisted.

"Now isn't that perfect?" Damien mused out loud. "You want to see him, and he wants to see you." The security chief drew a Glock 19 from his shoulder holster and pointed the pistol at the two of them. "Ladies first."

With the two guards flanking them, Kate exited the Medieval cell, holding her weak arm, with Shears and Damien close behind. She stumbled going up the first couple of stairs, wobbly from her injuries, but Shears put his arm around her waist to steady her. Damien allowed it as his gun stayed trained on their heads. They were marched up one flight of stairs and taken to the small office at the back of the Château near the conservatory.

Robert Devereaux was seated contentedly by the window, reading through the wine list his sister had printed for Kate, drinking the last of his coffee. One of the household staff, a butler dressed formally in a white jacket, white bow tie, and black slacks, was busily cleaning away the breakfast service. Damien waited for the butler to finish, then shoved his two captives onto the couch against the wall. He and his men stood back from Devereaux, yet still close at hand.

"Stevens, you can take this away, too," Devereaux instructed his butler, finishing his cup of coffee now cold, "and do bring back some fresh coffee and some more toast for my guests."

"Yes, sir," the butler replied, quickly exiting the room.

Devereaux held the wine list up, and said, "Well, Lieutenant Dawson, I've just been reading the wine list my sister put together for you, and they all say that customer service is dead. Fascinating list! I suppose I would have included a Riesling or two, several Rosés, and at least one good, old-fashioned 'Dago Red' for those customers without a discerning palate. But it is indeed a thing of beauty. I think you'll come to regret not working more closely with Renée on this list. But then, again, I forget you're not really a business owner. That was all a lie, wasn't it? You're really nothing but a stupid policeman who blundered in here trying to entrap me. Do you really think you were the first?"

"Don't be too sure of yourself, Devereaux," Kate warned through cracked and oozing lips, eyes filled with hate. "You're not going to get away, this time."

"On the contrary, Lieutenant, I am getting away with it. Take a look around. History is being made while we speak," he replied, with a great deal of confidence. "I'll admit this was a difficult operation and I made several errors; not fully vetting you, for example. Allowing your 'great-aunt, Matilda May,' through the front door, without bothering to check her references."

"And here I thought it was my sparkling personality," Shears joked, an octave higher, still partially clad in his costume of a wealthy dowager. Devereaux wagged his finger at them. "Yes, I made some mistakes, but we always knew there would come a time when we had to move our operation. Thankfully, we had all of the contingencies in place ahead of time. So, it was just a matter of a few choice phone calls and texts, and we were completely secure. Within the next few hours, if not sooner, your FBI or Justice Department will descend on my estate with search warrants and will find nothing. My attorneys will file huge lawsuits against the San Francisco Police Department and the Federal Government and will ultimately settle for hundreds of millions of dollars. Accusations of leaks will be tossed back and forth on Capitol Hill. A formal inquiry, calling for an independent prosecutor, will be made in the Senate and lawmakers from both sides of the aisle will be questioned about what they knew. The Director of the FBI or the Attorney General of the United States or both will be asked to tender their resignations. And the biggest story of the year will dominate the news media 24/7 for the next few months. My sister and I will be vilified at first, but we will ultimately be cleared, and our stock in Devereaux Wineries will double or triple in value on the stock exchange. You see, my plan is foolproof. I've anticipated every move and possible variation of counter move."

There was a knock at the door.

"Yeah," Damien LaMarca responded, answering the door. It was one of his security guards with an update. He listened, then approached Devereaux. "Excuse me, sir. It's all been confirmed. Your private jet is fueled, and ready to go. A chopper will be here shortly to take you to the airport."

"Very good, Damien," he replied. "Please monitor the aircraft's approach and get my luggage aboard once it lands. I'll be along shortly."

"Yes, sir," Damien responded, with a nod of his head, fixing his two security guards with a look as he exited the room.

"The only thing that remains is the two of you," Devereaux said, smiling genially at Kate and Shears. "I had considered just turning you lose, but the more I thought about it, the more I realized you know far too much about my organization. So, I've had to work overtime in coming up with a brand-new plan to fit the circumstances in which we now find ourselves. You know, it's not easy being a mastermind. Suffice it to say, my new plan involves blackmail, counterintelligence, and a tragic lover's quarrel in which the two remaining principals kill each other. It's simple, elegant, and without a lot of details that could go wrong."

"You don't actually think the authorities are going to buy that story, do you?" Kate asked, grasping at straws, head pounding, barely able to breathe.

"Why not?" Devereaux replied, satisfied with himself. "I have a near genius IQ. "No one would dare question it."

There was another knock on the door.

"Come in," Devereaux ordered, and in walked the butler carrying a tray of coffee cups, saucers, plates, toast, and fresh coffee. "Oh, thank you. Please put it down right here. Well, that's enough talk about what the authorities will believe or disbelieve. Please join me in a cup of coffee."

The butler laid out a complete serving set, with spoon, on the table in front of Kate and Shears, and then the same, in front of Devereaux. He then laid out the linen table napkins for each. The butler followed up with the toast and jam, and began serving the coffee, one person at a time.

"Coffee, sir?" the butler asked Shears.

The Army Colonel said, "Yeah, thanks," eyeing the man, wondering how he could ignore the sight of nearly-beaten-to-death people.

"The Senate will still move forward with its investigation," Dawson continued, trying to provoke him. "You won't be able to stop it."

"I'm actually counting on their investigation. It should make for a lot of laughs," said Devereaux, with delight. "May I recommend the Hurley Farms Apricot Jam? Rachael Ray calls it the 'best-tasting jam' she has ever sampled, and it comes from a farm in Napa Valley. You'll find it sweet like sorbet."

"Coffee, ma'am?" the butler asked Kate.

The police lieutenant declined through bleeding lips, "No, thank you."

"Now, let's see. Where were we? Ah, yes. You were about to come back at me with some pithy remark about the Senate and its investigation."

"I know all about 'squeeze play,'" Dawson bluffed, with a straight face.

"'Squeeze play,' what's that? Two simple words that you may have overheard at the reception on Friday night." Devereaux feigned ignorance of the words. "I have no clue what you're talking about."

"Don't insult my intelligence, Devereaux!" Dawson fed him back his own words, only seeing from one eye.

"I suppose what Kate's saying is that since it didn't take us very long to uncover your real plan, the Senate should discover it fairly quickly."

He shot them both a dirty look. "The two of you know nothing, 'Aunt Matilda.'"

"Aunt Matilda? Not one of my better moments," he laughed,

as he looked down at the remnants of his costume. "The name's actually Shears, Colonel Shears, Military Intelligence."

"Now, there's a misnomer if I ever heard one," Devereaux interrupted him. "Military Intelligence."

"Old joke. Only, I'm not laughing," Shears responded, with authority. "Me and my team have been trailing you for the last couple of years. An order for your arrest or termination was issued last month by the State Department after a witness came forward and fingered you and four members of Task Force Red in the downing of that plane over Cologne, Germany. They also know that you had the witness killed and murdered his wife when she threatened to tell all. They know all about you, Devereaux. They have known about you for years, and are right now, as we speak, moving to close down all of your bank accounts and seize all of your assets."

"Fascinating," Devereaux replied, trying to hide his inner thoughts and feelings, but the look of shock was all over his face. Had the information been a bullet to the head, the wealthy arms merchant would have been mortally wounded where he sat with his coffee and jam. He struggled to stand up from his chair, to keep it all inside, but his legs were stiff, as if frozen in a block of ice.

Suddenly, as if on cue, the distinctive "thump-thump" sound of a helicopter heralded the arrival of his air taxi as it approached the estate from the southeast. The aircraft swept across the sky overhead and searched the grounds until it pinpointed the landing zone next to the house.

"I regret having to break up our meeting, but I do have a plane to catch," he said finally, crossing the room, stiffly. When he reached the door, Devereaux called his men over, and whispered two words: "Kill them." Upon reflection, he added, "Take them down to the warehouse, put each body in a crate, weight the crate down, and bury them at sea."

"Yes, Mr. Devereaux," the first one said.

"Understood, Mr. Devereaux," the second one replied.

"Thanks, boys," he said, with all sincerity, and was off.

Damien LaMarca stood waiting for the helicopter from San Francisco International Airport as it landed on the north lawn of the estate. With the pilot's help, he loaded his boss's luggage aboard the small craft, its blades maintaining a constant "whoosh" as they continued to rotate above.

Robert Devereaux saw the chopper land from the house and hobbled towards the open door. Damien helped him board and, as his loyal servant, even aided in buckling him to one of the rear seats. He then climbed aboard, in front, next to the pilot. With a roar, the helicopter took off, straight up, and then zoomed past the line of squad cars as they raced down the streets nearest to the estate.

Kate Dawson and Colonel Shears were marched out of the office between two of Devereaux's security guards, taken through the conservatory, and walked around back to the stables. Both of them knew they were marked for execution, but Shears didn't seem to take Devereaux's orders too seriously. He knew his men were hiding out, waiting for a sign from him to strike. Also, he and Kate could hear the wailing sirens of police cars and law enforcement vehicles in the distance as they seemed to get closer and closer to the Devereaux estate. But at each juncture, on their way down to the warehouse, Shears started to worry. After they stepped off the elevator, below the stables, the Army colonel realized he was going to have to act first. He watched and waited for just the right moment to jump his guard.

When they reached the tunnel, Colonel Shears remembered that the pavement was uneven, loose, and that it was all downhill.

He waited for his guard to get sloppy, to get too close to him, to make a mistake, and then—WHAM! Shears drove his elbow into the guard's face, breaking his nose on contact. Blood exploded everywhere. Then, with a spinning karate kick, he slammed the guard against the wall, the weapon clattering to the floor. Shears followed his first couple of blows with a series of punches, his fists striking rapidly like bullets fired from a machine gun. The guard staggered backwards, hitting the floor hard.

Meanwhile, Kate Dawson took advantage of Shears' surprise explosion, and hurled herself at the second guard, grabbing his hand as they struggled to the floor over control of the MAC 10. Several automatic shots rang out, the ricochet of a bullet zipping by her ear. She struggled to keep two hands on his gun as he fought back, shoving an elbow into her ribs, which were already abused from the beating she'd taken. Kate got in one hard punch, maybe two, as she held onto him, like a cowboy riding a bucking bronco. The guard got a few more shots off, one narrowly missing Shears and his fellow guard.

Shears had had enough, grabbed Kate gently around the waist and set her down, then, in the same movement, punched the other man's shoulder and watched the weapon fly out of his hands. With his remaining strength, Shears drove the guard back with a sweeping head kick; another, and then another. The guard staggered back, and finally went down with one last, hard punch.

Shears stood off to the side, wringing his hand from that last punch, his fist trembling full of pins and needles.

"Oh, John!" Kate exclaimed, nearly fainting. "Hold me."

She fell into his arms and Shears held her tight. She sobbed on his shoulder for a few moments, then he softly took her head into his hands and kissed her gently. She held onto him tightly; refused to let him go.

"I've never been so frightened," she confessed.

"It's okay, sweetheart. You're safe now," he said, brushing away her tears. "To be honest, I was scared you wouldn't be here. We all feared the worse when Starke came back without you. I left almost immediately. I don't know what I would have done if I didn't find you."

"I missed you." She kissed him again and snuggled into his shoulder.

"Well, boys, it looks like the Colonel's back, and, like usual, he pulled the best duty assignment," one of his men observed, as he and two others double-timed their march down the tunnel. The three men were dressed in army fatigues but displayed no rank badges or company patches of any kind. They all carried automatic weapons and wore web belts with holstered Glock 19s, grenades, and additional rounds of ammunition. They gathered around Colonel Sheers and his "friend."

"Mission accomplished, Colonel?" one of his men asked, with a wink.

Another one shouted, "Isn't that letting the enemy get a little too close for comfort, sir?"

"Colonel, how many times have you warned us about fraternizing with the fairer sex?" the third one said, with a smile.

"Boys, you all remember Kate?" Shears asked, releasing their embrace.

Dawson was mortified. "Hi, guys," she managed to squeak out before hiding behind Shears, ashamed of the way she looked and what she'd been caught doing.

"That's Jimmy Crack Corn, Stevie, and Mitchie the Kid," Shears said, introducing three members of his team with a great deal of pride. "My men and I are going to be pulling out now. Nothing personal. It's just the clandestine nature of the work we do. We can't afford to get pulled into a local investigation or asked a lot of questions which might compromise national security."

"But when will I see you again?" Kate asked, near tears again.

"Jimmy Crack Corn, do you have victory dance?" Stevie asked, pulling a long cigar out of the zippered breast pocket of his fatigues.

Jimmy pulled his cigar out and examined it. "That is an affirmative. I have victory dance. Mmmmmmm."

"Mitchie the Kid, you got your victory dance?" Stevie asked.

"Affirmative, Stevie!"

Stevie looked over at the Colonel for approval and Shears nodded. "Then it's time to light those fires, kick the tires, and go home. The Fat Lady has sung the last song of the night."

Colonel Shears was handed a cigar, lit it, and took a couple of puffs. "I'll be around, Kate. Remember, we still need to figure out what the hell 'squeeze play' is." He held the cigar at bay long enough to kiss her, then chomped back down on it. Spinning about, he and his men headed back down to the warehouse and their two waiting submersibles.

Dawson watched, trying to control herself. Every breath hurt, and crying was not an option.

The late-model, California Highway Patrol car sped down Innes Avenue; its sirens wailing and red lights flashing. Two determined cops—one, a long-term veteran and the other, a rookie—wanted to be first car on the scene, so they accelerated past Malcolm X Academy and careened along India Basin Shoreline Park, raced down the lonely street at Hunter's Point, then turned suddenly off to the right. Taking the long path to the Castle, they skidded to a dusty halt outside the entrance to the house. The two CHP officers got out of the car and pulled their rifles, using the two front doors as shields to hide behind. They were the first to arrive, but within thirty minutes, the grounds were swarming with law enforcement agents.

Working quickly, as other squad cars began arriving and taking up flanking positions around the house, two field agents from the FBI commandeered the former gatekeeper's house and temporarily converted the one-room home into a small operations center with telephones, a police radio receiver, and a large map of Hunter's Point on the wall. Several detectives with shoulder holsters or guns strapped to their waists were busily making calls, while two patrolmen brought in the groundskeeper to go over the map with them. A tough, cigar-chewing, plain-clothed man, known as the "Sarge," soon took over the interrogation. Within a matter of moments, he was dispatching S.W.A.T. trained personnel with high-powered rifles to key positions in and around the grounds of the Devereaux estate. Their targets were the conservatory, the stables, and the Castle tower.

Sarge then ran out to a waiting squad car and hopped inside. The car sped off down the road, leading a phalanx of patrol cars and other vehicles with wailing sirens, down the main path to the house. The S.W.A.T. truck, which was the last in the long line, followed behind a long cloud of dust. Nearing the castle, police cars began peeling off, two at a time, to form a great big "v." The policemen jumped out of their cars, grabbed their rifles, and knelt behind their doors for cover. In time, the great big "v" stretched all the way back to Innes Avenue, the main road in and out of Hunter's Point. Last to arrive but certainly not least in importance, the limousine carrying the Chief of Police drove along the main highway, turned off onto the dusty road, and then followed the "v" all the way up to the front door.

In front of the Château, the limousine made a half-turn, circled the driveway around a small fountain, and stopped.

Nelson Gates, dressed in formal dress blues as the head cop, stepped out of the back of limo, and crunched down on the small graveled stones. He adjusted his formal, visor cap over his salt and pepper hair as he moved away from the vehicle. Alex Starke was next to get out right next to him. She was, after all, the head of the City's Counter- Terrorism Task Force and made him a good figurehead for the press.

He smiled at her once, then started barking orders, "I want everyone out of the house and lined up on the lawn. Domestics and other household personnel should line up on the right. Groundskeepers, groomsmen and stable boys, chauffeurs, and maintenance workers on the left. Security guards and anyone else authorized to carry firearms should line up right in front of me. I want them all searched, and I want to see picture IDs or passports for the lot."

Starke whispered to Gates, "There may still be celebrities in the Château from the weekend. I think you'll want to treat them with 'kid gloves,' or this could explode into a real media circus."

"Take a couple of police officers and handle it then," the Chief grumbled, as he walked towards the entrance of the Château with several of his officers. He liked to be seen with his men, and always made it a point of being accompanied by a select group of cops in uniform. They trudged through the small, graveled stones and marched towards the green path to the house, with all the pomp and pageantry of General MacArthur and his troops returning to the Philippines. He had a second thought and turned to Starke. "Oh, and when you find Dawson, I need to speak with her right away."

"I think that's going to have to wait, Chief," Starke replied, as she watched her boss rolled out of the house on a gurney.

"What are you talking about?" Gates asked, but as he turned back around, the Chief of Police had his own answer.

Flanked on one side by a doctor and two EMTs on the other, Kate Dawson laid there on the stretcher in great pain, blood on her face and clothes, as they wheeled her along the path. Her chest had been wrapped entirely in a white, gauze linen and taped tightly shut, much like a mummy bound for its sarcophagus. She was being fed oxygen through a cone mask and morphine through an IV drip. With the color all but drained from her face, Kate looked like a corpse on the gurney.

Gates pushed past the EMT and leaned over the gurney. Several members of the press hurried to snap pictures. He said, loud enough for the photo op, "You did a good job, Lieutenant. Hurry up and get well. We need good women like you out there. I'll see you around."

Starke simply smiled, and said, "Take care, Kate."

"Thanks, Alex," she replied, more of a whisper.

When they reached the ambulance, the two EMTs loaded her gurney in back and took great pains to see that Dawson was secure. They then closed the door and, within a matter of minutes, they were on their way to the hospital.

CHAPTER NINE

At the request of Lieutenant Matt Sheridan, Lenny Provolone's advocate, Kate Dawson drove the one hundred and twenty miles from San Francisco to the U.S. Army Garrison to testify as a character witness in Lenny's trial for treason and espionage. She pulled up to the Private Bolio Gate and was directed to the visitor's parking lot. Once she had her visitor's pass, Kate waited in the lobby outside the courtroom for her name to be called. She didn't know exactly what she was going to be asked to say, but she knew it must have been important to her friend's trial. Shortly after she arrived, an Army private escorted her into the courtroom and sat her down in the gallery near the back.

Kate had never been inside an Army courtroom and looked around to satisfy her curiosity. Other than the beautiful cherry wood that made up the judges' bench, witness box, bar, gallery, defense and prosecution tables, and jury box, the physical layout of the room mirrored that of a civilian courtroom. She did notice the defense and prosecution tables were reversed because Lenny Provolone and Matt Sheridan sat on the left side of the courtroom. The Bailiff was represented by a Sergeant at Arms and the Court Recorder sat within the bar. The jury was composed of not less than five Army officers, and of course the judge was a military judge. She also noticed there were no guards carrying firearms. In a civilian courtroom, there were always at least four or five police officers with side arms.

Lenny, in handcuffs, turned around to see Dawson in the gallery and smiled. He seemed genuinely pleased to see her. Kate raised her hand in a slight wave of acknowledgement, wishing their reunion had happened under different, perhaps happier circumstances. His eyes continued to traverse the courtroom; not one of his friends had bothered to show up there to support him, except Dawson. Not Harold, Jack, Vinnie, Lincoln, Sebastian . . . nor psycho Rebecca. Provolone slumped down in his chair, disappointed.

At exactly ten a.m., the door at the back of the courtroom opened and Daniel Overstreet, an aging Army colonel, entered and took his place at the bench. He had served on the bench longer than he could remember; had walked up that same aisle without a word for more than thirty-five years.

"All rise," the Sergeant at Arms ordered, very formally, and everyone in the courtroom stood. "All those having business with this court, stand forward and you shall be heard. Colonel Daniel Overstreet, presiding. God save the United States of America." Once the judge was seated, the five members of the jury marched into the courtroom and sat in the jury box. "Be seated."

Overstreet rapped the gavel.

"Where are we?" the Colonel asked, a bit confused, looking for glasses that were still on top of his head.

"Sir, Docket number 813298. VR-6. United States versus Leonard Provolone. The Defendant is charged with Treason and Espionage," the Sergeant of Arms replied, handing a file to the judge.

"Does the defense wish to enter a plea?"

"Judge, they've already entered a plea of 'not guilty.' This is our fourth day of trial. The prosecution rested its case yesterday, and we're waiting to hear additional testimony from the defense today."

"Yes, yes. I remember now," Overstreet replied, chasing the Sergeant at Arms away from the bench. The Judge continued looking for his glasses until he found them perched on his head. "I may be a little forgetful at times, but I'm not senile. Thank you for your assistance."

Provolone and his JAG attorney sat at the defense table, ready to get underway. They were waiting for papers being passed back and forth between the Government's attorney, Captain Larry Abbott, and the Sergeant at Arms.

"Is the Defense ready to call your next witness?" Overstreet asked.

"If it pleases the Court, Colonel, the Defense would like to call Lieutenant Kate Dawson," Sheridan said, wet behind the ears. "She does hold the legitimate rank of 'lieutenant' with San Francisco Police Department."

"Proceed," Judge Overstreet acknowledged.

While Kate Dawson, a civilian, was being sworn in, Sheridan sat back down at the defense table, and conferred with Provolone. They exchanged a few whispered words, then Sheridan was back on his feet, standing in front of the witness box. He looked very young and out of his league.

"Lieutenant Dawson, would you state your full name and occupation for the record, please?" Sheridan asked, politely.

She nodded her head. "Katherine Dawson. Lieutenant. Homicide Bureau. San Francisco Police Department." She still wore the scars of the beating she took and felt the stares of all those in the room.

"How do you know the defendant?"

"Mr. Provolone is my neighbor at the Bayside Village Apartments in San Francisco," she replied. Kate thought about the question, and then added, "But he is really much more than just a neighbor. He has become my friend for many years and has done work occasionally for me in connection with the SFPD."

"Would you tell us the nature of your 'friendship' with Mr. Provolone, Lieutenant Dawson?"

"We go out to dinner a couple of times a month. We watch the occasional movie on television together or see a film on the big screen. I've been his guest at a science fiction convention. We've attended the chance lecture or gone to the infrequent book signing together. We've both had our ups and downs in life the last couple of years, but we've always managed to be there for each other," she explained.

Sheridan shot her a sideways glance. "Are you and Mr. Provolone romantically involved?"

She shook her head. "No."

"Have you ever had sex with Mr. Provolone?"

"Never," Kate replied, feeling indignant. She looked hard at Sheridan and at the inquisitors at the prosecutors table. She wasn't on trial there, but their questions were probing areas that made her feel uncomfortable. They held each other's eye for another moment, or two, and she dared them to ask another leading question. She was ready to eat them alive and spit them out.

"In one of your previous answers, you state—and let me get this quote accurate—that Mr. Provolone 'has done work for you occasionally in connection with the San Francisco Police Department,'" Sheridan said, reading from his notes. "Please describe the nature of the work that he has done for you."

"Mr. Provolone has acted as a consultant for the department," she replied, trying to keep her answer as simple as possible.

"Consultant? Could you be more specific with your answer?"

Kate Dawson shifted uncomfortably in the witness chair, from the questions as well as the pain shooting from her still-bandaged ribs. "Back in 2016, my partner Frank Miller and I were assigned to bring in John Monroe, the 'Angel of Death' serial killer. He had already killed three people, and we were no closer to catching him than arresting the man on the moon. In fact, we didn't even know if we were chasing a man or a woman. One night, Lenny and I were having dinner and he mentioned that he was going to be running a series of simulations on the satellite he built for FEMA at Northrop Grumman, codenamed N.E.M.E.S.I.S.—"

"Objection, your honor," Abbott, the lead, prosecuting attorney, cut Kate off in mid-sentence. "Sidebar."

Both attorneys approached the bench and spoke privately with the Judge about the "objection."

"This is a top-secret government project and any further discussion in an open courtroom violates National Security," Captain Abbott said.

"I'll sustain your objection and warn counsel at both tables to speak only in very general terms about this project," Judge Overstreet replied, raising an eyebrow. "The terms 'FEMA,' 'Northrop Grumman,' and 'N.E.M.E.S.I.S.' are to be stricken from the record and recorded on the Errata sheet."

"I take exception," Sheridan said, in order to have his disapproval of the ruling added to the record.

"So noted," the Judge replied, then waved the two advocates back, away from the bench. They retreated hastily to their respective tables.

Overstreet sat quietly at the bench, weighing the issues and trying to make the right determination. When he shifted his gaze to the Jury box, the Judge could see that the Five Army officers awaited his ruling patiently. Finally, he decided it was time to get the show on the road.

"Jury members, you are instructed to disregard what you heard about a specific project, civilian contractor, service branch, or government agency," he stated, poised, cool, in complete command of himself. "Withholding and protecting certain secrets from our enemies has always been the primary goal of the National Security Act, regardless of whether we may personally believe the release of that top-secret information is critical to free an innocent man or convict a guilty one. Those decisions are thankfully reserved for a higher court than ours."

Redirecting, he said, "I believe the witness was yours, Lieutenant Sheridan, and I am instructing the witness on your behalf to steer clear of any discussion about top-secret projects or clandestine operations."

"What really happened that night after you had dinner with Mr. Provolone?" Sheridan questioned her, all business.

Kate Dawson shook her head. There was, in fact, a huge difference between civilian and military courts! "He promised me that he would use all of the resources at his disposal to help me track down the serial killer. He then collaborated with me and my partner, Frank Miller, over the next several weeks. We worked together on the project night and day, and I eventually brought John Monroe to justice."

Sheridan pressed. "To be clear, Lieutenant Dawson, you shot John Monroe three times in the chest and killed him."

"That's right," she said curtly.

"In addition to the aforementioned criminal investigation, Mr. Provolone assisted you with no less than four other homicide investigations? Did he also 'promise to use all of the resources' at his disposal to help you with them, too?" Sheridan asked, his features had hardened.

She hated to admit to herself the truth of the defense attorney's words. "Yes, and he also helped me complete my tax returns for a couple of years as well as repair my GPS when it wasn't working. He also loaned me his car once."

"A really helpful guy?"

"Naturally, I always thought so." Kate shrugged.

"No further questions," Sheridan said, turning her over to the prosecution for cross examination. "Your witness."

Captain Abbott studied Dawson's face for a long moment, wondering what the hell had happened to her, then looked down at his notes. "Lieutenant Dawson, when you conduct routine surveillance on a suspect, are you required to follow certain guidelines related to admissibility and evidentiary issues allowed in the courtroom?"

"Yes," she said simply.

"What about electronic surveillance?" Abbott added, again checking his notes. "Like attaching a 'bug' to a person's telephone line or to a phone booth and recording the person's conversation? Are there similar guidelines that must be followed related to admissibility and evidentiary issues?"

Kate was puzzled but went ahead and answered the question. "Yes."

"Why do you think these guidelines exist?"

"I am not a legal scholar, Captain," she replied, reading the rank on his military uniform, "just a lieutenant who works in the Homicide bureau for the San Francisco Police Department, but I will try to answer your question to the best of my ability to do so.

"Courts have held that this practice of 'wiretapping' constitutes a 'search' under the Fourth Amendment and requires police officials to obtain a warrant for electronic surveillance showing 'probable cause.' The Fourth Amendment protects an individual's privacy rights for situations in which the person has a legitimate expectation of privacy from any kind of surveillance."

"Thanks, Lieutenant. An excellent summary of the law," Abbott paid Dawson a compliment. "Were the rights to privacy of any individuals or groups violated when you worked with Mr. Provolone?"

Kate Dawson hesitated a moment. "Maybe? I'm not entirely sure."

"Why don't I put this another way?" he said, thinking about it. "Were proper warrants sought and issued by the Court to permit domestic surveillance of any individuals or groups under investigation by the Homicide Bureau of the San Francisco Police Department?"

Kate's head was whirling. She didn't know what to say. When she worked with Lenny to surveil the Black Rose or the End Times Ministries church compound or even the First Man's suite at the InterContinental Hotel, they weren't gathering evidence to be used in a court of law. They were protecting Kate from harm. But their surveillance was still not authorized or sanctioned by the courts.

"I'm not sure how to respond to your question, Captain," she replied, cleverly, "without going into the specific operating functions of a top-secret device, which I am prohibited from discussing in this courtroom." Abbott turned to the bench. "Your honor, will you instruct Lieutenant Dawson to answer the question?"

"Will both advocates please approach the bench?" Judge Overstreet ordered. He waited until both Captain Abbott and Lieutenant Sheridan were standing in front of him, and he said quietly, "Captain Abbott, you raised the issue of national security in objection to information the witness had intended to share with the court. You cannot now require her to speak and violate my ruling."

"Sir, I am merely intending to show that Mr. Provolone conspired with Lieutenant Dawson to violate the Fourth Amendment protections of individuals and groups from illegal search and seizure," Abbott explained fervidly.

Judge Overstreet shook his head. "You're fishing, Captain Abbott. You don't have the name of a single individual or group who filed a complaint against the witness or the defendant. Please move onto another question, or we will consider your cross-examination of this witness over."

"Your honor, I take exception," Abbott said, with the intention of having his disapproval added to the record.

"So noted," the Judge replied, then waved the two advocates back, away from the bench. Sheridan returned to the defense table, while Abbott resumed his cross examination of the witness. "How many people within the San Francisco Police Department know about Mr. Provolone's project?"

"Not many," Kate replied. "My partner knew, but he was killed in the line of duty in 2016. The assistant medical examiner also knew, but she was killed about a year ago in the line of duty, and my former boss knew. He had a recent stroke, so I don't know how much he remembers."

"A number will suffice," Abbott said, irritated.

"Four, including me."

"To the best of your knowledge, did Mr. Provolone ever profit from the work that he did for the U.S. Government?" he gazed at her intently.

Kate Dawson thought for a moment, then shook her head. "No, not that I'm aware of."

"Do you know Gwendolyn Bush?" Abbott asked. "'Wendy' to her friends?"

The name registered on Dawson's face, even though she tried to hide her surprise. "I don't know Gwendolyn Bush or 'Wendy.' I never met her," Kate replied, honestly. "Lenny told me a lot about her, however. He said that 'Wendy' seduced him, conned him into surrendering the WEP key access to his top-secret project, stabbed him with a butcher knife, and left him for dead. When 'Wendy' discovered that she had failed to kill him with the butcher knife, she hired an assassin to kill him in his hospital room. I saved Mr. Provolone's life on both occasions."

"Was Mr. Provolone in love with Gwendolyn Bush?"

"Yes, he told me that he was in love with her. And while I remain skeptical about his understanding of the word 'love,' I believe wholeheartedly that he believed he was in love with her."

"Do you know Renée Devereaux?" Abbott followed up with another question.

Dawson took too deep a breath and cringed, saying, "Yes, Captain Abbott, I know Renée Devereaux. Miss Devereaux is part of an ongoing criminal investigation into International Arms Dealing that my department is conducting," Kate explained, laying it all out for them. "She and her brother Robert Devereaux are suspects in the murder of a U.S. Army Ranger named Herbert Jefferson and his wife Sierra. They are also co-conspirators with a group of Army deserters known as Task Force Red in the alleged murders of one hundred and twenty-five people aboard a commercial jet that went down over Cologne, Germany; their alleged crimes also include drug trafficking, gun running, and money laundering."

"Objection, your honor," Sheridan said, standing up at the defense table. "With her answer to Captain Abbott's question, the witness has introduced a lot of unproven allegations and suppo-sitions that have no bearing whatsoever on Mr. Provolone's trial. And I would ask that most of it be stricken from the record."

Judge Overstreet took a deep breath and sighed. "Sustained. Jury members, you are instructed to disregard the witness's testimony about alleged murders, crimes, and conspiracies about arms dealers. They are part of an ongoing criminal investigation that has not yet been adjudicated."

"Thank you, your honor," Sheridan added, sitting down.

"Are you aware that Gwendolyn Bush, aka 'Wendy' and Renée Devereaux are one in the same person?" Abbott resumed his cross-examination.

"Yes, I do now," Kate replied. "At the time, when I began my own investigation, I thought I was dealing with two separate people. Eventually, I learned the truth and shared my findings with Mr. Provolone."

"Did you know that Renée Devereaux employed Mr. Provolone's surveillance satellite on thirteen separate occasions to aid persons hostile to the interests of the United States Government in their ongoing operations?"

"No," she answered truthfully, even though she had suspected as much.

Sheridan was out of his seat again. "Objection, your honor!"

"Sustained," the judge agreed. Captain Abbott picked up a book from his table and thumbed to a specific passage. According to *Article III, Section 3, Clause 1* of the *U.S. Constitution*: 'Treason against the United States, shall consist only in levying War against them, or in adhering to their Enemies, giving them Aid and Comfort. No Person shall be convicted of Treason unless on the Testimony of two Witnesses to the same overt Act, or on Confession in open Court.'" Abbott closed the book and put it down on the desk. "Lieutenant Dawson, you have maintained all along that Mr. Provolone, a civilian employee of a government contractor, did not commit treason. But I submit that is exactly what he did. He provided 'aid' and 'comfort' to a woman he 'loved' who was an international arms dealer. He showed her how to use his top-secret satellite and provided her with the WEP-key access to continue using it."

"Objection," Sheridan said, again standing up at his table. "Is my esteemed colleague, Captain Abbott, asking a question of the witness, or providing us with a preview of his closing arguments?"

"Sustained," Judge Overstreet replied. "That's all the questions I have for the witness," Abbott concluded, sitting down at the prosecution table. "Any redirect, Lieutenant Sheridan?"

"Your honor, I would like to ask the witness one final question," Sheridan said, standing up and walking around to the witness box.

"Proceed," the judge acknowledged.

Sheridan looked directly at Kate Dawson. "Lieutenant, you've stated that Mr. Provolone is your neighbor and friend. In the years that you've known him, has he ever done anything or said anything that would make you doubt his patriotism?"

"No, never," Kate replied.

"Thank you, Lieutenant. You're dismissed," Sheridan said, heading back to his table. "For my next witness, I would like to call . . ."

Dawson got up from the witness chair and headed down the center aisle to the exit. On her way past the defense table, she leaned over, painfully, and whispered, "I'll be praying for you, Lenny," then continued on, out the door.

Three days later, Kate learned from Matt Sheridan that Lenny had been convicted of treason but not espionage. As a civilian, the death penalty was not imposed. But he still faced a minimum penalty of five years in prison and a $10,000 fine. He was also stripped of his pension, his security clearance, and his government job, and forbidden from holding federal office at any time thereafter. All in all, better than she expected but still a difficult road ahead for her friend.

After three weeks convalescent leave, Kate Dawson returned to work on the first day of hearings in the U.S. Senate into the alleged ties between foreign governments, arms dealers, and sales of weapons by the Department of Justice. By contrast, the Iran-Contra Affair in 1985, the Fast & the Furious Scandal in 2006, and the Russian-Collusion Investigation in 2018 were considered insignificant. She remembered those scandals quite vividly and how long they had played out in the news, each consuming more than a year's worth of the news cycle. She was also surprised by the incredible rush to judgment on the part of the United States government, but then recalled everything that Robert Devereaux had told her was coming true. Kate was prepared to testify, if called upon by the Senate, but she was also quite content to let the reports she submitted to the Committee stand for themselves. Honestly, she had had enough testifying in court to last her a lifetime.

At 9:45 a.m., Kate walked into the conference room early and headed to the cantina. She poured herself a steaming cup of coffee, adding two sugars and a shot of milk. Kate picked up a couple of donuts and walked completely around the table until she found the chair that Lieutenant Roberts used to occupy; sliding into it at the head of the conference table. Clark had asked her to fill in for him during his absence. She had still not heard any word about her appointment as the new head of Homicide, and it pissed her off. She wondered what kind of game the Chief of Police was playing with her. Thanks to Jawara, a handful of photocopied materials sat on the table in front of each chair. He had agreed to help out making copies for departmental meetings. There was no money in the budget to hire an administrative assistant, so nearly everyone in the Bureau took turns pitching in, except Balardi. Matt Balardi felt it was beneath his talents to make coffee or run photocopies.

One by one the detectives filed into the conference room, poured themselves a cup of coffee, and sat down at the table. A few stopped to have a friendly word with Dawson before finding their seat.

"*Mi amiga, te ves genial*, [My friend, you look great,]" said Ramirez, with a great big smile.

"Looks like the rest did you some good, Kate," Mikhail added.

"Glad to see you back, Lieutenant," Starke said, adding her voice to those well-wishers.

Dawson wasted little time in getting their weekly meeting started. "Good morning. Clark asked me to sit in for him today, so let's go ahead and get our meeting started by discussing ongoing investigations."

"Lieutenant, Corcoran and I got one of those open-and-shut classroom shootings," Farris explained, shuffling noisily through the papers on the conference room table. "Fifty-three-year-old Marc B. Lee walked into Golden Gate Park Elementary School and opened fire on his estranged wife, Viola Smith Davies, also fifty-three, shortly before 10:30 a.m. local time on Monday, before taking his own life. Two students at the school were also wounded in the shooting. One of them, identified as seven-year-old Ricardo Jiménez, was later pronounced dead at the local hospital, while the other student, nine-year-old Sandy Smith, recovered from her injuries. Apparently, both students were standing behind Davies when the shooting began, but they were not targeted. Lee had a criminal record, including weapons and domestic violence charges. They had been married for a few months and had become estranged in the last month. A real tragic affair, especially when you consider the child was collateral damage. He just happened to be in the wrong place at the wrong time."

Kate shook her head, remembering her daughter's tragic murder. "Yes, you are so right, Farris."

Corcoran jumped into the conversation. "Dawson, we also pulled another murder-suicide in Pacific Heights," he said sourly. "Fifteen-year-old Joshua Rush fatally stabbed his mother, fifty-year-old Melissa Dougherty and then took his own life with a single gunshot wound to the head Tuesday afternoon. Apparently, Dougherty had removed her son from school earlier in the day at the request of administrators because of his behavioral problems. The bodies were found by seventy-two-year-old John Dougherty, returning home from a day-long outing with his senior citizen's group."

"What a nightmare that must have been," Dawson commented. "Can you imagine coming home and finding your grandson has fatally killed your daughter and taken his own life? In Pacific Heights, no less."

Farris interrupted her. "Lieutenant, do you remember that case from 2012 where the doctor was charged with killing the Stanford University physician over a dispute in the workplace? Well, Trista Wang finally pleaded 'no contest' Tuesday to lesser charges and agreed to serve thirty-two years in prison."

Kate nodded. "I barely remember that one. But if I recall correctly, the plea bargain ends nearly seven years of legal battles over Wang's competency to stand trial and her desire to represent herself in court. Wang had been under a judge's order to be forcibly medicated against her will for mental illness, so she could remain competent enough to stand trial. Didn't that issue go all the way to the Supreme Court a couple of years ago?"

"I believe it did. Had the case gone to trial, an insanity defense was likely," Farris concluded. Corcoran was silent for a minute or two, a surprised look in his face.

"How do you manage to keep it altogether, Lieutenant? We've just discussed three separate cases and you seemed to know something about each one even though you've been away for three weeks. Are you psychic or just incredibly well read?" Kate flashed him her most dazzling smile. "A little of both, I guess."

"I was wrong about you," Corcoran confessed. "I guess we all were."

"Thanks, Corcoran," she said, humbly. "Now, who's next?"

Walker, the quiet one who always sat with Corcoran and Farris, raised his hand politely, and caught Kate's eye. "Lieutenant Dawson, you asked Corcoran, Farris, and me to look into the chemicals that were needed to produce Botulinum Toxin," he said, standing up at his place. Walker seemed very nervous; kept wiping the perspiration from his upper lip with the back of his sleeve. "BTX contains sodium chloride, human albumin, a 5 ng/100 units of protein load, porcine gelatin, dextran, sucrose, and several other minor chemicals. It is prepared by laboratory fermentation of C botulinum cultures and can be produced nearly anywhere."

"Do you have any idea how it's stored?" Kate fired back.

"Crude botulinum is a protein with a molecular weight of about one hundred and ninety thousand Daltons, which suggests that it's cheaper to make in larger quantities," Walker reported, looking at his prepared notes. "After purification, the toxin is diluted with human serum albumin, bottled in vials, lyophilized, or freeze-dried, and sealed. Each freeze-dried vial contains about one hundred units. A one hundred units is enough to kill about fifteen thousand people."

Dawson nodded. "Okay. Do you know how it's triggered?"

"The freeze-dried BTX is reconstituted with preservative-free normal saline just before use. The saline solution in the form of eye drops or nasal spray can be purchased in any pharmacy or grocery store," he replied, hands shaking from his fear of speaking in front of others. "Studies suggest BTX must then be used within a four-hour window, or the toxin becomes inert and relatively harmless."

"So then, if I understand you correctly, before Mahmud Ibn Suri and his men could use the BTX to kill those twenty-four passengers who were on board the subway car, someone had to 'reconstitute' the toxin by combining it with a saline solution?" Kate repeated the obvious back to Walker.

"Yeah, that's about right," Walker acknowledged.

"*¡Espera un minuto!* [Wait a minute!]" Ramirez objected. "You didn't find a vial or broken glass on the subway car."

"*¡Claro!* [Exactly!]" Kate replied in Spanish to her former partner. "We'd always assumed that Mahmud Ibn Suri had spread the toxin in some unique way. Our best guess is that once the BTX was reconstituted and deadly, they could have showered droplets all around the car with an aspergillum in much the same way a Catholic priest sprinkles holy water during mass."

"We'll never know for certain," Jawara added. "I know, but at least we know how the neurotoxin is triggered," Kate said, with a shrug. "Walker, did you or any of your team ever get a line on where the chemicals were purchased or stolen?"

Corcoran relieved Walker by saying, "Farris and I were looking into recent thefts on college campuses and found a lab at Berkeley that had been burglarized in the last few weeks. Take a guess what they stole?" Kate didn't guess. She simply repeated what Walker had reported, "Sodium chloride? Human albumin? Protein load? Porcine gelatin?"

"The burglars stole only the chemicals they needed to make BTX," Corcoran said.

"Men, this is really excellent reporting," she complimented them, acknowledging each one of them in turn.

There was a knock at the conference room door. The Chief of Police entered, followed by William Clark, who immediately took a seat next to his partner Jawara at the table.

Kate's eyebrows furrowed but she stood up directly and took the Chief's hand. Her thoughts turned instantly to that day in the basement of the Hall of Justice. Still convinced she had done the right thing, she couldn't escape the feeling that he would, one day, try to get even with her. Maybe that particular day was finally upon her. She was apprehensive, to say the least.

"This is really an unexpected surprise, Chief Gates," she said, shaking his hand. "We were just reviewing our ongoing investigations."

"I need to speak to the detectives, Dawson," Gates said abruptly.

"Certainly. The floor is yours."

The Chief of Police swapped places with her and stood at the table, looking down at those who were gathered around it. "It is with a heavy heart that I report James Roberts passed away in his sleep early this morning."

Several gasps of surprise broke out around the table. A few others shook their heads, while the majority expressed their sadness with respectful silence. Kate bowed her head and folded her hands together in prayer under her chin. "As most of you already know, he suffered a stroke about seven weeks ago, and has been convalescing at UCSF Medical Center," the Chief continued, forcing back a single tear. "Let me just say that Lieutenant Roberts was a tireless and dedicated public servant and a very capable administrator. His untimely death has left a tremendous void in the San Francisco Police Department.

He will most assuredly be missed. Roberts is survived by his wife, Alma, and his daughter, Tiffany. There will be a formal ceremony on Saturday at noon in Colma when he will be laid to rest. All of you are invited to participate. The order of dress is formal dress blues."

Kate Dawson and the Chief of Police exchanged glances, like duelists on the field of honor. Dawson didn't have to hear any more from him. They were going to "white-wash" Roberts' record, make him out to be a saint, like Spencer Tracy from *Boys Town*, and sell it to the press, hungry for a story. Only she and a few others knew the real truth. She despised him for what he had done to her over the years, how he had belittled and mocked her, made fun of her, and turned life into a living hell. Whereas she sought a mentor, she had received a tormentor instead. Now that he was dead, Kate could not seem to muster any sympathy for him, but at the very least, she didn't feel anger or hatred towards him. She just felt sorrow and sadness for a man who could have done so much more with his life had he not surrendered to the petty jealousies and insecurities he must have felt deep down inside. She also knew that was a lesson she needed to learn if she was going to be an effective administrator.

"One more thing," Gates added, with some degree of hesitation. His eyes narrowed, flashing loathing like a torch at Dawson, but then turned back to face the detectives gathered around the table. "For the last seven weeks, in Lieutenant Roberts' absence, William Clark has done an excellent job, serving as the Interim Head of the Homicide Bureau. He has not only proven to be a very capable administrator but also a worthy friend and confidant of the chief's office."

Alex Starke started to clap, then was joined by Jawara and Ramirez. Eventually, the whole department, even Balardi, was clapping. They clapped for a couple of minutes, and then Kate brought the clapping to a close by walking up to Clark, shaking his hand, and patting him on the back.

"Well done, Clark," she said, smiling.

Gates wasn't about to be upstaged by Dawson. He took Clark's hand, shook it, and repeated, "Well done, William."

The rest of the department's detectives followed suit. They filed past him, shook his hand, and congratulated him.

A moment later, the Chief of Police continued, "Therefore, you can understand my dismay when I offered Clark the job on a permanent basis, and he turned me down flat. He said that he prefers to serve the department as a detective rather than lead as its bureau chief, and I can certainly respect that. The head of a bureau, like Homicide, is a thankless job, with lots of long hours and very little extra compensation. With Clark's mind all made up, the search went on for a properly qualified officer. We interviewed some of the best and brightest stars in law enforcement, but ultimately, we kept coming back to one of your own. I am pleased to announce that Kate Dawson will be assuming the role of bureau chief of homicide, effective November 1st."

The small conference room exploded with applause and cheers, as nearly everyone congratulated Dawson. William Clark was the most relieved and showed it by giving Kate a huge bear-hug. Jawara and Ramirez offered their congratulations, both kissing her politely on the cheek. Corcoran, Farris, and Walker shook hands with Dawson, and wished her well. Even Balardi, who rarely had anything positive to say, exchanged fist-bumps with her.

Gates turned to Dawson. "Well, I guess that's it," he said, extending his hand.

In order to maintain a façade of friendly cooperation, Kate shook his hand, and smiled. She then walked the Chief of Police to the door. "Thanks, Chief, for your visit. I know how busy you are. Lieutenant Roberts meant a lot to each of us. He will be sorely missed."

"Carry on, Dawson," Gates replied, without feeling, and left.

Kate returned to the conference room table. Before she sat down in her chair, she said, "I know Roberts' death comes as a shock to most of you. It certainly was a surprise to me. I had seen him on several occasions recently when I visited him in the hospital, and he always seemed to be in good spirits. He was also looking forward to getting back to work. James Roberts did a lot to make this department what it is today. It is now up to each of us to continue that legacy of hard work."

"Kate, do you suppose we could have a moment of silence?" Clark asked, tears in his eyes.

"Excellent idea, William. Let's all take a moment, and remember Lieutenant Roberts in our thoughts and prayers," Dawson replied, lowering her head, closing her eyes, the one turning yellow now from the massive contusion, and folding her hands together in prayer. After about a minute, she lifted her head, clearing her throat. "Well, let's get back to our meeting. Who's next?"

Balardi shot a look at Dawson, then let his eyes drop to his report. "Kate, you asked Ramirez and me to find the remainder of the Botulinum Toxin. Well, we searched and searched for it, even on the black market, but couldn't find a trace of the neurotoxin for sale. We also scoured the grounds at the Devereaux compound, hoping they tried to bury it there on the grounds. We found a broken crate of stolen AR-17 assault rifles that was missed during the initial sweep of the warehouse, and we've already surrendered those to ATF agents to strengthen their case against the Devereaux's, but we never found a single vial of BTX."

Kate Dawson glanced at her former partner, but Ramirez just shook his head. "There was nothing, Kate."

"We suspect a group of mercenaries, working with the Devereaux's, may have been responsible for stealing the remainder of vials," Balardi added. "Clearly, there is circumstantial evidence to suggest that one of their number played the role of 'fixer' after the warehouse fire. And the fact that none of the vials have hit the black market suggests the group may be hoarding the BTX for themselves; perhaps to use in some larger event they're planning."

"How many vials are we talking about?" she asked. Balardi smugly stated, "Based upon the amount of chemicals that were stolen from Berkeley, we could be looking at one hundred vials or more."

Kate folded her arms across her chest. "That's a hell-of-a large target."

"It's got to be the Super Bowl, Kate. Seventy thousand and eight hundred and seven people attended last year's Super Bowl game at NRG Stadium in Houston, Texas," Clark rattled off the facts, "and oddsmakers are suggesting that we could see record crowds well over eighty thousand people in Minneapolis next year."

"The Super Bowl is five months away," Kate reminded everyone. "Do we know what the 'shelf life' is for freeze-dried BTX?"

Balardi and Ramirez looked at each other, shaking their heads.

"Lieutenant Dawson," Walker said, raising his hand like a school boy asking permission to take the next turn, "I was born and raised in Saint Paul. Temperatures in February are quite frigid. Suppose they're so cold, the terrorists can't reconstitute the neurotoxin? What happens then?"

"Their big event is a bust," Kate shrugged.

"Don't you think they would have thought about that?

Planned for a warmer climate to carry out their operation?" Walker posed.

"Kate, maybe it's not just about the numbers," Jawara suggested. "The President said last week that he was going on a five-state tour, to include California, in order to sell his new economic agenda. He's also agreed to throw out the first pitch at Game One of the World Series between his beloved New York Yankees and the San Francisco Giants. There'll be over 42,000 fans at AT&T Park for that first game. What if they're targeting the World Series?"

"Major Denton did use the phrase 'squeeze play,' a baseball term, and Devereaux did say he would know more at the end of the month. We're well past that now. Aren't the champion teams already in place?" Kate asked rhetorically.

"Yeah," Jawara replied, without giving it much thought.

Clark and Walker nodded in agreement.

Dawson was silent for a moment or two, sitting at the table in the middle of the conference room, thinking matters through. She knew she had one chance to get it right or they'd never trust her again as their leader. Kate glanced at the watch on her wrist, a slim, delicate counterfeit meant to pass for Omega, but was nothing more than a twenty-dollar hunk of metal bought at the Wagon Wheel Flea Market. She was worth more than that, and it was time for her to start showing it.

"Get me everything you can on AT&T Park," she demanded. "We've got only three days to prepare for the possibility of a terrorist attack."

Sometime after midnight, Kate Dawson lay hunched over the conference room table, her arms supporting her head, sound asleep, like a student who had attempted but failed to do her all-nighter. She was the last one left of her team in the Homicide

Bureau. Papers, maps, brochures, and other documents littered the conference room floor, while the table itself was stacked high with Styrofoam coffee cups, boxes from Little Caesar's Pizza, and Chinese take-out from China Wok. The white board had extensive notes—obviously contributed by many different hands—dealing with several, very real scenarios of a terrorist attack on AT&T Park.

Colonel Shears opened the door to the conference room, soundlessly, so as not to disturb Kate, snatched a red marker from the white board's rail, and checked three items on the board with a bright-red checkmark. He also scribbled the words "rail yard" and circled them, the marker squeaking on the board.

Dawson shifted uneasily on the table, regarding him, eyebrows raised in silent question marks. "I've been wondering when you'd show up again," she said, her voice no louder than a whisper.

"I'm only a phone call away," he whispered back. You could never tell he had been beaten to an inch of his life.

"You'll have to remind me to get your number again."

Without waiting for another word, he turned to the white board and wrote his phone number in big, bold, red numerals. He set the marker down and turned back around to her, pointing at the number. "Is this subtle enough, Kate?"

"Now you'll have to remind me to copy it down," she said, dreamily. "Just take a picture of it with your cell phone," he suggested. "That way, you'll always have it at hand." Shears leaned against the white board and lit a cigarette, exhaling the smoke in the next breath. He didn't seem to take his time to enjoy it, but rather smoked instead of chewing gum or biting his nails.

"Can I have one, too?"

"I told you you'd start smoking again," he admonished,

offering her the cigarette that he was smoking and lit another for himself.

"Thank you," Kate whispered, then took a long drag and exhaled the smoke luxuriantly. "I don't know how I've managed without these."

"How can I help you, Kate?" He really wanted to.

"They've backed me into a corner, Shears." Dawson stood up and stretched, her hands reaching towards the ceiling, cigarette between her first two fingers. After a moment, she walked over to the white board. The three marks he'd made on the board had caught her attention. "The evidence all points to a terrorist attack, but I'm just not sure anymore."

"The jury's still out on that one, Kate."

"I have a meeting scheduled with the Chief of Police at nine tomorrow morning," she reported, analyzing the points on the white board. "He's asked me to make three specific recommendations, and I'm down for that. I just wish I had a better idea of what Task Force Red was going to do. If you were planning a hit on a major American city, what would you do?"

Colonel Shears walked over to a cutaway diagram of AT&T Park and its surrounding area that was thumb tacked to the wall. "There's no way to know exactly what they're planning to do," he cautioned her, wagging a finger. "But if it were me planning the hit, I'd target Game One of the World Series. I'd start by staging a diversionary action in the China Basin, like a collision between two small speed boats, with lots of fireworks to draw the attention of the police and Secret Service. But then the main strike would come from behind, using the railroad. I'd load two trains full of BTX and crash them at the terminus between 4th and King. The prevailing winds would drive the toxin over the park, which is less than a block away, and easily kill forty thousand people, including POTUS."

"Fuck!" Dawson exclaimed, taking a deep breath.

"It's a frightening thought, Kate, I know, but it's also something we need to deal with. We can't just bury our heads in the sand anymore and pretend that terrorism doesn't exist. Even home-grown terrorism."

Dawson nodded her head, contemplating it all. "Why not just fill two boats with the neurotoxin and crash them?"

"The China Basin is very narrow there, just beyond center field, and also very shallow. You'd need two large boats to carry enough BTX to do any damage, and then you'd have to worry about them running aground," Shears explained. "Besides the wind there is heading out into the Bay, not into the Park."

"Why not take a couple of boats out into the Bay, and start hurling vials of toxin into the Park?"

Shears chuckled, amused. "That doesn't sound like a particularly effective plan. Remember, Kate, the Police operate their own patrol boats in the Bay and along the China Basin. You'd probably manage to hurl a few vials before they stopped you. At that point, you might as well be catapulting rocks from the moon."

Kate Dawson looked at him, exhaustion and unrecovered injuries taking their toll. "Sorry, I've been at this for hours. Would you take me home?" She stubbed her butt out and waited for his reply.

"Sure, but we'll have to take your car."

"No problem," she replied, handing him her key fob.

Dawson's late model BMW was parked at the curb in front of the Hall of Justice, a parking ticket tucked under the windshield wiper blade. Shears read the green parking sign, "Two-hour parking 8 a.m.–6 p.m., except Sat–Sun." He snatched the ticket off the window for Kate, slid into the driver's seat, then reached across and held the passenger side door open for her.

As she slipped into the soft leather bucket seat, Kate yawned and stretched, her hands high in the air.

"You should be more careful where you park," he admonished her, handing her the parking ticket. Kate cocked her head and cut her eyes. "Oh, please, Shears. It's a little game we play. The meter maid puts the ticket on my car. I tear up the ticket. It's all very civilized."

"What if I ask you to call me something other than Shears? My men call me that all the time. It's not very 'personal.'"

"Then what should I call you?" Kate thought for a moment, then answered her own question. "What if I call you 'Johnnie'? How would you like that?"

Shears didn't look at her. "John would be sufficient."

She smiled playfully. "I know, but I like Johnnie." Kate spoke his name carefully, as if trying it out, seeing if she liked it. She did. Very much. "John sounds like a stuffed shirt, whereas Johnnie is playful, warm."

Shears smiled and nodded his head. "My grandmother from Sicily called me Johnnie."

"Not 'Giovanni'?" she tried to clarify.

"Johnnie," he repeated. "She always called me Johnnie."

"Then Johnnie, it is," she replied, the corners of her eyes drooping from fatigue.

Colonel Shears drove Kate's car towards South Beach, taking the long route along Bryant Street to Beale Street, instead of jumping on the Eisenhower Expressway to the Embarcadero. A light rain was starting to fall when he pulled onto Delancey Street and stopped in front of Kate's building at Bayside Village Apartments. Kate was out cold, her head back against the reclining bucket seat. The only sound was the rain tapping lightly on the roof as Shears leaned in and gathered her into his arms.

He carried her up the three flights of stairs and opened the door to her apartment with one of the keys on her key fob. Shears lay Kate down gently on her twin bed and politely unbuttoned the top two buttons of her Marc Jacobs blouse. He then pulled the blanket at the bottom of the bed over her.

The Army Colonel stood there for a couple of moments, admiring her. She was beautiful, even after hours and hours on the job. Moving in closer, their bodies almost touching, he could smell her perfume, feel her breath on his cheek, almost hear the rhythm of her heartbeats in her chest. He then leaned over and kissed her forehead before leaving her apartment.

On his way back down the stairs, Shears called one of his men on his cell phone and asked for an extraction from Bayside Village Apartments.

CHAPTER TEN

Kate Dawson was so deep in thought as she crossed the street at Bryant against the light, she never heard a single horn or holler or witness a single car screeching to a halt or slamming of its brakes. She seemed to be inside some kind of protective bubble as she replayed Shears' words over and over in her brain, thinking about diversionary tactics, plots, and counterplots. The world that Colonel Shears existed in was on the other side of the looking glass; a world that most people never saw but was there nonetheless. He had afforded her that rare look behind the curtain, but it had come at a great expense to Kate's own sanity. She could no longer ignore things the way that most people did. She had to be a witness to all things seen and unseen. Kate had to be the one to offer the one opinion no one wanted to hear. So, as she walked into the Hall of Justice and her meeting with the Chief of Police, she carried the news that no one wanted to know but everyone had better listen to.

Kate waited respectfully outside the Chief of Police's conference room, and when it was her turn, she walked in, briefcase in hand. She handed her flash drive to the young man handling tech and sat down, opposite Nelson Gates and two men from the Secret Service detail of the President, one blonde and one dark-haired. She pulled out some hand-written notes, with three bullet-pointed items, and eased her chair closer to the microphone.

"Good morning, gentlemen. My name is Lieutenant Kate Dawson, head of the Homicide Bureau," she spoke into the microphone, slowly but clearly. "My department and I have reason to suspect that a credible threat exists against the life of the President of the United States by four members of a former U.S. Army Ranger team, known as Task Force Red."

"Have you lost your mind, Dawson?" Gates responded, incredulous.

"No, sir," she replied, solid as a rock.

The blonde, blue-eyed secret service agent sitting next to the Chief put his hand over the microphone in front of him and whispered something to Gates. Gates replied, also in a whisper. The agent released the microphone, and asked, "Lieutenant Dawson, what do you know about Task Force Red?"

"According to my sources, Task Force Red was an elite five-member unit of the 75th Ranger Regiment, stationed at Bagram Airfield in Afghanistan," Kate reported, keeping to facts gleaned from the team's service records and information related to her by Colonel Shears. "The team was given the task of delivering a cache of diamonds to an Afghani warlord in the Parwan province in exchange for the location of a Taliban leader. The payment never reached the Afghani warlord. Task Force Red was reportedly ambushed somewhere near Charikar in the Parwan province, and every member of the team was killed."

The dark-haired secret service agent took over. "Lieutenant, if everyone was killed, then how can you subsequently report their involvement in an assassination plot against the President?"

"This is all very complicated, sir."

"Then, Lieutenant, I do hope you will try to simplify it for us."

"Instead of delivering the cache of diamonds to the Afghani warlord, as ordered, Task Force Red stole the diamonds for themselves, and then staged their own deaths with an elaborate hoax," Kate explained, waiting for all of it to sink in. "For the last eight months, they've been working together off the grid, stealing millions of dollars in military-grade weapons, munitions, and equipment. With the exception of one member, who may have disagreed with their methods, four members of Task Force Red are very much alive and are hitting even bigger targets."

"I want the names of those four members," the dark-haired agent demanded.

"Samuel Armbruster, Major; Victor Franco, Captain; James "Tex" Denton, Major, and Gideon McMaster, Captain," she rattled off their names and ranks. "I have reason to believe Herbert Jefferson was the lone holdout of the team. I think both he and his wife were murdered for that reason."

The other secret service agent stared her down. "If this is all true, Dawson, then why haven't we heard of it?"

Kate gave it right back. "I don't know, sir," she replied, with a half-truth. "It could be the Army is trying to clean up its own mess internally. You should probably talk to them."

"Where did you get all of this information?" the dark-haired agent asked.

Dawson thought about that for a moment. The last thing she wanted to do was implicate Shears. "I went undercover as a buyer at the Devereaux estate and learned that Robert and Renée Devereaux were not only buying and selling munitions but also bank-rolling terrorists and drug dealers," she revealed. "I'm convinced they killed Sierra Jefferson, Herb Jefferson's wife, while I was there. I was next in line to be killed, if it hadn't been for the timely arrival of the SFPD."

"Lucky for you," the dark-haired agent didn't seem too surprised.

"That's just what I thought," Kate agreed. The blonde secret service agent hesitated a moment. "How did you learn about the assassination plot?"

She looked like a moth that had gotten too close to the flame. "During the reception on the first night, Major Denton got drunk, and started shooting his mouth off about an operation, called 'squeeze play.'"

"'Squeeze play'? What's that?"

"I still have no idea what it means, but I know it's important. Vitally important," she replied. "Denton made the mistake of repeating those two words in front of Robert Devereaux who had a physical reaction, then quickly changed the subject. I wasn't the only one to notice it. Other guests saw it, too."

"'Squeeze play' is a term used in Major League baseball," the dark-haired agent explained. "It's a diversionary play used to move the runner on third base home, after a sacrifice bunt from the player at bat."

"So, I've been told," she said, with a shrug. "When I learned the President of the United States was going to throw out the first pitch at the World Series, I put two and two together, and came up with the possibility of an attempt on his life."

The two secret service agents covered their microphones and conferred privately with one another.

"You seem to know an awful lot about what's going on."

Kate's eyes bugged out. "Don't tell me you think I'm a suspect?"

"Let's just say you're 'a person of interest,'" the dark-haired agent replied, cool as a cucumber.

The other agent said, "Don't go planning any long trips."

"I wasn't planning on going anywhere," she replied, somewhat intimidated.

There was a natural pause while the Chief's tech assistant loaded Kate's PowerPoint slideshow on the main computer, then projected it on the conference room screen.

"Do you have any recommendations for the President's Secret Service Detail?" Gates asked, turning his attention to the screen.

Dawson bobbed her head up and down. "My team and I met for several hours yesterday, and we have three specific recommendations: One, we'd close off the airspace over AT&T Park, including to the Goodyear Blimp; Two, we'd search everyone going into the AT&T Park, and prohibit all coolers, backpacks, oversized bags and purses, camera equipment, the works! And finally, three, we'd increase police presence by adding more police officers on the ground, snipers on all the rooftops, and police boats in the Bay and along the China Basin."

"Thank you, Lieutenant," the Chief of Police said, dismissing her. "Next."

Kate Dawson gathered up her briefcase and notes, collected the flash drive, and stormed out of the Hall of Justice. "Shears, I need to see you immediately," she barked into her cell phone. After calling for him all over town, including leaving about a dozen heated messages at his phone number, Kate Dawson tracked Shears down to the old-fashioned Chinese laundry in Chinatown. The hulking Caucasian man met her at the front desk and led her into the back room where Shears was busy, packing his bags. She felt that "joss" was truly with her that day. Not only had she found her Army colonel but she had also survived yet another trip into the heart of darkness, Chinatown. She hoped that her luck would hold long enough to get back safely to police headquarters.

"The Secret Service didn't believe a word I told them," she complained to Shears, giving him a brief hug and kiss. "They seemed to think it was all some sort of fantasy that I made up. At the very least, they did call me a 'person of interest' and warned me not to leave town."

"I'm not surprised," Shears responded. "If, God forbid, something does happen to the President, they'll try to hang their incompetence around your head; make you out to be the fall guy."

"We've got to stop those assholes in Task Force Red."

"I will," he replied, with confidence.

"I'm coming with you, Shears," Kate insisted, putting her foot down.

"No, you're not going," he replied, stuffing a couple of pairs of BVDs and some heavy socks into his duffle bag. "It's far too risky. The boys and I can handle it. We don't need a fifth wheel gumming up the works."

Kate Dawson remained defiant. "You said so yourself, you need a five-member team. I've only counted four. I'm your fifth member."

"Do you know how to uncouple two freight cars while a train is in motion?" Shears asked rhetorically, already knowing her answer. "No, but you could teach me."

"How are your rappelling skills? Do you think you could rappel down a fifty-foot structure and land safely on the top of a boxcar? A moving boxcar?"

"Sure," Dawson replied, self-assured. "They taught us rappelling at the police academy—"

"—ten years ago."

"So, I'm a little rusty. I can pick it up again."

"That's impossible, Kate," Shears didn't falter, as he continued to pack up his bag. "I need men who know what they're doing. I don't need an amateur getting in the way; maybe getting killed."

"Dammit, Shears! Stop treating me like some kind of rookie!" she shouted, cutting him off with her voice raised in anger. "I've been on the SFPD for ten years. I caught this city's deadliest and most feared serial killer. I prevented a group of religious fanatics from detonating an atomic bomb in the San Andreas fault. I stood toe to toe with and brought down a sitting president on corruption and murder charges. I stopped a North Korean General from triggering World War III at the G-20 summit, and I survived numerous assassination attempts by the Morag Tong. You show me a member of your team who's done at least half of what I've done on my own, and I'll stand down."

Shears addressed her honorably, "Every one of us knows that you've got an impressive resume, Kate. You're a very accomplished woman. But every time I hear you talk about what you've done, I hear a lot of I's. 'I did this . . .' or 'I prevented that . . .' The last time I looked, there was no 'I' in the word 'team.'"

"Is it because I'm a woman?" she demanded, hands on her hips.

"You're totally missing the point, Dawson."

Kate was deeply offended. "That's it, isn't it? You're just another fuckin' Neanderthal who doesn't think a woman can cut it in combat. I can do anything that a man can do. Maybe even do it better." Kate Dawson stomped her foot angrily, and nearly shook the whole Chinese laundry down. Shears was caught off guard and flinched. She started to walk back to the front of the store, but he grabbed her wrist. She stared at him with aversion, her eyes flashing. Kate tried to turn away, but he held her.

"I could never put the woman I love in danger."

Shears pulled her to him and kissed her, deeply, passionately. He pushed her against the back wall, and his arms found their way around her waist, gripping her buttocks. He hesitated for a moment, hearing sounds out on the street, but Kate reached out and pulled him back to her.

Breathing heavily, she asked, "Now, what did you just say?"

He seized her into a desperate, loving embrace; kissing her again, his lips intimately locked with hers.

"That's what I thought you said," she whispered to herself, between kisses.

There they were, in the throngs of heated love, in the back room of the Chinese laundry, until their silence aroused curiosity. A short, round Chinese man peered out from behind the sheet that separated the two rooms, and when he saw them kissing, he ran back to the front of the store with a hand over his mouth, trying to hold back his giggles. In a few moments, it didn't matter. His whole staff was laughing.

Shears reached over the sheet and pounded on the wall. "*Tíngzhǐ xiào, fǒuzé wǒ huì bǎ nǐ de hěnduō dōngxī shāo kāi!* [Stop laughing, or I'll fire the whole lot of you!]" he barked at them in Chinese.

Kate put two fingers up to her lips. His kiss still lingered there. She could feel his heat all over her body. She grabbed his shirt and drew him back to her.

"I love you, Kate, but I've also got a job to do. Where I'm going, you can't follow. What I've got to do, you can't be any part of—"

Dawson cut him off. "I've heard this speech before, but this isn't Casablanca, it's not 1942, and my name isn't Ilsa."

Shears chuckled. "All my life, I've want to say those words to a woman on the eve of a great battle."

"Sweetheart, you're not leaving me behind."

Shears grabbed his duffle bag, backpack, and armament-tactical bag. He turned his back on her. "Get out of here, Kate," he said softly. "Please. Go home, take a long hot bath, and I'll call you tomorrow night."

"I wish you'd reconsider—"

"*Go, Kate,*" he practically shouted. Shears picked up his bottle of Jack Daniel's, took one last, long swig, and threw it in the waste basket.

She looked beseechingly at him for a moment, then he walked out. Kate ran after him and followed him around the back of the laundry. He loaded his bags in the backseat of an olive-drab U.S. Army Surplus Jeep, and then walked around to the driver's side, opened the door and put one leg inside.

Kate grabbed the lapels of his jacket and yanked hard. "Dammit, Shears!" she shouted right in his face. "I'm coming with you!"

"Oh, alright," he said, with a grin. "Get in. Just don't let me hear you bellyaching later when things get too hard. You're in the Army now and you'll get no special treatment where we're going."

Dawson ran around to the passenger side, and jumped in. "I love you," she said.

"I know," Shears said sourly. He fired up the big, Ford engine and revved it a couple of times, popped the clutch, and the fifty-year-old Jeep lurched forward out of the parking spot and hit the road, leaving a trail of black smoke behind him.

At 1:20 p.m., Shears and Dawson pulled into the 34th street entrance of the Desert Yard freight yard in West Oakland. Jimmy Crack Corn, Stevie, and Mitchie the Kid were waiting for them near an old boxcar, along with Alex Starke, and several other men.

Once part of the Union Pacific Railroad, the Desert Yard was bordered on the east by a residential/warehouse district and on the west by Oakland Army Base, located beneath a tangled mass of freeway interchanges, notably the I-880, I-580, and the San

Francisco-Oakland Bay Bridge. Since the Loma Prieta earthquake in 1989, units from Oakland Army Base frequently used the largely deserted freight yard for training soldiers in urban assault. Shears and his team had the Desert Yard signed out for the rest of the afternoon. Local lore among railroaders was that the Desert Yard got its name because there was no water tank available to refill steam locomotives back in the early part of the twentieth century. With little water, the "yard" lived up to its name and proved to be very hot and dry.

"I should have guessed Shears had chosen you for his team," Kate said, walking up to Starke, fist bumping her. "Glad to see you, Kate. I guess that means we're both AWOL today."

"I can't think of a better reason," Dawson sighed, glancing at the Army Colonel, who was having the time of his life. Surrounded by his team, he was mixing it up with them, telling jokes, laughing, backslapping, carrying on like men. Observing Shears, they had lifted him up to that rarest of places, exultation, and held him up on high, for the gods to bless. She had actually found a better reason.

"Ready to go to work?" Shears asked, after everyone had calmed down.

"Looks like you got yourself a fan club, Johnnie," Kate whispered.

"Nothing succeeds better than success. We've had a pretty good run, and the guys like being on a winning team. You see, they're not here for money or fame. They're here to get the job done."

"Well, so am I, but not dressed like this." She waved her hands over her body. "I know. I packed a set of fatigues for you in my duffle bag," he confessed.

"You rat," she said, giving him a shove. "I should have realized that you'd never leave me behind."

"Get dressed, soldier. You're out of uniform."

Kate Dawson went around to the back of the Jeep and dug out a set of army fatigues. She stripped out of her faux Versace jacket, slacks, and her Marc Jacobs blouse, and put on her ACU cargo pants, tan t-shirt, web belt, and brown boots. Kate took the band from her hair and shook her long mane to her shoulders, then twirled it into a loose French roll. She pulled her Army fatigue cap over it and headed back to the boxcar where the rest of the team was gathered. It didn't take Kate long to figure out what was going on.

Like a theatrical showman, Colonel Shears waited for the moment until the wind was kicking up the desert sand over his men and equipment to walk forward past them and take his place in front of the boxcar. He was a powerfully built man in his late forties, but he seemed larger than life when he turned to face them. He was General George Patton, G.I. Joe, and John Wayne all in one. Jimmy Crack Corn, Stevie, Mitchie the Kid, and the others shouting like thirty. Kate and Starke joined in, reluctantly, not really certain what they were supposed to do in all the whooping and hollering.

"HOORAH!" Shears shouted out load, over the noise, to acknowledge his men. "Heard! Understood! Acknowledged! We are the Triple T's, and we are here to kick some serious ass! *Hoorah!*"

His men continued to shout and scream for him.

"Gentleman, we are here to take down Major Denton and Task Force Red, and we *will* take him down," the Army colonel continued to excite his men with traditional rhetoric. "You see, I served with him in combat, and I taught him everything he knows. He and his men turned their backs on their fellow servicemen at Afghanistan. They betrayed our great country, and they are going down! *Hoorah!*"

"*Hoorah!*" his men shouted together. "Heard! Understood! Acknowledged!"

"All right, men, let's get our mind in the mission," he ordered.

"You heard the man, troop! Move out!" Stevie shouted, sounding like the team's unofficial drill sergeant.

Shears walked them around the old boxcar. Its original reddish-brown paint had nearly given way to a whitewashed appearance due to the elements, fading and peeling, chipped and splintered wood, and age. South Shore Railway could no longer be read on the side of the car, and the doors appeared to be rusted shut.

"What you're looking at is a typical, North American railroad car, also known as a 'box car,' because it is quite literally a box, which carries freight, livestock, automobiles, coal, and even people on wheels for the railroads," Shears explained, like a professor talking to his group of graduate students. "This particular car was built in the 1960s, but its design has changed very little in the one hundred and fifty years boxcars have been in use by the railroad. The most common boxcars are fifty to sixty feet in length, nine-and-a-half to ten feet wide, and twelve feet high. Tomorrow, the first train is likely to have six to ten of these boxcars in tow. We have no idea what the freight will be, other than fifty to sixty vials of the BTX. If we're lucky, that's all they'll be carrying. If not, then stopping each of these cars is going to be a real bitch."

"You mentioned the 'first' train?" Stevie asked, staring directly at Shears.

"Yes, there will most likely be two trains," he replied, deadly serious. "Mind you, this is all guess work at this point. We don't know exactly what Task Force Red is planning. Major Denton and I were at West Point together but didn't know each other because he was actually a year behind me. Nevertheless, we did take many of the same courses in strategic planning, military operations, and urban warfare. Whatever he knows, I know. If I was planning the hit, this is exactly what I would do. Based upon everything I know about Task Force Red, he won't deviate much beyond that."

"Colonel Shears, since I'm the new 'guy' here, would you mind walking all of us through what's going to happen?" Kate asked, playing her assigned role as the "rookie."

"I was just about to get to that," he replied, cockily. Shears retrieved a crumpled pack of cigarettes from his jacket pocket and, using his lucky, four-leaf clover Zippo lighter, lit one and took a couple of puffs. "Sometime around 1:15 p.m., minutes before the start of Game 1 of the World Series at AT&T Park, Denton will stage a diversionary action in the China Basin, out beyond center field. The diversion will be showy, with lots of fireworks, perhaps the collision of two small speed boats. Fans will drop everything they're doing to focus on it, so will the local police and Secret Service Officials will probably push back the official ball toss by the President and delay the start of the game by a couple of minutes. So, instead of being in the safety and comfort of the owner's suite, the President will be down on the field, perhaps in one of the dugouts, with his Secret Service detail, awaiting the ceremonial ball toss. The main strike will come at one-twenty or one-twenty-five from the railroad yard. Two trains loaded full of BTX will crash, one right after the other, into the terminus between 4th and King Streets. The crash will be huge, very literally turning two trains into a shower of burning splinters. Prevailing winds, southeasterly at that time of the day, will easily blow the neurotoxin over AT&T Park, less than a block from the railroad yard, and kill forty thousand people, including the President."

There was a moment, a long moment of silence, wherein his

team stared at each other without expression. The apocalyptic vision took a moment to sink in. Shears took advantage of the silence to draw heavily on his cigarette.

Kate was sorry she asked the question and wondered how she could take it back.

Starke felt as if someone had sucker punched her in the jaw. She reached up and took hold of it with her right hand and moved it back and forth. "Why don't we just climb on board the locomotive, and step on the brake?"

"There is no brake in the traditional sense of the word," Shears answered. "Apart from the engine, there's an emergency break in each car, but if I were Major Denton, I would have ordered my men to disconnect all of them first. Besides, the locomotive is likely to be heavily fortified or boobytrapped to prevent us from simply climbing aboard and stopping the train."

"Why don't we just throw one of those switches?" Dawson queried, her thought not fully formed.

"Which switch are you talking about, Kate?"

She struggled to remember. It had been a long time since she played with trains. "You know the one that has the train run off on a siding?"

"That's a completely different set of problems," Shears replied, running out of options. "All the tracks are now programmed by a computer. So, switching one train would only cause a collision with another train."

"What about derailing the train in the middle of the yard?" Starke asked. "We could do that, Alex," Shears confessed, "but then you're turning one potential problem into dozens of others. Can you imagine the destructive force of two hundred tons of locomotive smashing freely through a train yard?"

"Is there any way of stopping this train between here and there?" Kate asked bluntly.

"No, but I've got a plan to hijack both trains in transit and to bring them safely to a stop, without losing a single life," Shears boasted, a broad smile across his face.

"You've got to be kidding?" Starke said, with a healthy dose of skepticism. "You're going to need three times our number just to stop one train."

"We should discuss this further, Colonel," Kate recommended.

Shears beheld her knowingly. "There's a reason why we're training here today at the Desert Yard instead of the Presidio of Monterey or Camp Pendleton," he teased them, flicking away his cigarette. "This boxcar on the tracks and the overpass above us—I think that's I-580—approximate the conditions we'll be dealing with tomorrow. By drilling on my plan here today at the Desert Yard, you'll be more than ready for the mission tomorrow."

No sooner had Colonel Shears finished speaking that he climbed to the roof of the boxcar and shimmied up a rope to the highway high above them. He looked down on his men from I-580, walking briskly alongside the gleaming metal guardrail, which separated the road from the wall of the highway. He continued walking and striding, stopping and turning, with graceful movements of his arms. The Army Colonel was doing more than just play acting, as he held his men spellbound, walking from one side of the overpass to the other. He was letting them know just how safe and comfortable he felt at that great height.

Shears stopped, reached down to his feet, and picked something up. Cradled in his arms, as if it were a part of his muscular upper body, was a large, canvas-covered bundle. Shears looked down at his bundle, almost affectionately. It was filled with rope, about seventy-five feet of Bluewater 9 mm Canyonline rope. He took one end of the rope, threaded it through a carabiner on his belt, and then used his right hand as a guide to feed the rope back through a metal conical device for rappelling. He tied the rope around the cement base of the guardrail. Looking down, Shears gave a hand signal to Jimmy who nodded and backed up several feet. He then threw his bag over the precipice, his rappel line unspooling out of the canvas bundle as it hurtled through space, crashing to the sandy floor below inches in front of Jimmy.

"You don't know how much I missed this, Jimmy!" he shouted down to his man. "Once you get this in your blood, you never get it out!"

Jimmy Crack Corn smiled and gave him a huge "thumbs-up."

With a gloved hand grabbing onto the rope, Shears used his brake hand to snap his rappel device in place, and he started down. Every few feet, he adjusted the autoblock so that his brake hand could take in slack and weight of the rope. He kept his legs perpendicular to the highway overpass, and his torso leaning slightly in as his feet walked him backwards down the cement. All at once, his feet reached the end of the overpass, and he was airborne, maintaining his brake hand on the rope. Shears turned his head slightly to the right and left to watch for obstructions, but otherwise continued a slow but steady, controlled descent. Then, finally, like a well-trained acrobat, he landed on the roof of the boxcar, standing upright. He unclipped the rope from carabiner, and tossed it aside, now free to move around.

"We're going to rappel down from one of the overpasses that trains pass under heading into the City of San Francisco," Shears clarified, breathing normally. "There are at least five or six over-passes, starting at 25th Street, that we'll use. Since we don't want to get all bunched up on one overpass, we'll each be assigned our own overpass. We'll also be carrying a grappling hook if we fail to land on top of the boxcar."

"What's the likelihood we'll need it?" Starke asked. As a former paratrooper in the Israeli Army, she wasn't going to need one at all.

He was unruffled by the question. "If you rappel straight down, aiming for the middle of the roof, you won't need it at all. But I always say, I'd rather have something and not need it than to need something and not have it. Paratroopers with the 101st Airborne going into Normandy during the Second World War carried over one hundred pounds of equipment they didn't need."

"Are we all going to have to do that?" Kate shivered at the thought. Colonel Shears encouraged her, "You can do it, sweetheart."

Weakly, she said, "But I've got this thing about heights."

"Believe me, Kate. After you've rappelled a couple of dozen times today, you won't be bothered by heights again."

"That's comforting," she replied, as the typical smart ass she was.

Shears shrugged lightly. "The trickiest part of the rappel is landing on the roof of a moving boxcar, but you'll only have to do that once. Tomorrow."

"Now he tells us," Kate joked, chuckling uncomfortably.

"Once we've made it safely to the roof of the boxcar, we'll climb down a ladder and uncouple the cars," he explained, going onto the next step. "Boxcars typically have four sets of ladders built right into the side of the car. There are two on the front, port and starboard, and two in the back, port and starboard. It doesn't really matter which one you use but remember that we're planning on uncoupling the cars from the rear of the train first. So, use the ladders that are behind you as you look forward."

Shears climbed down from the roof of the boxcar using the

rungs of the ladder and hung onto the last rung. He then started pointing out details on the boxcar. "Boxcars are connected to other railcars and locomotives by couplers which look like these huge, iron knuckles. Left and right knuckles are always paired. These couplers are uncoupled by a cut bar, which is only accessible from the side ladders. When you lift the lever on the bar, it rotates and lifts the pin out of position on the coupler, allowing the knuckle to separate from its paired knuckle. Brakemen and conductors frequently 'kick' cars from the train by uncoupling them while moving. Well, that's exactly what we are going do, 'kick' boxcars from the train."

Jimmy and Stevie examined the cut bar and estimated what it would take to hold onto the ladder and lift the uncoupler.

"Go ahead. Lift it up," Shears ordered.

Following instructions, his men lifted the lever on the bar, and watched as it rotated and lifted the pin out of position on the coupler. The knuckle was now free to move. His men seemed satisfied.

"That's exactly what we're going to do to uncouple those boxcars. We'll uncouple them one at a time," he explained. "When the boxcars pull apart, that will bust open the air pressure lines and physical brakes will clamp down throughout the car. Separated from the train, the boxcar rolls to a stop harmlessly. No broken vials, and no deadly nerve gas."

"Do you mean that's it?" Kate asked the question that they all wanted answered but were afraid to ask themselves.

Shears was blasé, brushing off the query. "Well, you still have other cars to uncouple, but that's essentially it. So, when your boxcar starts to go, make sure you're standing on the one that's still coupled. Or you'll find yourself sitting in the middle of the yard on a box car that's no longer connected to a locomotive. There'll be no way for you to get back on board the train."

Kate Dawson nodded.

"I'll receive accurate, minute-by-minute reports in my headset from my people in the signal towers, and I'll relate those directly to you" he added, looking from man to man. "They'll also be following Major Denton's movements. If he or any of his men get even the slightest whiff of our plan, we'll be fighting ex-Army Rangers with automatic weapons as well as trying to complete our mission."

"What are our rules of engagement?" Starke asked.

After a pause, Shears answered, "There is no quarter. We're not taking prisoners, nor will they. Shoot to kill and be damned accurate. We're not going to get another chance at this."

They all seemed to hesitate, but only a split second before Kate Dawson replied. She looked squarely at the Army colonel, holding his gaze, no wise-ass remarks or bullshit. "We're behind you, sir."

Shears looked away and fumbled for a cigarette, lighting it and sucking the smoke hungrily into his lungs. "So, if you're ready to get started with your training, we'll start drilling on rappelling."

For several miles, the I-280 Southern Embarcadero Freeway ran directly above the railroad freight line going into the City of San Francisco. It always required regular maintenance work, especially at the 16th Street exchange. Trains slowed down to twenty-five miles-per-hour through the exchange there because of the number of city workers shoring up the numerous underpasses and damages to the highway above. In fact, for three weeks, the city workers had built an elaborate scaffold from the ground to the highway above and over the railroad line to complete their regular maintenance work. William Clark found the construction scaffolding for Kate while driving around the area looking for a place to park the police department's unmarked surveillance van. On Tuesday morning, Clark parked right at the corner.

Kate Dawson was relieved to know that she didn't have as great a rappel as the others to get aboard the train; figured her Chinese "joss" was still with her. She climbed into the back of the van, and with Mikhail Jawara's help, started suiting up in basic black, like a member of the SWAT team. She pulled on a pair of weather-proof tactical pants, one leg at a time, and then, added knee pads, adjusting the elastic behind each knee for a firm but comfortable fit. Next, she put on a long-sleeve black shirt and a bulletproof, top-of-the-line body armor vest. She zippered the vest up to her neck. Jawara handed her, one at a time, a pair of leather work boots with steel toes and shanks. They were tight on her feet, but she felt like she had excellent traction. She adjusted the web belt with carabiner and service pistol around her waist; securing at last the grappling hook. She was doubtful she would need it, but agreed with Shears, *'It was better to have it and not need it than to need it and not have it.'* Finally, she pulled on a helmet, which she snapped under her chin, and goggles for eye protection. The SWAT suit wasn't as bulky or cumbersome as ones that she had worn in the past. It certainly did give her much better freedom of movement, but she still wasn't crazy about it. *Maybe, it's the boots?* Kate felt like one of those Stormtroopers from *Star Wars*, a movie she and Lenny had seen together many times. *Heavily-armored, ready-for-bear, and not particularly effective.*

"One word about how big this suit makes my ass look," she warned Jawara, "and you're going home with a black eye."

Mikhail snickered. "Hey, you're talkin' to a brother here. You should know how much we love them big booties."

She fixed him with a look. "I warned you."

"Kate, be ready," Shears squawked over her radio headset. "The train is ten minutes out."

"Copy that," she replied.

Dawson climbed out of the back of the van, grabbing a pair of leather gloves on her way. She pulled them on her hands and, with Jawara's help, hurried across the street to the chain-link fence, marked "construction area." Clark held up traffic for her, and together they marched her along through the construction yard. A few of the city workers looked up from their lunches to see what was going on, but for the most part, they simply ignored her, choosing instead to ease back and enjoy the shade of the highway above on this hot and humid day. Finally, Clark and Jawara placed her hands on the scaffolding ladder.

"Happy hunting, Lieutenant," Clark said, almost in tears.

"You go get 'em, Kate," Jawara added, handing her a 9 mm HK submarine gun.

"Thanks, guys! See you later, I hope."

With the HK slung over her shoulder, she climbed up forty-five feet of ladder clumsily, not used to the steel-toed boots and worked her way across the scaffold plank, until she stood roughly right in the middle. A canvas bag with the rappelling rope marked the spot on the plank. She glanced down at the bag, then over her shoulder and saw the train at a distance, getting closer with every second. The train never looked more powerful or as menacing as it barreled down the tracks towards her. The words "sleek," "smooth," "beautiful," and "terrifying" raced through her mind as she tried to focus on two immediate tasks: threading the rope through the carabiner on her belt and tying the rope off on the metal bar above her head. With both tasks quickly accomplished, Kate tossed the canvas bag aside, and watched it hurtle through space, the end of her rappelling line tied to the bag crashing uneventfully to the ground.

She then lifted one leg over the scaffolding, followed by the other, until she was on the edge, ready to jump. She took hold of the rappel line with one hand and clamped down the rappel device with the other. Suddenly, a couple of city workers took an interest in what she was doing. But it was far too late. With its wheels spinning and its red lights flashing, the train slowed briefly through the work zone, and then raced on ahead into the vastness of the City of San Francisco.

Kate Dawson jumped at the very last second. She flew through the air for a few moments on the rappel line—the rope burning through her leather gloves as she tried to slow her descent—and then she crashed down on the roof of the boxcar hard; hard enough to shake the grappling hook loose from her belt. Hurriedly, in panic mode, she opened the carabiner and threw off the rappel line. But as she turned to grasp the grappling hook, its handle seared her newly rope-burned palms and slipped out of her reach. The hook tumbled forward, turning end over end, until it rolled off the edge of the roof and dropped to the gravel yard below. It took hold on one of the track's wooden crossbeams and tugged her sideways off the edge of the roof. Dawson scrambled madly to untie the long, lead rope from around her waist, but found herself rolling over and tumbling sideways to her doom. Freeing the knot, she stopped herself in time, holding tightly to the edge of the roof.

"Kate, are you okay? Do you copy?" Shears shouted in her earpiece. "Soldier, report your six. Immediately."

"I'm okay," she replied into her headset. "Got tangled up with my grappling hook on the jump. Heading now to uncouple first car. Do you copy?"

"Just received report from the signal towers," Shears reported. "Denton and Franco are in the locomotive of the first train. We're delivering them a first-class ticket to hell. Over and out."

"Don't get yourself killed, Shears! I'll never forgive you! Do you copy?"

"I hear you, Kate, loud and clear!"

The train sped towards the city limits, tearing along the tracks over bridges and freeways, leaving the lush meadows, lakes, and marshes of the countryside far behind it. In the distance, the skyline of San Francisco loomed. The Transamerica Pyramid, Salesforce Tower, 181 Fremont Building, Coit Tower, and the San Francisco-Oakland Bridge all stood tall against the horizon. Even AT&T Park could be seen. At the bend in Mission Bay, the railroad tracks were racing alongside the cars on the freeways that lead into the city.

Kate Dawson regained her footing. From there, she headed to the front of the boxcar, and down the ladder, the palms of her hands stinging on each rung. The bulky boots barely fit the rungs of the ladder, so she encountered some difficulty climbing down. At the bottom of the ladder, she locked her left arm around the rung, just as Shears had shown them, and reached for the lever on the bar. She got her hand around it, but she couldn't budge it, frozen solid as a block of ice.

"Oh, God, what I wouldn't give right now for a bottle of WD-40?" she said her prayer out loud.

Kate took the chance and removed her gloves; they were little more than tatters of leather at that point. Then she reached down to pull the lever up, but it was still stuck. She kept pulling at it, pushing through the pain of her palms, until she was flat against the wall of the boxcar. Bracing herself, she used the wall as leverage. The lever went up half way but refused to go up any further. Finally, taking a deep breath, she held it in, grunted, and pushed upward again. The lever went all the way up this time, rotated and lifted the pin out of position on the coupler. The large knuckle opened, and released its mirror-image knuckle from its grasp.

The train lurched forward, similar to an elevator car stuck between floors, and then the cars pulled apart from each other; hoses breaking, spewing oil everywhere; the air pressure exploded, and the brakes clamped down with an audible 'thunk.' Sparks flew from the wheels in every direction and piercing screeches filled the air as the wheels locked up and the boxcar slid harmlessly along the track until it stopped of its own accord.

Grabbing onto a rung of her boxcar's ladder with her injured palm, Kate clung tight, and watched as the other boxcar fell away into the distance. She and the rest of the train sped forward, shooting past the other trains in the yard, heading directly for the terminus, the end of the line.

Dawson knew she had no time to sit back and admire her handiwork. She had other cars to uncouple and the track was running out. She also realized she'd never get the job done if she had to keep worrying about the palms of her hands. Thinking quickly, she reached into her right pants pocket, and tore out the cotton lining; she then repeated the action with her left pocket. The pockets became make-shift mittens that she pulled on each hand and tied the excess fabric around her wrists.

Riding the train for another mile, Kate psyched herself up and began climbing the ladder to the roof with her newly-made mittens. *Next!* She tried to run down the center of the roof, feeling a bit more confident, perhaps a little too cocky. But with each step, she felt the pressure of the train's g-forces on her face and struggled to keep her balance as she moved down the narrow beam of the boxcar. Clutching the ladder down, she missed the first rung altogether and very nearly threw herself over the edge. For several heartbeats, she hung there, adrenaline rushing through her body, watching the landscape race by. Regaining her footing, Kate made it down the ladder, and held on for dear life at the bottom. The routine was the same as before, but thankfully, this time she had little trouble raising the lever and uncoupling the next set of knuckles. The hoses and air pressure escape valve screamed in retaliation as the boxcar came uncoupled from the train and rolled safely to a stop.

The train zoomed past a network of power lines and careened past other trains it met on the tracks towards the heavy wooden stop at the end of the line.

Starting up the rear ladder on the left side of the train, Dawson glimpsed a figure as it slipped into the shadows. She ducked her head back down, pressing her body flat against the car. Moments ticked by before she looked again. At the other end of the boxcar, a man carrying a MAC-10 had reached the top of the ladder. He stood upright, firmly on the roof, peered down the ladder on the left side of the train, then started moving slowly in her direction.

Kate looked back down the ladder—nowhere to go. She could always retreat to the bottom rung, but then that would make her a prime target. The only way off the boxcar was to jump, and she didn't relish the idea of jumping off a speeding train. One chance out of ten, she might survive, but then she realized she didn't have any chance of survival if and when he finally reached the end of the roof. Sixty feet, that's what Shears had told them. The boxcar was roughly sixty feet long.

Holding the rung with her left hand, she swung the HK in front of her, and clicked off the safety with her thumb. Right then, the train hit a bump in the tracks, lurched forward, and Kate's feet slipped off the ladder. She hung in the air by one hand, her body banging against the side of the train as she desperately tried to regain her footing; her boots too big for her feet and too big for the ladder as well. The train made a slight turn on the tracks and slapped her full force against the side, where she again gained purchase. Another bump or turn like that and Dawson knew she was history.

The gunman reached the end of the roof. Precariously perched, he peered over the right side, then turned to the left. Making eye contact, he laughed, and trained his MAC-10 on her.

BLAM! BLAM! BLAM! She fired a short burst of the HK and hit him center mass; his body flew off the roof at impact, careened downward, and landed in scrub brush alongside the tracks.

In shock, Dawson clicked the safety back on the HK, and let it fall back on its sling to her side. Then, slowly, almost methodically, she forced her feet into the last rungs of the ladder and climbed hand over hand to the roof, the wind fighting her every inch of the way.

The train sped along the mass of crisscrossing tracks, changing at the switches and scooting past the last of the signal towers, as Kate made her way sluggishly to the front, and down the next ladder. Fatigue began to set in as the rush of adrenaline started to wear off. She hung onto the last rung and reached for the uncoupling lever, but here was another one that didn't want to budge. Frustrated, she pulled the goggles from her face and wiped the sweat away. She'd had enough of that, too.

Adjusting the goggles back on her face, she pulled up with all her might and slammed the lever up against the bar. The pin released the mighty knuckle from its grasp on the other knuckle and the boxcar started blowing its hoses as it uncoupled from the car in front. Taking three deep breaths, Dawson reasoned that she had either one or two cars left, and time was running out.

As Kate started up the rear ladder, she heard gunshots and immediately drew her HK, clicking the safety off. She kept her head low as she crossed the length of the boxcar, low-crawling down the center of the roof, minimizing exposure. Another man with a MAC-10 knelt on the roof, his back to Dawson, firing down at the platform below. Alex Starke, his intended target, returned fire, keeping close to the ladder. She was a sitting duck for the second gunman.

Kate Dawson flattened herself on the roof, took aim and waited for Starke to stop shooting. Starke fired twice, then Kate squeezed off a short burst. BLAM! BLAM! BLAM! BLAM! The second gunman grabbed his shoulder and shouted madly, while Starke used the moment to reload another clip. Wounded but not down, he turned, wobbly, and fired a wild volley at Kate, bullets pinging off the car, then at Starke, then back at Kate. Watching him, Kate imagined that he had an unlimited supply of ammunition, but the opposite was actually true. The MAC-10 fired bursts of four bullets at a time, with a magazine of thirty. At most, the gunman could fire seven or eight bursts before he'd have to reload. And because of the weapon's poor recoil, the first shots were always better than the last couple. She'd have to wait him out and then hammer him on the reload.

"Are you okay, Starke?" Kate asked into her headset.

"Yeah, a little banged up," Alex replied, in a whisper, "but I'm okay."

"Do you think you can draw his fire?"

"Piece o' cake."

"On the count of three? One, two, three!"

Alex Starke let go several rounds from her Glock and the second gunman returned fire. He had not anticipated being out of rounds so quickly, had not counted, and scrambled for his next magazine. In the precious few seconds it took for him to reload, Kate Dawson fired a long burst. BLAM! BLAM! BLAM! BLAM! BLAM! BLAM! He was dead by the third shot, flipping off and into the railway ditch.

Kate clambered down the ladder, helping pull Starke to her feet. "Where's Shears?"

"I don't know," Alex replied, holding her arm. "He went after Denton on the locomotive, and I held Franco down here—"

"Shears! What's your six? Shears!" Dawson screamed into the headset. "We only have seven minutes," Starke reminded her, "maybe eight."

"Any word about the other train?" she said in panic, looking down the track. Starke smiled brightly at Dawson. "The boys took her down without a scratch! They're doing some kind of victory dance now."

"Then these were the last two cars," Kate said, her eyes boring into Starke's. "You've got to disable them. I'm going after Shears."

Starke grabbed Kate's hand. They shared a moment, albeit a brief moment, of admiration and mutual respect. "Bring him home, Kate." She braced herself to disconnect the trailing car.

"I'm going to try."

Kate Dawson climbed up her last ladder to the roof, ran down the center, bracing herself against the wind, and crossed to the locomotive engine. The train roared down the tracks, racing toward the heavy wooden stop at the end of the line. She could see it now as it loomed on the horizon; closer and closer with each second that ticked by. She inched along the iron railing to the train cabin, gun drawn. The door was closed but both of the cab windows had been shot out. Kate approached them cautiously, slowly, adrenaline pulsating throughout. Taking a deep cleansing breath, she glimpsed inside.

On one side of the cabin, near the driver's compartment, Major Denton leaned back in the engineer's chair, right leg propped up, a bloody mess. He held a gun out, about waist high, pointing at Shears. On the other side of the cabin, near the radio, Shears was sprawled on the ground, contorted with pain, also a bloody mess. He held a gun out, about the same height, pointing at Denton. They appeared to be in a kind of Mexican standoff.

Kate backed away from the window and blinked the sweat out of her eyes in order to figure out what to do. She had never been in such a situation before, but she knew what it meant. A Mexican standoff is a confrontation between two individuals in which no strategy existed that would allow either party to achieve victory. They'd sit there until doomsday unless some outside third party made it possible to resolve the standoff. Her thoughts ran wild. *I'm it. Oh, shit, I'm it! But what am I supposed to do? Shoot Denton, and pull Shears to safety? But if Denton has a boobytrap, he could trigger it and blow us all to kingdom come! Unless I kill Denton with a single shot . . .* She wasn't about to let anything happen to Shears. With the train mere moments from crashing, the power seemed all on Denton's side. He just had to wait it out for a few more seconds or shoot Shears dead at any time.

She pulled the SWAT helmet off her head and threw aside the goggles. Hair matted and glistening with sweat, her eyes burned with a determination that held the panic of a train wreck in her gut at bay. She checked the HK for rounds and ditched it when she realized it was out of ammo. Her fingers were slick and slippery on her 9 mil as she drew it from the holster on her belt. Kate Dawson was out of time. She had to make a decision, right or wrong.

Kate went back to the open window, sighted Denton where he sat in the driver's chair, peeked one final time, then came up shooting. BLAM! BLAM! The first struck him dead center in the forehead and the other right in his heart. Denton's dying reflexes managed to fire only one shot, which caught Shears in the chest and threw him backwards across the floor. Shears came up fighting like a madman, twisting and turning and clawing at his chest. He shucked out of his combat armor, dropping the smoking pieces to the floor. Kate Dawson came around through the door, then crouched down right next to Shears.

"Good shooting, Kate," he said, turning to her. "I wasn't sure how much longer I was going to be able to keep my gun raised at him."

"C'mon! We've got to get out of here!" she shouted over the roar. "We only have seconds!"

"It's no good. I'm all shot up. I won't be worth a damn after this. Go! Save yourself! I'll only slow you down."

Kate turned to face him, her eyes flashing. "Stop giving me fuckin' orders! I'm gonna save your life if it's the last thing I do!"

"Bitch, bitch, bitch," he said, all out of energy.

"I want you to put your arms around my neck and hang on—now! Hang on tight!"

Groggy and a bit bleary-eyed, Shears hooked his arms around her shoulders, and she half-carried him to the rear exit door of the locomotive. They stumbled out onto the platform, Dawson supporting Shears who was doubled over in agony.

"Come on, you can make it. We're almost there."

She sat him down on the steel floor between two iron posts, then placed his hand on the iron railing and grabbed hold of the other side of the railing.

"Okay, Shears, we're as far as we can go," Kate said, breathing heavily. She didn't sugarcoat anything, but just told him straight, "We're going to have to jump off the train."

"All right," he replied, with a shrug.

"I'll tell you when."

He shook his head. "I'd prefer you just give me a good push." She did.

They tumbled down together into the train yard. Eyes shut,

holding each other tight, they hit the rock bed as close to a tuck and roll as possible and came to skidding halt in a cloud of dust and gravel. Moments later, as the air cleared, Kate pushed herself up, desperate to see his face, to know he was alive. She cradled his face with her hands, tears of joy and relief coursing down her cheeks. Covered in blood, in tremendous pain, and weak, he reached up and vigorously brought his lips to hers.

Starke frantically ran down the tracks towards them. Gasping for breath, she dropped to her knees and hovered over Shears, checking his wounds. Kate lay his head gently to the ground, rocked back on her ankles, and tried to stand up. She was faint, shaky, covered in cuts and blood.

"How much time, Alex?" Kate asked.

"Plenty! Twenty-six seconds!" Starke joked.

Barreling through the last of the rail yard, the engine was going way too fast for the end of the line. The train wheels began sparking on the rails as an attempt was made by those in the signal towers to slow it down. At the terminus, it smashed into the wooden stop, hurling hundreds of matchsticks in the air, yet continued on, grinding on the concrete for over a thousand feet, until it came to a stop.

Kate kneeled down and threw her arms around Shears. "I love you," she whispered, kissing him passionately, urgently, through blood, sweat, and tears.

Pushing her back just enough to lock her gaze unswervingly, he replied, "I love you, too," then collapsed securely in her arms.

EPILOGUE

Kate Dawson walked into the Homicide Bureau at the Hall of Justice a few minutes after seven o'clock that morning. The Police Department was burying her former boss out at Woodlawn Memorial Park in Colma, California, and she had not only agreed to say a few words about Lieutenant James Roberts but was also to be part of the miles' long caravan out to the cemetery. At the same time, a heavy blanket of fog had fallen over the city, making the morning commute a hazardous one for everyone. The mist was especially thick over the downtown streets, enshrouding most of the buildings and high rises along Bryant Street.

Nothing ran in the newspapers or on television about a small group of men saving the President and forty thousand fans at AT&T Park from a terrorist strike with a deadly nerve gas. As far as anyone was concerned, it never happened.

However, on the day after the San Francisco Giants posted a big win against New York in the first game of the World Series, Dawson received a telex from Interpol. The telex confirmed that Robert and Renée Devereaux had been arrested in Rome, while attempting to flee to nearby neutral Switzerland. All of their bank accounts had been frozen, and in conjunction with an FBI extradition warrant, they were to be returned to the United States to stand trial. More arrests related to illegal arms and drug smuggling were expected in the next few days.

When she arrived at police headquarters, the building looked deserted, even though many of the parking spots along the street were filled with vehicles belonging to police detectives. The halls were dark and gloomy, all of the shades drawn, and office doors closed the night before. If Kate didn't know any better, she would have imagined the building was in mourning, possessed by the spirit of some great police officer who had recently passed. She couldn't shake the feeling that she was not alone there, that there was someone watching her every step.

She stood in the middle of the darkened hallway, just outside the Homicide Bureau, and listened. Just beneath the deafening sounds of silence, she heard a sound, a tiny sliver of noise that could have been a mouse squeaking. But this particular sound was a measured one, a creak rather than a squeak, every few seconds, as regular as the hands on a clock. She walked along the hallway, following the sound like a predator tracking its prey, stopping every few steps to listen. Kate continued to follow the sound, looking around, remembering . . .

Suddenly, it was fully daylight, no fog, no rain, just glorious sunlight. The drawn shades were all up, the doors open, and the lights were on. Frank Miller, her late partner, stood next to her, practically holding her steady on her feet. She was so nervous that she thought she might lose it, but as she looked at him, Kate found the courage necessary to do what she needed to do. She looked at him a second time. He was young again, close to the age when she first met him. At last, Dawson realized she had stepped through a portal into her past.

"You're going to do just fine," he reassured her, just as he had reassured her on that first day, ten years earlier, when she met

Lieutenant Roberts, the bureau chief of Homicide. She was in another time, another place, experiencing that moment from the past all over again.

Miller knocked on the door for her, and whispered, "Good luck."

"Come in," Roberts growled, his familiar guttural sound.

Kate opened the door. The Lieutenant was sitting in rocking chair near his desk, pitching gently back and forth on the wooden rocker, the creak of the chair keeping perfect tempo with the hands on his office clock. He was reading a file on his desk; refused to acknowledge her right away.

"Lieutenant Roberts, I'm Kate Dawson," she said, stumbling into the room on unsteady legs, closing the door behind her. She gazed at him with wide, red-rimmed eyes. She had been out partying the night before, celebrating her promotion from patrolman to detective. Her hair was a tangled mess; her cheeks drawn and hollow from the lack of sleep. She should have looked much better. The self-confidence and calm reassurance that she had worked a lifetime to perfect had vanished in an instant with the stumble; quickly replaced by fear and doubt.

Roberts finally looked up, scratching the stubble of beard that was growing on his face, then reached to adjust the small, horned-rim glasses on the end of his nose as if to bring the microscopic image of the female detective into focus. He didn't know what to make of her.

"Yes, I know who you are," he replied gruffly. "Frank Miller seems to think you'll make a good detective. I'm not so sure. Your eyes are so bloodshot you can barely see out of them, and I can spot a hangover from a mile away. Must have been one hell-of-a party last night, Dawson."

Kate folded her arms across her chest, and looked down, ashamed. "I'm sorry, sir. I was celebrating my promotion last night. I guess I got carried away. It won't happen again, Lieutenant."

"Honesty? I like that, Detective. I will not tolerate a liar."

"Miller taught me to stick with the truth," she said, with great pride. "He seems to think that it's always easier to remember the truth than some convoluted lie you made up on the spot."

Roberts picked up her folder from the desk and glanced through it. "Miller tells me that you frequently disobey orders."

"No, sir," she replied. "Only the orders worth disobeying."

"He also says you're one of the best trainees he's ever had," the Lieutenant added, reading through the report.

Kate nodded. "Well, like I was saying, he's been a great mentor to me."

"You graduated at the top of your class at the Police Academy?"

"Yes, sir."

Roberts shot her one of his patented steely looks. "Detective Dawson, in a real crisis situation, will you cause me any trouble?"

"Probably, sir," she responded honestly.

He was silent for a long moment, then extended his hand, saying, "Welcome to Homicide, Dawson."

Kate took his hand, and shook it . . .

As she stood there, the portal to the past started to close and the room went dark again; the shades drawn, doors closed, and all of the lights out. The people who were there faded away until they were nothing but shadows of a former time. She turned back to Roberts, who smiled, unlike the first time he laid eyes on her, then also faded away into memory.

For a good slowly-ticking minute, Kate Dawson stood, planted in the middle of the darkened hallway, not just simply remembering but also trying desperately to hold onto the images from the past. However, as the lights began to come on, the office doors opened, and the shades were lifted, she realized that a brand new day was dawning for her and the San Francisco Police Department. She could no longer hold onto the past but had to be content with the knowledge that it would always be there, lurking in the shadows. For now, it was time for her to move forward, to embrace the new dawn. She crossed the hallway, stepped through the door into her new office, and sat down at her desk. The brass-engraved name plate, mounted on mahogany wood, read: Lieutenant Kate Dawson, Head of the Homicide Bureau.

Kate smiled, as she proudly ran her hand down the wood grain of the new desk, but her face really lit up when she spotted a small note card tucked into the corner of her blotter. She hoped it was from him as her fingers raced nervously across the desktop. The note card had several Chinese characters, hand-written by Shears. It didn't take her long to decipher his message: "Congratulations. A colonel still outranks a bureau chief. See you around, soldier." Dawson held his note to her heart, and closed her eyes, thinking about nothing but him, as her first day began.

ACKNOWLEDGMENTS

As the author of this book, I am grateful to those friends, colleagues, and family members who continued on life's journey with me. While it would be impossible for me to list the names of everyone in my life who helped, I want to give a shout-out to certain people who were there during the abnormally long gestation period of this book. The original idea for *Merchants of Death* came from watching a report on "60 Minutes" (from five or six years ago) about the very lucrative trade of selling weapons to third-world counties. At the same time, I was also interested in writing a book about siblings and sibling rivalry. I am fortunate to have both an incredible brother and a wonderful sister in my life. And while I love them both dearly, we have differences that clearly set us apart. Bob is solid as a rock, a family man with a forty-year marriage, wife, two sons and a daughter; Jackie is a fellow creator, artist with a camera, and master of all things digital. They are both alike me, and different in so many ways.

Finally, I also wanted to write about transitions that happen in life and how people change because of those transitions. One of my "pet peeves" about series books that feature the same character is that the lead character rarely, if ever, changes over the course of the books. Read any of the Ian Fleming books or Robert Ludlum books and you'll see that James Bond nor Jason Bourne ever ages or goes through any serious transitions in life. I didn't want that to happen to Kate Dawson's character, so I have been subtly aging her and maturing her throughout the series. In the first book, she's still very much a rookie. In this book, her job changes and she must adjust to the next phase in life. If I'm lucky enough to continue writing Kate Dawson thrillers, she will eventually become Chief of Police. I am keen on seeing her mature and change as a character. In this book, she is introduced to a rival, not unlike a sibling, who is younger, smarter, and more competitive than she is, and has to deal with the fact that she is no longer the favored one in the department.

In the last couple of years, I went through several transitions of my own. I retired as a college dean (after more than thirty years in higher education) and moved to South Florida to be near my siblings. My brother and his family had lived in Miami prior to moving to Destin, Florida and my sister had lived in Pompano Beach, Florida prior to moving to Pasadena, California. So, with plenty of material to write, the book went through a longer gestation period than normal but eventually found its way into print. Thank you, Jackie and Bob, for being the best siblings ever. Thank you, Matt and Lenny, for being the best "brothers" from other parents. Thank you, Catherine for your love and help finding the right word or turn of phrase. And thank you Jeanie, for the Herculean tasks that you accomplish every year as my agent. I am really blessed to have you. A book has one author but many loving friends, family, and colleagues who help and nourish it along the way. Thanks to all of you!

ABOUT THE AUTHOR

Born in Chicago, Illinois, in the 1950s, Dr. John L. Flynn is a three-time Hugo Award–nominated author, psychologist, teacher, and college dean. In 1977, he received the M. Carolyn Parker Award from the University of South Florida for excellence in creative writing. He received his Bachelor's and Master's degrees in English from the University of South Florida and worked as an English teacher in Baltimore, Maryland. He published his first book *Future Threads* in 1985. In 1998, he earned his PhD as a clinical psychologist from the University of Southern California. He has published nearly twenty books and dozens of articles. He currently resides in Lake Worth, Florida.

THE KATE DAWSON MYSTERIES

FROM OPEN ROAD MEDIA

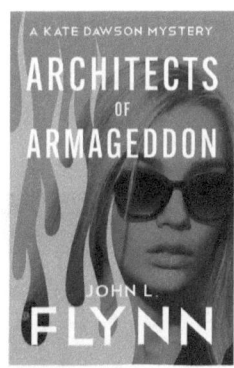

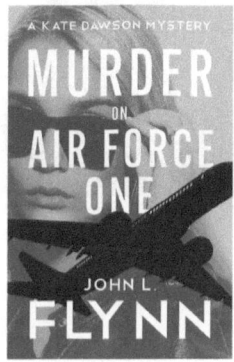
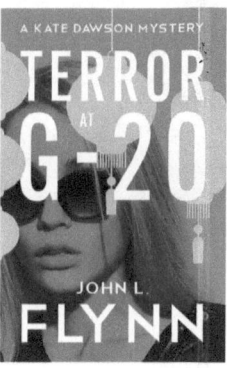

INTEGRATED MEDIA

Find a full list of our authors and
titles at www.openroadmedia.com

FOLLOW US
@OpenRoadMedia